## Welcome to
### *THE CAMEL CLUB*

Existing at the fringes of Washington, D.C., the Club consists of four eccentric members. Led by a mysterious man known as "Oliver Stone," they study conspiracy theories, current events, and the machinations of government to discover the "truth" behind the country's actions. Their efforts bear little fruit—until the group witnesses a shocking murder...and they become embroiled in an astounding, far-reaching conspiracy. Now the Club must join forces with a Secret Service agent to confront one of the most chilling spectacles ever to take place on American soil—an event that may trigger the ultimate war between two different worlds. And all that stands in the way of this apocalypse is five unexpected heroes.

### ACCLAIM FOR DAVID BALDACCI'S CAMEL CLUB THRILLERS

### *THE CAMEL CLUB*

"A terrific read."

—*Toronto Sun*

"Baldacci knows exactly what his readers want—just enough high-tech suspense to while away a few hours in front of a warm winter fire."
—*Fort Worth Star-Telegram*

"An original, effervescent thriller...page-turning fiction that grips and scares, and offers plenty to think about later."
—*Toledo Blade* (OH)

"Cleverly constructed...If you pick this book up, you'll stick with it all the way."
—*St. Louis Post-Dispatch*

"Features Baldacci's trademark plot twists and cat-and-mouse chases, as well as a superbly tense grand finale."
—*Richmond Times-Dispatch*

"Baldacci is a master at building suspense...will leave readers breathless."                                              —*Booklist*

"Fascinating...Baldacci is an author who promises a good story and then delivers it."                                    —*Publishers Weekly*

"Enjoyable."                                                        —*New York Daily News*

"An exciting and impressive read in Baldacci's style of fast-paced and breathtaking fiction."                          —ArmchairInterviews.com

"The story is very complicated but well worth the read...offers a lot of food for thought."                           —BestsellersWorld.com

"Another page-turner from the master of the art."
                                                                    —FreshFiction.com

"Utterly relentless...with more twists and turns than a good auto-cross circuit. This is one scary book."             —BookReporter.com

"Exciting...highly enjoyable and truly something special from this great author."                                     —NewMysteryReader.com

"Excellent...top-notch...one great book...tight and filled with much suspense."                                       —CurledUp.com

"Sure to be a bestseller."                                         —*Kirkus Reviews*

## HELL'S CORNER

"Strap on your Glock. Grab an extra magazine of shells. There's danger and excitement lurking around this Corner."
                                                                    —*Kirkus Reviews*

"Camel Club fans and thriller aficionados will rejoice at having a new action-packed, conspiracy-laden, politically intriguing mystery to solve."                                                       —*Sunday Denver Post*

"Car chases, gunfights, and explosions...The Club rides again... Baldacci has spiked his post-9/11 thrillers with a splash of real-world urgency...Throw in a handful of nifty double-crosses and misdirections, and you've got the perfect thriller for a weekend of reading."

—*Richmond Times-Dispatch*

"Four stars! Outstanding...demands to be read in one sitting, and readers will be begging for more adventures with Stone and company...The intense puzzle, twists and turns, and characters all showcase why Baldacci is a #1 *New York Times* bestselling author."

—*RT Book Reviews*

"Grade A...Intelligent and quickly paced."

—*Cleveland Plain Dealer*

"Another winner...Skillfully constructed and very difficult to put down. Baldacci keeps peeling back layers of Stone's psyche, revealing him to be a man full of unresolved conflicts and a potentially self-destructive amount of guilt over his past actions."     —*Booklist*

"Strap on your Glock. Grab an extra magazine of shells. There's danger and excitement lurking around this *corner*."

—*Kirkus Reviews*

"Will literally have readers at a loss for breath...*Hell's Corner* is David Baldacci at his best and features writing and plotting that only a master at the peak of his talent could accomplish...a contemporary thriller packed with relevant and well-researched plot elements, combined with a whodunit style of murder mystery...I anxiously await what Baldacci will do next to top this thrill ride."

—BookReporter.com

## DIVINE JUSTICE

"A rousing success...Baldacci shows once again that he is a sort of thriller Renaissance man: a master of plot, dialogue, and character."

—*Booklist* (starred review)

"Lots of action...cinematic...fast-moving and furious."
—*Pittsburgh Post-Gazette*

"Cunning chases will keep readers avidly turning the pages."
—*Richmond Times-Dispatch*

### STONE COLD

"Superb...This time he outdoes himself. The result is exhilarating... It's a sign of Baldacci's skills as a storyteller that he brings so many revenge-themed plots together into a single, riveting thriller. In *Stone Cold*, he ups the ante." —*Richmond Times-Dispatch*

"An exhilarating thriller: fast paced, with a cast of engaging characters, a couple of mind-wrenching plot twists, and a general air of derring-do. Let's hope this isn't Oliver Stone's last appearance."
—*Booklist* (starred review)

"Exciting...Gripping, chilling, and full of surprises, Baldacci's latest reveals the anarchy that lurks under the slick facade of corrupted governments." —*Publishers Weekly* (starred review)

"Baldacci's intricately woven plotlines, well-developed characters, fast-paced action, and surprise ending will leave readers satisfied and wanting more. A sequel worthy of its predecessors; highly recommended for all fiction collections."
—*Library Journal* (starred review)

### THE COLLECTORS

"An intelligent and rousing thriller." —*Booklist*

"You'll be rooting for his likable underdog protagonists."
—*Entertainment Weekly*

# THE CAMEL CLUB

## DAVID BALDACCI

GC

**GRAND CENTRAL**
PUBLISHING

NEW YORK   BOSTON

Copyright © 2005 by Columbus Rose, Ltd.
Excerpt from *Memory Man* copyright © 2015 by Columbus Rose, Ltd.

Grand Central Publishing
Hachette Book Group
1290 Avenue of the Americas
New York, NY 10104
www.HachetteBookGroup.com

Printed in the United States of America

LSC-C

Originally published in hardcover by Hachette Book Group.
First trade edition: September 2014
Reissued: March 2015

10   9   8   7   6

Grand Central Publishing is a division of Hachette Book Group, Inc.
The Grand Central Publishing name and logo are trademarks of Hachette Book Group, Inc.

The Hachette Speakers Bureau provides a wide range of authors for speaking events. To find out more, go to www.hachettespeakersbureau.com or call (866) 376-6591.

The publisher is not responsible for websites (or their content) that are not owned by the publisher.

Library of Congress Cataloging-in-Publication Data

Baldacci, David.
    The camel club / David Baldacci.—1st ed.
      p. cm.
    ISBN 0-446-57738-3 (regular ed.)
    ISBN 0-446-57880-0 (large print ed.)
    1. Secret societies—Fiction.   2. Nuclear warfare—Fiction.   3. Conspiracies—Fiction.   I. Title.
    PS3552.A446C36   2005
    813'.54—dc22                                      2005015534

ISBN 978-1-4555-3340-4 (pbk.)

This novel is dedicated to the men and women
of the
United States Secret Service

And to Larry Kirshbaum, a first-rate editor,
a great publisher, and a wonderful friend

# THE
# CAMEL
# CLUB

# PROLOGUE

THE CHEVY SUBURBAN SPED DOWN the road, enveloped by the hushed darkness of the Virginia countryside. Forty-one-year-old Adnan al-Rimi was hunched over the wheel as he concentrated on the windy road coming up. Deer were plentiful here, and Adnan had no desire to see the bloodied antlers of one slashing through the windshield. Indeed, the man was tired of things attacking him. He lifted a gloved hand from the steering wheel and felt for the gun in the holster under his jacket; a weapon was not just a comfort for Adnan, it was a necessity.

He suddenly glanced out the window as he heard the sound overhead.

There were two passengers in the backseat. The man talking animatedly in Farsi on a cell phone was Muhammad al-Zawahiri, an Iranian who had entered the country shortly before the terrorist attacks on 9/11. The man next to him was an Afghan named Gul Khan, who'd been in the States only a few months. Khan was large and muscular with a shaved head. He wore a hunter's camouflage jacket and was checking his machine gun with nimble fingers. He clicked the mag back in place and put the firing switch on two-shot bursts. A few drops of rain fell against the window, and Khan idly watched them trickle down.

"This is nice countryside," Khan said in Pashto, a dialect Muhammad spoke but one Adnan had little familiarity with. "My country is filled with the metal carcasses of Soviet tanks. The farmers just plow around them." He paused and added with a deeply satisfied look, "And some American carcasses too, we have."

Adnan kept glancing in the rearview mirror. He didn't like a man with a machine gun sitting behind him, fellow Muslim or not. And neither was he overly trusting of the Iranian. Adnan had been born in Saudi Arabia but migrated to Iraq as a young boy. He fought for Iraq in the horrific war between the two countries, and his enmity toward Iran still ran very deep. Ethnically, Muhammad al-Zawahiri was Persian, not Arab, like al-Rimi. It was another difference between the two men that caused al-Rimi not to trust him.

Muhammad finished his phone call, wiped a smudge of dirt off one of his American-made cowboy boots, checked the time on his very expensive watch and lay back against the seat and smiled as he lit a cigarette. He said something in Farsi and Khan laughed. The big Afghan's breath smelled strongly of onions.

Adnan gripped the steering wheel tighter. He had never been a careless man, and Adnan didn't like the Iranian's flippancy about serious matters. Seconds later Adnan looked out the window again.

Muhammad had clearly heard it too. He rolled down his window and poked his head out, looking up at the cloudy sky. When he saw the wink of red lights overhead he barked to Adnan, who nodded and hit the gas; both men in the back strapped on their seatbelts.

The Chevy flew along the snaking country road, banking so hard around some curves that the men in the rear held on to the hand straps with all ten fingers. Yet even the fastest car in the world couldn't outrun a helicopter on a serpentine track.

Speaking again in Farsi, Muhammad ordered Adnan to pull off under some trees and wait, to see if the chopper kept going. Continuing in Farsi he said, "Car accident, Adnan? Medical evacuation helicopter perhaps?"

Adnan shrugged. He didn't speak Farsi very well, and oftentimes nuances in that language escaped him. One didn't need to be a linguist, however, to sense the urgency in his colleague's voice. He drove under a cluster of trees, and all three men got out and crouched down by the vehicle. Khan pointed his machine gun at the sky and Adnan slid his pistol out as well. Muhammad just gripped his cell phone and looked nervously overhead. For a moment it appeared that the chopper had left, but then a searchlight beam cut through the tree canopies directly over them.

The next word Muhammad spoke was in English: "Shit!" He nodded at Adnan, instructing him to go for a better look.

The Iraqi ran in a crouch until he reached the edge of the tree line

and cautiously gazed up. The chopper was hovering sixty feet overhead. Adnan returned to his companions, reporting what he'd seen.

"They may be looking for a place to land," he added.

"Do we have an RPG in the truck?" Muhammad asked, his voice
slightly trembling. He was used to being the brains behind these sorts
of operations rather than one of the foot soldiers who actually did the
killing—and often died in the process.

Adnan shook his head. "We didn't think we'd have need of a rocket-
propelled grenade tonight."

"Shit," Muhammad said again. "Listen," he hissed. "I think they're
landing." The tree canopies were starting to shake from the chopper's
rotor wash.

Adnan nodded at his companions. "It is only a two-person helicopter. There are *three* of us," he added firmly. He stared at his leader.
"Take out your gun, Muhammad, and be ready to use it. We will not
go quietly. We will take some Americans with us."

"You fool," Muhammad snapped. "Do you think they haven't already called for others? They will simply keep us pinned down until
help arrives."

"Our cover papers are in order," Adnan countered. "The best
money can buy."

The Iranian looked at him as though he were insane. "We are *armed
Arabs* in the middle of pig farmers in Virginia. They will fingerprint
me and know in seconds who I really am. We are trapped," he added in
another hiss. "How could this be? How?"

Adnan pointed at the man's hand. "Perhaps that cell phone you're
always on. They can track these things. I've warned you before about
that."

"Allah's will be done," Gul Khan said as he put his gun's firing selector on full auto, apparently in accordance with God's wishes.

Muhammad stared at him incredulously. "If we are stopped now,
our plans will not succeed. Do you think God wants that? Do you!"
He paused and took a deep, steadying breath. "Here is what I want
you two to do. What you *must* do!" He pointed a shaky finger at the
vibrating tree canopies and said in a firm voice, "I want you to hold
them off, while I make a run for it. There is another road a half-mile

through these trees to the west. I can call Marwan to come and pick me up in the other truck at that location. But you must hold them off. You must do this!"

Adnan stared sullenly at his leader. By his expression, if there were a literal translation for "chickenshit" in his native tongue, Adnan would've certainly used it.

"Go, now, draw them off, it is your sacrifice for the cause," Muhammad cried as he started backing away.

"If we are to die while you escape, then give me your gun," Adnan said bitterly. "*You* will have no need of it."

The Iranian pulled out his pistol and tossed it to Adnan.

The burly Khan turned toward the chopper and smiled. "How about this plan, Adnan?" he said over his shoulder. "Firing into their tail prop before they can land worked very well against the Americans in my country. Their spines snap like twigs when they hit the ground."

The bullet hit him in the back of the neck, ironically snapping Khan's own spine like a twig, and the big Afghani fell dead.

Adnan swiveled his pistol away from his first victim and pointed it at Muhammad, who, seeing this traitorous attack, had started to run. He was not fleet of foot, however, and the cowboy boots he favored were not built for running. Adnan caught up to him when Muhammad fell over a rotting tree trunk.

Muhammad looked up at his colleague as Adnan pointed Muhammad's own pistol at him. The stream of invectives in Farsi from Muhammad was followed by pleas in halting Arabic and then finally in English: "Adnan, please. Why? Why?"

In Arabic Adnan answered, "You deal drugs, you say, to make money to support the effort. Yet you spend more time shopping for your precious cowboy boots and your fancy jewelry than you do on the work of Islam, Muhammad. You have lost the way. You are American now. But that is not why I do this."

"Tell me why then!" the Iranian shouted.

"It is *your* sacrifice for a greater end." Adnan didn't smile, but the triumph was very clear in his eyes. He fired a contact shot into the man's left temple, and no more pleas in any language flowed from the Iranian. Adnan pressed Muhammad's hand around the gun, then set it down and made his way quickly back to the clearing, where the chopper had landed and one of the passenger doors was now opening. Adnan had lied. It was actually a four-person chopper. Two men got out. They were Westerners wearing grim features, and carrying something between them. Adnan led them back to Muhammad's body after stopping to retrieve a shotgun from the Suburban.

The object the men toted was a body bag. They unzipped it. Inside was a man, a man who looked remarkably like Adnan and was dressed identically to him. The man was unconscious but still breathing. They set him up against a tree near where the dead Iranian lay. Adnan handed his wallet to one of the men and he placed it in the unconscious man's jacket pocket. Then the other man took the shotgun from Adnan, pressed Muhammad's dead hands around it, pointed it at the unconscious man, and fired a blast into his head, instantly wiping away part of his face. A living human to a corpse, in seconds. Adnan was an expert in such things, and not by his choosing. *Who would select that vocation, except a madman?*

A minute later Adnan and the two men were racing to the helicopter, and they climbed in; it immediately lifted into the air. There were no insignias on the chopper's sides or tail, and none of the men wore uniforms. Indeed, they barely looked at Adnan as he settled himself in one of the backseats and pulled on his safety harness. It was as though they were trying to forget he was even there.

Adnan was no longer thinking about his dead companions. His thoughts had pushed on, to a far greater glory that awaited him. If they succeeded, humanity would speak of it for generations to come in awed tones. Adnan al-Rimi was now officially a dead man. Yet he would never be more valuable.

The chopper took a northerly route, on its way to western Pennsylvania. To a town called Brennan. A minute later the rural Virginia sky was quiet once more except for the fall of a gentle rain that took its time washing away all the blood.

# CHAPTER

# 1

HE WAS RUNNING HARD, BULLETS *embedding in things all around him. He couldn't see who was shooting, and he had no weapon to return fire. The woman next to him was his wife. The young girl next to her was their daughter. A bullet sliced through his wife's wrist, and he heard her scream. Then a second bullet found its target and his wife's eyes widened slightly. It was the split-second bulge of the pupils that signaled death before one's brain could even register it. As his wife fell, he raced to his little girl's side to shield her. His fingers reached for hers but missed. They always missed.*

He awoke and sat straight up, the sweat trickling down his cheeks before finally creeping onto his long, bushy beard. He poured a bit of water from a bottle over his face, letting the cool drops push away the heat-filled pain of his recurrent nightmare.

As he got up from the bed, his leg brushed against the old box he kept there. He hesitated and then lifted the top off. Inside was a ragged photo album. One by one he looked at the few pictures of the woman who'd been his wife. Then he turned to the photos of his daughter; of the baby and toddler she'd been. He had no more pictures of her after that. He would have given his life to have seen her, even for a moment, as a young woman. Never a day went by that he didn't wonder what might have been.

He looked around the cottage's sparsely furnished interior. Looking back at him were dusty shelves crammed with books covering an array of subjects. Next to the large window that overlooked the darkened grounds was an old desk stacked with journals filled with his precise handwriting. A blackened stone fireplace provided much of his heat, and there was a small kitchen where he prepared his simple meals. A minuscule bathroom completed his modest living arrangements.

He checked his watch, took a pair of binoculars from the rickety wooden table next to his bed and grabbed a frayed cloth knapsack off his desk. He stuffed the binoculars and a few journals in the knapsack and headed outside.

The old grave markers loomed before him, the moonlight glancing off the weathered, mossy stone. As he stepped from the front porch to the grass, the brisk air helped carry away the burning sensation in his head from his nightmare, but not the one in his heart. Thankfully, he had somewhere to go tonight, yet with some time to spare. And when he had extra time, he invariably headed to one place.

He walked through the large wrought-iron gates where the scroll-work announced that this was Mt. Zion Cemetery, located in north-west Washington, D.C., and owned by the nearby Mt. Zion United Methodist Church. The church was the oldest black congregation in the city, having been organized in 1816 by folks who didn't enjoy practicing their faith at a segregated house of worship that had some-how missed the concept of equality in the Scriptures. The three-acre parcel had also been an important stop along the underground rail-road, shepherding slaves from the South to freedom in the North dur-ing the Civil War.

The graveyard was bracketed on one side by the massive Dumbar-ton House, headquarters of the National Society of the Colonial Dames of America, and on the other side by a low-rise brick residen-tial building. For decades the historic cemetery had suffered from ne-glect, with toppled tombstones and waist-high weeds. Then the church had enclosed the graveyard with the fence and built the small care-taker's cottage.

Nearby was the far larger and far better known Oak Hill Cemetery, the final resting place of many notable people. However, he preferred Mt. Zion and its place in history as a gateway to freedom.

He'd been engaged as the cemetery's caretaker some years ago, and he took his work very seriously, making sure the grounds and grave sites were kept in good order. The cottage that came with the job was his first real home in a long time. The church paid him in cash with no bothersome paperwork; he didn't make nearly enough to pay income taxes anyway. In fact, he made barely enough money to live. Yet it was still the best job he'd ever had.

He walked south on 27th Street, caught a Metro bus and was soon dropped a block or so from his "second home" of sorts. As he passed the small tent that at least technically belonged to him, he pulled the binoculars out of his knapsack and from the shadow of a tree used them to eye the building across the street. He had taken the government-issued binoculars with him after serving his country proudly before completely losing faith in its leaders. His real name he had not used in decades. He had been known for a long time now as Oliver Stone, a name he'd adopted in what could only be termed an act of cheeky defiance.

He related well to the irreverent film director's legendary work, which challenged the "official" perception of history, a history that often turned out to be more fiction than fact. Taking the man's name as his own seemed appropriate, since *this* Oliver Stone was also very interested in the "real" truth.

Through the binoculars he continued to study the comings and goings at the mansion that never ceased to fascinate him. Then Stone entered his small tent, and, using an old flashlight, he carefully noted down his observations in one of the journals he'd brought in his knapsack. He kept some of these at the caretaker's cottage and many more at hiding places he maintained elsewhere. He stored nothing at the tent because he knew it was regularly searched. In his wallet he always kept his official permit allowing him to have his tent here and the right to protest in front of the building across the street. He took that right very seriously.

Returning outside, he watched the guards who holstered semiautomatic pistols and held machine guns or occasionally spoke into walkie-talkies. They all knew him and were warily polite, as folks were with those who could suddenly turn on you. Stone always took great pains to show them respect. You were always deferential with people who carried machine guns. Oliver Stone, while not exactly in the mainstream, was hardly crazy.

He made eye contact with one of the guards, who called out, "Hey, Stone, I hear Humpty Dumpty was pushed, pass it on."

Some of the other men laughed at this remark, and even Stone's lips curled into a smile. "Duly noted," he answered back. He had watched this very same sentry gun down someone a few feet from where he was standing. To be fair, the other fellow had been shooting at him.

He hitched his frayed pants up tighter around his slender waist, smoothed back his long grayish white hair and stopped for a moment to retie the string that was trying and failing to hold his right shoe together. He was a tall and very lean man, and his shirt was too big and his trousers too short. And the shoes, well, the shoes were always problematic.

"It is new clothes that you need," a female voice said in the darkness.

He looked up to see the speaker leaning against a statue of Major General Comte de Rochambeau, an American Revolutionary War hero. Rochambeau's stiff finger was pointing at something, Stone had never known what. Then there was a Prussian, Baron Steuben, to the northwest, and the Pole, General Kosciuszko, guarding the northeast flank of the seven-acre park that Stone was standing in. These statues always brought a smile to his face. Oliver Stone so loved being around revolutionaries.

"It really *is* the new clothes that you need, Oliver," the woman said again as she scratched her deeply tanned face. "And the hair cut too, yes. Oliver, it is a new everything that is needed."

"I'm sure that I do," he replied quietly. "Yet it's all in one's priorities, I suppose, and fortunately, vanity has never been one of mine."

This woman called herself Adelphia. She had an accent that he'd never been able to exactly place, although it was definitely European, probably Slavic. She was particularly unsympathetic to her verbs, wedging them into very awkward places in her speech. She was tall and spare with black hair shot through with gray that she wore long. Adelphia also had deeply set, brooding eyes and a mouth that was usually cast into a snarl, though Stone had sometimes found her to be kindhearted in a grudging sort of way. It was difficult to gauge her age, but she was certainly younger than he. The six-foot-long, freestanding banner outside her tent proclaimed:

A FETUS IS A LIFE. IF YOU DON'T BELIEVE IT,
YOU'RE GOING STRAIGHT TO HELL.

There was very little that was subtle about Adelphia. In life she only saw the rigid lines of black and white. To her, shades of gray were non-existent, whereas this was a city that had seemingly invented the color. The small sign outside of Oliver Stone's tent read simply:

I WANT THE TRUTH

He had yet to find it after all these years. Indeed, was there ever a city created where the truth was more difficult to discover than the one he was standing in right now?

"I go to get the café, Oliver. You would like some? I have money."

"No thank you, Adelphia. I have to go somewhere."

She scowled. "Another meeting is where you go? What good does it give you? It is not young you are no more and you should no be walking in the dark. This is dangerous place."

He glanced at the armed men. "Actually, I think it's fairly secure here."

"Many men with guns you say is safe? I say you crazy," she responded testily.

"Perhaps you're right and thank you for your concern," he said politely. Adelphia would much rather argue and looked for any opening to pounce on. He'd long since learned never to allow the woman such an opportunity.

Adelphia stared at him angrily for another moment and then stalked off. Meanwhile, Stone glanced at a sign next to his that read:

HAVE A NICE DOOMSDAY

Stone had not seen the gentleman who erected that sign for a long time.

"Yes, we will, won't we?" he muttered, and then his attention was caught by the sudden activity across the street. Policemen and marked cruisers were assembling in groups. Stone could also see lawmen taking up positions at the various intersections. Across the street the imposing black steel gates that could withstand the push of an M-1 tank opened, and a black Suburban shot out, its red and blue grille lights blazing.

Knowing instantly what was happening, Stone hurried down the street toward the nearest intersection. As he watched through his binoculars, the world's most elaborate motorcade streamed out onto 17th Street. In the middle of this imposing column was the most unique limousine ever built.

It was a Cadillac DTS model loaded with the latest in navigation and communication technology, and it could carry six passengers very comfortably in rich blue leather with wood trim accents. The limo boasted automatic-sensor reclining seats and a foldaway storable desktop and was fully airtight with its own internal air supply in case the outside oxygen wasn't up to par. The presidential seal was embroidered on the center of the rear seat, and presidential seals were also affixed on the inside and outside of the rear doors. On the right front fender rode the U.S. flag. The presidential standard flew from a post on the left front fender, signaling that America's chief executive was indeed inside.

The exterior of the vehicle was constructed of antiballistic-steel panels, and the windows were phone-book-thick polycarbonate glass that no bullet could penetrate. It ran on four self-healing tires and sported double-zero license plates. The car's gas mileage was lousy, but its price tag of $10 million did include a ten-disc CD changer with surround sound. Unfortunately, for those looking for a bargain, there was no dealer discount. It was known affectionately as the Beast. The limo had only two known weaknesses: It could neither fly nor float.

A light came on inside the Beast, and Stone saw the man perusing some papers, papers of enormous importance, no doubt. Another gentleman sat beside him. Stone had to smile. The agents must be furious over the light. Even with thick armor and bulletproof glass you didn't make yourself such an easy target.

The limo slowed as it passed through the intersection, and Stone tensed a bit as he saw the man glance his way. For a brief moment the president of the United States, James H. Brennan, and conspiracy-minded citizen Oliver Stone made direct eye contact. The president grimaced and said something. The man next to him immediately turned the light out. Stone smiled again. *Yes, I will always be here. Longer than both of you.*

The man seated beside President Brennan was also well known to

Stone. He was Carter Gray, the so-called intelligence czar, a recently created cabinet-level position that gave him ironfisted control of a $50-billion budget and 120,000 highly trained personnel in all fifteen American intelligence agencies. His empire included the spy satellite platform, the NSA's cryptologic expertise, the Pentagon's Defense Intelligence Agency, or DIA, and even the venerable CIA, an agency Gray had once headed. Apparently, the folks at Langley thought that Gray would show them preference and deference. He had done neither. Because Gray was also a former secretary of defense, it was assumed that he would show the Pentagon—which consumed eighty cents out of every intelligence dollar—loyalty. That assumption had also turned out to be completely erroneous. Gray obviously knew where all the bodies were buried and had used that to bend both agencies to his considerable will.

Stone did not believe that one man, one fallible human being, should have that much power, and certainly not someone like Carter Gray. Stone had known the man very well decades ago, though Gray certainly would not have recognized his old mate now. *Years ago it would've been a different story, right, Mr. Gray?*

The binoculars were suddenly ripped out of his hands, and Stone was staring at a uniformed guard toting a machine gun.

"You pull these out again to look at the man, Stone, they're gone; you got it? And if we didn't know you were okay, they'd be gone right now." The man thrust the vintage field glasses back into Stone's hands and marched off.

"Simply exercising my constitutional rights, Officer," Stone replied in a low voice that he knew the guard couldn't hear. He quickly put his binoculars away and stepped back into the shadows. Again, one should not argue with humorless men carrying automatic weapons. Stone let out a long breath. His life was a precarious balance every day.

He went back inside his tent, opened his knapsack and, using his flashlight, read over a series of stories he'd clipped from newspapers and magazines and pasted into his journals. They documented the doings of Carter Gray and President Brennan: "Intelligence Czar Strikes Again," claimed one headline; "Brennan and Gray Make Dynamic Duo," said another.

It had all come about very quickly. After several fits and starts

Congress had dramatically reorganized the U.S. intelligence community and essentially put its complete faith in Carter Gray. As secretary
of intelligence, Gray headed the National Intelligence Center, or NIC.
The center's statutory mandate was to keep the country safe from attacks within or without its borders. Safe by any means necessary was
perhaps the chief unwritten part of this mandate.

However, the beginning of Gray's tenure had hardly matched his
impressive résumé: a series of suicide bombers in metropolitan areas
with enormous casualties, two assassinations of visiting foreign dignitaries and then a direct but fortunately unsuccessful attack on the
White House. Despite many in Congress calling for his resignation
and the dismantling of the secretary's authority, Gray had kept the
support of his president. And if power slots in Washington were compared to natural disasters, the president was a hurricane *and* an earthquake all rolled into one.

Then slowly, the tide had begun to turn. A dozen planned terrorist
attacks on American soil had been thwarted. And terrorists were being
killed and captured at an increasingly high rate. Long unable to crack
the inner rings of these organizations, the American intelligence community was finally starting to attack the enemy from within its own
circles and damaging its ability to hit the United States and its allies.
Gray had understandably received the lion's share of the credit for
these outcomes.

Stone checked his watch. The meeting would be starting soon.
However, it was a long walk, and his legs, his usual mode of getting
around, were tired today. He left the tent and checked his wallet.
There was no money in it.

That's when he spotted the pedestrian. Stone immediately headed
after this gentleman as he raised his hand and a taxi pulled up to the
curb. Stone increased his pace, reaching the man as he climbed into the
cab. His eyes downcast, his hand out, Stone said, "Can you spare some
change, sir? Just a few dollars." This was said in a practiced, deferential
tone, allowing the other man to adopt a magnanimous posture if he so
chose. *Adopt one,* Stone thought. *For it's a long walk.*

The man hesitated and then took the bait. He smiled and reached for
his wallet. Stone's eyes widened as a crisp twenty-dollar bill was
placed in his palm.

"God bless you," Stone said as he clutched the money tightly.

Stone walked as quickly as he could to a nearby hotel's taxi stand. Normally, he'd have taken a bus, but with twenty dollars he'd ride by himself for a change. After smoothing down his long, disheveled hair and prodding his equally stubborn beard into place, Stone walked up to the first cab in line.

On seeing him the cabby hit the door lock and yelled, "Get the hell outta here!"

Stone held up the twenty-dollar bill and said through the half-opened window, "The regulations under which you operate do not allow you to discriminate on any basis."

It was clear from the cabby's expression that he would discriminate on any basis he wanted to and yet he eyed the cash greedily. "You speak pretty good for some homeless bum." He added suspiciously, "I thought all you people was nuts."

"I am hardly a nut and I'm not homeless," Stone replied. "But I am, well, I am just a bit down on my luck."

"Ain't we all?" He unlocked the doors and Stone quickly climbed in and told the man where he wanted to go.

"Saw the president on the move tonight," the cabby said. "Pretty cool."

"Yes, pretty cool," Stone agreed without much enthusiasm. He glanced out the rear window of the cab in the direction of the White House and then sat back against the seat and closed his eyes. *What an interesting neighborhood to call home.*

# CHAPTER

## 2

THE BLACK SEDAN CREPT DOWN the one-lane road that was bracketed by thick walls of trees, finally easing onto a gravel path branching from the road. A hundred feet later the car came to a stop. Tyler Reinke, tall, blond, athletically built and in his late twenties, climbed out of the driver's side while Warren Peters, early thirties and barely five foot seven with a barrel chest and thinning dark hair, extricated himself from the passenger seat. Reinke unlocked the car's trunk. Inside lying in a fetal position was a fellow in his mid-thirties, his arms and legs bound tightly with rubber straps. He was dressed in blue jeans and a Washington Redskins jacket. A heavy cloth covered his mouth, and a plastic tarp had been placed under him. Yet, unlike most people bound and stuffed in car trunks, he was still alive, although he appeared deeply sedated. Using the tarp, the men lifted him out of the trunk and set him down on the ground.

"I scouted this out before, Tyler," Peters said. "It's the best location, but a bit of a hike. We'll carry him using the tarp. That way nothing from us gets on him."

"Right," Reinke replied as he stared warily down the steep, uneven terrain. "Let's just take it nice and slow."

They made their way carefully down, leaning heavily into tree trunks along the way. Luckily, it had not rained lately and the ground provided firm footing. Still, carrying the man between them on the plastic was awkward, and they had to take several breaks along the way, with the stout Peters puffing hard.

Their path finally leveled out and Reinke said, "Okay, almost there. Let's set him down and take a recon."

The two men drew out night-vision binoculars from a duffel bag that Reinke had strapped to his back, and took a long look around.

Satisfied, they took up their trek once more. Fifteen minutes later they reached the end of the dirt and rock. The water was not deep here, and flat boulders could be seen in several locations poking through the surface of the slow-moving river.

"All right," Peters said. "This is the place."

Reinke opened the duffel bag, pulled out two objects and set them down on the ground. Squatting next to the larger object, he felt along its contours. Seconds later his fingers found what they were searching for. A minute later the dinghy was fully inflated. The other item he'd pulled from the duffel was a small engine prop that he attached to the boat's stern.

Peters said, "We'll keep to the Virginia side. This engine's pretty quiet, but sound really carries over the water." He handed his colleague a small device. "Not that we'll need it, but here's the GPS."

"We have to dunk him," Reinke pointed out.

"Right. Figured we'd do it by the shore here."

They took off their shoes and socks and rolled up their pant legs. Carrying the captive, they stepped along the soft dirt and rocks lining the water's edge and then waded in up to their knees and lowered him into the warm water until his body—but not his face—was submerged and then quickly pulled him up again. They did this maneuver twice more.

"That should to it," Peters said as he looked down at the soaked man who moaned a bit in his sleep. They hadn't dunked his face because they thought that might rouse him, and make it more difficult to transport him.

They waded back to shore and then placed him in the inflatable dinghy. The men made one more careful sweep of the area and then carried the small boat out to the water and climbed in. Peters started the engine, and the dinghy sped out into the river at a decent clip. The tall Reinke squatted next to the prisoner and eyed the GPS screen as they made their way downriver hugging the forested side.

As he navigated the craft Peters said, "I would've preferred doing this somewhere more private, but that wasn't my call. At least there's a fog rolling in. I checked the weather forecast and for once it was right. We'll put into a deserted little cove a couple hundred yards down from here, wait until everything is cleared out and then head on."

"Good plan," Reinke replied.

The two men fell silent as the tiny craft headed into the gathering fogbank.

# CHAPTER

## 3

Alex Ford stifled a yawn and rubbed his tired eyes. A clear voice shot through his ear fob. "Stay alert, Ford." He gave a barely noticeable nod of his head and refocused. The room was hot, but at least he wasn't wearing the Kevlar body armor that was akin to strapping a microwave to your body. As usual, the wires leading from his surveillance kit to his ear fob and wrist mic were irritating his skin. The ear fob itself was even more aggravating, making his ear so sore it was painful to even touch.

He touched the pistol in his shoulder holster. Like all Secret Service agents, his suits were designed a little big in the chest, to disguise the bulge of the weapon. The Service had recently converted to the .357 SIG from the nine-millimeter version. The SIG was a good gun with enough stopping power to do the job; however, some of his colleagues had complained about the switch, clearly preferring the old hardware. Alex, who wasn't a big gun buff, didn't care. In all his years with the Service he'd infrequently pulled his gun and even more rarely fired it.

This thought made Alex reflect on his career for a moment. How many doorways had he stood post at? The answer was clearly etched in the wrinkles on his face and the weariness in his eyes. Even after leaving protection detail and being reassigned to the Secret Service's Washington Field Office, or WFO, to do more investigative work at the tail end of his career, here he was again taking up space between the doorjambs, watching people, looking for the needle in a haystack that intended bodily harm to someone under his watch.

Tonight was foreign dignitary protection at the low end of the threat assessment level. He'd been unlucky enough to draw the overtime assignment to protect a visiting head of government, finding out about it an hour before he was about to go off duty. So instead of having a drink in his favorite pub, he was making sure nobody took a shot at the prime minister of Latvia. Or was it Estonia?

The event was a reception at the swanky Four Seasons Hotel in Georgetown, but the crowd was definitely B-list, many here only because they'd been ordered to attend. The few marginally important guests were a handful of junior levels from the White House, some local D.C. politicos hoping for decent newsprint and a portly congressman who was a member of some international relations committee; he looked even more bored than Alex felt.

The veteran Secret Service agent had already done three of these extra-duty soirées in the past week. The months leading up to a presidential election were a manic swirl of parties, fund-raisers and meet-and-greets. Members of Congress and their staffers would hit a half dozen of these events every evening, as much for the free food and drink as to shake constituents' hands, collect checks and sometimes even discuss the issues. Whenever one of these parties had in attendance anyone under Secret Service protection guys like Alex would trudge out after a long day's work and keep them safe.

Alex glanced at his partner for the night, a tall, beefy kid out of WFO with a Marine Corps buzz cut who'd been called in at the last minute too. Alex had a few more years until he could retire on his federal pension, but this kid was looking at more than two decades of riding the Secret Service's career roller coaster.

"Simpson got out of this again," the kid muttered. "Second time in a row. Tell me this: Whose ass is getting kissed upstairs?"

Alex shrugged noncommittally. The thing about duty like this, it gave you time to think; in fact, way too much time. Secret Service agents were like jailhouse lawyers in that respect: a lot of clock on their hands to mull things over, creating complicated bitch lists as they silently guarded their charges. Alex just didn't care about that side of the profession anymore.

He glanced at the button on his wrist mic and had to smile. The mic button had been problematic for years. Agents would cross their arms and accidentally turn it on, or else the mic would get stuck on somehow. And then coming over the airwaves would be a graphic description of some hot chick wandering the area. If Alex had a hundred bucks for every time he'd heard the phrase "Did you *see* the rack on that one?" he could've retired already. And then you'd have everyone yelling into his mic, "Open mic." It was pretty funny to watch all the agents scrambling to make sure it wasn't *them* inadvertently broadcasting their lust.

Alex repositioned his ear fob and rubbed at his neck. That part of his anatomy remained one large train wreck of cartilage and fused disks. He'd been pulling motorcade duty on a presidential protection detail when the truck he'd been riding in rolled after the driver swerved to avoid a deer on a back road. That little tumble fractured Alex's neck. After a number of operations and the insertion of some very fine stainless steel, his six-foot-three frame had been reduced by nearly a full inch, though his posture was much improved, since steel didn't bend. Being a little shorter didn't bother him nearly as much as the constant burn in his neck. He could've taken disability and left the Service, but that wasn't the way he wanted to go out. Single and childless, he didn't have any place to go to. So he'd sweated and pushed himself back into shape and gotten the blessing of the Secret Service medicos to return to the field after months on desk duty.

Right now, though, at age forty-three, after spending most of his adult life on constant high alert amid numbing tedium—a typical Secret Service agent's daily existence—he seriously wondered just how demented he'd been to keep going. Hell, he could have found a hobby. Or at least a wife.

Alex bit his lip to mitigate the smoldering heat in his neck and stoically watched the prime minister's wife cramming foie gras into her mouth.

*What a gig.*

# CHAPTER

## 4

O LIVER STONE GOT OUT OF THE TAXI.

Before driving off, the cabby said with a snort, "In my book you're still a bum no matter how fancy you talk."

Stone gazed after the departing car. He'd long since stopped responding to such comments. People would think what they wanted to. Besides, he *did* look like a bum.

He walked toward a small park next to the Georgetown Waterfront Complex and glanced down at the brownish waters of the Potomac River as they licked up against the seawall. Some very enterprising graffiti artists, who obviously didn't mind working with water right under their butts, had elaborately painted the concrete barrier.

A little earlier there would have been traffic racing along the elevated Whitehurst Freeway that ran behind Stone. And a jet-fueled nightlife would have blared away near the intersection of M Street and Wisconsin Avenue. Georgetown had many tony places that promised good times for those with lots of ready cash or at least passable credit, neither of which Stone possessed. However, at this late hour most revelers had called it a night. Washington was, above all, an early-to-bed-and-early-to-rise sort of town.

The Potomac River was also quiet tonight. The police boat that regularly patrolled the waters must have headed south toward the Woodrow Wilson Bridge. That was very good, Stone thought. Thankfully, he didn't pass any police officers on land either. This was a free country, but somewhat less free for a man who lived in a cemetery, wore clothes only a couple of levels above rags and was out after dark in an affluent area.

Stone walked along the waterfront, skirted the Francis Scott Key

Park, trudged under the Francis Scott Key Bridge and finally passed a memorial to the famous composer. A bit of overkill, Stone thought, for a fellow who had written song lyrics no one could remember. The sky was an inky black with splashes of clouds and dots of stars; and, with the recently reinstated curfew at nearby Reagan National Airport, there were no aircraft exhaust streams to mar its beauty. However, Stone could feel the thick ground fog rolling in. Soon, he would be lucky to see a foot in front of him. He was drawing near to a gaudily painted building owned by one of the local rowing clubs when a familiar voice called to him from the darkness.

"Oliver, is that you?"

"Yes, Caleb. Are the others here?"

A medium-sized fellow with a bit of a paunch came into Stone's line of sight. Caleb Shaw was dressed in a suit of clothes from the nineteenth century, complete with a bowler hat that covered his short, graying hair; an old-fashioned watch graced the front of his wool vest. He wore his sideburns long, and a small, well-groomed mustache hovered over his lip.

"Reuben's here, but he's, uh, relieving himself. I haven't seen Milton yet," Caleb added.

Stone sighed. "Not a surprise. Milton is brilliant but absentminded as always."

When Reuben joined them, he didn't look well. Reuben Rhodes stood over six foot four and was a very powerfully built man of about sixty with a longish mass of curly dark hair dappled with gray and a matching short, thick beard. He was dressed in dirty jeans and a flannel shirt, with frayed moccasins on his feet. He was pressing one of his hands into his side. Reuben was prone to kidney stones.

"You should go to the clinic, Reuben," Stone implored.

The big man scowled. "I don't like people poking around inside me; had enough of that in the army. So I'll suffer in silence and in privacy if you don't mind."

As they were speaking, Milton Farb joined them. He stopped, pecked the dirt with his right foot three times, then with his left two times and finished this off with a series of whistles and grunts. Then he recited a string of numbers that obviously had great significance for him.

The other three waited patiently until he finished. They all knew if they interrupted their companion in the midst of his obsessive-compulsive ritual, he would have to start again, and it was getting rather late.

"Hello, Milton," Stone said after the grunts and whistles had ceased.

Milton Farb looked up from the dirt and smiled. He had a leather backpack over his shoulder and was dressed in a colorful sweater and crisp-pressed khaki pants. He was five foot eleven and thin with wire-rim glasses. He wore his graying sandy-blond hair on the long side, which made him resemble an aging hippie. However, there was an impish look in his twinkling eyes that made him appear younger than he was.

Milton patted his backpack. "I have some good stuff, Oliver."

"Well, let's get going," said Reuben, who was still holding his side. "I've got the early shift at the loading dock tomorrow." As the four headed off, Reuben drew next to Stone and slipped some money into his friend's shirt pocket.

"You don't have to do that, Reuben," Stone protested. "I have the stipend from the church."

"Right! I know they don't pay much to pull weeds and polish tomb-stones, especially when they throw in a roof over your head."

"Yes, but it's not like you have much to spare yourself."

"You did the same for me for many a year when I couldn't pay any-one to hire me." He then added gruffly, "Look at us. What a ragtag regiment we are. When the hell did we get so old and pathetic?"

Caleb laughed, although Milton looked stunned for a moment until he realized Reuben was joking.

"Old age always sneaks up on one, but once it's fully present, the ef-fects are hardly subtle," Stone commented dryly. As they walked along, Stone studied each of his companions, men he'd known for years and who'd been with him through both good and bad times.

Reuben had graduated from West Point and served three distin-guished tours in Vietnam, earning virtually every medal and commen-dation the military could confer. After that, he'd been assigned to the Defense Intelligence Agency, essentially the military counterpart of the CIA. However, he eventually quit the DIA and became a vocal protester of war in general and the Vietnam War in particular. When the country quit caring about that "little skirmish" in Southeast Asia, Reuben found himself a man without a cause. He lived in England for a time before returning to the States. After that, heavy doses of drugs and burned bridges left him with few options in life. He'd been fortunate to run into Oliver Stone, who helped turn his life around. Reuben was currently on the payroll of a warehouse company, where he unloaded trucks, exercising his muscles instead of his mind.

Caleb Shaw held twin doctorates in political science and eighteenth-century literature, though his bohemian nature found comfort in the fashions of the nineteenth century. Like Reuben, he'd been an active protester during Vietnam, where he lost his brother. Caleb had also been a strident voice against the administration during Watergate, when the nation lost the last vestiges of its political innocence. Despite his academic prowess, his eccentricities had long since banished him from the mainstream of scholarship. He currently worked in the Rare Books and Special Collections Division at the Library of Congress. His membership in the organization he was meeting with tonight had not been included on his résumé when he sought the position. Federal authorities frowned on people who affiliated with conspiracy-theory groups that held their meetings in the middle of the night.

Milton Farb probably possessed more sheer brilliance than the other members put together, even if he often forgot to eat, thought that Paris Hilton was a place to stay in France and believed that so long as he possessed an ATM card that he also had money. A child prodigy, he had the innate capacity to add enormous numbers in his head and a pure photographic memory—he could read or see something once and never forget it. His parents had worked in a traveling carnival, and Milton became a very popular sideshow, adding numbers in his head faster than someone else could on a calculator, and reciting, back, without faltering, the exact text of any book shown him.

Years later, after completing graduate school in record time, he was employed at the National Institutes of Health, or NIH. The only things that had prevented him from having a successful life were his worsening obsessive-compulsive disorder, or OCD, and a strong paranoia complex, both problems probably caused by his unorthodox childhood on the carnival circuit. Unfortunately these twin demons tended to erupt at inappropriate times. After sending a threatening letter to the president of the United States decades ago and being investigated by the Secret Service, his NIH career quickly came to an end.

Stone first met Milton in a mental health facility where Stone worked as an orderly and Milton was a patient. While he was hospitalized Milton's parents died and left their son penniless. Stone, who'd come to know of Milton's extraordinary intellectual ability, persuaded his destitute friend to try out for, of all things, *Jeopardy!* Milton qualified for the show, and, his OCD and other issues temporarily kept in check with medication, he went on to defeat all comers and earn a small fortune. He now had a thriving business designing corporate Web sites.

They headed down closer to the water where there was an old abandoned junkyard. At a spot nearby there was a great clump of ragged bushes, half in the water. From this hiding place the four managed to pull out a long, crusted rowboat that hardly looked seaworthy. Undaunted by this, they tugged off their socks and shoes and stuffed them in their bags, carried the boat down to the water and climbed in. They took turns at the oars, with big Reuben pulling the longest and hardest.

There was a cooling breeze on the water, and the lights of Georgetown and, farther south, Washington were inviting, though fading with the encroaching fog. There was much to like about the place, Stone thought as he sat in the bow of the little vessel. Yes, much to like, but more to loathe.

"The police boat's up near the 14th Street Bridge," Caleb reported. "They're on a new schedule. And they've got Homeland Security chopper patrols circling the Mall monuments every two hours again. It was on the alert e-mail at the library today."

"The threat level was elevated this morning," Reuben informed them. "Friends of mine in the know say it's all bullshit campaign posturing; President Brennan waving the flag."

Stone turned around and stared at Milton, who sat impassively in the stern.

"You're unusually quiet tonight, Milton. Everything all right?"

Milton looked at him shyly. "I made a friend." They all stared at him curiously. "A *female* friend," he added.

Reuben slapped Milton on the shoulder. "You old dog you."

"That's wonderful," Stone said. "Where did you meet her?"

"At the anxiety clinic. She's a patient too."

"I see," Stone said, turning back around.

"That's very nice, I'm sure," Caleb added diplomatically.

They moved slowly under the Key Bridge, keeping to the middle of the channel, and then followed the curve of the river south. Stone took comfort that the thickening fog made them practically invisible from shore. Federal authorities didn't tolerate trespassers very well. Stone watched as land came into view. "A little to the right, Reuben."

"Next time let's just meet in front of the Lincoln Memorial. It requires much less sweat on my part," the big man complained as he huffed and puffed on the oars.

The boat made its way around the western side of the island and into a small strip of water known appropriately as Little Channel. It was so isolated here that it seemed impossible that they'd glimpsed the U.S. Capitol dome just minutes ago.

Reaching shore, they climbed out and hauled the boat up into the bushes. As the men trudged single file through the woods toward the main trail, Oliver Stone carried an extra spring in his step. He had a lot he wanted to accomplish tonight.

# CHAPTER

# 5

The Latvian entourage finally retired, and Alex immediately hitched a ride to a federal cop hangout, not far from the Secret Service's WFO. The establishment was called the LEAP Bar. The acronym LEAP probably meant nothing to the layperson but was very well known to federal law enforcement types.

LEAP stood for "Law Enforcement Availability Pay." In exchange for being available at least ten hours a day for work that required a badge, a gun and more than a modicum of guts, federal officers received from their respective agencies a 25 percent bump in their base pay. Naming the bar LEAP was a brilliant marketing move by the saloon owners because the place had been packed from day one with pistol-toting men and women.

Alex passed through the front door and edged up to the bar. On the wall facing him were dozens of arm patches with the insignias of law enforcement agencies. Adorning the other walls were framed newspaper articles of heroic deeds by the FBI, DEA, ATF, FAM and other such agencies.

When Alex saw her, he grinned, in spite of wanting to remain cool and unaffected by her presence.

"Beefeater martini on the rocks with not two, or four, but three plump olives," she said, eyeing him with an accompanying smile.

"Good memory."

"Yeah, it's really tough considering you never order anything else."

"How's DOJ treating you?"

Kate Adams was the only bartender of his acquaintance who was also a Department of Justice lawyer.

She handed him his drink. "Hunky-dory. How's the Service treating you?"

"The paychecks keep coming and I keep breathing. That's all I ask."

"You really should raise your standards."

Kate mopped up the bar as Alex kept shooting discreet glances her way. She was five-seven with slender curves and shoulder-length blond hair curling around a long neck. She had high cheekbones with a slim, straight nose between, leading down to a shapely chin. In fact, everything about her was cool and classical until you got to the eyes. They were large and green and, to Alex, evidenced a fiery, passionate soul lurking within. Single, a GS-15 and in her mid-thirties—he'd checked on the government database—Kate looked five years younger than that. It was a pity, Alex thought, since he looked every bit his age, though his black hair had not yet started to thin or gray. Why, he didn't know.

"You're getting skinny," she remarked, breaking into his thoughts.

"Being out of protection, I'm not standing around shoveling in hotel food, and I actually get to work out instead of sitting my butt on a plane for ten hours at a crack."

He'd been coming here for over a month and chitchatting with the woman. He wanted to do more than that, though, and now tried to think of something that would hold her attention. He suddenly glanced at her hands. "So how long have you played the piano?"

"What?" Kate said in a surprised tone.

"Your fingers are calloused," he observed. "A sure sign of a piano player."

She looked at her hands. "Or from a computer keyboard."

"No. Computer keys callous the tips only. Piano keys hit the full upper part of the finger. And that's not all. You chew your nails down to the nubs. You have a dent in your left thumbnail, a scar on your right index finger, and your left pinkie is a little crooked, probably from a break when you were a kid."

Kate stared at her fingers. "What are you? Some sort of hand expert?"

"All Secret Service agents are. I've spent a good chunk of my adult life looking at hands in all fifty states and a bunch of countries overseas."

"Why?"

"Because people kill with their hands, Kate."

"Oh."

He was about to say something else when a group of FBI agents who'd just gotten off the last shift burst in, strode en masse to the bar and started ordering in loud voices. Alex, pushed away by their sheer number, took his drink and sat alone at a small table in a corner. However, his gaze remained fixed on Kate. The Bureau boys were giving the lovely bartender their fawning attention, which irritated the hell out of the Secret Service agent.

Alex finally turned his attention to the TV bolted to the wall. It was tuned to CNN, and a number of bar patrons were listening intently to the person speaking on the screen. Alex carried his drink over near the set so he could hear better, and watched a repeat of an earlier press conference held by Carter Gray, the nation's intelligence chief.

Gray's physical appearance instantly gave one assurance. Though short in stature, he had the weighty presence of granite with his burly shoulders, stout neck and wide face. He wore glasses that gave him a professional air, which wasn't simply a façade; he was the product of some of the finest schools in the country. And everything the schools hadn't taught him, he had learned through almost four decades in the field. He did not seem capable of being either intimidated or caught off guard.

"In rural southwest Virginia three *alleged* terrorists were found dead by a farmer looking for a lost cow," the secretary of intelligence announced with a completely straight face. The mental image this conjured made Alex want to laugh, but Carter Gray's grave demeanor extinguished any desire to chuckle.

"Forensic evidence suggests these men had been dead for at least a week and perhaps longer. Using the information database at the National Intelligence Center, we have confirmed that one of them was Muhammad al-Zawahiri, who we believe was connected to the Grand Central suicide bombing and is suspected of running an East Coast drug ring as well. Also killed were Adnan al-Rimi, believed to be one of al-Zawahiri's foot soldiers, and a third man whose identity is still unknown. Using intelligence developed by NIC, the FBI has arrested five other men with connections to al-Zawahiri and confiscated a large quantity of illegal drugs, cash and weapons."

Gray knew how to play the Washington game perfectly, Alex

thought. He'd made sure the public knew that NIC was the one who'd done the heavy lifting, but he'd also credited the FBI. Success in D.C. was measured in budget dollars and extra scraps of turf. Any bureaucrat who forgot this did so at his extreme peril. Yet every agency occasionally needed favors from its sister organizations. Gray had clearly covered his bases there.

Gray continued. "One of the most interesting facets of this incident is that, based on the investigation so far, it seems that al-Zawahiri killed his two companions and then committed suicide, although it may turn out that his death was somehow related to his drug trafficking. Regardless, we believe that this latest development will send another shock wave through terrorist communities at a time when the United States is making clear inroads in the fight against terror." He paused and then said in a crisp voice, "And now I'd like to introduce the president of the United States."

This was the standard drill for these press conferences. Gray would report the actual details in straightforward language. Then the charismatic James Brennan would follow and knock the political baseball out of the park with a hyperbole-laced speech that left no doubt as to who could protect the country best.

As Brennan began his remarks, Alex turned his attention back to the bar and the lady there. He knew that a woman like Kate Adams probably had twenty guys gunning for her, and most of them were probably better prospects than he was. She also probably realized how he felt; hell, she'd probably known how he felt about her even before *he* did.

He squared his shoulders and made up his mind. *Well, there's no reason I can't be the one guy out of twenty who sticks.*

However, halfway to the bar he stopped. Another man had come in and walked right up to her. The immediate smile on Kate's face was enough to tell Alex that this person was special. He sat back down and continued to watch as they moved off to the end of the bar where they could talk in private. The fellow was a little shorter than Alex, but younger, powerfully built and handsome. To Alex's practiced eye the man's clothes were very expensive. He was probably one of those high-priced corporate attorneys or lobbyists who plied their trade on K Street. Every time Kate laughed it was like a meat cleaver directly in the Secret Service agent's skull.

He finished his drink and was about to leave when he heard his name. He turned and saw Kate motioning to him. He reluctantly walked over.

"Alex, this is Tom Hemingway. Tom, Alex Ford," she said.

When they shook hands, there was such strength in Hemingway's grip that Alex, who was pretty strong, felt a pain shoot up his arm. He stared down at the man's hand, amazed at the thickness of the fingers and the knuckles that looked like wedges of steel. Hemingway had the most powerful set of hands the Secret Service agent had ever seen.

"Secret Service," Hemingway said, glancing at Alex's red lapel pin.

"You?" Alex asked.

"I'm with one of those places where I'd have to kill you if I told you," Hemingway replied with a knowing smile.

Alex could barely conceal his contempt. "I've got buddies at the CIA, DIA, NRO and the NSA. Which one are you?"

"I'm not talking anything that obvious, Alex," Hemingway answered with a chuckle.

Alex glanced at Kate. "Since when is DOJ mixed up with funny guys like him?"

Hemingway said, "Actually, we're working on something together. My agency and DOJ. Kate's the lead counsel. I'm the liaison."

"I'm sure you couldn't ask for a better partner than Kate." Alex put his empty glass down. "Well, I better get going."

"I'm sure I'll see you in here soon," Kate said quickly.

Alex didn't answer her. He turned to Hemingway. "Hang in there, Tom. And don't let it slip where you do your Uncle Sam time. I wouldn't want you to get busted for having to kill some poor bastard who asked too many questions." He strode off. With the eyes in the back of his head that all Secret Service agents seemed to possess, Alex felt the man's gaze burning into him. What he didn't sense was Kate's worried look following him out.

Okay, Alex thought as the crisp night air hit him, that was a real crappy end to what up until then was just your average shitty day. He decided to go for a stroll and let his Beefeater with a trio of fat olives pickle his soul. Now he wished he'd had a second.

# CHAPTER

## 6

THE PRESIDENTIAL MOTORCADE was returning to the White House after the fund-raising event, passing swiftly through empty streets and closed intersections. Thanks to the meticulous work of the Secret Service advance team, U.S. presidents never spent one idle moment in traffic. That perk alone would be sufficient motivation for some frustrated D.C. commuters to vie for the job. On the drive over, Gray had given his boss an end-of-the-day briefing on all pertinent intelligence matters. Now, in the backseat of the Beast, Brennan was intently studying some poll results while Gray stared straight ahead, his mind, as always, juggling a dozen things at once.

Finally, Gray glanced at his boss. "With all due respect, sir, going over the polls every five minutes won't change the result. As a presidential candidate Senator Dyson is not in your league. You will win this election by a landslide." Gray added diplomatically, "Thus, you have the luxury of focusing on other concerns of critical importance."

Brennan chuckled and put the poll results away. "Carter, you're a brilliant man but clearly no politician. A race isn't in the bag until the last vote has been counted. But I'm certainly aware that my considerable lead in this race is due in part to you."

"I truly appreciated your support during my very rough beginning."

Actually, Brennan had considered dumping Gray on multiple occasions during that "rough" period, a fact Gray knew well. However, while Gray had never been an ass-kisser, if one were inclined to smooch someone's buttocks on occasion, the derriere of the leader of the free world wasn't a bad place to target.

"Are you on to any more al-Zawahiris out there?"

"That incident was a very rare thing, Mr. President." Gray still wasn't sure why al-Zawahiri had seemingly turned like that. The NIC chief wanted to assume that his strategy of infiltrating terrorist organizations and employing other tactics to turn them against each other was really starting to pay dividends. However, Gray was far too suspicious a man to rule out alternatives.

"Well, it got us some great press."

As he had in the past, Gray mastered an urge to say what he really thought about such a comment. The veteran spy had served under several presidents, and they were all much like Brennan. They were not inherently bad people. However, considering their exalted status, Gray found them far more prone to traditional human failings than their fellow citizens. At their core Gray considered them to be selfish and egotistical creatures formed and then hardened in the heat of political battle. All presidents could claim it was about doing good, about furthering the right agendas, about leading their political party, but in Gray's experience it really all came down to the throne of the Oval Office. Power was the greatest high in the world, and the presidency of the United States represented the greatest power there was; its potency made heroin seem like a placebo.

However, if Brennan dropped dead tonight, there was an adequate vice president ready to step into his shoes, and the country would continue to run. In Gray's opinion, if Brennan somehow lost the upcoming election, his opponent would simply move into the White House and America wouldn't miss a beat. Presidents weren't indispensable, the NIC chief knew, they only thought they were.

"Rest assured, Mr. President, you would know of any more al-Zawahiris the moment I did."

Brennan was far too wily a politician to accept that statement at face value. It was a Washington tradition that intelligence chiefs kept things from their president. Yet Brennan had every incentive to allow the very popular Gray free rein to do his job. And Carter Gray was a spy, and spies always held things back; it was apparently in their genes never to be entirely forthcoming. It was as though, if they did reveal all, they'd disappear.

"Get some sleep, Carter, I'll see you tomorrow," the president said as they left the Beast.

Brennan's entourage poured out of the other cars in the motorcade. The president's top advisers and handlers hated the fact that Brennan had chosen to ride alone with Gray both to and from the fund-raiser. It had been a bone thrown Gray's way for the al-Zawahiri coup, but it benefited the president as well. At the fund-raiser Gray scared the fat checkbooks out of the well-heeled attendees with his stirring talk on terrorism. The tuxedoed crowd coughed up a million dollars for Brennan's political party. That was certainly worth a private ride in the Beast.

Gray was whisked away from the White House moments later. Contrary to the president's advice, Carter Gray had no intention of going to bed, and forty-five minutes later he was striding onto the grounds of the National Intelligence Center headquarters in Loudoun County, Virginia. The facility was as well protected as NSA in Maryland. Two full army companies—four hundred soldiers strong—were devoted to the exterior security. However, none had the necessary security clearances to set foot inside any of the structures except in the event of a catastrophe. The main building looked like it was all glass with commanding views of the Virginia countryside. There actually wasn't a window in the place. Behind the glass panes, the bunker-thick concrete walls, lined with specialized material, prevented human or electronic eyes from peering in.

Here more than three thousand men and women armed with the most sophisticated technology labored 24/7 to keep America safe, while the other intelligence agencies fed NIC with more data every second of every day.

After the intelligence failures surrounding 9/11 and the CIA's WMD disaster, many U.S. leaders were left wondering if "American intelligence" was an oxymoron. Subsequent governmental attempts at reform had met with little success and had actually created more confusion at a time when clarity and focus in the intelligence sector were national goals. A National Counter-Terrorism Center with its own director reporting to the president and a brand-new Intelligence Directorate at the FBI were added to the plethora of existing counterintelligence ranks that still largely refused to share information with each other.

At least in Gray's mind, saner heads had prevailed and shredded all these unnecessary layers in favor of a single national intelligence director with his own agency personnel, operations center and, of critical importance, budget *and* operational control over all other intelligence agencies. It was an old adage in the spy business that analysts got you in political hot water but covert op people landed you in prison. If Gray ever went down, he wanted to be responsible for his own professional demise.

Gray entered the main building, went through the biometric identification process and stepped into an elevator that whisked him to the top floor.

The room was small and well lighted. He entered, took a seat and put on a headset. There were four other people in the room. On one wall was a video screen, and on the table in front of Gray was a dossier labeled with the name Salem al-Omari. He knew the file contents by heart.

"It's late, so let's get to it," Gray said. The lights dimmed, the screen came to life and they saw a man sitting in a chair in the middle of a room. He was dressed in blue scrubs with neither hands nor feet bound. His features were Middle Eastern, his eyes haunted but also defiant. They were all defiant, Gray had found. When he looked at someone like al-Omari, Gray couldn't help but think of a Dostoyevsky creation, the displaced outsider, brooding, plotting and methodically stroking a weapon of anarchy. It was the face of a fanatic, of one possessed by a deranged evil. It was the same type of person who'd taken away forever the two people Gray had loved most in the world.

Though al-Omari was thousands of miles away in a facility only a very few people even knew existed, the picture and sound were crystal clear thanks to the satellite downlink.

Through his headset he asked al-Omari a question in English. The man promptly answered in Arabic and then smiled triumphantly.

In flawless Arabic Gray said, "Mr. al-Omari, I am fluent in Arabic and can actually speak it better than you. I know that you lived in England for years and that you speak English better than you do Arabic. I strongly suggest that we communicate in that language so there is absolutely no misunderstanding between us."

Al-Omari's smile faded, and he sat straighter in his chair.

Gray explained his proposal. Al-Omari was to become a spy for the United States, infiltrating one of the deadliest terrorist organizations operating in the Middle East. The man promptly refused. Gray persisted and al-Omari refused yet again, adding that "I have no idea what you're talking about."

"There are currently ninety-three terrorist organizations in the world as recognized by the U.S. State Department, most of them originating in the Middle East," Gray responded. "You have confirmed membership in at least three of them. In addition, you were found with forged passports, structural plans to the Woodrow Wilson Bridge and bomb-making material. Now you're going to work for us, or it will become distinctly unpleasant."

Al-Omari smiled and leaned toward the camera. "I was interrogated years ago in Jordan by your CIA and your military and your FBI, your so-called Tiger Teams. They sent females in wearing only their underwear. They wiped their menstrual blood on me, or at least what they called their menstrual blood, so I was unclean and could not perform my prayers. They rubbed their bodies against me, offered me sex if I talk. I say no to them and I am beaten afterward." He sat back. "I have been threatened with rape, and they say I will get AIDS from it and die. I do not care. True followers of Muhammad do not fear death as you Christians do. It is your greatest weakness and will lead to your total destruction. Islam will triumph. It is written in the Qur'an. Islam will rule the world."

"No, that is *not* written in the Qur'an," Gray rejoined. "Not in any of the 114 suras. And neither is world domination mentioned in the sayings of Muhammad."

"You've read the *Hadith*?" al-Omari said incredulously, referring to the collections of sayings and the life of the Prophet Muhammad and the first Muslims.

"And I've read the Qur'an in Arabic. Western scholars have never done a good job of translating that language, unfortunately. Thus, Mr. al-Omari, you should know that Islam is actually a peaceful, tolerant religion, though it *is* a religion that defends itself vigorously. That's understandable, since some 'civilized' cultures have been trying to convert Muslims to their faith ever since the Crusades, first with the sword and then the gun. But the *Hadith* says that even in jihad, innocent women and children must be spared."

"As if any of you are *innocent*," al-Omari shot back. "All of Islam must fight back against those who would oppress us."

"Islam represents one-fifth of the face of humanity, and the overwhelming numbers of your brethren believe in the freedoms of speech and press and also equal protection under law. And more than half of the world's Muslims live under *democratically* constituted governments. I know that you were trained at a madrasa in Afghanistan, so that your knowledge of the Qur'an is limited to rote memory, thus I'll forgive your seeming ignorance on these issues." Gray didn't add that at the madrasa al-Omari's training would have also included automatic weapons and how to fight holy wars, earning such a training center the dubious title of Islamic West Point.

Gray continued. "You aspired to be a *shahid*, but you had neither the nerve nor the zealotry to be a suicide bomber, nor did you have the backbone and instincts to be a mujahid."

"You shall see whether I have the courage to die for Islam."

"Killing you does me no good. I want you to work for me."

"Go to hell!"

"We can do this easy or hard," Gray said, checking his watch. He had been up for thirty hours now. "And there are many ways to attain *Janna*."

Al-Omari leaned forward. "I will get to Heaven *my* way," he said, sneering.

"You have a wife and children living back in England," Gray noted.

Al-Omari folded his arms across his chest and assumed a stony look. "Bastards like you will serve us well in the next life."

"A son and a daughter," Gray continued as though he hadn't heard the man's retort. "I realize that the women's fate may not overly concern you. However, the boy—"

"My son will gladly die—"

Gray interrupted in a very firm voice. "I will *not* kill your son. I have other plans for him. He just turned eighteen months old?"

A trace of concern crossed al-Omari's face. "How did you know that?"

"You will raise him in the Muslim faith?"

Al-Omari did not answer; he simply stared at the camera.

Gray continued. "Well, if you do not agree to work with us, I will take your son from his mother, and he will be adopted by a loving couple who will raise him as their own." Gray paused for the emphasis he would place on his next words. "He will be raised in the Christian faith in America by Americans. Or not. It's all up to you."

So stunned was al-Omari that he rose from the chair and staggered toward the camera, until hands appeared and forced him back into his chair.

The next words out of his mouth were in Arabic, but were nonetheless clear enough. Moments later, his rage uncontrollable, al-Omari had to be physically restrained as the threats continued to flow. Finally, his mouth was taped shut.

Gray pushed the man's file away. "Over the last few years 7,816 Americans have died at the hands of people like you. All of these deaths have taken place on American soil. Counting attacks overseas, the death toll is nearly ten thousand. Some of these victims were children who were denied the opportunity to grow up to practice any religious faith at all. I will give you twenty-four hours to make your decision. I ask you to consider it carefully. If you work with us, you and your family will live out your lives in comfort. However, if you choose not to work with us . . ." Gray nodded to the man next to him, and the screen went blank.

Gray looked at six more files in front of him. Four represented other Middle Easterners, much like al-Omari. The fifth was a neo-Nazi based in Arkansas, and the sixth, Kim Fong, was a member of a Southeast Asian group with ties to known Middle East terrorist organizations. These men were "ghost detainees" in the unofficial nomenclature. No one other than Gray and a few select people at NIC knew they were even in custody. Like the CIA, NIC maintained clandestine paramilitary squads in hot spots all over the world. One of their tasks was to capture alleged enemies of America and afford them no due process whatsoever.

Gray would put similar proposals to all the ghost detainees, although the inducements would vary depending on the intelligence Gray had gathered on each man's background. Money worked with more of them than one would think. Rich people rarely blew themselves and others to bits for religious or any other reasons. However, they often manipulated other people to do it for them. Gray would be lucky if half accepted his offer, but he would gladly take those odds.

An hour later Gray left NIC. Only the skinhead had agreed outright to help, doubtless spurred on by Gray's threat to turn him over to a radically violent anti-Nazi group headquartered in South America if he didn't cooperate. Other than that, the night had been a disappointment.

As Gray walked to his car he reflected on the situation confronting him. The violence was mounting on each side, and the harder one side hit, the harder the other tried to hit back. Using just a fraction of its nuclear arsenal, the United States could wipe out the entire Middle East, vaporizing everyone in the blink of an eye, along with every holy site for two of the world's major religions. Barring that unthinkable scenario, Gray did not see any clear resolution. This was not a war of professional armored battalions versus turbaned rabble in the streets toting rifles and RPGs. And it was not simply a difference of religions. It was a battle against a mind-set, of how people should conduct their lives, a battle that had political, social and cultural facets melded together into an exceedingly complex mosaic of humanity under enormous strain. At times Gray humbly wondered whether the conflict should be fought with psychiatrists and counselors instead of soldiers and spies. Yet all he could do was get up each day and do his job.

Gray sat back against the worn leather of the Suburban he was riding in while the armed guards all around him kept a close lookout. Gray closed his eyes for fifteen minutes until he felt the vehicle slow. Then came the familiar rattle as the motorcade rolled across the gravel drive leading up to Gray's modest home. It was as well guarded as the VP's digs at the Naval Observatory. President Brennan was not about to let anything happen to his intelligence chief.

Gray lived alone, but not by choice. He went inside, allowed himself a beer to unwind and then headed upstairs to sleep for a few hours. As was his habit before retiring, he picked up the two pictures on the fireplace mantel across from his bed. The first was his wife, Barbara, a woman who'd shared most of his adult life. The second photo was of his only child, his daughter, Margaret, or Maggie as everyone had called her. *Had?* He had never grown comfortable referring to his family in the past tense. Yet how else did one refer to the dead and buried? He kissed both of the pictures and set them back down.

After he had climbed into bed, the horrible weight of depression lasted thirty minutes, less than usual, and then Carter Gray fell into an exhausted sleep. In five hours he would rise and again engage in the only battle he now considered worth fighting.

# CHAPTER

# 7

ALEX FORD'S WALK THAT NIGHT took him east, and he soon found himself in familiar territory: 1600 Pennsylvania Avenue. Now gracing the area between the White House and Lafayette Park were elm trees and retractable bollards, interspersed with guard booths camouflaged so they didn't stand out like prison gun towers. However, the key here was, and always would be, security, regardless of how many new trees and pretty flowers they planted.

"Hey, Alex," a man in a suit said as he walked out of the front security gate.

"You going on or off duty, Bobby?"

Bobby smiled. "You see an ear fob sticking out my ass? I'm going home to the little woman and kids, unless they moved out and forgot to tell me, which isn't exactly beyond the realm of possibility, since I'm never there. What brings you back here?"

Alex shrugged. "You know, once you get POTUS duty inside you, you can't get it out."

"Right! I'm counting the days till I see my family more than once a year."

"You on the campaign travel team?"

Bobby nodded. "We leave day after tomorrow to shake some more hands and make some more speeches from Iowa to Mississippi. Because of all the campaign stuff, we were shorthanded and had to pull in some WFOs on twenty-one-day rotations to post POTUS' and the VP's families."

"I know. The halls at work are pretty empty."

"Brennan did a fund-raiser tonight. Kiss-up for dollars. Lucky me, I got to stay here."

"Yeah, lucky you."

Bobby laughed. "I don't know if you heard, but the man's hometown in Pennsylvania changed its name to Brennan. He's going up there during the campaign to attend the dedication. Talk about your ego trips." Bobby drew closer and said in a low voice, "He's not a bad guy. Hell, I voted for him. But he's a slick one. Some of the stuff he's done on the side . . ."

"He's not the first."

"If John Q. Public knew what we did, huh?"

As he headed off, Alex glanced over at Lafayette Park where the remaining "White House protesters" were located, or at least that's how Alex and other Secret Service agents politely referred to them. The signs and tents and odd-looking folks had always held a fascination for him. There used to be far more of them, with elaborate signs erected everywhere. Yet even before 9/11 a crackdown had been enforced, and when the area in front of the White House was redone, this created a good excuse to shove these people away. Yet even the powerless in America had rights, and a few of them hooked up with the ACLU and sued in court for the right to return and the Supreme Court eventually sided with them. However, only two of the protesters had elected to come back.

During his stint at the White House Alex got to know some of the protesters. Most were certifiably crazy and therefore closely watched by the Secret Service. There was one fellow he remembered who dressed only in neckties, strategically placing them over his body. Yet not all of the protesters were asylum candidates, including the man he'd come to visit.

Alex stopped by one tent and called out, "Oliver? It's Alex Ford. You there?"

"He no here," a female voice said contemptuously.

Alex glanced over at the woman as she walked up with a paper cup of coffee in hand. "How's it going, Adelphia?"

"Doctors are immorally killing babies all over this country, that's how it *goes*."

The woman was nothing if not passionate, Alex thought. Adelphia might've carried her passion somewhat to an extreme, but Alex still respected her for at least having one.

"Yeah, that's what I hear." He paused respectfully. "Uh, where's Oliver?"

"I tell you, he no here. He have somewhere to *go!*"

"Where?" Alex knew where both Stone and Adelphia lived but didn't want to let on to the woman that he had this information. Adelphia, he'd come to learn, was paranoid enough.

"*Not* am I his keeper." She turned away.

Alex smiled. When he'd been on presidential protection detail, he'd always suspected that the lady had a thing for Mr. Stone. Most of the agents who knew Oliver Stone had written him off as a harmless crackpot who adopted the name of a famous film director for some ridiculous reason. Alex had taken the time to get to know the man, however, finding Stone erudite and thoughtful, and more in touch with the political and economic complexities of the world than some wonks who worked across the street. In particular, the man knew by heart every detail of seemingly every conspiracy ever reported on. Some of the agents called him King Con for this attribute. *And* Stone played one hell of a game of chess.

Alex called out to Adelphia, "If you see Oliver, tell him Agent Ford was looking for him; you remember me, right?" Adelphia made no sign that she'd heard him, but then again, that was just Adelphia.

He headed back on foot to where his car was parked. Along the way Alex passed something that made him stop. On the far corner two men, one black and one white, were working on a freestanding ATM housed in a sliver between two buildings. They were dressed in overalls that had "Service Staff" printed across the back. Their van was parked at the curb. It had a company name and phone number printed on the side.

Alex slipped into the shadows, pulled out his cell phone and called the number shown on the van. An official-sounding recording answered, giving the business hours for the company and so on. Alex did a quick look-see in the van, then pulled out his Secret Service badge and walked over to the men.

"Hey, fellows, you servicing the machine?"

The short man eyed the badge and nodded. "Yeah. Lucky us."

Alex looked at the ATM, and his very experienced eye saw what he thought he would see. "Hope you guys are union."

"Proud members of Local 453," the smaller man said with a laugh. "At least we're getting double time to do this crap."

*Okay, here we go again.*

Alex drew his pistol and pointed it at them. "Pop the machine open."

The black guy said irately, "You Secret Service, what business you got checking out an ATM?"

"Not that I need to give you a reason, but the Secret Service was originally formed to protect the official currency of the United States." Alex pointed the gun directly at the black man's head. "Open it!"

Stuffed inside the ATM were no fewer than a hundred cards.

Alex gave the pair their Miranda speech while he put PlastiCuffs on them. Then he called the arrest in. As they were waiting, the black guy looked over at him.

"We been doing this a long time and had no trouble. How the hell you figure it?"

"There's a skimmer reader attached to the card slot. It captures the PIN so you can clone the card. And on top of that banks are cheap. So there's no way one's going to pay some union guys double overtime to schlep down here in the middle of the night to service this thing."

After the police took the men away, Alex walked down the street to his car. Even after the successful if unexpected bust, all he could think about was one Kate Adams, who fought for justice by day and poured out highballs by night and seemed very close to the big-knuckled Tom Hemingway of the undisclosed supersecret agency.

Alex could only hope tomorrow would start on a better note.

## 8

STONE, MILTON, REUBEN AND Caleb walked along the main trail on
Theodore Roosevelt Island, a ninety-acre memorial to the former
president and Rough Rider that sat in the middle of the Potomac
River. They soon reached a clearing where an immense statue of Teddy
Roosevelt stood with his right arm raised to the heavens as though he
were about to retake the oath of office nearly ninety years after his
death. The area was elaborately laid out with brick pavers, two curved
stone bridges over man-made canals of water, and a pair of huge foun-
tains that flanked the statue.

Oliver Stone sat cross-legged in front of the statue, and the others
joined him there. Stone was an enthusiastic fan of T.R., which was the
reason they were here, albeit as trespassers, since the island officially
closed at dark. He announced in a solemn voice, "The regular meeting
of the Camel Club is officially called to order. In the absence of a formal agenda I move that we discuss observations since the last meeting
and then open the floor for new business. Do I have a second?"

"I second the motion," Reuben said automatically.

"All in favor say aye," Stone added.

The ayes carried the motion, and Stone opened the notebook he
pulled from his knapsack. Reuben slipped some crumpled pieces of
paper from his pocket, and Milton slid his laptop computer out, then
took a small bottle of antibacterial lotion out of his pocket and thoroughly washed his hands. Stone used a small penlight to see his notes,
while Reuben read by the flickering flame of his cigarette lighter.

"Brennan went out late tonight," Stone reported. "Carter Gray was
with him."

"Those two are joined at the hip," Reuben noted hotly.

"Like J. Edgar Hoover and Clyde Tolson," Caleb added jokingly as he took off his bowler hat.

"I was thinking more of Lenin and Trotsky," Reuben growled.

"So you don't trust Gray?" Stone asked.

"How can you trust any prick who actually likes being called a czar?" Reuben replied. "And as far as Brennan goes, all I can say is he should thank his lucky stars for terrorists because but for them his ass would be headed for the unemployment line."

"Reading the newspapers again, are we?" Stone said in an amused tone.

"I use the papers to get my laughs, just like everybody else."

Stone looked thoughtful. "James Brennan is a gifted politician, and his intellect is first-rate. But more than that, he has the power to make people trust him. Yet inside, a darker beast lurks. He has an agenda that is not available to the public."

Reuben eyed him closely. "It seems to me that you're describing Carter Gray more than you are the president."

Milton broke in excitedly. "I've compiled facts on several conspiracies of global proportion that have not been reported by any news media."

"And I," Reuben said as he eyed his notes, "have personally noted three occasions when the present Speaker of the House has been unfaithful to his quite fetching wife."

"Personally noted?" Caleb asked skeptically as he stared at his friend.

Reuben barked, "Two of my close acquaintances in the know keep me abreast of things. Clearly, despite the trouble some of his amorous predecessors have gotten into, it still seems our esteemed congressman continues to cavalierly insert his dinky in places it should not be." He waved his notes. "It's all here."

"What close acquaintances?" Caleb persisted.

"High-placed sources that desire to remain anonymous, if you must damn well know," Reuben snapped as he stuffed these allegedly libidinous revelations back in his pocket.

Milton interrupted impatiently. "Yes, but let me tell you about my theories." He spent the next twenty minutes enthusiastically discussing theoretical ties between North Korea and Great Britain for purposes of worldwide terrorism, and a possible attack on the euro and yen by a cabal in Yemen sponsored by a top member of the Saudi royal family.

"I consider these facts material to the worldwide apocalypse that is most certainly on the horizon," Milton concluded.

The other members of the Camel Club sat there looking a bit overwhelmed; it was a normal reaction after Milton had delivered one of his convoluted diatribes.

Finally, Reuben said, "Yes, but that North Korea/Great Britain thing is a bit of a stretch, don't you think, Milton? I mean the bloody Koreans are absolutely humorless, and whatever else you say about the Brits, they are a very witty people."

Stone looked at Caleb. "Anything interesting on your end?"

Caleb thought for a moment. "Well, we had a real scare when we couldn't find our Dutch Bible."

They all looked at him expectantly.

Caleb exclaimed, "Our Dutch Bible! It has hand-colored illustrations by Romeyn de Hooghe. He's generally thought to be the most important Dutch illustrator of the late seventeenth and early eighteenth centuries. But it turned out all right. It was there the whole time, simply a clerical error."

"Thank God," Reuben said sarcastically. "We wouldn't want a de *Hoose* on the loose."

Disappointed, Stone turned back to Reuben. "Other than your lascivious congressman, do you have anything of real interest?"

Reuben shrugged. "I've been out of the loop too long, Oliver. People forget you."

"Then why don't we move on to something a little more concrete?"

The other men eyed him curiously.

Stone drew a long breath. So many birthdays had passed by uncelebrated that he had to actually think about how old he was. *Sixty-one,* he said to himself. *I am sixty-one years old.* He'd founded the Camel Club long ago with the purpose of scrutinizing those in power and raising the public cry when they believed things to be awry, which they very often were. He had kept vigil outside 1600 Pennsylvania Avenue watching and noting his observations and fighting for things that other people apparently didn't believe were important anymore, like truth and accountability.

He was beginning to wonder if it was worth it.

Yet he said aloud, "Have you noticed what is going on in this country?" He stared at his friends, who didn't answer. "They may have us believing that we're better protected. Yet being safer doesn't necessarily mean that we're more *free*."

"You sometimes have to sacrifice freedom for security, Oliver," Caleb said as he fiddled with his heavy watch. "I don't necessarily like it but what's the alternative?"

"The alternative is not living in fear," Stone answered. "Especially in a state of fear from exaggerated circumstances. Men like Carter Gray are quite good at that."

"Well, Gray's first year on the job you would've thought the man would have been run out on a rail, but he somehow managed to turn it around," Reuben admitted grudgingly.

"Which proves my point," Stone retorted, "because I don't think anyone is that good or that *lucky*." He paused, obviously choosing his words with care. "My opinion is that Carter Gray is bad for this country's future. I open the meeting to discuss relevant possibilities."

His three companions simply stared dully at him. Finally, Caleb found his voice.

"Uh, what exactly do you mean, Oliver?"

"I mean what can the Camel Club do to make sure that Carter Gray is relieved of his post as intelligence secretary?"

"You want *us* to take down Carter Gray!" Caleb exclaimed.

"Yes."

"Oh, good," Reuben added in mock relief. "Because I thought it might be something difficult you were wanting."

"There is ample historical precedent for the powerless overcoming the powerful," Stone noted.

"Yeah, but in real life, Goliath kicks the shit out of David nine times out of ten," Reuben replied grimly.

Stone said, "Then what exactly is the purpose of continuing the club? We meet once a week and compare notes, observations and theories. To what end?"

Caleb answered, "Well, we've done some good. Although we never got any credit for it. Our work helped reveal the truth behind the scandal at the Pentagon. That came from a scrap of conversation the White House chef's assistant overheard and told you about. And don't forget about the mole at NSA who was altering transcription files, Oliver. And then there was the DIA subterfuge that Reuben stumbled onto."

"Those events were a long time ago," Stone replied. "So again I ask, what is the purpose of the club *now*?"

Reuben said, "Well, maybe it's like lots of other clubs, except without a building, refreshments or the pleasure of female companionship. But what can you expect when you don't pay any dues?" he added, grinning.

Before Stone could answer, all four of them had turned their heads in the direction of the sounds filtering through the woods. Stone instantly put a finger to his lips and listened. There it was again: a boat's engine, and it sounded as though it was right at the edge of the island. They all took their bags and made their way quietly into the surrounding brush.

# CHAPTER

# 9

Oliver Stone eased a branch out of the way and peered through this small gap toward the paved area in front of the Roosevelt monument. His companions were also riveted on what was happening nearby.

Two men appeared on one of the gravel paths carrying something on a plastic tarp. One man was tall, lean and blond, the other short, thick and dark-haired. When they laid the tarp on the ground, Stone could see that they were carrying a man bound with straps. They slid the plastic from under him and then swept the area with their flashlights, going grid by grid. Fortunately, as soon as Stone saw the flashlights come out of their pockets, he motioned for his friends to hunker down behind the cover of bushes, with their faces hidden from the beams.

Satisfied that they were alone, the men turned back to their captive. One of them removed the cover from his mouth and placed it in his pocket.

The man made a few sounds, none of them coherent. He appeared drunk.

The short man put on a pair of rubber gloves and pulled a revolver from his coat while the other man undid their captive's bindings. The short man took a nearly empty bottle from the duffel bag and pressed the semiconscious man's hands around it and then splashed a bit of the remaining liquid on his clothes and around his mouth.

Reuben was about to charge out of the bushes, but Stone put a hand on his arm. The other man was also armed; a pistol was clearly visible in his belt holster. The Camel Club stood no chance. To reveal themselves now would mean a death sentence.

Meanwhile, the man holding the gun knelt down next to the captive. He took the man's right hand and placed it around the gun. Perhaps because of the touch of the cold metal, the captive opened his eyes. As he stared up at the other man, he suddenly cried out, "I'm sorry. Please don't. I'm sorry."

The short man slid the pistol into the man's mouth, pushing it against the roof of the mouth. The captive choked for an instant, and then the short man forced the trigger down. At the sound of the shot all four members of the Camel Club closed their eyes.

When they reopened them, the four men continued to stare transfixed as the gun and bottle were placed near the body. A plastic baggie was taken out of the knapsack carried by the other man, and this was laid next to the murder weapon. Finally, a piece of folded paper was placed in the pocket of the dead man's windbreaker.

Finished, the two men looked around the area even as the Camel Club members shrank farther back in the bushes. A minute later the killers trudged off. As soon as the sounds of their footfalls disappeared, the Camel Club let out a collective sigh of relief. Holding his finger to his lips, Stone quietly led the way out of their hiding place and into the clearing.

Reuben squatted down next to the body. He shook his head and said in a very low voice, "At least he was killed instantly. As if that somehow makes up for being murdered." He looked at the nearly empty bottle. "Dewar's. Looks like they got the poor bastard drunk so he couldn't fight back."

"Is there any ID on the body?" Stone asked.

"This is a crime scene," Caleb said shakily. "We shouldn't touch anything."

"He's right," Reuben agreed. He glanced over at Milton, who was making frantic motions with his hands as he sped silently through his OCD ritual. Reuben sighed. "We should get the hell out of here, Oliver, is what we should do."

Stone knelt down beside him and spoke quietly but urgently. "This was an execution made to look like suicide, Reuben. Those were professional killers, and I'd like to know who the target was and what he knew that led to his death." As he was speaking, he wrapped a handkerchief pulled from his pocket around his hand, searched the dead man's pockets and slid out a wallet. He nimbly flipped it open, and they all gazed at the driver's license in the see-through plastic. Reuben pulled out his lighter and flicked it on so Stone could read the information on the license.

"Patrick Johnson," Stone read. "He lived in Bethesda." Stone put the wallet back, searched the other pocket and pulled out the piece of paper the killer had placed there. By the flickering flame of the lighter he read the contents of the letter in a soft voice.

" 'I'm sorry. It's all too much. I can't live with this anymore. This is the only way. I'm sorry. So sorry.' And it's signed Patrick Johnson."

Caleb slowly took his bowler hat off in respect for the dead and mouthed a prayer.

Stone continued, "The writing is very legible. I suppose the police will assume it was written before he supposedly drank himself into a suicidal stupor."

Reuben said, "He said he was sorry right before they killed him."

Stone shook his head. "I think he was speaking about something *else* he was sorry for. The note's words are just a subterfuge, a typical suicide's last plea."

Stone put the note back. As he was doing so, his hand nudged against something else in the dead man's pocket. He pulled out a small red lapel pin and squinted at it in the darkness.

"What's that?" Reuben asked, holding his lighter closer.

Caleb said in a hushed whisper, "What if they come back?"

Stone put the pin back and felt Johnson's clothes. "They're soaked through."

Reuben pointed to the plastic baggie. "What do you make of that?"

Stone thought for a moment. "I think I understand its purpose and the soaked clothes as well. But Caleb's right, we should leave."

They set off and then realized that Milton wasn't with them. They turned back and found him crouched over the dead man counting, with his hand reaching over the body.

"Uh, Milton, we really need to leave," Caleb said urgently.

However, Milton was apparently so traumatized that he couldn't stop counting.

"Oh, for chrissakes," Reuben moaned. "Why don't we all just bloody well count together until they come back and give *us* some bullets to suck on?"

Stone put a steadying hand on Reuben's arm and stepped forward next to Milton. He looked down at Patrick Johnson's face. He was young, though death had already begun to hollow him. Stone knelt and placed his hand gently on Milton's shoulder and said quietly, "We can do nothing for him now, Milton. And the comfort you take in your counting, the safety and security that you're striving for, can be defeated if those two men come back." He added bluntly, "They have guns, Milton, we don't."

Milton halted his ritual, stifled a sob and said in a quivering voice, "I don't like violence, Oliver." Milton clutched his knapsack closer to his chest and then pointed at the corpse. "I don't like *that*."

"I know, Milton. None of us do."

Stone and Milton rose together. With a sigh of relief Reuben followed them to the path leading to their boat.

Warren Peters, who'd fired the shot that killed Patrick Johnson, was walking along the trail back to their dinghy when he stopped short.

"Shit!" he whispered.

"What?" Tyler Reinke asked as he nervously looked around. "Police boat?"

"No, almost a big mistake." Peters scooped up some dirt and pebbles in his hand. "When we dunked him, it cleaned his shoe soles off. If he walked here through the woods, his soles wouldn't be clean. The FBI won't miss that."

The two men hurried back along the path and over to the body. Peters squatted down next to the murdered man's shoes and pressed dirt and pebbles into the soles.

"Good catch," Reinke said.

"I don't want to even think about what would've happened if I'd blown that." He finished his task and started to rise, but his gaze caught on something.

"Son of a bitch!" Peters exclaimed between clenched teeth. He pointed to the note he had pressed into the victim's pocket: A corner of it was sticking out. "I shoved that all the way in because I didn't want it to look too obvious. So why's it visible now?" He pushed the note back in the pocket and looked at his partner searchingly.

"Could an animal have taken a go at the body?"

"After a few minutes? And why would an animal go after paper instead of flesh?" He rose, pulled a flashlight from his pocket and checked the stone floor.

Reinke said, "You must've made a mistake with the paper. You probably didn't push it in as far as you thought."

Peters continued to search the area and then stiffened.

"What now?" his companion asked impatiently.

"Listen, do you hear that?"

Reinke remained still and silent and then his mouth gaped.

"Somebody running. That way!" He pointed to the right, down one of the trails in the opposite direction they had come.

The two men pulled their weapons and sprinted toward the sound.

# CHAPTER

# 10

Stone and the others had just jumped into their boat and pushed off. The fog was now dense enough to make navigation tricky. They were perhaps ten feet from the island in the Little Channel when the two men burst out of the trees and saw them.

"Pull as hard as you can and keep your face turned down," Stone said to Reuben, who needed no such prompting. His broad shoulders and thick arms moved with a Herculean effort, and the little boat sprang away from the shore.

Stone turned to the others in the boat and whispered, "Don't let them see your faces. Caleb, take off your hat!" They all immediately bent low, and Caleb swept off his bowler and jammed it between his quivering knees. Milton had started counting the minute he climbed onto the boat. The two men on shore took aim at their quarry, but the fog made their targets very elusive. They both fired, but their shots splattered harmlessly into the water a good foot from the boat.

"Pull, Reuben, pull," a terrified Caleb gasped as he ducked even farther down.

"What the hell do you think I'm doing?" Reuben snapped, sweat trickling down his face.

The pursuers took careful aim and fired twice more. One slug found its mark, and splintered wood flew up and hit Stone in the right hand. The blood trickled down his fingers and onto the boat's gunwale. He quickly staunched the flow with the same handkerchief he'd used to search the body of Patrick Johnson.

"Oliver!" a frantic Milton called out.

"I'm all right," Stone answered. "Just stay down!"

The two gunmen, realizing the futility of their attack, raced away.

"They're going to get their boat," Stone warned.

"Well, then we have a bit of a problem, because *their* boat has a motor," Reuben retorted. "I'm going as fast as I can, but there's not much gas left in my tank."

Stone pulled on Caleb's sleeve. "Caleb, you take one oar and I'll take the other." Reuben moved out of the way, and the two men rowed with all their strength.

Ordinarily, after leaving the inlet they would have gone north on the river and returned to their original launching site. Now they simply wanted to get to the mainland as fast as possible, which meant a straight path east. They passed the western tip of the island and made their turn toward Georgetown.

"Oh, shit!" Reuben was staring back toward the island as he heard the boat engine coming. "Row like your lives depend on it," he bellowed to Stone and Caleb. "Because they sure as hell do."

Seeing that Caleb and Stone were growing tired, Reuben pushed them out of the way and took up the oars again, pulling with all his considerable strength.

"I think they're gaining," Caleb said breathlessly.

A shot hit right next to him, and Caleb joined a cowering Milton in the bottom of the boat.

Stone ducked down as another shot passed by, and then he heard Reuben cry out.

"Reuben?" He turned to look at his friend.

"It's all right, just a glance, but I'd forgotten how much they burn." Reuben added grimly, "They've got us, Oliver. It'll be *five* corpses for those bastards tonight."

Stone looked toward the wispy lights of sleeping Georgetown. Even though the river was fairly narrow here, with the fog they were still too far away for anyone on shore to see what was going on. He glanced back at the oncoming boat. He could now make out the silhouettes of the two men on board. His mind raced back to the businesslike manner in which the unfortunate Patrick Johnson had been dispatched. Stone envisioned the gun being placed inside his own mouth, the trigger pulled.

Suddenly, the motorboat veered away from them.

"What the—" Reuben said.

"It must be the police boat. Listen," Stone whispered, pointing south of their position and cupping his ear.

In a relieved voice Caleb cried out, "The police? Quick, get their attention."

"No," Stone said firmly. "I want everyone to remain as silent as possible. Reuben, stop rowing."

Reuben looked curiously at his friend but stopped pulling at the oars and just sat there. "We'll be damn lucky if they don't run right into us," he complained in a low voice.

All of them could now clearly hear the whine of the big engine. Through the fog they saw the green starboard side running lights of the patrol boat passing by less than thirty feet away. The policemen on board wouldn't have been able to hear the engine of the other boat over their own, nor could they have seen the rowboat, which had no lights. The members of the Camel Club held their collective breath and watched as the patrol boat slowly glided along. When it was finally out of sight, Stone said, "Okay, Reuben, get us to shore."

Caleb sat up. "Why didn't you want us to alert the police?"

Stone waited until the sharp outline of land came into view before answering.

"We're out on a boat we're not supposed to have, going to a place we're not supposed to be. A man has been killed and his body left on Roosevelt Island. If we tell the police we witnessed a murder, we're admitting that we were there. We can tell them we saw two men who then tried to kill us, but we have no proof of that."

Now Milton sat up. "But you and Reuben were hurt."

"My hand is only scratched and Reuben's was just a glance, so there's no conclusive proof a bullet was involved. Thus, the police are left with the fact that there is a dead body that was transported by boat to the island we were on. We have a boat that could have performed that task quite easily, and there isn't another such vessel around, since that motorboat will be long gone by the time we explain things. We are persons whom the police might not put much credibility in. So what do you think would be the most logical result of our telling them our story?" Stone looked at each of them expectantly.

"They'd arrest us and throw away the key," Reuben muttered as he ripped off a piece of his shirt and tied it around the minor wound on his arm. "What I'd like to know is how those two bastards suddenly realized we were on the island."

"They must have heard us," Stone said. "Or else they came back for some other reason and noticed something amiss. Maybe I didn't put the note or the pin back properly."

"You didn't say what the pin was," Caleb noted.

"It was the lapel pin customarily worn by Secret Service agents."

"You think he was an agent?" Reuben asked as they drifted to shore.

"Presumably, he has some connection."

When they reached land they swiftly pulled the boat ashore and hid it in an old drainage ditch near the seawall.

"So now what?" Reuben asked as they trudged along through the quiet streets of Georgetown.

Stone ticked the points off on his fingers. "We find out who the murdered man was. We find out why someone would want to kill him. And we find out *who* killed him."

Reuben looked incredulous. "And I thought your idea of bringing down Carter Gray was a toughie. Jesus, man, do you understand what you're saying?"

"Yes, I do," Stone replied impassively.

"But why do we have to do anything?" Caleb asked.

Stone stared at him. "Men who kill like that tend to clean up all loose ends, which means they'll do everything they can to track us down and kill us too. We can't go to the police for the reasons I've already outlined. So my very strong suggestion is—"

Reuben broke in. "That we get them before they get us."

Stone walked on, the rest of the Camel Club hurrying along in his wake.

# CHAPTER

# 11

As THE VAN PASSED AROUND A bend in the road, the elaborate sign set in foot-high reflective letters came into view:

WELCOME TO BRENNAN, PENNSYLVANIA,
BIRTHPLACE OF PRESIDENT JAMES H. BRENNAN

A rendering of Brennan had been carved into the wood beside these words. It was a good likeness. The man in the van's passenger seat looked at his two companions and smiled. Then he raised an imaginary gun, pointed it at Brennan's head and "fired," placing three shots right into the brain of the most powerful man on earth.

The van entered the downtown area: With a population of fifty thousand and fast becoming a major bedroom community of Pittsburgh, Brennan had high hopes for a major renaissance, and the new jobs, emerging business and construction going on around town were a testament to this dream becoming a reality. Much of this hope was based upon it being the hometown of the very popular incumbent president.

Even the unused water tower situated in the middle of downtown had not escaped this push for greatness. At first the town fathers had wanted to put Brennan's picture and the seal of the president of the United States on the tower. When told that this would neither be legal nor in good taste, they instead painted it in the Stars and Stripes, thereby connecting the man and the town. The three men in the van were also very interested in the nation's chief executive, for an entirely different reason.

The three men were tall, and possessed the leanness of people unfamiliar with a western diet of saturated fat and sugar. Two were Arab and the other Persian, though they had downplayed their Middle Eastern origins by shaving off their beards and assuming the style typical of college students—namely, baggy jeans, sweaters, athletic shoes and plenty of attitude. They were enrolled as part-time students at the local community college studying basic engineering. In reality each was proficient in certain areas of science that had to do with barometric pressure, wind deflection, air drag and coefficiency as well as more esoteric subjects like the Coriolis effect and gyroscopic precession.

Two of the men were from Afghanistan and in their late thirties, though they looked much younger. The other man, the Persian, was thirty years old and hailed from Iran. Their professors and classmates believed them to be from India and Pakistan. The three Muslims had found that to most Westerners the term "Middle Eastern" covered more than 3 billion people, from Indians to Muslims, with not much attention given to the nuances of nationality or ethnicity. And it wasn't as though they were an oddity in Brennan. Over the last decade there had been a large influx of Middle Easterners into the United States, particularly in and near major metropolitan areas. Many new businesses in Brennan were owned by hardworking Saudis, Pakistanis and Indians.

When they reached their apartment, a block from Main Street, someone was waiting for them. The man didn't look at them when they entered, but continued gazing out the window.

He was nearly sixty, though as lean and wiry as the younger men. He was Caucasian and an American, although from the immediate deference paid to him by his companions, he was clearly the leader of this small band. The Muslims referred to him, with respect, as Captain Jack. He had given himself this title based on his preferred brand of liquor. They did not, nor would they ever, know his real name. Captain Jack lived outside of Brennan, in a rental house on the road to Pittsburgh. He had come here, ostensibly, to look for locations for the "business" he was thinking about starting. This had given him ample reason to examine many of the vacant properties in the area.

Captain Jack was looking through his binoculars at Mercy Hospital across the street. Built right after the end of World War II, it was a squat white building with little in the way of architectural interest. It was the only hospital in the immediate vicinity, which was why it had attracted his interest.

There was a drop-off entrance in the rear of the hospital, but the space was very tight, and it was a long hike once inside to get to the admitting desk. Thus, even ambulances almost always dropped off their patients in front, using a wheelchair ramp next to the steps. For Captain Jack, that was a very important element, so critical, in fact, that he had videotaped an entire twenty-four-hour cycle of these comings and goings. They also had floor plans for Mercy Hospital and knew every exit and entrance, from the most obvious to the most obscure.

He continued to watch as a patient was unloaded from an ambulance and whisked through the front doors on a gurney. The trajectory here was excellent, Captain Jack thought. And high ground was almost always good ground in his line of work.

He sat down and watched as one of the men worked away on a laptop while the other two went over some equipment manuals.

"Current status?" he asked.

The Iranian on the laptop answered, "We've switched to another chat site." He glanced at a piece of paper taped to his screen. "Tonight it's *Gone with the Wind*."

"Not one of my favorites," their leader said dryly.

"What's so great about a wind blowing?" one of the Afghans commented.

They had chosen a movie chat site listing the fifty greatest American movies of all time. It was highly doubtful that law enforcement agencies would be monitoring people cyber-gabbing about films, so their method of encryption was relatively simple. And then they would move on to another film the next day.

"Everyone progressing on schedule?" Captain Jack asked as he scratched his trim beard.

There were several other operation teams in Brennan. The authorities would of course call them terrorist cells, but to Captain Jack that was simply splitting hairs. American operations teams overseas could just as easily be deemed terrorist cells by the folks they were intending to harm. He should know: He had been on many of those teams. Once he'd gotten past the patriotic claptrap, he'd seen the truth: One should do what Captain Jack did for a living only for those willing to pay the

most money. That simple change in philosophy had vastly uncompli-
cated his life.

The Iranian read through the chat lines. He had done this so often
he could decipher the encrypted messages in his head. "All accounted
for and all on schedule." He added with an element of disbelief, "Even
the woman is progressing well. Very well."

The American smiled at this comment. "Women are far more capable than you give them credit for, Ahmed. The sooner you learn
that, the better off you'll be."

"The next thing you'll be telling me is that men are the weaker sex,"
Ahmed said scornfully.

"Now you're getting close to something called wisdom."

Captain Jack looked at the two Afghans. They were both Tajiks,
members of the Northern Alliance before they'd been recruited for
this assignment. He spoke to them in their native language, Dari.

"Do they still sell off the daughters for marriage in your country?"

"Of course," one replied. "What else do you do with them?"

"Times are changing, my friend," Captain Jack said. "It's not exactly
the fourteenth century anymore."

The other Afghan piped in, "We have nothing against modern
women, so long as they obey their men. If they do that, no problems.
They are free."

Free in that sense was relative, Captain Jack knew.

In Afghanistan, if a woman demanded divorce she lost everything, including the children. An adulterous wife, even one whose husband had
taken another wife, was executed, sometimes by her own family. The
men in their lives controlled everything: whether they went to school,
worked outside the house, who they would marry. These were not conditions originated by the Taliban or Islam, but they wouldn't necessarily run afoul of them either. They were based on ancient Afghan tribal
customs.

"It's not just the women," the first Afghan said. "*I* have to obey my
father, even if I disagree with him. His word is final. It is a matter of respect, of honor."

*And so it was,* Captain Jack thought. *And good luck trying to change
that way of thinking considering it's been around for thousands of
years.*

Captain Jack rose. "We don't have a lot of time before the advance team arrives."

"If we have to work twenty-four hours a day, it will be done," Ahmed declared.

"You're in school, remember?" Captain Jack said.

"Only part-time."

"*Brennan,* Pennsylvania. I thought only despots named places after themselves," one of the Afghans said.

Captain Jack smiled. "*Brennan* didn't do it, the people named it after him. This is a democracy, after all."

"Does that make Brennan any less of a dictator?" the other Afghan said.

Captain Jack stopped smiling. "I don't really care. All you have to remember is we only get one chance at this."

Across the street at Mercy Hospital an emergency room doctor was walking down the hallway with one of the hospital administrators. The physician was a recent and welcome addition to Mercy, since the hospital was habitually understaffed. As they walked along, the doctor glanced nervously at an armed security guard posted at a doorway.

"*Armed* guards? Is that really necessary?" he asked.

The administrator shrugged. "Afraid so. Our pharmacy's been burglarized twice in the last six months. We can't afford another hit."

"Why wasn't I told this before I agreed to come here?"

"Well, it's not exactly something we wanted to publicize."

"But I thought Brennan was a peaceful town," the doctor said.

"Oh, it is, it is, but, you know, drugs are everywhere. But no one will try anything with armed guards here."

The physician glanced over his shoulder at the security man who stood rigidly against a wall. From the look on the doctor's face he didn't appear to share the positive sentiments of his colleague.

As the men passed down the hallway, a uniformed Adnan al-Rimi, his appearance much changed since his "death" in rural Virginia, walked off to patrol another part of the hospital. There were many such dead men walking the streets of Brennan right now.

# CHAPTER

# 12

On the outskirts of Brennan, Pennsylvania, was a faded strip mall that had as its meager tenants a pawnshop, several low-rent mom-and-pop operations, a bail bondsman's establishment and a fried chicken eatery. All of the other lease space was empty except for one office. The windows of this unit were still covered up, as the build-out had not yet been completed. Actually, the work had never been started, nor would it ever be.

In the far back room behind a makeshift plywood partition were two Arab men and a third fellow. One of the Arabs was an engineer specializing in medical devices, the other a chemist, though both men had other skills as well. The third man, a former U.S. National Guardsman, was sitting in a chair looking nervously at the various pieces of equipment stacked neatly on a long table against the wall; these included wrenches, power screwdrivers, electrical wires and other, more sophisticated equipment. The former National Guardsman was looking nervously at where his right hand had been. A cast had been made of the stump, and a shiny metal socket with metal fingers had been attached to this spot.

"Just relax," the chemist advised, and he put a gentle hand on the nervous fellow's shoulder.

The engineer lifted an object out of a long box and held it up. It looked like a human hand. "It's made of silicone, and we have copied your vein patterns, simulated your natural skin color and even matched it to your skin's hair color. The metal socket and inner hand attached to your wrist are internally wired, with powered movement and flexibility in all five fingers. The older models only had mobility in the thumb, index and ring fingers. And they were able to engineer down the scale of the wiring so the new generation's size approximates that of an actual human hand." He held his hand up against the prosthetic one. "You can see that it's barely an inch longer than normal."

The man nodded and smiled. His thoughts were obvious. It did look like a real hand.

The chemist said, "You have a solid wrist joint and good remaining wrist muscles; that will help greatly. The electrodes embedded in the inner hand will have solid connection to the muscle."

"Yeah, I'm a real lucky bastard," the man said bitterly.

The silicone hand was put over the socket and the hand securely attached. When that was done, they took the man through some simple exercises.

The engineer said, "When you push your wrist muscles upward, the hand opens. When you relax your wrist muscles, the hand closes. Practice that."

The man did so about a dozen times while the men watched closely. Each time, he became more comfortable with the manipulations.

The chemist nodded approvingly. "That is good. You are getting it. But you must keep practicing. Soon you will be able to do it without thinking. It will feel natural."

The man in the chair rubbed the fake hand with the steel hook that constituted his other hand. "Does it feel real?" he asked. "I can't tell."

The engineer said, "Someone shaking hands with you will be able to tell it's not real, simply by the texture and the colder temperature of the skin, but in all other respects it will look very real."

The man seemed disappointed by this explanation and stopped looking at his new hand.

"You can never be what you were," the chemist said bluntly. "But it is better than what you had, and we can do your other hand too, if you want."

The man shook his head and held up his hook. "I want to keep this one. I don't want to forget what happened to me."

"You have your uniform?" the engineer asked.

The man nodded as he rose from the chair, still opening and closing his new hand. "That's *another* memory, not that I need it."

"What was your rank?"

"Sergeant. National Guard." He flexed his new hand again. "And after it's over?"

"You will be taken care of, as agreed," the engineer answered.

"It's nice, to be finally taken care of."

"We will be in touch, in the usual way."

They shook hands.

"Feels good to finally be able to do that," the ex–National Guardsman said.

After he had left, the two men went back to work. There was another box on the table that was marked in Arabic. One of the men opened it. Inside wrapped in plastic was a stainless-steel canister. Inside the canister was a bottle filled with liquid. He lifted out the bottle and held it up to the light.

He well knew that, according to the FBI, the three deadliest substances in the world were, in descending order of lethality, plutonium, botulism toxin and ricin. The liquid in the glass vial was not nearly as deadly as any of those poisons. However, in its own way the substance was still very effective.

The hand he had just placed on the former National Guardsman had a pouch inside. When a tiny release button built into the skin was pushed and the wrist bone was flexed a very special way, the pouch opened and any liquid inside it would be secreted through the artificial pores.

As they worked away, the chemist said, "He is bitter, that National Guardsman."

"Wouldn't you be?" the other answered.

# 13

T OM HEMINGWAY SAT IN HIS modest apartment near Capitol Hill. He had taken off his suit and put on shorts and a T-shirt and was barefoot. Though it was very late, he was not tired. In fact, adrenaline was ripping through his veins. He had just received the news: Patrick Johnson was dead. Hemingway felt no remorse. The man had no one to blame but himself. But there had been witnesses to the killing, and they had gotten away. Of course, that potentially changed everything.

He went into his bedroom, unlocked a hidden floor safe, took out a folder and sat down at his kitchen table. Inside the folder were photographs of over two dozen men and one woman. All were Muslims. The authorities would classify them as enemies of America. The assembling of these people represented two full years of Tom Hemingway's life. And for those in the group who had run afoul of the law in some way, Hemingway had achieved a miracle. He had made the living appear to be dead.

Hemingway's father, the Honorable Franklin T. Hemingway, had been a statesman, when that word still carried some actual meaning. He had risen through the ranks to become ambassador to some of the most diplomatically challenging countries on earth. Before his untimely death, he had been hailed as one of the great peacemakers of his generation, a dedicated and honorable civil servant.

Tom Hemingway eventually came to terms with his father's violent death; however, he knew it was not something he would ever get over, nor should he. He had loved and respected his father, learning civility and compassion by the man's example. Unlike many other ambassadors who "purchased" their title with large campaign donations and who never even bothered to adequately learn the language and culture of the country they were sent to, Franklin Hemingway immersed himself and his family in the language and history of whatever land he was assigned. Thus, Tom Hemingway had a far better understanding and appreciation of both the Islamic and Asian worlds than virtually any other American.

He had not gone the route of his diplomatic father, however, because Tom Hemingway didn't believe he had the temperament for such a career. He had instead entered the spy world, beginning with the National Security Agency before transferring to the CIA and working his way up. It seemed an important even honorable career, and he'd thrown himself at it with the work ethic his father had instilled in him.

He'd become a superb field agent, assigned to some of the most dangerous hot spots in the world. He had survived, sometimes just by minutes, attempts to kill him. He had, in turn, killed, on behalf of his government. He helped orchestrate coups that toppled popularly elected governments. He also oversaw operations that created instability in fragile third-world countries, because this was deemed the best way to foster an atmosphere most beneficial to the United States. He had done all that was asked of him, and more.

And ultimately, it had been for nothing. The precious work that he'd performed was a sham, fueled more by business interests than national ones, accomplishing nothing other than making a bad situation worse. The world was as close to destruction as he had ever seen, and Tom Hemingway had seen a lot.

There were many reasons, beginning with critical shortages of water, oil and gas, steel, coal and other natural resources. Rich countries like the United States, Japan and China took the lion's share of these precious commodities, leaving scraps for the poorest nations. But it was more than the historically complex issue of the haves and the have-nots. It was a fundamental question of ignorance and intolerance. Hemingway had always considered ignorance and intolerance to be like commas, because you often found them in pairs, and almost never did you find one, ignorance, without its evil twin, intolerance.

At age forty Hemingway's father had helped create peace in lands that had known only war. At the same age his son had helped to rip peace from lands all over the world, leaving much of it in shambles. It had been a devastating revelation, given his provenance.

And then he had sat down and looked at his options, and a plan had slowly coalesced. There were many who would have looked at what he intended and called him hopelessly naive. That was not the way the world worked, they would have argued. You are doomed to pitiful failure, they would have pronounced. And yet these were the same people who had performed atrocities in certain parts of the world under the pretense of helping them. They committed these "crimes" for reasons as crude as money and power and expected to have their own way without ever being seriously challenged by those they had so clearly wronged. Now who was the naive one? Hemingway thought.

His "official" occupation had allowed him to crisscross the Middle East over the last few years. During that time he slowly formed the pieces to his puzzle, meeting with people he needed assistance from. He found skeptics aplenty, but then one man, someone he deeply respected and a longtime friend of his father's, agreed to help. The man gave Hemingway not only access to people but the necessary funds to construct an elaborate operation. Hemingway did not believe for an instant that this gentleman didn't have reasons of his own to do so. However, Tom Hemingway, American-born and -bred, even with all his contacts in that region and familiarity with its language and culture, couldn't have possibly pulled off something this monumental on his own. And if he suffered from a certain idealism that bordered on naiveté, he was brutally realistic about how best his plan could be successfully carried out.

He often wished his father were still alive so that he could ask for his advice. He knew, though, what Franklin Hemingway would say: *It is wrong. Don't do it.* But the son was going to do it.

And what was his true motivation? Hemingway had asked himself that question often as the process was unfolding. He had come up with different answers at times. He had finally concluded that he was not doing this for his country, and he was not doing this for the Middle East. He was doing this for a *planet* that was quickly running out of second chances. And perhaps also as a tribute for a father who was a man of peace but who died a violent death, because people patently refused to understand each other.

Perhaps it was as simple, and complex, as that.

# CHAPTER

# 14

THE BODY OF PATRICK JOHNSON was discovered early the next morning by a group of fifth graders and their teachers from a Maryland elementary school, who wanted to learn more about Teddy Roosevelt. Unfortunately, they learned far more than they'd bargained for.

Later that morning Alex Ford was driving his creaky government Crown Vic into work and thinking about what he'd be doing that day. If nothing else, duty at the Washington Field Office provided a lot of variety. The head of WFO, the special agent in charge, or SAIC, believed that agents with broad experience in all areas of concern to the Service were better agents because of it. Alex generally agreed with this approach. Already this week he'd performed surveillance on a couple of ongoing cases, pulled a few hours of prisoner transport, stood post for several visiting foreign dignitaries and been called in once as part of the Gate Caller Squad maintained 24/7 at the WFO's duty desk.

The Gate Caller Squad, part of the Secret Service's Protective Intelligence Squad, was summoned whenever someone walked up to the White House, knocked on the gate and wanted to see the president without an appointment, which happened more frequently than most people imagined. There was one guy who showed up every six months and informed the guards that this was "his" house and they were all trespassing. There was also increased activity like this when the moon was full, the Service had discovered. Such bizarre behavior would win the gate caller a visit from the Secret Service, some shrink time and possibly a trip to jail or St. Elizabeth's, depending on how deranged the agents found the person.

Alex parked his car, walked into the WFO, nodded to a broad-hipped female guard in the lobby, swiped his security card in the slot in the elevator and rode up to the fourth floor, where the Metro Area Task Force was located. For part of his work, Alex was assigned to the task force, as were many of the more veteran agents at WFO. The task force worked closely with Virginia and Maryland state police and other federal law enforcement on myriad financial felony cases. That was the good news. The bad news was that criminals were so active the task force had more work than it could reasonably handle.

The Service had three floors in the building, and he headed to his wall-less work cubby in a large open area of the fourth floor. There was an e-mail from Jerry Sykes, his ATSAIC, or assistant to the special agent in charge, telling him to come up to the sixth floor as soon as he got in.

Okay, that was a little out of the ordinary, he thought. Had he violated some civil rights he was unaware of when arresting the two ATM goofballs last night?

Alex rode the elevator to the sixth floor, got off and walked down the hallway, nodding to people he knew along the way. He passed the duty board that hung on one wall in the corridor. It had magnetic pictures of all the agents at WFO arranged in clusters according to their current assignments. It was a good, if not exactly high-tech way of keeping abreast of people's whereabouts. There was also an electronic backup duty roster, because some pranksters would switch the pictures of agents on this board to other assignments. So an agent tasked to Criminal could suddenly find himself, at least according to the board, being in the desk-bound insomniac land of the Recruitment Division.

A few of the pictures were hung upside down; that meant that an agent was leaving the WFO for an assignment elsewhere. There were also red or blue dots on many of the pictures. This didn't designate whether an agent was a Republican or Democrat, though some agents tried to sell that line to their friends and families who visited here; it designated whether the agent lived in Virginia or Maryland.

Sykes rose from his desk when Alex appeared in the doorway.

"Have a seat, Alex," Sykes said, motioning to a chair.

Alex sat and unbuttoned his suit jacket. "So am I in trouble, or is this just a fun date?" Alex smiled and, thankfully, Sykes grinned in return.

"Heard about your heroics last night. We love agents who work *unpaid* overtime like that. Feel free to do it more often."

"Well, I wouldn't turn down a nice bump in salary as a thank-you."

"In your dreams. Got a brand-new toy for you, something really hot." He tapped a file lying on his desk. "This came on a slingshot from HQ to the SAIC here and then on to me."

Alex looked doubtful. "My load's pretty full, Jerry. So long as people use money, other people will try and steal it or forge it."

"Forget that for now. How about making a run at a homicide?"

"I don't remember that being in our statutory mandate," Alex said slowly.

"Check your badge and your paycheck. It says Homeland Security now and not Treasury, so we have lots of new goodies in our bag to hand out." Sykes glanced at the file. "A man named Patrick Johnson was found this morning on Roosevelt Island with a gunshot wound in his mouth, a revolver and bottle of Scotch next to him and a suicide note in his pocket."

"And he is?" Alex asked.

"Employed at N-TAC," Sykes replied, referring to the National Threat Assessment Center. "In other words, he's one of us. That's where you come in."

"But N-TAC's not really part of the Service anymore, not after the intelligence shake-up. It's with NIC now. Along with damn near everything else."

"Right but we still have our fingers in that pie, and Johnson at least technically was a joint employee of the Secret Service and NIC."

"Gunshot wound to the mouth, guy was probably drunk, revolver right there and a note. What's to investigate?"

"Suicide is what it looks like so far, and it'll probably stick. Since it occurred on federal property and he was a federal employee, the FBI and Park Police are investigating. But we want somebody looking out for our interests too. If it was a suicide, we can handle the spin okay. But if it's something else, well, then, we need to run that down. That's where you come in."

"Why Roosevelt Island? Was Johnson a T.R. freak?"

"That's for you to find out. But don't let the Bureau run you off."

"So why am I so lucky, Jerry?" Alex asked. "I mean isn't this something for the Inspections Division to do?"

"Yes. But I like you," Sykes replied sarcastically. "And after all that time on protection, you really need as much real work as you can get."

"Funny, that's what they said when I went *into* protection detail."

"Whoever said life was fair?"

"No one who's ever worn a badge," Alex shot back.

Sykes took on a serious expression. "You've seen the kids running around here. They're good and they're smart and they work their butts off, but their average experience is less than six years. You've got three times that. And speaking of baby agents, take Simpson with you. Rookie needs some breaking in."

"I'm curious," Alex said. "Has Simpson got any strings upstairs?"

"Why?" Sykes asked, although Alex thought he saw a smile flit across the man's face.

"Because the crap duty doesn't seem to stick to that rook, that's why."

"All I can say is Simpson's the blessed relation of some big muckety-muck, and people tend to give '*that rook*' a little slack. Do not feel so inclined. Here's the file. The crime scene awaits you. Go get 'em."

As Alex rose, Sykes added, "The ninety-day report cycle is out on this one. We want daily *detailed* e-mails. And just so you know, they'll be going directly to the SAIC and HQ."

"Okay."

"Like I said, Alex, this one is hot, treat it accordingly."

"I get the point, Jerry."

Alex returned to his desk, hung his jacket over his chair and opened the file. The first thing he encountered was a photo of Patrick Johnson looking very much alive. There was a hand-scribbled note that said Johnson was engaged to be married. The name and phone number of his fiancée were underneath this note. Alex assumed the woman had already been told of the man's death. Johnson's employment history looked pretty routine.

Johnson had been with the N-TAC division of the National Intelligence Center, or NIC as the D.C. bureaucrats referred to it. In layman's terms N-TAC put together information and strategies that cops could use to prevent everything from presidential assassinations to terrorist attacks to another Columbine. No Secret Service agent ever wanted to *arrest* an assassin. That meant the person you were guarding was dead.

Alex remembered the huge battle that erupted when NIC made clear it wanted to absorb N-TAC into its intelligence empire. The Service had put up a vigorous counterattack, but in the end the president sided with Gray and NIC. However, because the Service had such a unique relationship with the president, it had been able to keep some connection to N-TAC, which was why Johnson had still technically been a joint employee of the Service, if in name only.

Alex flipped through the rest of the file making mental notes. Finally, he stood and put on his jacket. He grabbed Simpson on the way out.

Jackie Simpson was petite and dark-haired with an olive complexion and strong facial features dominated by a pair of startling blue eyes. Though a rookie at the Secret Service, she was no novice when it came to detective work, having spent nearly eight years as a police officer before joining the Service. When she spoke, no one could miss Simpson's southern origins, in her case Alabama. She was dressed in a dark pantsuit and carried her sidearm on a belt clip riding near her left hand. Alex raised his eyebrows at the three-inch blocky heels she wore that still left her six inches shorter than he was. Then his gaze took in the wedge of red handkerchief poking out from the lady's breast pocket. That was a little fashion statement that could get you killed. Alex also knew that her pistol was a custom piece that she had somehow gotten approval for. The Service liked uniformity when it came to its agents' weapons, in the event they had to share ammo during a shoot-out.

Like many people in a new job, she was full of bountiful enthusiasm as well as a startling lack of tact. When told of their new assignment, she responded, "Sweet."

"It wasn't too sweet for Patrick Johnson," Alex pointed out.

"I didn't mean it that way."

"Glad to hear it. Let's go." Alex walked off fast, leaving Simpson to scurry after him.

# CHAPTER

# 15

DJAMILA, THE NANNY, CHANGED the diaper of the youngest boy, then turned her attention and considerable patience to feeding the one-year-old's two brothers, aged two and three. After she'd finished this task, she played with them and then put the boys down for naps. She took her prayer rug out of the bag she brought with her to work and prepared to perform the *salat*, or prayer, by undertaking the ablution, or *wudu*, of the face, head, hands, arms up to the elbows, and the feet up to the ankles. Barefoot, Djamila faced the *qibla*, the direction of Mecca, and performed her prayer. It was a ritual she did five times each day beginning two hours before sunrise and ending with the last prayer at nightfall, when the twilight disappears. This was Djamila's second prayer of the day, performed at noon, when the sun begins its decline.

A few minutes after she'd finished, the boys' mother, Lori Franklin, came downstairs and gazed admiringly at her well-kept house and then looked in at her sons sleeping very soundly in their respective berths in the large playroom. Franklin was barely thirty and very attractive, with a slim, yet curvy figure and well-toned muscles. She carried a small bag with her.

"Going to the club, miss?" Djamila said.

"Yes, Djamila; a set of tennis and then who knows." She laughed lightly and drew a contented breath in the way that young, well-off people often did. She nodded at her sons. "I see you have the army down already."

"Yes, they are good boys. They play hard and sleep harder."

"They're good boys with *you*. They aren't so good with me, or the three nannies that came before you. Now I can actually have a life even if my husband works twenty hours a day. Men, Djamila, can't live with them, can't live without their W-2s."

"In my country a man he is head of the home," Djamila noted as she put some toys away in a storage box. "A woman's duty is to help her husband, keep the home in a good way, and to take care of the children. But you must marry a man you respect and whose wishes you can carry out with a good conscience. Your husband is not your master; only God is."

The American rolled her eyes. "Oh, men are kings here too, Djamila, at least in their own minds." She laughed again. "And I gave George the family he wanted. And I give him his *wishes* when he really needs me to. It's not such a bad bargain."

"So you won't be back this afternoon," Djamila said, frowning, as she hurriedly changed the subject. She had found her employer far too frank sometimes.

"I'll be here in time to make dinner. George is out of town again. You can eat during the day now, can't you? Your fasting thing is over?"

"Ramadan has passed, yes."

"I can never keep the dates straight."

"That is because they change. Ramadan is celebrated in the ninth month of the Islamic year. It was then that Muhammad received the first revelation of the Qur'an from the angel Gabriel. But Muslims use the lunar calendar, so Ramadan comes earlier every year. My parents have celebrated Ramadan during winter and also during summer."

"Well, I wouldn't want to celebrate Christmas in July. And I can't imagine fasting like that. Djamila, it can't be healthy for you."

"Actually, it is *very* healthy. And the women with child or nursing, they do not have to fast. The *sawm*, how you say, the fasting, it purges the body of bad thoughts. It is a cleansing, focusing time of life. I enjoy it very much, and I do not feel hungry at all. I eat the *sahur* before dawn, and after sunset I can eat the meal. It is not much of a sacrifice."

Djamila didn't add that one American meal typically equaled three of hers. "Then at the end of Ramadan we celebrate. It is called '*id al-fitr*. We wear new clothes and exchange nice meals and visit with our friends and family. It is very much fun."

"Well, I still think it's unhealthy." Lori Franklin looked out the window. "It's a beautiful day, so why don't you drive the boys to the park and let them burn some energy up? That way the house will be a little quieter when I get home."

"I will take them, miss. I like to drive very much."

"Women aren't allowed to drive in your country, are they?"

Djamila hesitated and then said, "It is true that a woman cannot drive a car in Riyadh, but that is just a local law that has nothing to do with Islam."

Franklin looked at her with pity. "You don't have to make excuses. There were lots of things you weren't allowed to do over there. I know. I watch the news. Forced marriages and men having lots of wives. And you had to wear all those veils and things to cover up your body. And no education. You have no rights at all."

Djamila looked down for a moment so Franklin wouldn't see the resentment reflected in her features. When she looked back up, she forced a smile and said in a positive tone, "What you say is not Islam that I know or that most Muslims know. Muslim women are not forced to marry. It is a contract between man and woman, and also between their families. If a divorce happens, God forbid, the woman she is entitled to much property from the man. This is her right by the law, you understand. And a man may have more than one wife, but only if he can support them all equally. Unless a man he is very rich, he only has one wife. And Islam says all should learn, men and women. I receive a good education.

"As for dress, the Qur'an does not say wear this or that. It tells both men and women to be modest and righteous in their dress. God is loving. He knows if one believes in him, that person will make the right choices. Some women choose the veil and the *abaya,* what you call a body cloak. Others do not."

"Well, it's *very* different here, Djamila. In America you can do anything you want to. *Anything.* That's what makes this country so great."

"Yes, I have heard that. And yet sometimes is doing *everything* you want to do really that good?"

Franklin smiled. "Absolutely, Djamila, especially if you don't get caught."

"If you say so," Djamila replied, but she didn't believe any of it.

"Women really run this country, Djamila, we just let men think they do."

"But women in America, they were not allowed to vote until the twentieth century, is that not so?"

Franklin looked a little put off by this comment but then waved her hand dismissively. "That's ancient history. Let's just say we've made up for lost time. And the sooner the Muslim women figure that out, the better."

Djamila chose not to respond to this. She had been instructed not to address such issues with her employer, and yet sometimes she could not help herself.

Franklin said, "I wish you'd reconsider and come live with us. This house is huge."

"Thank you. But for now I would like to keep our arrangement the same."

"Okay, whatever you want. I can't afford to lose you."

She blew kisses at her sleeping family and left. As Franklin pulled out of the driveway, she glanced at the white van parked there. It had never occurred to her that it was somewhat odd that a woman who before coming to the United States had never driven a car would have shown up for a new job with her very own van and valid driver's license. However, Franklin already had far too much to occupy her mind than to worry about such a trivial incongruity.

She was in fact not going to play tennis or cards at her country club. In the small bag she carried was a negligee of breathtaking sheerness. She was already wearing the matching thong, and she had seen no reason to wear a bra for what she would be engaged in doing that afternoon. Her only problem would be convincing her very young lover not to tear them off her body.

Djamila went to the window and watched her employer drive away in her little Mercedes sports car. On one afternoon when George Franklin took the day off to spend some time with his sons, Djamila followed Lori Franklin to the country club, where she got into the car of a man who was not her husband. Djamila followed them to a motel. She suspected that that was where the woman was heading now. After all, it was a bit difficult to play tennis without a tennis racket, and Franklin's was still hanging on a peg in the garage.

Men were clearly not kings in America, Djamila had concluded after only a few weeks in the States. They were fools. And their women were whores.

After her charges' nap she took them to the park, where they played to exhaustion. Djamila smiled as she watched the oldest boy take great pleasure in running circles around his brothers. Djamila wanted sons, lots of them. And then her smile faded. She doubted that she would ever live to become a mother.

She fed the boys snacks from a picnic basket she'd prepared. After that, Djamila had to chase down the oldest boy, Timmy, to retrieve her cell phone and car keys from him. He'd done this before whenever she left her purse in a place he could reach. She didn't mind; all children were curious. She loaded the boys into the van, where they immediately fell asleep. Then she took out her rug and performed her midafternoon prayer next to the van. She had brought a small bottle of water and a pan with her to perform her ablution.

While the boys slept, she drove all around Brennan, Pennsylvania. As had often been the case in this area, the town existed because the railroad gods had long ago decided to put a station stop here. These trains carried some passengers but mostly coal and coke to the steel mills and the eastern ports. Now Brennan was rebuilding itself into a posh suburb of Pittsburgh. The town had quaint shops and restaurants, regentrified homes and a sparkling new country club.

Djamila stopped often to take pictures with a small digital camera no bigger than her index finger. As she did so, she spoke into a small recorder, describing things that should have held little importance to a foreign-born nanny shepherding three slumbering boys around; however, all of it interested her. Then she covered the outlying areas, paying particular attention to road configurations.

Finally, she pulled up in front of a beautiful fieldstone estate that was set well back from the road and behind a low wall of locally quarried stone. Such a pretty home, she thought, but far too big. In America everything was too big: from the meals to the houses to the cars to the people. The only things that weren't big were the clothes. Djamila had seen more butts, breasts and bellies in the last few months than she had seen in all the preceding years of her life. It disgusted her.

Give Djamila the *jilbab* and a *khimar* to cover her body, give her even three other wives to compete with, over such "freedom."

She frowned as she glanced at the sleeping children. Yes, her employers disgusted her with their money and loveless marriage. Even the children in the backseat in one sense disgusted her because they would grow up one day and believe they ruled the world simply because they were Americans. She put the van in gear and drove off.

Djamila would report in tonight on her computer, at the movie site. According to her memorized schedule, the chat room for this night dealt with a film called *To Kill a Mockingbird*. It was a strange name for a movie, but Americans, she knew, were strange. Yes, strange, violent and, most frightening of all, completely unpredictable.

# CHAPTER

# 16

OLIVER STONE HAD RETURNED to his cottage and attempted sleep, but the night's extraordinary events rendered that act impossible. He built a small fire to battle the chill in the air and sat and read until dawn, though his thoughts continually wandered to the death of Patrick Johnson. Or rather, *murder*. Then he made some coffee and had a bit of breakfast. After that, he spent the next several hours attending to his duties in the cemetery. As he weeded, cut the grass, cleared debris and cleaned off aged tombstones, he focused on how close he and his friends had come to losing their lives last night. It was a feeling he'd had many times earlier in his life, and he'd learned to deal with it. Now it would not go away so easily.

After he'd finished his work, he went inside the cottage and showered. Looking at his appearance in the mirror, Stone made a decision; only he didn't have the necessary tools to implement that decision. Caleb and Reuben would be at work by now. And he just didn't trust Milton to do the job properly.

There was really only one alternative. He headed to Chinatown.

"Adelphia?" Stone called out. It was forty-five minutes later, and he was standing outside her apartment, which was situated over a dry cleaners. "Adelphia?" he said again. He wondered if she'd already gone out. Then he heard approaching footsteps and Adelphia opened the door, dressed in a pair of black pants and a long sweater, her hair pulled back in a bun. She looked at him crossly.

"How you know where I live?" she demanded.

"You told me."

"Oh." She scowled at him. "How did meeting go?" she said irritably.

"Actually, there were a few surprises."

"What is it you want, Oliver?"

Stone cleared his throat and launched into his lie. "I've thought about your advice about my appearance. So I was wondering if you could give me a haircut. I suppose I could do it myself, but I'm afraid the result would be worse than how I look right now."

"It is not so bad you look." This comment seemed to slip out before the lady realized it. She coughed self-consciously and then gazed at him in mild surprise. "So, you take my advice?"

He nodded. "I'm going to get some new clothes too. Well, new in the sense that they'll be new to me. And shoes."

She looked at him suspiciously. "And the beard? That thing that makes you look to be, how you say, that Rumpelstein person."

"Yes, the beard will go too. But I can shave that off myself."

She waved dismissively. "No, I do. I have dreamed many times of disappearing that beard." She motioned him into her apartment. "Come, come, we do it now. Before your mind it is changed."

Stone followed her in and looked around. The inside of Adelphia's apartment was very clean and organized, which surprised him. The woman's personality seemed far too impulsive and fractured to manufacture such order.

She led him into the bathroom and pointed to the toilet. "Sit."

He did so while she busied herself with getting necessary instruments. From where he was sitting Stone could see a shelf in the hallway that held books on many subjects, a few in languages Stone did not recognize, though he had spent many years traveling the world.

"Do you know all those languages, Adelphia?" he asked, pointing at the books.

She stopped assembling her tools and looked at him suspiciously. "And why would books like that I keep if I could not *read* them? Does my apartment look so big that I keep things I no use?"

"I see your point."

She draped a sheet over him and knotted it behind his neck.

"How much cutting is it you want?"

"Over the ears and off the neck will do nicely."

"You are sure of this?"

"Absolutely sure."

She started clipping. Finished, she combed his hair into place, gelling down a few stubborn cowlicks. Next she attacked his thick beard with her shears, whittling it down quickly. Then picked up another object.

"It is this I use on my legs," she said, holding up a lady's razor. "But it will do too for your face."

When he saw what he looked like in a small mirror Adelphia handed him after she'd finished, Stone almost didn't recognize his reflection. He rubbed at facial skin he had not seen in years. With the bundle of long, scraggly hair and beard gone he noted that he had a long forehead with stacks of wrinkles and a smooth, slender neck.

"It is a nice face you have," Adelphia said sincerely. "And your neck is like baby's skin. Me, I have got no nice neck. It is old woman's. Like the turkey. "

"I think you have very pleasing features, Adelphia," he said. Stone was still looking at his face in the mirror, so he didn't see her blush and quickly look down.

"You have visitor last night."

Stone glanced up at her. "A visitor. Who?"

"A man in suit. His name it is Fort, or is something like that. I not remember exactly. He say to tell you of his coming by."

"Fort?"

"I see him talking to those men, the ones across the street. You know him, Oliver. The Secret men."

"The Secret Service. Do you mean Ford? Agent Alex Ford?"

Adelphia pointed at him. "That is it. A big man he is. Taller than you."

"Did he say what he wanted?"

"Only that he say hello."

"What time was this?"

"Do I look like keeper of time? I tell you he say hello." She hesitated. "I think it is midnight he come by. It is nothing else I know."

His mind now preoccupied with this latest news, Stone hurriedly rose and took off the sheet. "I would like to pay you," he began, but she waved this offer away. "There must be something I can do to return this kindness."

She glanced at him sharply. "There is a thing you can do." She paused and he stared at her curiously. "We get the café sometime." She added with a scowl, "When you not have big meeting in middle of night."

Stone was a little taken aback but decided what was the harm in talk and coffee? "All right, Adelphia. I guess it's time we did things like that."

"Then that is good." She put out her hand for him to shake. He was surprised by how strong her long fingers were.

As Stone walked along the streets a few minutes later, he thought about his late night visitor. Alex Ford had been closer to Stone than any of the other Secret Service agents. So his visit could be simply a coincidence.

Stone headed to a nearby Goodwill store. There, with the money Reuben had given him, he purchased two pairs of dungarees, a pair of sturdy walking shoes, socks, shirts, a sweater and a faded blue blazer. The clerk, whom he knew well, threw in two pairs of brand-new underwear.

"You look years younger, Oliver," the man commented.

"I feel it. I really do," he answered. He returned to Lafayette Park with his purchases to make a quick change inside his tent. However, as he started to enter his little sanctum, a voice called out.

"Where the hell do you think you're going, bud?"

Stone looked up to see a uniformed Secret Service agent staring at him. "That tent's already occupied, so move on."

Stone replied, "Officer, this is *my* tent."

The guard walked over to him. "Stone? Is that really you?"

Stone smiled. "A little less hair and a little less beard, but, yes, it's me."

The guard shook his head. "Who you been to see, Elizabeth Arden?"

"And who is this Elizabeth woman?" a female voice cried out.

They both turned to see Adelphia striding toward them and looking at Stone accusingly. She was still dressed in the same clothes as earlier, but her hair was now down around her shoulders.

"Don't get your conspiracy theories in a wad, Adelphia," the guard said playfully. "It's a spa where you go to get all pretty. My wife went there once, and let me tell you, for what it cost, I'll take the woman just the way she is." He chuckled and walked off, as Adelphia edged up to Stone.

"You would like to go for a café now and talk?" she asked.

"I would love to but I have to meet someone. However, when I get back."

"We will see," Adelphia replied in a disappointed tone. "I too have things to do. I no can wait for you all the time. I have job."

"No, of course not," Stone said, but the woman had turned and stormed off.

Stone slipped inside his tent, changed and put the rest of his newly acquired clothes in his knapsack. He wandered through the park until he found what he was looking for in a trash can: the morning newspaper. There was nothing in the paper about a body being discovered on Roosevelt Island; it had obviously occurred too late to make the morning edition. He found a payphone and called Caleb in his office at the Jefferson Building of the Library of Congress.

"Have you heard anything, Caleb? There's nothing as yet in the papers."

"I've had the news on all morning. All they're saying is that Roosevelt Island is closed due to an investigation of an undisclosed nature. Can you come down here around one o'clock so we can talk about it?"

Stone agreed and added, "You've taken precautions?"

"Yes, and so have the others. Reuben's at work but he called on a break. I spoke with Milton. He's staying inside his house. He's really terrified."

"Fear is a natural reaction to what we all saw." And then Stone remembered. "Uh, Caleb, you might not recognize me immediately. I've changed my appearance somewhat. I felt it necessary because I was the most likely to have been spotted by the killers."

"I understand, Oliver."

Stone hesitated and then added, "Since I'm fairly well presentable, would it be possible for me to meet you in the reading room instead of outside the building? I've always wanted to see the place, but didn't want to, well, embarrass you at work."

"Oliver, I had no idea. Of course, you can."

As Stone walked to the Library of Congress, he thought about Patrick Johnson's killers. They would know soon that the eyewitnesses had not gone to the police. And they might see an opportunity there that could lead to the extinction of the Camel Club.

# CHAPTER

# 17

ALEX PULLED HIS CAR OFF THE George Washington Parkway before it ascended sharply along the Potomac River, and parked in the lot for Roosevelt Island. The only access to the island from the parking lot was a long footbridge.

The parking lot was filled with police cruisers and unmarked federal vehicles. A team from the D.C. Medical Examiner's Office was here as well as an FBI forensics squad. Alex knew he'd be running a gauntlet of suits and uniforms by the time their visit was over.

"Busy place," Simpson commented.

"Yeah, it'll be fun to see the Bureau and the Park Police fight out jurisdiction on this one. The D.C. cops will run a distant third."

They stepped onto the bridge and flashed their credentials at a guard posted there.

"Secret Service?" the uniformed cop said, looking a little confused.

"President sent us. Top secret stuff," Alex answered, and kept on walking.

They quickly made their way to the crime scene along the marked paths. As they drew closer, Alex caught snatches of conversation and the sounds of cell phones playing a cacophony of downloaded tunes. Alex was proud of the fact that his phone simply *rang* when someone called him.

The two agents stepped into the paved area in front of the T.R. statue, where Alex looked around, mentally assembling the players working the homicide.

The D.C. and Park Police stood out because of their uniforms and somewhat deferential manner. The forensics techs were also easy to spot. The suits standing around looking like they owned the place were the Bureau boys undoubtedly. Yet there were some other suits Alex couldn't identify.

He stepped toward what he'd picked out as the ranking park policeman. Getting the uniforms on your side was a very good rule to live by.

"Alex Ford, Secret Service. This is Agent Simpson."

The policeman shook their hands.

Alex inclined his head at the body. "What do we have so far?"

The cop shrugged. "Probable suicide. Looks like the guy shot himself in the mouth. We won't know for sure until the M.E. does the post. The guy's in full rigor. We can't get his mouth open without screwing things up for the autopsy."

"That the FBI over there?" Alex inclined his head at two suits standing near the body.

"How'd you guess?" the cop said with an amused expression.

"Superman capes sticking out of their jackets," Alex replied. That comment drew a chuckle. "How about those guys?" he asked, pointing at the other men he'd noted earlier and who were talking quietly together.

"Carter Gray's boys from NIC," the man said. "They're probably analyzing what Al Qaeda has against Teddy Roosevelt."

Alex grinned and said, "You mind copying us on whatever you find? My boss is one of those real anal-retentive types."

"Sure thing, though we don't have much interest in the case so far. His wallet's still on him, and there's a suicide note and a handgun with one round fired. And it looks like the guy sucked down nearly a quart of Scotch. You can still smell it. There're prints on the gun and bottle, and the revolver's registered to him. We'll run the prints to confirm they match the deceased."

"Gunpowder residue on the hand?" Simpson asked.

"None that we could see. But the weapon looks very new and well maintained. And even with a revolver you may not get residue."

"Any sign of a struggle?" Alex asked. The cop shook his head.

"One thing," Simpson said. "Did he drive here to do the deed?"

"No car in the parking lot," the cop said.

"Well, somebody could have shot him and driven off," said Simpson. "But if it *was* a suicide, how else could he have gotten here?"

"There's an elevated pedestrian bridge on the north end of the parking lot that crosses the GW Parkway and connects to the Heritage Trail and Chain Bridge," the cop said. "And a bike path crosses the bridge and ends in the parking lot for the island. But we don't think that's how he came. Somebody would've seen him if he'd used those routes." He hesitated. "We have another theory. His clothes are soaked, too much for it to be just dew."

Alex finally got it. "What? You're saying he *swam* here?"

"Looks that way."

"Why? If he was in the water already and wanted to commit suicide, why not just go out by sucking in a bunch of the Potomac?"

"Well, if he just swam across Little Channel from the Virginia side, it's not very far," the cop pointed out.

"Yeah," Alex retorted. "But if you're going to come from that direction, why not just take the footbridge that goes *over* Little Channel, instead of sloughing through it? And if he was stone drunk, he would've drowned."

"Not if he drank the Scotch when he got here," the cop answered. "And there's something else."

He called out some instructions to a member of the forensics team canvassing the area. The man brought over something and handed it to the cop, who held it up. "We found this." It was a plastic evidence baggie with another plastic baggie inside it.

Alex and Simpson studied it. Alex got the answer first. "He used this to put his gun in so his ammo wouldn't get wet while he was swimming here."

"You win the prize. It was a .22 revolver with jacketed rounds."

"I understand there was a suicide note," Alex said.

The cop pulled out his memo book. "I wrote it down verbatim." He read it to the two Secret Service agents, and Simpson copied it down in her notebook.

"Do you have the original note?" Alex asked.

"And you are?" a strident voice asked.

Alex turned and was confronted by a short, compact man in a two-piece Brooks Brothers, muted tie and shiny banker wing tips.

Alex flashed his creds and introduced himself and his partner.

The man barely glanced at the creds before announcing, "I'm FBI

Special Agent Lloyd. We already have agents from NIC here to represent the Service's interests."

Alex assumed his beleaguered federal lawman pose. "Just following orders, Agent Lloyd. And quite honestly, the Service likes to rep its own interests. I'm sure the Bureau can understand that losing someone from N-TAC is a sensitive area, what with us being part of Homeland Security instead of Treasury now." Alex knew that Homeland Security carried a lot more beef than Treasury ever had in law enforcement circles. And if nothing else, the eight-hundred-pound gorilla Bureau tended to respect the nine-hundred-pound gorilla that Homeland Security had become.

Lloyd looked like he was going to shoot back some ripping comment but then seemed to think better of it. He shrugged. "Fine. Go play Sherlock Holmes. The body's right over there. Just don't contaminate the crime scene."

"I really appreciate it, Agent Lloyd. I was asking about the note that was found."

Lloyd motioned to one of the other FBI suits, and the note was brought over.

Lloyd said, "They're going to fume the clothes and other stuff for latent prints, but I'm not confident they'll find much. It's a suicide."

Simpson spoke up. "Cloth isn't great for capturing latents, but that jacket he's wearing isn't a bad surface, particularly since it was damp and the weather last night was good for holding prints. Your tech guys have a Superfume stick in the truck? You can't beat cyano for popping latents on surfaces like that."

"I don't know if they do or not," Lloyd said.

"It might actually be better if you take the clothes to the lab. You can fume them in a heat-accelerated chamber or a megafume. I know the FBI lab has those." She pointed to the suicide note. "Pop that in a heat chamber with ninhydrin or DFOSPRAY, and it'll pull whatever's there right out."

"Thanks for the pointer," Lloyd said tersely, although it was obvious he was impressed with her knowledge of fingerprint lift techniques.

Alex looked at Simpson with new respect, and then his gaze returned to Lloyd, who was staring darkly at her.

"You'll need to confirm it's his handwriting on the note," Alex added.

"I'm aware of that," Lloyd said.

"I can get the Service's lab to run it. And whatever fingerprints that might be there."

"The FBI lab has no peer," Lloyd shot back.

"But our lab has less of a backlog. We *are* on the same team here, Agent Lloyd."

This comment seemed to strike some cooperative nerve buried deeply within the stubborn FBI man. After a few moments his manner totally changed. "I appreciate that, Agent Ford."

"Make it Alex, she's Jackie," Alex said, inclining his head at Simpson.

"Good enough, I'm Don. We'll actually take you up on that offer. The FBI lab *is* pretty full with terrorist-related matters. You'll have to sign for it for chain of custody. The M.E.'s a stickler for that."

Alex did so and then examined the paper closely through the plastic before giving it to Simpson to hold. "So we have any motive for the suicide? I heard he was getting married."

"That'll sure drive some men to kill themselves," the cop said.

That comment drew a laugh from everyone except Simpson, who looked for a moment like she might pull her gun and produce some dead men of her own.

Lloyd said, "Too early to tell. We'll investigate, but it certainly looks like Patrick Johnson killed himself."

"No signs of anyone else having been here?" Simpson asked.

The cop answered, "There might have been, but then fifty schoolkids came marching through. It was still foggy here this morning. They almost tripped over the body. Scared the crap out of them. The stone pavers here won't be of much help for footprints or other trace."

"What path did he use to get here?" Alex asked.

"Probably that one." The cop pointed to his left. "If he swam across Little Channel, that path would've been the one he'd use after he walked through the trees and crap."

Lloyd added, "We're making a search along the shore for his car. He lived in Bethesda, Maryland. He had to drive down here reasonably close and then swim for the island. If we find his car, we can better pinpoint where he entered the water."

Alex glanced toward the Virginia side. "Guys, if he swam across Little Channel, the only place to leave his car would be in the parking lot."

The cop shrugged. "But he didn't. Unless someone drove him to his suicide spot and then left. That doesn't make much sense."

"The police boat usually runs through here," Simpson noted.

Lloyd nodded. "They did in fact come by here last night. But the fog was so thick they didn't see anything, certainly no swimmer in the water."

"How long has he been dead?" Alex asked.

"M.E. thinks about twelve hours give or take."

"Any thoughts on why he picked Roosevelt Island?"

"It's private, quiet, but still close to everything. And maybe he was a Roosevelt groupie," Lloyd added. The FBI agent glanced over at the men from NIC, frowned and then turned back to Alex. "We'll be heading over to NIC to ask some questions, see if we can find out why Johnson would want to kill himself. What we learn might get those guys"—he motioned to the NIC folks—"a little more paranoid than they already are."

"Meaning Johnson might have been doing something at NIC he shouldn't have?" Alex said.

"Hard for me to say, since I'm not really sure what it is they do over at NIC," Lloyd commented before walking off.

"Join the club," Alex muttered. He motioned Simpson to follow him over to the body. "Your stomach gonna be okay with this?" he asked her.

"I was a homicide detective in Alabama. I've seen plenty of gunshot wounds and dead bodies."

"I didn't know Bama was such a killing field."

"Are you kidding? Alabama has more guns than the entire United States military."

Alex squatted down and looked at Johnson's body. He felt one of the stiffened arms. The sleeve was soaked through, and the body was still in full rigor.

There was dried blood coming from the ears, nose and around the mouth.

"Basilar fracture," Simpson deduced. "The blood seeps down from the base of the fractured skull. The M.E. will probably find the slug near the top or the back of the head. Since it was only a .22 caliber, he would've had to really shove it up there to get a clean trajectory."

"There's some blood spatter on the sleeve but only one small blood drop on the right hand," Alex added. "That's a little surprising."

"Yeah, but sometimes there's less bleeding when the slug stays in the head."

"Probably right."

Over his shoulder Alex called out, "Where was the gun and note found?"

The cop answered, "Gun was on the right side of the body, about six inches away. The note was in the right side pocket of his windbreaker."

When Alex rose, he bit back a searing pain in his neck. It almost always gave him a jolt when he stood quickly. Simpson looked at him.

"You okay?"

"Old yoga injury. What do your Alabama homicide detective instincts think?"

Simpson shrugged. "I learned that the prelim manner of death was usually right."

"That's not what I asked you. What does your *gut* say?"

She spoke quickly. "That we need to know a lot more before we close the book on this one. This wouldn't be the first case where the preliminary findings were misleading." She nodded over at the NIC guys. "I doubt they're going to be very cooperative."

Alex stared at the men. If there was one agency that was more shrouded in secrecy than the CIA and even the NSA, it was NIC. He could easily envision the roadblocks being erected with a foundation of national security interests outweighing everything else. While it was true that the Secret Service used that tactic at times, Alex had a lot more confidence in his agency invoking that authority properly. He wasn't nearly as comfortable with NIC chambering that particular silver bullet.

"So what do *you* think?" Simpson asked him.

Alex studied the ground for a long minute and then looked up at her. "Not to sound too selfish about it, but I think this is going to be a pain in my ass that I don't really need at this point in my career."

As Alex and Simpson were leaving Roosevelt Island, the two men who'd been identified as being with NIC hustled over to them.

"We understand you're Secret Service," the tall blond one said.

"That's right," Alex replied. "Agents Ford and Simpson out of WFO."

"I'm Tyler Reinke and this is Warren Peters. We're with NIC. Since Johnson was a shared employee between our two agencies, it'll probably be best if we work together."

"Well, it's pretty early on in the game, but I don't mind sharing so long as I get something in return," Alex answered.

Reinke smiled. "That's the only way we play the game."

"Okay, so can you arrange for us to interview the people Johnson worked with?"

Peters said, "I think so. Do you know anyone at NIC?"

"Well, you're the first two I've ever found who would admit you worked there."

Both Reinke and Peters looked a little chagrined at this comment.

"Here's my card," Alex said. "Let me know when you've got it set up." He pointed to the bagged note in Simpson's hand. "We'll also run a comparison on the handwriting on the note, to make sure it's Johnson's."

Peters said, "I actually wanted to talk to you about the note. We've got lots of handwriting experts on staff. They can turn that around pretty fast."

"The Service can get it done quickly too," Alex countered.

"But NIC has a hundred samples of Johnson's handwriting at work. I'm just offering to help make things go faster. Cooperation is the key these days, right?"

Simpson piped in, "That note is evidence in a homicide investigation. The M.E. might have a problem letting you take it. It's one thing to give it to the FBI or Secret Service, we're sworn law enforcement."

"Actually, we are too," Reinke said. "And I've already talked to the M.E. and pointed out that there are national security interests here. He was fine with us taking custody of it so long as the chain of evidence was properly maintained."

"Well, I'm sure that scared the hell out of him," Alex said. He pondered for a moment and then shrugged. "Okay, let us know ASAP. And check it for prints too."

After Peters had filled out the appropriate paperwork with the M.E., he gingerly took the note. "Carter Gray's going to be on the warpath. Probably already is."

"I can see that," Alex replied.

After the NIC men had left them, Simpson asked, "So what do you really think?"

"I think they're assholes who're gonna pitch my card in the nearest trash can."

"So why'd you give them the note, then?"

"Because now that they have control of material evidence in a homicide case, that gives us a great excuse to go to NIC and see things for ourselves."

# CHAPTER

# 18

Carter Gray had risen at six-thirty and arrived back at NIC forty-five minutes later. In the NIC lobby were a series of stark black-and-white photos that every employee had to pass each day. One showed the World Trade Center towers ablaze. The photo next to it graphically captured the rubble and empty space where the towers had stood. The crippled Pentagon was in the third photo, a hole punched in its face by the American Airlines jet. A fourth photo showed the stark crater in the Pennsylvania field, the final resting place of the doomed United Airlines flight. The picture beside that one captured the blackened and blistered skin of the White House where two rocket-propelled grenades had hit and actually entered the East Room of the president's house, and the one next to it showed the devastation of the Oklahoma City bombing.

These horrific pictures continued down one side of the NIC lobby and then marched down the opposite wall. For many, though, the last photo was the most devastating. Virtually all of the victims had been under the age of sixteen, their lives ripped from them by a squad of four suicide bombers who detonated simultaneously during a special ceremony overseas honoring America's best and brightest school-children. They had won the trip to France because of their academic prowess and stellar community service back home. They returned to the States wrapped in coffins instead of accolades.

"Never forget," Gray had lectured his people. "And do all you can to make certain these things never ever happen again."

NIC kept an unofficial tally of how many lives and property had been saved by its stopping potential terrorist attacks in the United States and overseas. The estimated number of deaths prevented stood at 93,000 Americans and 31,000 foreigners, and the value of property saved at nearly $100 billion. No one outside the highest intelligence circles knew of these statistics; certainly, the American public would never know, and for good reason. If they ever found out how many "near misses" there had been, the American people would probably never leave their homes again.

Gray rode the elevator to the same floor as he had the night before but entered a different room. In here were five men and two women seated around a rectangular conference table. Gray sat and opened a laptop in front of him.

"Results of last night?" he said.

"Al-Omari refused to cooperate," one of his lieutenants answered.

"Not that surprising actually."

"About al-Omari's son, Mr. Secretary, do you want us to take him?"

"No. The boy can stay with his mother. A child needs at least *one* parent."

"Understood, sir," the man said, acknowledging the death sentence just handed out to the unfortunate father.

"Take one week, and by any means at your disposal you will extract as much useful intelligence as possible from Mr. al-Omari."

"Done," one of the women said.

"Ronald Tyrus, our resident neo-Nazi?" Gray asked.

"We've already started debriefing him."

"And the others?"

"Kim Fong has given us a confirmed lead on a shipment of a new-generation explosive allegedly invisible to airport X-ray. According to him, it's being smuggled into L.A. next week."

"Follow it to the buyer. I want the scientists, equipment and their financial backers, the whole spectrum. The others?"

"None of them would cooperate." The man paused. "The usual exit strategy?"

Each of the people in this room had worked with Gray before in some capacity and stood in awe of the man. They had collectively made decisions and taken actions that were illegal and often immoral as well. Over the years these highly educated and trained men and women had been given orders to find and kill those persons deemed to be enemies of the United States; and they had dutifully carried out those commands, because that was their job. Yet the potential death of another human being, while certainly not new territory for this group, never failed to garner their respectful attention.

"No," Gray said. "Let them go, but with tracers. And let it be known through discreet channels that they've talked to the authorities."

"The result will be they'll be killed by their own people," the other woman present said.

Gray nodded. "Film the murders. We'll use that as leverage. And if they won't turn to our side, terrorist killing terrorist never fails to make the six o'clock news. Okay, give me the latest."

The man charged with responding to this query was the youngest person in the room. However, in many ways he had more experience in the field than most agents far his senior. Tom Hemingway looked just as dashing and was dressed just as impeccably as he had been last night at the LEAP Bar. He was a rising star at NIC and its reigning expert in Middle East affairs. He also had an excellent grounding in the Far East, having spent the first twenty years of his life in those two places with his father, who'd been a U.S. ambassador, first to China, then Jordan, and, for a brief time, Saudi Arabia, before returning to China.

Because of his father's travels, Tom Hemingway was one of the few operatives in American intelligence who could speak Mandarin Chinese, Hebrew, Arabic and Farsi. He had read the Qur'an in its original Arabic and knew the Muslim world as well as any American other than his father. It was these attributes, plus physical and mental indefatigability and a gift for spy craft, that had fueled his meteoric rise through the ranks to his current position as one of Gray's inner circle.

Hemingway clicked a key on his computer, and a screen hanging on the far wall sprang to life showing a detailed satellite-imaging map of the Middle East.

He said, "As outlined here, CIA and NIC operatives on the ground have made significant inroads in Iran, Libya, Syria, Bahrain, Iraq, UAE and Yemen as well as the new Kurdish Republic. We've infiltrated over two dozen known terrorist organizations and splinter cells at the deepest levels. All are on track to pay big dividends."

"It helps when your field agents aren't all blond and blue-eyed who speak no Arabic," one of the other men commented dryly.

"Well, for decades that's all we had," Gray shot back. "And we still don't have nearly enough operatives who can speak the language."

"Kabul and Tikrit aren't exactly popular career paths these days," commented one of the men.

"What are the losses currently running?" Gray asked.

"Two operatives killed per month," Hemingway answered. "It's as high as it's ever been, but with more reward obviously comes more risk," he added.

Gray responded, "I can't emphasize enough the importance of getting these people out safely."

There was a murmur of largely unenthusiastic agreement around the table. Middle East terrorists dealt with suspected spies very directly. They filmed the beheading of the person and released it to the world to dissuade others from replacing the fallen. It had proved a very effective strategy.

"We're losing soldiers over there at the rate of a dozen a day, seven days a week," Hemingway pointed out. "And with the new front that just opened on the Syrian border, the casualty rate will only get worse. Meanwhile, the Muslim independence movements in Chechnya, Kashmir, Thailand and Mindanao are allowing the spread of radical Islamic ideology to grow unabated. And Africa's a whole other problem. Most of northern Nigeria had adopted strict sharia law. They're stoning women to death for committing adultery and cutting the limbs off petty thieves. The terrorists' recruiting and training operations are largely conducted over the Internet, and they use identity theft and other scams to hide their movements and conduct financing through the *hawala* system of informal money transfers. There's no centralized command for our military to hit. Clandestine, undercover operations are the only viable strategy."

"There's a democratic government in power in Iraq, duly elected by the people," another man said. "Despite suicide bombers and bullets flying everywhere, the people came out and voted. And look at the gains in Lebanon, Kuwait, Afghanistan and Morocco. In fact, democracy is slowly spreading across the region. That truly is a miracle and something both we and the Muslim community can be proud of."

Hemingway looked at Gray. "It's cost this country half a trillion dollars and counting to get to the election stage in Iraq. At that rate we'll be bankrupt in five years. And when the Kurds declared their independence, it hardly set well in Baghdad. And the Sunnis may not be far behind in revolting from the Shia control. Meanwhile, the Baathist exiles and foreign insurgents are continuing to escalate the violence. On top of that, word is the Iraqi government will soon be asking the U.S to leave because it's struck a deal with the Baathists for a bloodless coup. And then the Baathists will fight a final battle with the insurgents who favor a Taliban-style government. Iraq will end up far more destabilized than it ever was, with a legion of newly minted terrorists ready to attack us. So what has our money and the blood of our soldiers really bought us?"

Gray said, "I'm aware of that. We knew the day would come. Unfortunately, from our side we really can't leave. The situation is far too volatile."

Hemingway threw his hands up. "That's what happens when you have a country that was artificially created by a colonial power, jamming three distinct and incompatible groups into one boundary. A one-size-fits-all democracy is not an effective foreign policy when you're dealing with such different cultures. Western democracy is predicated on separation of church and state. That's a difficult sell to Muslims. That's why Mali and Senegal are the only Muslim nations rated fully free."

Gray said calmly, "We don't make the foreign policy of this government, Tom, we just try and clean up the mess and limit the damage. India and Pakistan?"

Hemingway drew a deep breath. "Situation continues to worsen. The current casualty estimates of a nuclear war between the two countries have twenty-five million dying the first day, with another twenty million critically injured. That is a disaster beyond the world's collective ability to respond. And China and India are closer every day, both economically and militarily. That's a real concern."

"Egypt?" Gray asked.

"Ready to erupt, along with Indonesia and Saudi Arabia," Hemingway responded. "Ever since the Temple of Hatsheput massacre, Egypt's tourist trade's been in the toilet. And a bad economy equals opportunities for an overthrow."

Gray sat back in his chair. "Well, understandably, people on vacation are averse to being shot and hacked to death."

"And then there's North Korea," Hemingway said.

Gray nodded. "A madman in charge, the world's third largest army, with nukes that can hit Seattle and whose lead export is counterfeit American money. I want the updated detailed scenarios on my desk in twenty-four hours. Okay, narcoterrorism?"

Hemingway clicked another key and the wall screen changed. "In the highlighted areas Middle East terrorists are hooking up with Far East drug cartels in a much more formal way. In some cases they're actually taking over the drug operations completely. The Central Asian republics are imploding. Drug production is the fastest-growing part of the economy. And since the republics were the former Soviet Union's toxic waste dumps, we could soon have Middle East terrorist groups selling *radioactive* heroin and crack in the States."

"Ironic considering Muslims don't even touch liquor, much less crack," another man said.

Hemingway shook his head. "I've been on flights with some Saudis where the *hijab* comes off and the booze comes out as soon as the plane was wheels-up."

"Thank you for your report, Tom. Is this current hit list fundamentally accurate?" Gray asked another man.

"Yes, sir. It's based on very credible evidence."

"In my experience a term very often confused with *incredible* evidence," Gray said. "As usual, ground-level operatives are to be given the broadest possible latitude to accommodate different tactics by the enemy. Preemptive action is encouraged whenever possible. We'll take care of any lingering details on the other end."

Everyone in the room understood Gray's words to mean: kill them and don't worry about the legal or political niceties.

Gray next asked for and received a report on the domestic terrorist front, which included groups of militia and religious cults.

"Give me the current hot reads," Gray ordered next.

And on it went for the next two hours as one potential crisis after another was carefully dissected. And yet at any moment all this analysis could be thrown out the window as another building or world leader toppled or a jumbo jet exploded in midair.

Gray was about to adjourn when one of the women, who'd left the room in response to a hurried summons, returned and handed him a new file.

Gray took two minutes to scan the four pages. When he looked up, he was clearly not pleased. "This happened last night. The police and FBI have been investigating since eight-forty-five this morning. And this is the first I hear of it?"

"I don't think its potential importance was appreciated as quickly as it should have been."

"Patrick Johnson?" Gray asked.

"He's an analyst with—"

"I know *that*," Gray said impatiently. "It's in the report you just handed me. Regardless of how he died, does it have something to do with his work?"

"The FBI's heading up the investigation."

"That gives me no comfort whatsoever," Gray said bluntly. "Do we at least have people on the scene? This report was inexplicably silent on that."

"Yes."

"I want Patrick Johnson's entire life history in one hour. Get on it."

The woman shot out of the room. After she'd gone, Gray rose and walked down the hall to another conference room where representatives from CIA, NSA and Homeland Security were waiting. For the next hour Gray received a briefing and asked a series of questions that made half the people in the room feel uncomfortable and the other half seriously intimidated.

After that, he walked to his office, a modest room wedged between two far larger ones used for crisis command centers that were full of activity on most days. His office was devoid of any personal mementos or the ubiquitous photo wall of fame. Gray had no time to consider his past triumphs. Sitting at his desk, he stared for a moment at a wall where windows would normally be. He had vetoed them out of the NIC facility's design; windows were a weakness, an avenue for spies and a source of distraction. Still, it had not been an easy decision because Gray was an avid outdoorsman. Yet here he was spending his "golden years" in a place without windows and sunlight trying to prevent the destruction of his world. Ironic, he mused, the mightiest intelligence agency ever created could not even see out of its own building.

A noise sounded on his computer. He hit a key and started to read about Patrick Johnson with great interest.

# CHAPTER

## 19

THE RARE BOOKS DIVISION at the Library of Congress Jefferson Building holds more than 800,000 precious volumes. For many bibliophiles the crown jewel of this literary treasure was the Lessing J. Rosenwald collection of antique books and prints. Many of these were classified as "incunabula," meaning they were created before 1501 and without benefit of the Gutenberg printing press technology. The Rosenwald collection, along with over a hundred others, is housed in numerous vaults next to the Rare Books reading room. It was in this sanctuary that patrons were allowed to read, and occasionally touch, volumes that were more works of art than simply books.

Although the reading room is open to the public, security is very tight. The entire area is monitored 24/7 by closed-circuit camera with time stamp. Clerks monitor the usage of all books in the room, and no volume is ever allowed out of the room except on loan to another institution or by order of the Librarian of Congress. The most rare publications are often not even taken out of the vault except under special circumstances. In many of these exceptional cases the staff handles the books while the visitor merely reads the exalted pages from a few inches safe distance.

No bags or notebooks that could be used to secrete the precious tomes are allowed; nor are pens, as they could smudge the ancient pages. Only pencils and loose-leaf paper are permitted in this sanctified place. And even then, some clerks will often draw nervous breaths when a lead pencil draws within a foot of one of their cherished "wards."

Oliver Stone made his way to the reading room on the second floor and passed through the large leather and brass inner doors with port-hole windows. Enormous bronze metal doors—which some claimed were symbolically stamped with three panels to show the importance of the history of printing—were open against the inner wall. When the reading room was closed, these doors were locked over the inner ones, creating a formidable barrier even if one could get past all the electronic security and armed guards. The room itself was one of the most beautiful in the whole of the Library of Congress. It had been fashioned after the Georgian simplicity of Independence Hall in Philadelphia with the intent of creating a soothing environment for scholarship and contemplation. This result had been achieved, because as soon as Stone entered the space, he felt a wondrous sense of calm.

Caleb Shaw was working at his desk at the far end of the room. As a reference specialist he was an expert in several antiquarian periods, and he also helped scholars with important research. When Caleb saw his friend, he came forward to meet him, buttoning up his cardigan as he did so. The room was very cool.

"Oliver, you're right, I'm not sure I would have recognized you," he said, gazing at his friend's altered appearance.

"It actually feels good." Stone eyed one of the security cameras. "This place seems very well guarded."

"It has to be. The collection is priceless, the only one like it in the world. The safeguards they go through to make sure nothing is lost, you wouldn't believe it. If a book gets misplaced, no one leaves until it's found. The person who buys the books for the collection can't access the database and alter the descriptions in the catalog, and the person who accesses the database can't purchase books."

"Because otherwise a person could buy a book for the collection and make it 'disappear' on the database, and then take the book and sell it and no one the wiser?"

"Exactly. My goodness, what a morning it's been!" Caleb exclaimed. "A very elderly gentleman came in, not a scholar known to anyone here, just someone off the street. And he wanted to see a William Blake. A William Blake! 'Any William Blake will do,' he said. Well, that was a red flag right there. You might as well have asked to see our Mormon Bible, for all the sirens that set off. No one gets to see a Blake without senior-level approval, and that is not frequently given, I can tell you."

"Blake is rare?" Stone said.

"Rare doesn't even begin to describe the situation with Blake. God-like perhaps."

"So what did you do?"

"When we talked to him a little further, we discovered that he was quite probably descended from one of Blake's siblings. So we brought out some of his illuminated works, his engravings, you know. He wasn't allowed to touch them, of course, because very few people know how to handle old books. But this episode had a nice ending. The gentleman was quite overwhelmed by the entire experience. In fact, I thought he might start weeping. But many of our volumes *are* things of beauty. I think that's why I love working here."

All of this came thundering out in the fashion of a man passionately engaged with his work and eager to spread this enthusiasm to others.

Caleb and Stone took a staff elevator to the lower level, where they walked through the tunnels that connected the Jefferson, Adams and Madison Buildings of the Library of Congress complex, arriving at the cafeteria in the lower level of the Madison. They purchased lunch there and carried it outside, where they ate on a picnic table set up on the Madison's raised frontage that looked out on Independence Avenue. The massive Jefferson Building was on the other side of the street, and just beyond that was the U.S. Capitol.

"Not a bad view," Stone commented.

"I'm afraid it gets taken for granted by most."

Stone finished his sandwich and then leaned toward his friend.

"Patrick Johnson?"

"I looked him up in the government database but found nothing. I don't have the security clearances to make a really thorough probe. You thought he might be with the Secret Service because of that pin you found. If so, that's out of my league. Law enforcement and librarians don't share the same databases, I'm afraid."

"There's a new development. That Secret Service agent I'm friendly with, Alex Ford? He came by to visit me last night at my tent."

"Last night! Do you think there's a connection?"

"I don't see how there can be, since he came by before the murder even happened. But it is troubling."

There was a buzzing sound, and Caleb pulled out his cell phone and answered it. His features became very animated as he listened. When he clicked off, he said, "That was Milton. He was able to hack into the Secret Service's database."

Stone's eyes widened. "He was able to do that! Already?"

"Milton can do anything with a computer, Oliver. He could make a fortune doing illegal things on the Internet. Three years ago he hacked into the Pentagon because he said he wanted to make sure they weren't planning on nuking one of our own cities and blaming it on terrorists as an excuse for an all-out war against Islam."

"That certainly sounds like something Milton would think of. What did he find?"

"Johnson worked as a data management supervisor at NIC."

"NIC? Carter Gray."

"Exactly."

Stone rose. "I want you to call Reuben and Milton and tell them to be ready to go out tonight. And we'll need your car. You can pick me up at the usual spot. We'll meet Reuben at Milton's house. It's closest to where we're going."

"And where is that?"

"Bethesda. To the late Patrick Johnson's home."

"But, Oliver, the police will be there. It's a murder investigation."

"No," Stone corrected. "It's a *homicide* investigation right now with the police no doubt leaning toward suicide. But if the police are there, we might be able to pick up some valuable information. Oh, and, Caleb, bring Goff."

As his friend walked off, a puzzled Caleb stared after him. Goff was Caleb's *dog*! However, Caleb was well acquainted with his friend's odd requests. He threw his trash away in a garbage can and headed back to his world of rare books.

# CHAPTER

# 20

As soon as Tyler Reinke and Warren Peters left Roosevelt Island, they headed directly back to NIC. They dropped the "suicide" note off to have it compared against samples of Patrick Johnson's handwriting *and* to have it checked for fingerprints. They instructed the labs that there might be useful latent fingerprints on the paper that would rule out suicide. That's what they said, but not, of course, what the NIC men intended. If any of the witnesses last night had touched the note and they were on a database somewhere, Peters and Reinke would have a golden opportunity to tie up the loose ends.

After that, they drove to Georgetown, parked their car and began walking toward the riverbank.

"They haven't come forward," Peters said. "We'd know if they had."

"Which might give us some breathing room," Reinke replied.

"How much do you think they saw?"

"Let's just go with worst-case scenario and assume they saw enough to pick us out of a police lineup."

Peters thought for a bit. "All right, let's also go with the theory that they haven't told the police what they saw because they were on the island doing something illegal, or else they're scared to for some other reason."

"You were in the bow of the inflatable; how good a look did you get?"

"It was so damn foggy I didn't see much of them. If I had, they wouldn't be a problem."

"Boat they were in?"

"Old and wooden and long enough to accommodate at least four."

"Is that how many you saw?"

"Only two, maybe three. I'm not really certain. I might have winged one of them. I thought I heard somebody cry out. One was an old guy. I remember seeing a whitish beard. Pretty crappy clothes."

"Homeless?"

"Maybe. Yeah, that could be it."

"Now we've got the police, FBI and Secret Service to worry about."

"We knew that going in," Peters replied. "A homicide gets investigated."

"But the original plan didn't take into account eyewitnesses. What's your take on this Ford character?"

"He's no kid, so he probably knows how to hedge with the best of them. We'll find out more on him and his partner later. I'm more worried about the Bureau."

When they reached the riverbank, Reinke said, "We know they were headed this way. I made a preliminary recon of the riverbank earlier this morning and didn't find it, but the boat has to be here. I'll go north, you go south. Call if you spot anything."

The two men headed off in opposite directions.

Patrick Johnson's fiancée had finally stopped sobbing long enough to answer a few standard questions posed to her by Alex and Simpson, who sat across from the devastated woman in her living room. The FBI had already been by to interrogate her, and Alex doubted that Agent Lloyd had exhibited the greatest bedside manner. He decided to try a gentler approach.

Anne Jeffries lived in a one-bedroom apartment in Springfield, Virginia, where eighteen hundred a month in rent bought you considerably less than a thousand square feet, a single bedroom and one toilet. She was medium height and a little on the plump side, with a puffy face engraved with small features. She wore her brunet hair long, and her teeth had been bleached to a startling white.

"Our wedding was to be on May first of next year," Jeffries said. She sat dressed in a rumpled sweat suit with her hair unkempt, her face unmade and a pile of used Kleenex next to her feet.

"And there were no problems that you were aware of?" Alex asked.

"None," she answered. "We were very happy together. My job was going great." However, she made each of these statements as though they were questions.

"What is it that you do?" Simpson asked.

"I'm director of development for a nonprofit health care group based in Old Town Alexandria. I've been there about two years. It's a great position. And Pat loved his job."

"So he spoke about it to you?" Alex asked.

Jeffries lowered her tissue. "No, not really. I mean I knew he worked for the Secret Service, or something like that. I knew he wasn't an agent, like you two. But he never spoke about what he did or even where he did it. It used to be that old joke between us, you know, the 'if he told me, he'd have to kill me' thing. God, what a stupid line." The tissue went back up, and the eyes filled with fresh tears.

"Yeah, it is a stupid line," Alex agreed. "As I'm sure you know, your fiancé was found on Roosevelt Island."

Jeffries took a deep breath. "That was where we had our first date. It was a picnic. I still remember exactly the food that I brought and the wine we had."

"So he maybe committed suicide at the site of your first date?" Simpson asked. "That might be symbolic." She and Alex exchanged glances.

"We weren't having problems!" exclaimed the woman, who'd sensed their suspicion.

"Maybe from your perspective you weren't," Simpson said in a blunt tone. "Sometimes the people we think we know best we don't really know at all. But the fact is a bottle of Scotch and a gun were found with his prints on them."

Jeffries stood and paced the small room. "Look, it's not like Pat was leading some secret double life."

"Everyone has secrets," Simpson persisted. "And killing himself at the place where you had your first date, well . . . ? It may not be a coincidence."

Jeffries whirled around to look at Simpson. "Not Pat. He didn't have secrets that would cause him to take his own life."

"If you knew about them, they wouldn't be secrets, would they?" Simpson said.

"His suicide note said that he was sorry," Alex interjected, shooting Simpson an angry look. "Any idea what he was sorry about?"

Jeffries dropped back onto her chair. "The FBI didn't tell me about that."

"They were under no obligation to tell you, but I thought you would want to know. Any idea what he might have meant?"

"No."

"Was he depressed about anything? Any change in emotions?" Alex asked.

"Nothing like that."

"The gun he used was a Smith & Wesson .22 caliber revolver. It was registered to him. You ever see it around?"

"No, but I knew he'd purchased a gun. There'd been a couple of break-ins in his neighborhood. He got it for protection. I hate guns personally. After we were married, I was going to make him get rid of it."

"When was the last time you spoke with him?" Alex asked.

"Yesterday afternoon. He said he'd call me later if he got the chance. But he never did."

She looked like she might start bawling again, so Alex spoke quickly. "No idea what he was working on lately? Anything he might have mentioned, even just in passing?"

"I told you, he didn't talk about work to me."

"No money problems, ex-girlfriend, things like that?"

She shook her head.

"And what were you doing last night between the hours of eleven and two?" Simpson asked.

Jeffries looked stonily at her. "Is that supposed to mean something?"

"I think the question is pretty straightforward."

"You said Pat killed himself, so why does it matter where *I* was?"

Alex cut in. He was finding his partner's interrogation technique very annoying. "Technically, it's a homicide, which can include anything from suicide to murder. We're just trying to establish the whereabouts of everyone involved. We'll be asking lots of people that same question. Don't read anything more than that into it."

Slowly, Anne Jeffries' defiant look dissolved. "Well, I left work around six-thirty. Traffic, as usual, was a bitch. It took me an hour and ten minutes to crawl a few miles. I made some phone calls, had a bite to eat and went back down to Old Town to meet with the woman who's making my wedding dress." Here she paused and let out a sob. Alex handed her a fresh tissue and nudged the glass of water she'd earlier poured for herself closer to the woman. She gulped from it and continued. "I finished with her around nine-thirty. That's when I got a call from a girlfriend who lives in Old Town, and we met for a drink at Union Street Pub. We were there for about an hour or so, just chitchatting. Then I drove home. I was in bed by midnight."

"Your friend's name?" Simpson asked, and wrote it down.

The two agents rose to leave, but Jeffries stopped them.

"His . . . his body. They didn't tell me where it is."

"I would imagine it's at the D.C. morgue now," Alex said quietly.

"Can I . . . I mean would it be possible for me to see him?"

"You don't have to do that. They've already positively identified him," Simpson added.

"That's not what I meant. I . . . I just want to see him." She paused and said, "Is he, is he terribly disfigured?"

Alex answered, "No. I'll see what I can do. By the way, is his family nearby?"

"They live in California. I've spoken with them; they're flying in with Pat's brother." She gazed up at him. "We were really very happy together."

"I'm sure you were," Alex said as he walked out the door with Simpson.

Outside, he faced off with his partner. "Is that what the hell you call effective interrogation techniques?"

Simpson shrugged. "I was the bad cop and you were the good cop. It worked pretty well. She's probably telling the truth. And she doesn't know zip."

Alex was about to respond when his phone rang.

He listened for a minute and then turned to Simpson. "Let's go." He started walking off fast.

"Where to?" she asked, hustling after him.

"That was Lloyd from the FBI. They think they just found out what Patrick Johnson was sorry about."

# CHAPTER

## 21

WHEN ALEX AND SIMPSON arrived at Patrick Johnson's Bethesda residence, they were surprised, for two reasons. One, there was no visible police presence, not even a marked vehicle or yellow police tape. A couple of Suburbans in the driveway were the only evidence of someone being on-site.

The second surprise was the house itself.

Alex stopped on the front sidewalk, put his hands on his hips and surveyed the single-family home. It wasn't huge, but it wasn't attached to another house either, and the upscale neighborhood was within walking distance of the thriving Bethesda downtown area. Alex said, "At Johnson's pay grade I thought we'd be looking at a one-bedroom apartment like his fiancée. Hell, this thing's got a *yard*. With *grass*."

Simpson shook her head. "When I got assigned to WFO and didn't know squat about the D.C. housing sticker shock, I priced some places around here just for the hell of it. This is over a million dollars, easy."

Inside, Agent Lloyd was waiting for them. Alex said, "Where'd he get the money for this place?"

Lloyd nodded. "And it's not just the house. There's a new Infiniti QX56 in the garage. Runs over fifty grand. And we found his other car. He left it on the Virginia side of the river before he took his last swim. Lexus sedan, another forty grand."

"Selling secrets?" Simpson asked.

"No. We think it's a more reliable source of illegal cash."

"Drugs," Alex said quickly.

"Come up and see for yourself."

As they were being led upstairs, Alex mentioned to Lloyd, "Bureau securing crime scenes differently these days?"

"Special marching orders on this one."

"Let me guess. Since it involves NIC, discretion is valued over all other things."

Lloyd didn't answer but he did smile.

In the master bedroom closet there was a set of drop-down stairs leading to an attic access panel. On the floor of the closet they saw bundles of something stacked in clear plastic.

"Coke?" Simpson asked.

Lloyd shook his head. "Heroin. That brings ten times the return coke does."

"And his fiancée knew nothing? Where'd she think he got all this money?"

"I haven't asked her that yet because we interviewed her before we found this. But I will," Lloyd added.

"How'd you get onto the drug angle so fast?" Alex asked.

"When we saw where he lived, we ran Johnson's name through SEISINT and pulled up the property records on his purchase of this place. He bought it last year for one point four million and put a half million in cash down from a financial source we haven't been able to trace. He financed the cars and then paid them off soon after, again using a bank account we can't track. I knew it had to be an inheritance, drugs or selling secrets. The point of least resistance was the drugs. So I pulled in a dog from DEA. It started barking its head off when it went into the closet. We didn't find anything until we saw the panel to the attic. We lifted the dog up there and bingo! He had it stacked between the rafters with insulation over it. "

"Well, I guess other things being equal, it's better he was selling drugs than selling his *country* down the river," Simpson commented wryly.

"I'm not even sure he had access to secrets worth selling," Lloyd replied. "And now we don't have to go down that road. But this is going to be a big enough mess as it is. Hell, I could write the *Post* headline myself: 'Carter Gray, Intelligence or Drug Czar?' "

It seemed to Alex his FBI counterpart was looking forward to every last bit of dirt thrown up on the only federal law enforcement agency that rivaled his in terms of budget and bite. He said, "Now the question is, did he kill himself because he was a drug dealer getting married to a respectable woman and suddenly couldn't handle it, or did his druggie associates kill him and try to make it look like a suicide?"

Lloyd said, "I'd vote for him taking his own life. He died on the spot where he and his fiancée had their first date. Drug dealers would've just popped a new hole in his head while he was sitting in his car or sleeping in his bed. The whole murder-suicide subterfuge is way too sophisticated for those types."

Alex considered this, then said, "Did you find anything else connected to the drugs? Transaction journal, list of drop-off spots, computer files, anything like that?"

"We're still looking. But I doubt he would've been careless enough to leave stuff like that around. We'll let you know what we do find so you can close your file out."

As Alex and Simpson walked back to the car, Simpson glanced at her partner. "Well, there goes the pain in your ass that you didn't really need. Congratulations."

"Thanks," Alex said curtly.

"But a drug dealer at NIC, they're still going to take heat over that."

"That's how the cards fall sometimes."

"So back to WFO?"

He nodded. "I'll shoot off my e-mail upstairs, follow with a more detailed one when friend Lloyd fills in the rest of the spaces, and we go back to busting counterfeiters and standing in doorways looking to catch a bullet."

"Sounds like a thrill."

"I hope you believe that, because you're going to be doing it for a long time."

"I'm not complaining. I joined the ranks, nobody pushed me here." She didn't sound very convincing, though.

"Look, Jackie, I usually mind my own business, but here's a piece of real honest advice for a healthy career with the Service from someone who's seen it all."

"I'm listening."

"Do your share of the crap work, no matter who's looking out for you upstairs. One, it'll make you a better agent. Two, you'll leave the Service with at least one friend."

"Oh, really, who's that?" Simpson said irritably.

"Me."

# CHAPTER

## 22

AT THE NIC HELIPAD GRAY boarded a Sikorsky VH-60N chopper. It was the same model the president used as Marine One, although in the coming years it would be replaced by a Lockheed Martin–built version. Gray usually rode the Sikorsky to the White House for his meetings with Brennan, causing some understandably anonymous souls to snidely dub it "Marine One and a Half." However, there was one distinct difference between how Gray and Brennan were ferried on choppers. When the president rode in from Andrews Air Force Base, Camp David or elsewhere, there were three identical VH-60Ns in the convoy. Two served as decoys, giving any would-be assassin with a surface-to-air missile only a one-in-three shot of hitting his intended target. Carter Gray was on his own in that regard. After all, there were numerous cabinet secretaries, but just one president.

Traditionally, it was only Marine One that was allowed to land on the White House grounds. It was Brennan who'd authorized Gray to travel this way, over the very heated protests of the Secret Service. It saved Gray what could have been a tortuous daily commute from Loudoun County, and the intelligence czar's time was very valuable. However, there were still grumblings at the Secret Service. Understandably, they didn't care to see anything flying at 1600 Pennsylvania Avenue unless it had the president on board.

At a speed of 150 knots the ride was quick and uneventful, though Gray was too busy to have noticed. He strode across the White House grounds knowing full well that the countersnipers arrayed on the surrounding rooftops were drawing practice beads on his wide head. Inside the West Wing Gray nodded at people he knew. Until 1902 greenhouses stood on this plot of ground. That's when Teddy Roosevelt finally decided he needed a private place, away from his numerous children and their large coterie of pets, in order to competently conduct his business as the nation's leader. His successor, the rotund William Taft, made the West Wing even bigger and the Oval Office a permanent fixture in the lives of all future presidents.

Gray's daily visit had already been scheduled and approved. No one went into the Oval Office unannounced, not even the First Lady. Brennan always received Gray in the Oval Office and not the adjacent Roosevelt Room, as he often did visitors and other underlings.

Brennan looked up from his thirteen-hundred-pound desk built from the wood of the British ship HMS *Resolute,* which American whalers discovered after it had been caught in the ice and abandoned by its crew. The ship had been repaired by the U.S. government and sent back to England as a gesture of goodwill. Queen Victoria reciprocated by presenting the desk as a gift to President Rutherford B. Hayes. Thereafter, the Resolute Desk, as it became known, had been used by every president since, except for a period of time when it was at the Smithsonian Institution.

Gray had had his antennae on high since he stepped inside the West Wing. He had seen the Web casts on Patrick Johnson's death. More of them had trickled out that afternoon. He got the last of them on the chopper ride over. Gray had also received a briefing by the FBI that included the discovery of the drug cache at Johnson's home. He also knew of Secret Service agents Ford and Simpson's involvement in the investigation. When he heard Simpson's name, it allowed him a rare smile. That could be his ace in the hole down the road, should he need one.

As befitted any respectable spymaster, Gray had eyes and ears in the White House and had already been warned that Brennan was concerned about the Johnson matter and its possible negative effects on his reelection campaign. Therefore, he did not let his boss initiate the discussion.

As soon as the two men sat down across from each other, Gray said, "Mr. President, before we go into the daily briefing, I'd like to take up the unfortunate issue of Patrick Johnson's death on Roosevelt Island."

"I'm surprised you hadn't called about it, Carter." There was an edge to the man's voice that Gray understood but didn't particularly like.

"I wanted to have a firm grasp of the facts before I did, sir. The last thing I wanted to do was waste your time."

"You certainly wouldn't be the first one to waste it today," Brennan snapped.

*This is the President, and I serve at his pleasure,* Gray reminded himself.

Gray gave the president a brief background on the matter, information that doubtless the man already knew. When Gray got to the drug discovery, Brennan put up his hand.

"Are there any others involved?" he asked sharply.

"Good question, Mr. President, and not one that's been answered to my satisfaction. I will personally conduct an internal investigation of this matter, aided, at my request, by the FBI." Getting the Bureau involved was loathsome to Gray, but better he suggest it than allow someone else to do it.

"Carter, if the FBI is coming in, you have to give them a free hand. Nothing swept under the rug."

"I wouldn't have it any other way. However, at this point it does not appear that the case goes any further. That is to say, if Johnson was selling drugs, it was separate from his work at NIC."

The president was shaking his head. "That's not an assumption we can make yet. What exactly did he do for you?"

"He oversaw our electronic intelligence files containing background information on terror suspects and other targeted individuals and organizations, both outstanding and those that had been apprehended or killed. Johnson actually helped to design the system."

"Worth selling?"

"It's hard to see how. It was basic info. A lot of it is contained on our public Web site. Then there's the confidential information such as fingerprints, DNA info, if applicable, that sort of thing. However, the files Johnson managed did not contain, for example, any specific intelligence that we'd uncovered to aid us in capturing the targets."

The president nodded, sat back and rubbed a kink out of his neck. At his desk since seven a.m., he had already crammed fourteen hours' worth of work into eight, and he had a full afternoon ahead of him with a state dinner to follow. And then it was off the next day to the Midwest to campaign for an election that he had in the bag but was far too paranoid to let his guard down about. "To put it bluntly, Carter, I'm not happy about this at all. The last thing I need right now is some damn scandal."

"I will do everything in my power to prevent that from happening, sir."

"Well, vetting your employees a little better would've been good," the president admonished.

"I absolutely agree with that." Gray paused and then added, "Sir, obviously, we cannot allow this development to interfere with our main work."

Brennan looked puzzled. "Come again?"

"As you know, the media has a way of creating something out of nothing. It's a terrific way to sell newspapers, but not necessarily good for national security."

Brennan shrugged. "That's First Amendment territory, Carter. That's sacrosanct."

Gray leaned forward. "I'm not saying otherwise. But we *can* do something about leaks, and also the content and timing of the information flow. Right now the media knows about as much as we do. They'll report it, and NIC will be giving an official statement regarding the matter. I think at this stage all that is fine, but it's certainly not in our best interests to see NIC's mission derailed for something like this."

He paused again and then delivered the lines he had practiced on the chopper ride over. "There are only a few ways you are politically vulnerable, sir. And your opponents are so desperate now they'll seize on anything to hit you with. In that desperation they may see this as such an opportunity. Historically, such a strategy has a certain precedent of success. To put it *bluntly,* we cannot let them use this to defeat you in November. Whatever the truth is, it's not important enough to prevent you from winning a second term."

Brennan thought about this for some time. Finally, he said, "Okay, together we'll keep a tight leash on the media. I mean this is national security, after all. And if you run into any flack from the Bureau or others, you let me know about it." He paused and then said, in his best politician's baritone, "You're right, this nation's security will not be sidetracked by some guy selling drugs on the side."

Gray smiled. "Absolutely." *Thank God it's an election year.*

Brennan went to his desk and pressed the intercom button. "Tell Secretary Decker to come in."

Gray looked surprised at this. "Decker?"

Brennan nodded. "We need to talk about Iraq."

Decker walked in a minute later. He was in his fifties with close-cropped gray hair, handsome features and lean body from running five miles every day wherever he happened to be in the world. A widower, Decker was deemed one of the city's most eligible bachelors. Although he'd never served in the military, he'd begun in the defense industry, working his way up and earning a sizable fortune before jumping to the public arena. His rise there had been equally swift and included stints as secretary of the navy and deputy defense secretary. He was the total D.C. package—smart, articulate, ruthless, ambitious and well respected—and Gray loathed him. As defense secretary, Decker headed up the Pentagon, the sector that used the vast bulk of all intelligence dollars, a purse that Gray technically controlled. Thus, while Decker was cooperative with Gray and said all the right things in public, Gray was well aware that behind the scenes Decker tried to circumvent and backstab him at every opportunity. He was also Gray's major rival for the president's ear.

Decker opened the conversation in his usual brisk manner. "The Iraqi leadership has made it clear that they want us gone very soon. However, there are enormous problems there, even more than the Kurds forming their own republic. The Iraqi army and the security forces are simply not ready. In some critical ways they may never be ready. But the country is growing weary of our presence. And now the Iraqis have publicly taken the position that Israel must be exterminated, following the hard line of their new ally, Syria. It's an untenable situation but hard for us to reject since it's a democratically-elected government saying it."

"We know all this, Joe," Gray said impatiently. "And the Baathists are negotiating with the leadership to come back to power in exchange for stopping the violence," he added, looking directly at the president.

Brennan nodded. "But how can we leave Iraq in that way? The last thing we want is Syria and Iraq teaming up, with Hussein's cronies in control again. With the Sharia Group and Hezbollah headquartered in Syria, we could soon have their presence in Iraq and beyond," Brennan added, referring to the two anti-Israeli terrorist organizations. "And France sliced off the coastline of Syria and formed Lebanon in the 1920s. Syria has always wanted it back and may unite with Iraq to do so. And then they might go after the Golan Heights, sparking a war with Israel. That could destabilize the entire region more than it already is."

Gray said, "Well, if another country came here and lopped off New England and unilaterally formed another country with it, we'd be upset too, wouldn't we, Mr. President?"

Decker cut in. "Besides the Baathists, there are extremist Islamic factions in the Iraqi legislature that are growing in power. If they take over, they'll be far more dangerous to the U.S. than Saddam Hussein ever was. But we also promised the Iraqi people that we would leave when they had adequate security forces in place and officially asked us to withdraw. That moment is almost upon us."

"So get to your point, Joe!" Gray snapped.

Decker glanced at Brennan. "I haven't discussed this fully with the president yet." He cleared his throat. "By taking out some of these extremist factions in the legislature, we can tip the power in favor of the government in Iraq that's best for the *U.S.* and keep the Baathists from coming back to power. And there is all that oil to consider, sir. Gas is approaching three dollars a gallon now. We need the leverage of the Iraqi reserves."

"Take out? As in, what, assassination!" Brennan said, scowling. "We don't do that anymore. It's illegal."

"It's illegal to assassinate a head of state or government, Mr. President," Gray corrected.

"Exactly," Decker agreed. "These people are not in that category. To me it's no different than putting a price on bin Laden's head."

"But the targets you're talking about are duly appointed members of the Iraqi legislature," Brennan protested.

"The insurgents are murdering *moderate* legislators with impunity over there right now. This is simply evening the playing field, sir,"

Decker rejoined. "If we don't do something, there won't be any moderates *left*."

"But, Joe," Gray said, "if we go in and do that, it'll ignite a civil war."

"We'll make it look like the Iraqi moderates did it in retaliation so there's no heat on us. I've been promised full cooperation from them."

"But the resulting civil war . . . ," Brennan said.

"Will give us a perfectly legitimate reason to keep our military presence in Iraq for the foreseeable future," Decker responded quickly, obviously pleased with himself. "However, if we allow the Baathists back in, they'll crush all opposition, and Iraq will return to a Hussein-style dictatorship. We can't let that happen. All the money spent and lives lost will have meant nothing. And if that happens in Iraq there's no reason to think the Taliban can't reemerge in Afghanistan."

Brennan looked at Gray. "What do you think?"

Actually, Gray was chagrined he hadn't thought of it first. Decker had clearly outflanked him on this. *The little son of a bitch.* "You wouldn't be the first U.S. president to authorize something like that, sir," he grudgingly admitted.

Brennan didn't look convinced. "I need to think it over."

"Absolutely, Mr. President," Decker replied. "But it is on a tight time frame. And as you well know should Iraq and Afghanistan fall back under the control of governments hostile to us, the American public will raise holy hell." He paused and added, "That is not a legacy you want or deserve, sir."

For all his hatred of the man Gray had to admit, from the concerned expression on Brennan's face, Decker had played it perfectly.

After Decker had left, Brennan sat back and took off his reading glasses. "Before we start the briefing, I want to run something by you, Carter. I'm heading up to New York on September 11 to give a speech at the memorial site." Gray knew where this was going but stayed silent. "I wanted to know if you'd like to accompany me. After all, you've done more than almost anyone to ensure something like that never happens again."

It was unheard-of to decline an invitation by a United States president to travel to an event. However, Gray really didn't care about protocol or tradition with this particular subject.

"That is a kind offer, sir, but I'll be attending a private service here."

"I know it's painful for you, Carter, but I just thought I'd ask. You're sure?"

"Very sure, Mr. President. Thank you."

"All right." Brennan paused. "You know about my hometown renaming itself after me?"

"Yes, sir. Congratulations."

Brennan smiled. "It's one of those things that come along that's both flattering and embarrassing at the same time. My ego's not so large that I can't see that the town's hope in profiting by the change is at least equal to their wanting to pay homage to a local boy made good. I'm going up to give a speech at the dedication and shake some hands. Why don't you join me?"

If the most important rule was you never declined a president's invitation, the second most important rule was you never turned the man down twice.

"Thank you, I'd like that very much."

The president tapped his glasses against his briefing book. "It's likely that I'll be here for another four years."

"I'd say it's more than likely, sir."

"I want you to speak frankly, Carter. This will stay between you and me." Gray nodded. "Despite your successes in protecting this country, do you believe that the world is safer today than it was when I took office?"

Gray carefully considered this question, trying to ascertain the answer his chief wanted. However, Brennan remained inscrutable, so Gray decided to tell him the truth. "No, it's not. In fact, it's far more volatile."

"My people tell me that at its present consumption the planet could run out of fossil fuel in fifty years. No more plane travel, a few electric cars, cities shutting down for lack of energy. How we communicate, work, travel, get our food, all radically transformed. *And* this country won't have the means to adequately maintain its nuclear weapons and other military resources."

"That's all certainly possible."

"Yes, but without our military, how do we remain safe, Carter?"

Gray hesitated and then said, "I'm afraid I don't have the answer for you, sir."

Brennan said quietly, "I believe the difference between a mediocre president and a great one is *opportunity*."

"You've done a good job, Mr. President. You should be proud." Actually, in Gray's opinion, the man hadn't done anything special, yet he was not about to tell his boss *that*.

As Gray walked out of the West Wing an hour later, his mind, for once, wasn't on stopping America's enemies or pleasing his commander in chief. As he climbed aboard the chopper, Gray was thinking about purple. That was his daughter's favorite color until she was six. And then orange became her favorite. When he asked her why the change, she informed him with hands on little hips and her stubborn chin angled up that orange was a more grown-up color. Even to this day that memory never failed to make him smile.

Warren Peters finally found the boat where the Camel Club had hidden it. He immediately called Tyler Reinke and the man joined him quickly.

"You're sure this is it?" Reinke asked as he gazed at the boat.

Peters nodded. "There's blood on the gunwale. So I was right. I hit one of them."

"If they took the boat and brought it back, someone might have seen them."

Peters nodded and then stared out at the water. "But there might be an easier way to track them down. Johnson had ID in his pocket."

"Right, so?"

"So what if our witnesses saw where he lived, and get curious?"

"It might save us a lot of legwork," Reinke agreed. "We'll go there tonight."

# CHAPTER

## 23

CHOOSING HIS WORDS WITH CARE and hedging as much as he possibly could without drawing the ire of his superiors, Alex wrote up his report and e-mailed it to Jerry Sykes. He finished up some other paperwork and decided to call it a day before someone grabbed him for post duty. Alex had no desire to spend another evening watching a king or prime minister stuff his face with crab dip.

He passed an agent who was stashing his pistol in a wall locker before going in to interrogate a suspect.

"Hey, Alex, bust any more ATM bandits?" the agent asked. The story had made its way through WFO with the swiftness only a water cooler broadcast network could inspire.

"Nope. Couldn't find anybody else that stupid."

"Hear you and Simpson make a nice team," the man commented, barely suppressing a grin.

"We have our moments."

"Heard of J-Lo?"

"Who hasn't?" Alex replied.

"Well, Simpson is J-*Glo*. Didn't you know you were partnering with a celeb?"

"J-Glo? What's that supposed to mean?"

"Come on, Alex, she's got a halo over her. The light is shining from heaven above on that little southern pistol. They say it's blinding from at least five hundred yards. I'm surprised you can still see."

The agent walked off, laughing.

As luck would have it, Alex ran into his partner on the way out of the building.

"Going home?" he asked.

"No, I'm going to see if I can find any friends. I can't seem to dig up any here. "

She started to walk off, but Alex put a hand on her shoulder. "Look, what I said was meant as constructive criticism, nothing else. I would've paid good money for tips like that when I was just starting out and didn't know squat."

For an instant Simpson actually looked like she wanted to take a swing at him, but with what seemed immense self-control she regained her composure.

"I appreciate your interest but it's different for a woman. The Service is still very much a man's world."

"I'm not denying that, Jackie. But the fact is you're not doing your career any favors by letting yourself be treated differently from every-body else."

Simpson's face flushed. "I can't help it if people are treating me with kid gloves."

Alex shook his head. "Wrong answer. You *can* help it. In fact, you better make damn sure it stops." He paused and then asked, "Who *is* your guardian angel?" Simpson didn't appear to want to answer. "Look, just spill it. It's not like I can't find out."

She snapped, "Fine! My father is Senator Roger Simpson."

Alex nodded, impressed. "Chairman of the Intelligence Oversight Committee. That's a pretty big angel."

In a flash Simpson was right in Alex's face, almost stepping on his size 13 loafers as she attacked. "My father would *never* use his influ-ence to help me. And for your information, being his only child didn't make my life easier. I had to fight for every damn thing I got. I've got the bruises and thick skin to show for it."

Alex backed up a step and put out a hand to keep her at bay. "This town isn't built on fact, it's based on perception. And the perception is that you get out of the crap work more than you should. And that's not all. "

"Oh, really?"

He pointed at her jacket. "You usually wear a blazing red handker-chief in your breast pocket."

"So what?"

"So, to a Secret Service agent, that's a no-no. It not only draws attention to you in a profession that prides itself on keeping a low profile *except* on protection detail. It also makes a damn fine target for somebody looking to take a shot at you. So not only does it label you as a maverick, it labels you as a *stupid* maverick."

Simpson's jaw clenched as she stared down at this crimson mark, as though it were a scarlet letter.

Alex continued. "And your gun. It's a custom piece. Another sign that you think you're different—translate, better—than everybody else. That doesn't sit well with agents here, men or women."

"My daddy gave me this gun when I became a police officer." Alex noted that the angrier Simpson became, the more pronounced her Alabama drawl.

"So put it in a shadow box on your wall and carry the Service's standard issue!"

"And what, then all my problems just go away?" This shot out of the woman's mouth with such an attitude that now Alex felt like decking her.

"No, then you just have all the problems everybody else has. Why don't you just file that one away under 'Life's a Bitch'?" *And so are you.*

Alex turned and walked off. He'd had enough of the rookie for one day. The LEAP Bar was seriously calling his name.

Kate Adams had just come on duty after a full day at Justice when Alex walked in. It was relatively early yet, so the place was mostly empty. Alex marched up to the bar, a man on a mission. She'd seen him coming and had the martini with three fat olives waiting for him by the time Alex's rear hit the stool.

"My imagination, or are you a little upset about something?" she said in a teasing manner that immediately eased the tension from him.

The mingled scents of coconut and honeysuckle drifted across the width of the mahogany bar and settled in his nostrils. He wondered if she'd washed her hair before coming to work, or if it was her perfume, or both. Regardless, it was doing a number on him.

"Just work. It'll pass." He took a sip of his drink, popped one of the olives into his mouth and chased it down with a handful of peanuts he grabbed from a bowl next to him. "How goes it with you? Your super-spy friend Tommy come calling?"

She raised her eyebrows at this comment. "Hemingway? I wouldn't exactly call him a friend." He gave her such a skeptical look that she put down the glass she was drying off and leaned across the bar.

"You have another opinion you'd like to express, Agent Ford?"

He shrugged. "None of my business really."

"A girl can flirt and not mean anything by it."

Alex took another hit of his martini. "That's good to know."

"You have to admit, he's very cute, well traveled, intelligent. The man's the whole package really."

Alex started to launch a blistering rejoinder but then realized she was just pulling his chain, and enjoying herself immensely. "Yeah, he is. Hell, I was thinking about asking the guy out myself."

She leaned across the bar again and grabbed his tie so hard Alex was jerked toward her, spilling part of his drink.

She said, "Well, since you can't seem to get around to it, I will. Do you want to go out?"

Alex felt his mouth hanging open but had the good sense to shut it a second later. "You're asking me out?"

"No, I'm asking the guy behind you. *Yes,* I'm asking you out."

Alex couldn't help but glance around him on the outside chance that he was being set up with a hidden studio audience that was just waiting to erupt into belly laughs.

"You're really serious?"

She tightened her grip on his tie. "When I flirt, I flirt. When I ask, it's a whole other ball game."

"Yes. I want to go out with you."

"See, that wasn't all that hard, was it? Now, since we've finally gotten that settled, why don't we negotiate a date? Because you seem a little slow on the social uptake, I'll go first. I'm assuming you enjoy eating as well as drinking. How about dinner?"

"You just threw me a curve. I thought for sure you'd be safe and propose lunch."

"I'm not into safe these days," she said. Then Kate let go of his tie very, very slowly, sliding her hand down the fabric until the tie fell free.

Alex eased himself back, not seeming to mind at all that half his martini was now on his jacket sleeve.

"Dinner sounds fine with me," he managed to say without mangling the words too badly.

"Okay, let's set a date and time. I'm into instant gratification; are you free tomorrow night?"

Even if he'd been assigned to guard the president on his deathbed, Alex would've found a way to be available. "Sounds good."

"Say around six-thirty. I'll make dinner reservations unless you'd care to."

"No, go ahead."

"Do you want to meet at the restaurant or pick me up at my place?"

"Your place is fine."

"My, you're so agreeable, Agent Ford. I can't tell you how refreshing that is for me after being around lawyers all day. Lawyers don't agree on anything."

"Yeah, I've heard that."

"Why don't you come by around six?"

She wrote her phone number and address down and slid it across to him. He handed her one of his cards with his home address and phone number penciled in on the back.

"You like it out in Manassas?" she asked, eyeing his card.

"My wallet likes it a lot." He glanced at her address and got a funny look. "R Street? Georgetown!"

"Don't get your hopes up, mister. I'm not an heiress masquerading as a DOJ do-gooder. I live in the carriage house behind the mansion. The woman who owns the place is a widow and likes having someone around. She's really nice. Quite the pistol actually."

"You don't owe me an explanation."

"But that doesn't mean that you don't want one." She poured him a fresh drink. "On the house, since you seemed to have spilled yours." She handed him a rag.

"While you're in a cooperative mood, where does the 'total package' work and what project are you two involved in?"

Kate put a finger to her lips. "Lawyer confidentiality thing, you understand. But without breaking any state secrets I can tell you I'm working with his agency on its request to reuse an old building. But I don't think we're going to reach such an agreement. So what's going on at work that has you ticked off?"

"You don't hear enough sob stories as it is?"

"We're officially going out. So, in for a dime, in for a dollar."

Alex smiled. "Okay. There's this rookie at work I'm partnering with on an investigation. She's got a bigwig daddy who's pulling strings for her upstairs. I'm trying to explain to her that that's not how you make friends at the Service."

"And she's not getting the concept?"

"If she doesn't soon, it'll come down on her like a ton of bricks."

"So what's the case you're working on with her?"

"Now it's my turn to plead confidentiality." Suddenly, Alex's gaze was riveted on the plasma screen TV on the wall behind the bar.

A camera shot of Roosevelt Island was in the foreground of the screen as the big-toothed news anchor teleprompted her way through the story of a mysterious suicide. There was no report on the Secret Service's involvement, Alex noted. However, the heroin find at Patrick Johnson's house was prominently mentioned.

"Is that your case?" Kate asked.

He glanced back at her. "What?"

"I was hoping that'd be the only reason you were so totally ignoring me."

"Hey, I'm sorry," he said sheepishly. "Yeah, that's it. But no more details."

They both turned to the TV when they heard a familiar voice.

The man was articulating NIC's official response to the tragedy. And it wasn't Carter Gray, who probably didn't want to make this an ongoing national story by lending his considerable presence to it. However, Tom Hemingway was polished and efficient, the total package, as he presented NIC's spin to the country.

Alex looked back at Kate, who for the first time seemed at a loss for words. He smiled triumphantly. "Busted."

# CHAPTER

## 24

Caleb picked up Oliver Stone near the White House in his ancient pewter-gray Chevy Malibu with a fidgety tailpipe. They headed to Milton Farb's house near the D.C. and Maryland line, where Reuben would meet them. Stone sat in the front seat holding Caleb's dog, Goff, a small mongrel of unknown provenance named after the first chief of the Rare Books Division, Frederick Goff. As they pulled up in front of Milton's modest but well-kept home, Reuben jumped up from the front steps, walked over to the car and climbed in. He was dressed in his usual jeans, moccasins and a wrinkly red-checked flannel shirt; a pair of work gloves stuck out of his back pocket, and he carried his safety helmet in his hand.

"Grabbed some overtime at the loading dock," he explained. "Didn't have a chance to go home." He looked in surprise at Stone's new haircut and clean-shaven appearance. "Don't tell me you're rejoining mainstream America."

"Just trying to remain incognito and alive. Is Milton ready?"

"Our friend will be delayed a bit," Reuben said with a wink.

"What?" Stone said.

"He's entertaining, Oliver. You remember? His new lady friend?"

"Did you meet her?" Caleb asked excitedly. "Maybe she has a friend for me." Although a confirmed bachelor, Caleb was always on the lookout for new prospects.

"Just got a glimpse. She's actually a lot younger than Milton and damn nice-looking," Reuben replied. "Hope the poor fellow doesn't go and commit himself. I've had three trips down the aisle, and there won't be a fourth unless I am ungodly drunk. Blasted women. Can't live with them, and they sure as hell can't live with me."

"Your third wife was quite a nice woman," Stone noted.

"I'm not saying that the ladies don't have their uses, Oliver. I'm just of the opinion that long-lasting relationships are not the product of legal commitment. There have been more good times bashed by the covenant of marriage than I could count in several lifetimes."

"So your logic is what, ban marriage and you'll see the divorce rate plummet?"

"That too," Reuben said gruffly.

They all looked over as the door to Milton's house opened.

"She *is* good-looking," Caleb said, peering around Stone.

Milton and the woman kissed lightly on the lips, and then she walked down the steps to her car, a yellow Porsche that was parked in front of Caleb's Malibu.

"I wonder if Milton's OCD creates a problem for her," Caleb said thoughtfully. They had all spent hundreds of hours of their lives waiting through Milton's rituals. Yet they'd accepted it as an element of their friend's personality. They all had such "elements," and Milton had been diligent in seeking help for his disorder. And after years of medication, counseling and occasional hospitalization, he led a fairly normal existence, only resorting to his OCD for brief periods when locking his doors, sitting, washing his hands, or during moments of intense stress.

"I don't think that'll be a problem for her," Reuben said, pointing.

They all watched as the woman tapped the pavement with her high heels and then pecked on the car window with her finger, silently counting and muttering before opening her car door. Then she performed a similar exercise checking her seat, before climbing in. She left a considerable amount of rubber on the pavement as she hit sixty miles an hour six seconds later, before she slammed on her brakes at the next intersection. Then she roared off again, the deep-throated decibels of the Porsche's turbo actually causing Caleb to wince.

"Where the hell did he meet the woman, at a NASCAR event?" Caleb asked as he stared wide-eyed at the smoke still rising off the tire marks on the street.

"No, he told us he met her at the anxiety clinic," Reuben reminded them. "She was there getting treatment for OCD too."

Milton closed his front door, went through a brief ritual and came out to join them carrying his knapsack. He climbed into the backseat next to Reuben.

"She's a real looker," Reuben said. "What's her name?"

"Chastity," Milton replied.

Reuben snorted. "Chastity? Well, for your sake, I hope she doesn't live up to her name."

Traffic was fairly heavy, and by the time they got to Patrick Johnson's neighborhood it was quite dark. This suited Stone well. The nighttime was where he was most comfortable.

He checked house numbers as they drifted down the street. "All right, Caleb, it's coming up in the next block on the left. Park the car here."

Caleb pulled the Malibu to the curb and looked at his friend.

"Now what?" he asked nervously.

"We wait. I want to get the lay of the land a bit, see who's coming and going." Stone pulled out his binoculars and gazed through them up the street. "Assuming that those Suburbans parked out front are Bureau cars, I'm guessing that the third house up on the left is Johnson's."

"Nice digs," Reuben commented, following his friend's gaze.

Meanwhile, Milton had been studying his laptop computer. He said, "It was reported that they found heroin in the house. And Roosevelt Island was where Johnson spent his first date with his fiancée. They're theorizing that he killed himself there symbolically; with his upcoming marriage he couldn't live his double life anymore."

"How can you be on the Internet in a car?" Caleb exclaimed.

"I'm pure wireless," Milton replied. "I don't need hot spots. You know, Caleb, you really should let me bring you into the twenty-first century."

"I use a computer at work!"

"Only for word processing. You don't even have a personal e-mail account, only a library one."

"I prefer pen, paper and stamps to compose *my* mail," Caleb responded indignantly.

"Are you sure you don't mean foolscap and a quill, Brother Caleb?" Reuben asked with a grin.

Caleb said heatedly, "And unlike those Neanderthals on the Internet, I use complete sentences and, heaven help us, punctuation. Is that a crime?"

"No, it's not, Caleb," Stone said calmly. "But let's try to keep the discussion relevant to our mission tonight."

"You know, you would've thought that an NIC employee would've been vetted well enough that his drug dealer status showed up," Reuben said.

"Well, presumably, he was clean when he signed on with them but turned dirty sometime after," Milton replied. "Look at Aldrich Ames. He had a big house and drove a Jaguar, and the CIA never even thought to ask him how he could afford it."

Caleb said, "But apparently, Johnson was selling drugs, not secrets. He ran afoul of his business associates, and they killed him. That seems pretty clear."

"Did those two gentlemen look like drug dealers to you?" Stone asked.

"Since I don't *know* any drug dealers, I'm not in a position to really answer that question," Caleb said.

"Well, I *do* know some," said Reuben. "And despite what damn bigots might think, they're not all young black gang members with nine-millimeters stuffed in their prison shuffle pants, Oliver."

"I'm not implying that they are. However, let's consider the facts. They brought him to a place where he had his first date. That implies intelligence gathering unless he was in the habit of sharing his romantic history with his alleged criminal associates. They carried him in a powered boat that was so *silent* we didn't even hear it until they reached the island. Now, that may be a technology drug dealers employ in, say, South America where there is a good deal more water. But in the nation's capital?"

Reuben said, "Who the hell knows what sort of high-tech toys they're using around here nowadays?"

Stone ignored this. "In addition, the two killers undertook a fairly military-style reconnaissance of the area and used a killing technique that smacks of the professional assassin. And they were well aware of potential incriminating forensic residue and took appropriate steps accordingly. They even had the foresight to bring a plastic baggie to give the impression that he'd used it to keep the gun dry while he swam to the island."

"That's right," Caleb said. "But even drug dealers want to avoid jail."

Stone ignored this comment too. "And when they realized there were witnesses to their crime, they gave not a second thought to disposing of us. These men are expert killers, but I very seriously doubt that they are drug dealers."

The other three pondered their friend's logic as Stone raised the binoculars to his eyes again.

The silence was broken a minute later by Caleb, who asked Milton, "What does Chastity do?"

"She's an accountant. She used to work for a big firm, but they fired her because of her OCD. She has her own company now. And she helps me with my Web design business. I'm awful with money. She keeps the books and does the marketing too. She's really terrific."

"I'm sure she *is* terrific," Reuben said. "It's those quiet professional types you have to watch out for. You think they're mild-mannered and then they just *jump* you. I dated this woman once, prim and proper, dresses past the knees. But I swear to God that lady could do things with her mouth that defied—"

Stone broke in quickly. "Firing Chastity because of her medical condition doesn't seem right unless it prevented her from doing her work."

"Oh, she could do the work. They said she embarrassed the firm in front of clients, which was a crock. Two of the partners just didn't like her, one of them because Chastity wouldn't sleep with him. She sued and won a lot of money."

"That's the country we all know and love," Reuben said. "The United States of Lawyers. But don't let the rich pretty ones get away, Milton. I'm not telling you to marry the woman, God forbid, but if a man can keep a woman in these enlightened times, there's nothing wrong with a woman keeping a man."

"She does buy me things," Milton said quietly.

"Really," Reuben said with sudden interest. "What sorts of things?"

"Software for my computer, clothes, wine. She knows a lot about wine."

"What sorts of clothes?" Reuben persisted.

"Personal clothes," a pink-faced Milton said. He immediately looked down at his computer and started hitting some keys. Reuben started to say something, but Stone silenced him with a very severe look.

Finally, Stone said, "All right, here's what I want each of you to do."

After laying out his plan, Stone put on an old hat he pulled from his backpack, placed Goff on a leash and got out of the car. Milton's spare cell phone was in his pocket. Reuben and Caleb would stay in the car and keep watch, while Milton walked on the other side of the street toward Johnson's home. His task was to note anyone who was paying Stone too much attention. Milton had been chosen for this role because he had remained in the bottom of the boat while they were being pursued, making it nearly impossible for the killers to have seen him. If Milton spotted anyone, he would ring Stone's cell phone.

Stone strolled slowly along the street, stopping to bag some waste that Goff deposited next to a tree. "Good dog, Goff," Stone said, petting him. "That's very helpful in keeping up our cover." When he reached the front of Johnson's residence, a man wearing an FBI windbreaker came out carrying a large box wrapped with police evidence tape.

"A terrible tragedy, Officer," Stone said in an inquiring tone to the man. The man didn't answer, however, hurrying past Stone and handing the box to a woman who sat in one of the Suburbans. Stone let Goff sniff around a tree in front of Johnson's house. While the animal did so, he was able to take in many details of the house and the adjacent properties. As he continued down the street, he passed a sedan that was idling at the curb. He managed not to even flinch when he saw who was sitting in the driver's seat.

Tyler Reinke's gaze bored into Stone briefly before returning to his surveillance of Johnson's house. He obviously didn't recognize the man he had come close to shooting the night before. Stone inwardly said thanks for his prescience in radically altering his appearance. Now the question became, where was the other man?

Stone continued down the street, turned left at the next corner and immediately called Caleb, relaying what he'd just seen. He then phoned Milton, who joined him a minute later.

"You're sure it's him?" Milton asked.

"No doubt. Now I want to know where the other one is." His cell phone buzzed. Caleb's voice was taut.

"Reuben just spotted the other man."

"Where is he?"

"Speaking with one of the FBI agents outside of Johnson's home."

"Come and pick us up," Stone said, relaying to Caleb where he and Milton were. "Don't come down the street you're on. I don't want you to pass the house or the car he's in. Turn left at the next corner and then make a right. We'll meet you on the next block."

As the two men were waiting at the arranged spot, Stone watched as Milton picked up a page from a newspaper that had blown across the street. He folded it neatly and deposited it in a trash can that sat in front of a driveway.

Stone said, "Milton, did you touch the note in Patrick Johnson's pocket last night?"

Milton didn't answer right away. However, his embarrassed look was all the response Stone really needed.

"How did you know, Oliver?"

"Those men knew we were there somehow. I don't think it was because they saw us. I think they must have come back to the body for some reason and noticed that the note had been disturbed or was in a different place."

"I . . . I . . ."

"You just wanted to check it, I know." Stone was deeply worried for a very simple reason. Damp paper held fingerprints extremely well. Were Milton's prints on any database anywhere? He didn't want to ask him that question right now, for fear of sending his already upset friend into a panic attack.

When the Malibu pulled up, Stone and Milton climbed in. Caleb drove ahead a bit, found a parking spot on the crowded street and wedged in.

"Do we risk following them?" Reuben asked.

"Unfortunately, Caleb's car rather sticks out," Stone said. "If they pick up that we're following them and run the license plate, they'll be at Caleb's house waiting before he even gets back there."

"Oh, dear God," Caleb said as he gripped the steering wheel and looked like he might be sick to his stomach.

"So what do we do?" Reuben asked.

Stone replied, "You said one of them was talking to the FBI. But the FBI wouldn't be talking to just an ordinary citizen. I know. I tried. That could very well mean they're law enforcement."

"Which means they could be with NIC," Milton chimed in. "That's where Johnson worked."

"A thought that had occurred to me," Stone replied. "Carter Gray," he muttered.

"Not a man you take on lightly," Reuben commented.

Oh, shit!" Caleb whispered. He was staring in the rearview mirror. "That might be their car coming up behind us."

"Don't look in that direction," Stone commanded sharply. "Caleb, take a deep breath and calm down. Reuben, slump down a little in your seat to disguise your size in case they look this way." As he was talking, Stone took off his hat and slid forward in his seat until he had disappeared from view. "Caleb, can they see your license plate from the street?"

"No, the cars parked in front and back of us are too close."

"Good. As soon as they pass, I want you to wait ten seconds and then pull out, and turn in the opposite direction from them. Milton, you're pretty well hidden from view in the backseat. I want you to very carefully glance over and see if they look at us. And I want you to get a good look at them."

Caleb took a deep breath and then held it as the car passed by slowly.

"Don't look over, Caleb," Stone whispered again from his hiding place.

As the car headed on and turned left at the next intersection, Stone said, "Milton?"

"They didn't look over."

"Okay, Caleb, go ahead."

Caleb slowly pulled his car out and turned right at the next corner as Stone sat back up. "Everyone keep a sharp lookout to make sure they don't return," Stone said.

Stone looked back at Milton. "What did you see?"

Milton gave a fairly complete description of both men as well as the Virginia license plate number of the car.

Reuben looked at Stone. "I say now we go to the cops. We'll back each other up. They'll believe us."

"No!" Stone said sharply. "We have to get them before *they* get to us."

"How?" Reuben asked. "Especially if the killers are the *authorities*?"

"By doing what the Camel Club used to do very well: seek the truth."

Milton broke in. "We can start by running their license plate number. It wasn't a government plate, so we might just have lucked out, and it's his personal car."

Reuben said, "Do you know someone at DMV who can run the tag?"

Milton looked offended. "If I can hack into the Pentagon's database, Reuben, DMV should prove no challenge at all."

# CHAPTER

## 25

AT NIC HEADQUARTERS THERE was a state-of-the-art gymnasium in the lower level that virtually no one used for lack of time. However, in a small room off the main area there *was* one person working out.

Tom Hemingway wore only a pair of loose-fitting shorts and a white tank shirt, and his feet were bare. He sat cross-legged on the floor with his eyes closed. A moment later he rose and assumed a martial arts stance. Most people watching him would have concluded that Hemingway was about to start practicing kung fu or karate. These same people would probably be surprised to learn that "kung fu," literally translated, meant a skillful ability attained through hard work. Thus, someone could be a baseball player and be deemed to have good "kung fu."

There were four hundred types of martial arts disciplines that had originated other than in China, whereas there were only three indigenous to that country: Hsing-I Chuan, Pa-Kua Chang and Tai Chi Chuan. The key difference between the four hundred and the three was *power,* as the whole body was used as a means to transfer all kinetic energy of the attacker on to the target. It was roughly equivalent to the speed of a slap with the shock of being hit by a car. A blow struck by a skilled practitioner of any of the three so-called internal martial arts had the power to rupture organs and kill.

During his years in China, Hemingway had found himself drawn to these internal martial arts, if for nothing more than to create a sense of identity that blended better with his surroundings than his blond hair and blue eyes did. Although he practiced the other forms of internal martial arts, Hemingway had become most proficient in the ShanXi House of Hsing-I.

Prior to starting his practice forms, Hemingway had sat motionless for almost an hour meditating. This exercise allowed one to intuitively take in his surroundings, sensing presence long before anyone could actually be seen. This talent had served Hemingway well in the field. As a CIA agent his life had been saved on more than one occasion by his ability to be aware of his enemy in a manner that defied the five human senses.

Through long years of practice Hemingway's joints, tendons, ligaments, muscle groups and fascia were enormously strong. Decades of spine stretching while executing the twists and turns of his discipline had kept each of his vertebrae in perfect alignment with its neighbor. His sense of balance almost defied human comprehension. He had once stood for six hours on a skyscraper's one-inch-wide ledge, twenty-one stories up in a driving wind and rain, while a Colombian death squad circled below looking for him. So strong were his fingers that he had to consciously hold back when he shook hands, and even then people frequently complained of his crushing grip.

He now assumed the bamboo stance, which was the critical maneuver in Hsing-I. The bamboo technique was simple physics, and also where the famed power of Hsing-I emanated. Hemingway had killed highly skilled men with just one vector strike off the bamboo stance.

He next picked up a pair of crescent swords, the traditional *neijia* weapons of the Pa-Kua internal martial art. They were his favorite form of practice weapon. He flew around the room using highly intricate bilateral movements of the curved swords, coupled with astonishingly tight footwork and tremendous centrifugal force that were characteristic of the Pa-Kua discipline

After he had finished his workout, Hemingway showered and changed into his street clothes. As he was dressing, he unconsciously rubbed the tattoo that he carried on the inside of his right forearm. It was composed of four words in Chinese. Translated, it meant "Ultimate loyalty to serve country." There was a story behind the marking that intrigued Hemingway.

A famous general in the Southern Song dynasty named Yueh Fei had served under a field marshal who had defected to the enemy. This betrayal had sent Fei home in disgust. There his mother lectured him that a soldier's first duty is to his country. She sent him back to battle with those four words tattooed on his back as a permanent reminder. Hemingway had heard the story as a young boy and never forgotten it. He'd gotten the tattoo when a particularly troubling mission he performed for the CIA caused him to consider quitting. Instead, he had the words engraved on his skin and went on with his work.

Hemingway drove to his modest apartment on Capitol Hill and went into the kitchen to make wulong black tea, his favorite. He brewed a pot and placed two cups on a tray and carried it into the small living room.

Hemingway poured out the tea and then called out, "Cold wulong isn't very good."

There was a stirring in the next room, and the man walked out.

"Okay, what gave me away? I'm not wearing anything scented. I took off my shoes. I've been holding my damn breath for thirty minutes. What?"

"You have a powerful aura that you can't hide," Hemingway said, smiling.

"You scare me sometimes, Tom, you really do." Captain Jack tipped back his head and laughed and then accepted a cup of tea. He sat down, took a sip and nodded at a painting of a Chinese landscape that hung against the far wall. "Nice."

"I've actually been to the area depicted in the painting. My father collected that artist's work and some sculpture from the Shang dynasty."

"Amazing man, Ambassador Hemingway. I never met him but I certainly knew of him."

"He was a statesman," Hemingway said as he sipped his tea. "Unfortunately that's a breed that's nearly extinct these days."

Captain Jack remained silent for a few moments, studying the man across from him. "I tried reading the poetry you told me about."

Hemingway looked up from his tea. "The Red Pepper collection? What'd you think?"

"That I should work on my Chinese."

Hemingway smiled. "It's a beautiful way to communicate, once you get into it."

Captain Jack set his teacup down on the table. "So what was so important that it had to be done in person?"

"Carter Gray will be going to the dedication in Brennan."

"Damn, I'd say that was worth a face-to-face. How do you want to play it, then?"

"The exit strategy has always been problematic. No matter how we tried to tweak it, there was too much uncertainty. Now, with Gray coming, we have certainty."

"How exactly do you figure that?"

Hemingway explained his plan and his colleague looked suitably impressed.

"Well, I think it'll work. In fact, I think it's brilliant. Brilliant and ballsy."

"Depending on whether it succeeds or not," Hemingway replied.

"Don't be modest, Tom. Let's call this what it is. A plan that will rock the entire world." He paused and added, "But don't underestimate the old man. Carter Gray's forgotten more than you and I will ever know about the spy business."

Hemingway opened his briefcase. Inside was a DVD. He tossed it to his companion. "I think you'll find what's on there helpful."

Captain Jack fingered the DVD and watched Hemingway closely. "I did over twenty years with the Company, quite a few under Gray, and you did what?"

"Twelve, all in the field, with two years at NSA before that," Hemingway answered. "I started at NIC a year after Gray became secretary."

"I hear they're grooming you for the top spot. Interested?"

Hemingway shook his head. "There's little future there that I can see."

"Back to the CIA, then?"

"It's a useless anachronism."

"Right! There'll always be a CIA, even after the Iraqi WMDs that never were."

"You think so?" Hemingway said curiously.

"Oh, when I was helping support a host of 'acceptable alternatives' to communism, mostly monster dictators, or feeding crack to black neighborhoods to help fund illegal operations overseas, or blowing up democracies in other countries because they wouldn't support American business interests, I thought to myself, there's got to be a better way of doing this. But I got over that thinking a long time ago."

"We can't win this particular fight with soldiers and spies," Hemingway said. "It's not that simple."

"Then it can't be won," Captain Jack answered bluntly. "Because that's the only way countries know to settle their differences."

"Dostoyevsky wrote that 'while nothing is easier than to denounce the evildoer, nothing is more difficult than to understand him.'"

"You and I have both spent a lot of time there, but do you really think you'll ever understand the 'evildoer' mentality of the Middle Eastern terrorist?"

"How do you know that's the 'evildoer' I'm referring to? We certainly don't have clean hands when it comes to events overseas. In fact, we *created* many of the problems we face today."

"That's why there's only one sensible motivation these days: money. As I've told you before, I don't care about anything else. I will go back to my beautiful little island, and I will not stir again. This is it for me."

"That's being brutally honest," Hemingway remarked.

"Would you rather I tell you that my twitching ideology is screaming for me to help make the world better?"

"No, I'll take the brutal honesty."

"And why are you doing it?"

"For something better than what we have."

"Idealism again? I'm telling you, Tom, you'll live to regret it. Or die."

"Not idealism, or even fatalism, but simply an idea put into action."

Captain Jack shook his head slowly. "I've fought for and against pretty much every cause there is. There will always be war of some kind. At first it was over fertile soil and good water, then precious metal and then the most popular version of human disagreement, 'My God is better than your God.' Whether you draw your faith from Jeremiah and Jesus, Allah and Muhammad or Brahma and Buddha, it doesn't matter. Someone will tell you you're wrong, and he'll fight you over it. Me, I believe in aliens, and to hell with all earthly gods. In the grand scheme of a trillion planets in the universe we're just not that damn important anyway. And humans are rotten to the core."

"Buddha rose above materialism. Jesus was champion of embracing one's enemies. As was Gandhi."

"Jesus was betrayed and died on the cross, and Gandhi was murdered by a Hindu who was ticked off Gandhi tolerated Muslims," Captain Jack pointed out.

Hemingway paced the room. "I remember my father telling me about England's redrawing of India's boundaries when it became independent. They wanted to separate the Hindu from the Muslim, but they used outdated maps. Twelve million people had to relocate because the Brits screwed it up so badly. And a half million people died during the resulting chaos. And before that, Iraq was unilaterally cobbled together, causing many of the conflicts we see today. There are dozens of such examples. The strong countries smashing the weaker ones and then avoiding responsibility later for the very problems they caused."

"You keep proving my point, Tom, that we're rotten to the core."

"*My* point is we *never* learn!"

"And what, you think *you* have a better answer?" Hemingway didn't respond. Captain Jack rose but then paused at the door. "I doubt that I'll see you again, unless you end up heading to a small island in the South Pacific. If you do, you'll be welcome. Unless you're a fugitive. Then, my friend, you're on your own."

# CHAPTER

## 26

AFTER HE'D LEFT THE BAR, ALEX Ford grabbed a bite to eat at a nearby diner, wedging his butt between the wide frames of two hefty D.C. cops at the counter. He shared some shoptalk with his law enforcement brethren and also swapped some old doomsday gossip. Alex's personal favorite was, "At all costs, stay out of the Metro on Halloween." What Alex really wanted to do was stand on the counter and shout for all to hear that a beautiful woman had just asked him out. Instead, he quietly finished off his cheeseburger, french fries and wedge of blueberry pie washed down with black coffee. Afterward, he headed back to WFO to check his e-mails.

Sykes still hadn't responded, although Alex had received an electronic receipt that the man had opened the e-mail report. He wandered the halls of WFO, half hoping to run into Sykes and see where he stood on the investigation. Alex had written up thousands of reports, but this one went right to HQ, something not all that common for street grunts like him, who weren't being groomed to move up the agency's leadership ladder. When you knew the director's eyes were going to be running over your feeble attempt at logical composition, it tended to make the neck hairs stand up and start twitching.

He passed by the assignment board and noted that his photo and Simpson's had been placed under the heading "Special Assignment." As he looked at the olive-skinned lady staring back at him out of the photo, he muttered the name "J-Glo." Maybe she should just go back to Alabama. Daddy would probably love that.

He killed some more time at his desk and then decided that if Sykes really wanted to talk, he'd find him.

Out on the sidewalk he sucked in a chest full of crisp night air and smiled as he thought of Kate Adams, and then he walked down the street with a lift in his step that had been absent for a long time. He thought about heading home, but what he really wanted to do was talk to someone. However, all his good friends were married Secret Service agents, which meant if they weren't on duty, they were spending some rare quality time with their families. And Alex shared little in common with the young bucks at WFO.

This made him realize that in three short years he was going to have to make some pretty major decisions. Would he just retire? Or would he go to another agency, live mostly off his pension from the Service and stockpile the paychecks from the new job? This was known as double-dipping. It was completely legal, and many feds did it to pad their retirement funds. It was a way to even out things after they'd worked for below market-value in the public sector.

Much of Alex's adult life had been a blur, learning the ropes at the Service, busting bad guys in eight different field offices, then on to protection detail, where he had spent every waking hour hopping planes and running from one city, one country to the next. He had been so busy worrying about everybody else that he had never spent much time worrying about *himself*. And now that it was time to think about his future, Alex suddenly felt totally incapable of doing so. Where did he start? What did he do? He felt a panic attack coming on, and not one that another martini would've cured.

He was standing paralyzed on a corner deciding what to do with the rest of his life when his cell phone rang. At first the name and number on the caller ID screen didn't register, but then it clicked. It was Anne Jeffries, the late Patrick Johnson's fiancée.

"Hello?"

"You don't think I would know if the man I was going to marry, the man I was going to spend the rest of my *life* with, was a damn drug dealer!" She screamed this at him so loudly that he jerked the phone away from his ear.

"Ms. Jeffries—"

"I'm going to sue. I'm going to sue the FBI and the Secret Service. And *you*. And that *bitch* of a partner of yours!"

"Whoa, hold on, now. I can understand that you're upset—"

"Upset? Upset isn't even in the universe of what I'm feeling. It's not enough that Pat had to be murdered, now his reputation is being destroyed too."

"Ms. Jeffries, I'm just trying to do my job—"

"Save your pathetic excuses for my lawyer," she snapped, and then hung up.

Alex put his phone away and took a deep breath. He wondered whom the woman might call next? *The Washington Post? 60 Minutes?* Every boss he'd ever had? He called Jerry Sykes' private cell number. It went into voice mail, but Alex left a detailed message about his brief but explosive conversation with the bereaved fiancée. Okay, he'd done what he could. The shit was probably going to fly anyway.

He definitely didn't want to go home now. He wanted to walk. And think.

His wandering took him, as it often did, to the White House. He nodded to some of the uniformed Secret Service that he knew, and stopped and chatted with an agent who was sitting in a black Suburban gulping down black coffee. Alex and the man had started out together at the Louisville Field Office, though their paths had parted after that.

POTUS was hosting a state dinner tonight, his friend told Alex. And then it was off to campaign in the Midwest the next day, with a 9/11 ceremony in New York City after that.

"I like to see a president who keeps busy," Alex replied. Some chief executives worked their butts off, pulling a full twelve hours during the day, changing into a tux and doing the Washington social two-step and then working the phones from their private quarters until the wee hours. Other presidents liked to cruise through the day and knock off early. Alex had never thought the presidency was a "cruising" sort of job.

He passed into Lafayette Park and was surprised to see a light on in Stone's tent. Maybe he'd finally found somebody he could really talk to.

"Oliver?" he called out softly while standing next to the lighted tent.

The tent flap fell open, and he stared at a man he didn't recognize.

"I'm sorry," Alex said, "I was looking for—"

"Agent Ford," Oliver Stone said as he stepped outside.

"Oliver? Is that you?"

Stone smiled and rubbed his clean-shaven face. "A man needs a fresh start every once in a while," he explained.

"I came by looking for you last night."

"Adelphia told me. I miss our chess matches."

"I'm afraid I didn't give you much competition."

"You improved a lot over the years," Stone replied kindly.

While Alex was on presidential protection detail, he'd visited Stone as often as his busy schedule allowed. At first it was to check up on potential problems near the White House. Back then, Alex considered anyone within a square mile of the place who didn't carry a Secret Service badge as the enemy, and Stone had been no exception.

What had really intrigued Alex about Oliver Stone was that the man didn't seem to have a past. Alex had heard rumors that Stone had at one time worked for the government. So Alex went on every database he could think of looking for some history on the fellow, but there was simply none. He didn't search under "Oliver Stone," an obviously fake name. Instead, he surreptitiously got Stone's fingerprints and ran them through AFIS, the FBI's massive automated fingerprint identification system. That came back negative. Then he passed them through the military databanks, the Secret Service's own computer files and through every other place he could think of. They all came back zip. As far as the United States government was concerned, Oliver Stone didn't exist.

He'd once followed Stone to his caretaker's cottage at the cemetery. He checked with the church that owned it, but they would tell him nothing about the man, and Alex had no probable cause to force the issue. He'd watched Stone working in the cemetery a few times, and when he'd gone off, Alex considered searching the cottage. Yet there was something about Stone, an intense measure of dignity and also a profound sincerity, that caused Alex to finally reject this idea.

"So what did you come to see me about?" Stone asked.

"Just passing through. Adelphia said you were at a meeting."

"She likes to embellish. I met some friends over on the Mall. We like walking there at night." He paused and added, "So how are things going at the WFO?"

"It's nice working cases again."

"I heard that an employee of yours was killed."

Alex nodded. "Patrick Johnson. He worked at the National Threat Assessment Center. That's really been blended with NIC now, but I'm involved because Johnson was still sort of a joint employee of ours."

"*You're* involved?" Stone said. "Do you mean that you're working the case?"

Alex hesitated. There didn't seem to be any reason not to acknowledge his involvement. It wasn't exactly confidential. "I was assigned to poke around, although it seems to have been solved."

"I hadn't heard."

"They found heroin in Johnson's home. They think whoever he was dealing with killed him." He didn't mention Anne Jeffries' call. That part wasn't publicly known.

"And what do *you* think?" Stone said, eyeing him keenly.

Alex shrugged. "Who knows? And we're just really piggybacking on the FBI."

"And yet a man *has* been killed."

Alex looked at his friend questioningly. "Yeah? I know that."

"Over the years I've watched you, Agent Ford. You're observant, diligent, and you have sound instincts. I think you should use those talents on this case. If the man's work was sensitive to this nation's security, a second pair of eyes is certainly in order."

"I've covered the bases, Oliver. If it wasn't drugs?"

"Exactly. If not drugs, what? I think someone should answer that question very thoroughly. Perhaps the answer lies with his work. Consider that planting drugs at his home would be an easy way to cover something up."

Alex looked doubtful. "That's highly unlikely. And quite frankly, NIC is a big can of worms to open for a guy looking to retire in three years."

"Three years isn't such a long time, Agent Ford; not nearly as long as the years you've already served your country. And unfortunately, fair or not, the *end* of one's career is what a person is usually remembered for."

"And if I make a misstep on this one, maybe I don't have a career left."

"But the other important point to realize is this: The end of one's career is also what *you* remember most vividly. And you'll have decades to possibly regret. And that *is* a very long time."

Leaving Stone, Alex slowly walked back to his car. What the man said made sense. There were issues that were not clear in Alex's mind about Patrick Johnson's death. The drug discovery *did* seem a little too convenient, and other details just didn't add up. In truth, he had been only halfheartedly investigating the case, more than ready to follow the Bureau's lead and its conclusions.

And Stone had been right on another level. Alex had stayed at the Service after his accident because he didn't want to go out on a disability ride. Well, sleepwalking through a major case wasn't the way he wanted to go out either. There was something to be said for professional pride. And if U.S. presidents shouldn't cruise through their duties, Secret Service agents shouldn't either.

Oliver Stone watched Alex pass out of sight and then quickly walked to his cottage at the cemetery. From there he used the cell phone Milton had given him to call Caleb and tell him of this latest development. "It was a stroke of good fortune that I couldn't ignore," Stone explained.

"But you didn't say anything about us seeing the murder, did you?"

"Agent Ford is a federal policeman. Had I told him that, his duty would've been clear. My best hope is that he will dig up something at NIC that would have been beyond our means to do."

"Won't that place him in jeopardy? I mean if NIC's gunning down its own employees, they might not stop at killing a Secret Service agent."

"Agent Ford is a capable man. But we'll also have to act as his guardian angels, won't we?"

Stone clicked off and, suddenly remembering he hadn't eaten any dinner, went into his kitchen and made some soup, which he ate in front of a small fire he'd built. Cemeteries always seemed to be cold, no matter the season.

After that, he sat down in his old armchair next to the fire with a book that he'd been reading from his very eclectic collection that

Caleb had helped him assemble. That's all he had left: his friends, his books, some theories, a few memories.

He glanced at the box with the photo album again, and, despite intuitively knowing it would be a bad thing, he put his book down and spent the next hour drifting through his past. Stone lingered over the pictures he had of his daughter. One showed her holding a bunch of daisies, her favorite flower. He smiled as he remembered how she would pronounce it: *dayzzzees*. There was another picture of her blowing out candles on a cake. It wasn't her birthday. She'd gotten stitches in her hand after she'd fallen on some broken glass, and the cake was her reward for being so brave. The cut left a scar in the shape of a crescent on her right palm. He'd kissed it every time he held her. He had so few memories of her that Stone clung desperately to every one.

At last his mind went back to that final night. Their house had been situated in a very isolated area; his *employer* had insisted on that. It was only after the attack that Stone understood the reason for this requirement.

He remembered the creak of the door as it was opened. Cut off from their child, he and his wife barely slipped through the window when the muffled shots commenced. Stone remembered visualizing the suppressor cans on the ends of the muzzles. *Thump—thump—thump*. They nipped at him like lethal gnats. And then his wife screamed once, and that was all. She was dead. Stone killed two of the men sent to execute him that night, using their own guns against them. And then he'd gotten away to a safe place.

That night was the last time Stone saw his wife or his daughter. The next day it was as though they'd never existed. The house had been emptied and all signs of the murderous attack obliterated. All attempts to find his daughter over the years had failed. *Beth.* Her full name was Elizabeth, but they had always called her Beth. She was a beautiful child and the pride of her father. And he had lost her forever on a hellish night decades ago.

When he eventually learned the truth of what had happened, Stone was consumed with the idea of revenge. And then something happened that struck those thoughts from him. He read in the paper of the violent death of a man, an important man, in a country overseas. The killing was never solved. The man left behind a wife and children. Stone recognized the fingerprints of his former employer all over that killing. It was a scene personally very familiar to Stone as well.

That's when he realized he was not a man who deserved revenge even for his wife being murdered and his child taken from him. His past sins were many, piled high under the dubious cloak of patriotism. For Stone, it effectively disenfranchised him from seeking justice for the wrong committed against his family.

He disappeared and traveled the world under a number of aliases. It had been relatively easy; his government had trained him very well to do just that. After many years of wandering he embarked on the only option left to him. He became Oliver Stone, a man of silent protest, who watched and paid attention to important things in America others didn't seem drawn to. And still, it had not been nearly enough to balance the pain of losing the two people he cared most about. That would be his burden until his last breath.

When he fell asleep in the chair as the fire died low, the wetness of his tears still shimmered on the album's slick pages.

DJAMILA ROSE AT FIVE O'CLOCK in her small apartment on the outskirts of Brennan, Pennsylvania. Shortly after dawn she performed her first prayer of the day. After she had cleansed herself and removed her shoes and covered her head, Djamila went through the Islamic rituals of standing, sitting, bowing and prostrating herself on her prayer rug. She began by reciting the *shahada*, the central statement of Muslim faith: *La ilaha illa'Llah*, or "There is no god but God." After that, she recited the opening sura, the first chapter of the Qur'an. The invocations were performed silently, only her lips moving as she formed the words. After she'd finished her *salat*, she changed her clothes and readied herself for work before sitting down to breakfast.

As she surveyed her tiny kitchen, Djamila reflected on her conversation with Lori Franklin the day before. Djamila had lied to her employer, though the American would have no way of knowing of the deceit. Djamila's official papers showed her to be a Saudi. That, and her being a woman, had allowed her entry into America to go very smoothly, even in post-9/11 times. Djamila was actually an Iraqi by birth, and a Sunni Muslim by religious practice, as were over 80 percent of all Muslims, although in Iraq the Sunnis were in the minority. In early times the Sunnis clashed with their Shia counterparts largely over the issue of the successor to the Prophet Muhammad. Now the differences were far more numerous and bitter.

The Shiites believed that the fourth rightly guided caliphate, Ali ibn Abi Talib, Muhammad's son-in-law and also his cousin, was the true blood successor to the Islamic Prophet. Shia Muslims performed a pilgrimage to Mazar-i-Sharif to the blue mosque where Ali was entombed.

Sunni Muslims believed that Muhammad had not appointed his successor, and thus they established the caliphates to take over for the Prophet after his death. The Sunnis and Shiites agreed that none of the caliphs rose to the level of a prophet; however, the fact that three of the four caliphs had died violent deaths was a testament to how fervently divided the Muslim population was over this issue.

Under the secular regime of Saddam Hussein, Djamila had been allowed to drive a car, whereas in Saudi Arabia this wouldn't have been possible. The Saudis followed a very strict form of sharia, or Islamic law. This strictness required women to be completely covered at all times, and it prohibited them from voting and even from going out of the house without a permission note from their husbands. These rules were scrupulously enforced by the tenacious, whip-wielding religious police.

There was also the notorious "Chop-Chop Square," the main square in downtown Riyadh. It was here every Friday where those who broke the sharia were punished for all to see. Djamila had been there once and watched in horror as five people lost both their hands and two others their heads. Far more subtle punishment was the *fallaga*, the beating of the bottom of the feet in a way that left no marks, although the victim was typically unable to walk, so great was the pain.

The rest of the world had largely looked the other way ever since King Ibn Saud, conqueror of Arabia and the ruler who had given his name to the country, hired geologists to come look for water but who struck oil instead. With fully one-quarter of the world's black gold reserves under the country's sands, a resource eagerly coveted by the industrialized world, the Saudis could usually do what they wanted without fear of repercussions.

However, Djamila had not entirely lied to Franklin. Living in Baghdad, and being a Sunni Muslim like Saddam Hussein, she *had* worn clothes mostly of her choosing, and she *had* been well educated. Despite that, she had hated living under the Iraqi dictator. She had lost friends and family who "disappeared" after speaking out against the despotic ruler. During the American invasion of Iraq she prayed that Hussein would be toppled, and those prayers were answered. She and her family at first welcomed the Americans and their allies as heroes for giving them back their freedom. But then things rapidly began to change.

Djamila returned from the market one day to find her family's home reduced to rubble after an errant air strike. All of her family, including her two young brothers, perished. After that tragedy Djamila went to live with relatives in Mosul. But they fell victim to a car bombing in the resulting insurgency against the American presence in Iraq.

Next Djamila traveled to Tikrit to stay with a cousin, but the war had forced her to flee there as well. Since that time she'd been home-less, joining a growing number of people who had essentially become nomads, constantly caught in the fighting between an ever-larger army of insurgents, and America and its allies. In one of these groups she had met a man who spoke out against the Americans as being nothing more than imperialists after precious oil. He argued that all Muslims had the duty to strike back against this enemy of Islam.

Like most Muslims, the only jihad Djamila had ever practiced was the "greater jihad," the internal struggle to be a better follower of Islam. This man was obviously speaking of another jihad, the "lesser jihad," the holy war, a concept that originated with Islam in the sev-enth century. At first Djamila dismissed the man and his advocacy as mindless ravings, yet as her situation grew bleaker, she found herself beginning to listen to him and others like him. The things he was say-ing, added to the horrors she had seen firsthand, started to make sense to the young woman who'd lost everything. And soon her dismay and hopelessness turned to something else: anger.

Before long, Djamila found herself in Pakistan and then Afghanistan, being trained to do things she would never have contemplated before. While in Afghanistan she wore the burka, held her tongue and obeyed the men. She would go to the market and soon her clothing would swell because she shoved all the items she purchased under it. The burka had a grill in front of the opening for the face. It was designed to take away a woman's peripheral vision. If she wanted to look at some-thing she had to turn her entire head. In this way, it was said, the hus-band would always be able to tell what was holding his wife's interest. Even with the Taliban gone, many burkas remained. But even women who took the burkas off were not really free, Djamila could see, since

their husbands and brothers and, indeed, even their sons still controlled every aspect of their lives.

After months of training, she was on her way to the United States,
along with scores of others like her, all with forged documents and all
with a burning ambition to strike back against an enemy that had destroyed their lives. Djamila had been taught that everything about
America was evil. That the Western life and values were in complete
opposition to the Muslim faith and, indeed, had as its core mission the
complete destruction of Islam. How could she not fight against a monster such as that?

Her first weeks in America had been divided between monotony
and eye-opening experiences. For weeks she had little to do except
carry messages back and forth. Yet she was seeing America, the great
enemy, for the first time. She had visited some of the shops with an
Afghan woman. The woman was shocked to see pictures of people on
the products in the stores. Under the Taliban all such graphics had
been blotted out.

Americans were large people with huge appetites and the cars they
drove, Djamila had never seen such enormous cars. The stores were
full, the people wore all sorts of different clothes. Men and women
embraced in the streets, even kissing in front of strangers like herself.
And things moved so fast she could barely follow them. It was as
though she had been hurled far into the future. She found herself terrified but also curiously intrigued.

Then she had been taken from the group she had come to America
with and brought to another city, where she received still more training. She was given a new identity, complete with references. And she
was also given the very special van that she now drove. She was next
sent to Brennan and became the Franklins' nanny. She enjoyed the
work and loved being with the boys, but as time passed she longed to
go home. America was simply not for her.

Djamila had always looked forward to the time when she would
perform the hajj, the pilgrimage to the most holy site in Islam, Mecca,
the town in Hejaz where Muhammad was born. As a child she had
heard stories from family who'd undertaken this most significant
event in a Muslim's life. She envisioned standing in a circle around the

Great Mosque, or Al-Masjid *al-Haram,* in Mecca, performing her prayers.

The pilgrimage continued in Muzdalifa, where the Night Prayer was observed and twenty-one pebbles were picked up for symbolic stoning of Satan at Mina. Two or three days were spent in Mina for various ceremonies before the return to Mecca. Families who made the pilgrimage were allowed to add the term "hajj" to their name.

As a little girl Djamila had been especially drawn with anticipated delight to stories of the four-day celebration afterward, the *'id al-adha,* the Festival of Sacrifice, also known as the Major Festival. She had also looked forward to painting the mode of transportation she used to make the pilgrimage on her front door, an old Egyptian custom that other Muslims sometimes copied. However, Djamila had never gotten the chance to go to Mecca before her country had exploded into war. Now she doubted she would ever be able to do so. Indeed, she felt it very unlikely that she would return to her homeland in anything other than a coffin.

She packed her things for work and went down to her van. She glanced at the back cargo area of the vehicle. Hidden there was an add-on feature that the car manufacturer would never have dreamed of offering.

In the center of downtown Brennan, Captain Jack closed on the purchase of his new property, an automobile repair facility. Dressed in an elegant two-piece suit, the distinguished-looking "entrepreneur" took the keys, thanking the seller and his agent as he drove away in his Audi convertible. They had smiled and counted their money and wished him luck. *Good luck to you too,* he wanted to say. *And good luck to the town of Brennan. It's certainly going to need it.*

A few minutes later Captain Jack parked his car at a curb, flipped open his iPAQ, went online and entered the chat room. Today's film was *The Wizard of Oz.* He remembered watching it as a child. Probably unlike most viewers, he'd always sympathized with the plight of the enslaved flying monkeys. He left his message arranging a meeting at the park.

The auto repair facility would be one of the most critical elements of this operation, and that was where the woman came in. If she didn't come through, none of his work would matter. Some things a person couldn't get from faceless e-mails, like whether someone had the will necessary to do the job.

Sometimes you had to go see for yourself.

The day was overcast and a bit chilly, so the park was nearly empty. Captain Jack sat on a bench, read his newspaper and drank his coffee. He had spent half an hour making a careful reconnoiter of the park before ever leaving his car. The odds that anyone had him under surveillance were astronomically small. Yet one didn't survive long in his line of work by tripping over the small but crucial details.

The front pages were filled with very important news: The stock market, amazingly, had gone up yesterday after having gone down the day before. American football was thick in the air; war on the gridiron they called it. Well, at least those who had never been in the real thing called it that. Captain Jack also learned that, shockingly, one movie star was actually leaving his wife for another movie star. And then he read of the revelation that a rock musician had been found lip-synching during a live concert. And that a car bombing had killed three Israelis in that never-ending struggle. Retribution would be swift, proclaimed Israeli officials. Yes, it would, Captain Jack knew. You didn't screw with the Israelis. Captain Jack was a very brave, battle-scarred man. Yet even he avoided directly antagonizing the Israelis.

Buried in the far back pages of the newspaper, Captain Jack read how AIDS in Africa continued to kill millions. He next skimmed an article on how civil wars on that continent had claimed millions more. Half the world lived in complete poverty, stated another story. Thousands of children were dying every day simply because they had nothing in their bellies.

Captain Jack put down the paper. He was not much of a moralist; he'd killed many people in his lifetime. If there was a heaven and a hell, he knew where his eternal lodgings would be. *But, really, lip-synching on the front page?*

He heard the children first, but didn't look in that direction. Next he listened to the swing being swung, and then the whirligig started going round and round. He smiled at the screams of delight from the young ones.

Finally, the sounds of the children quieted down. More minutes passed, and then he heard car doors open and close. Next he listened to the footsteps coming toward him. They were measured, calm treads. Then came a slight squeak from the bench directly behind his as the person sat down. He immediately lifted up his paper.

"I think the Steelers could go all the way this year, don't you?" he said.

"No, my money is on the Patriots," the other replied.

"Are you sure?"

"I am very sure of what I say. If I were in doubt, I would say nothing."

With their identifying code out of the way, Captain Jack got down to business.

"Things are good with the Franklins?"

"Yes, very good," Djamila replied.

"Routines all square, no curves thrown at you?"

"Their life is simple. He works all the time. She plays all the time."

He caught the edge behind her words. "Oh, you think so?"

"I know so." She paused and added, "Americans disgust me."

"Do they, now?"

"They're pigs! They are evil, all of them!"

He said one word in Arabic that froze Djamila.

"Listen to me," Captain Jack said firmly. "A few Americans are bad and a few Muslims are bad. But most want to live in peace and relative happiness, make a home, have a family, pray to God and die with dignity."

"They destroy my country! They say Iraq is united with Al Qaeda and Taliban. That is insane. Hussein and bin Laden were mortal enemies; we all know that. And fifteen of the nineteen 9/11 hijackers, they are Saudis. Yet I do not see American tanks roll down streets of Riyadh, only Baghdad."

"Deposing a man they helped keep in power, I know. But Iraq doesn't own a chunk of America as the Saudis do. Besides, all 'great' civilizations slaughter others who stand in their way. You can talk to the American Indians about that one. But if you want to hear about Muslim cruelty against other Muslims, go see the Kurds."

"You tell me this. You tell me this now! Why? Why!"

Captain Jack's voice was calm but still very firm. "Because the anger you mistake for passion is the one thing that could destroy all that we've worked for. I need you to focus, not hate. Hate makes you do irrational things. I do not tolerate irrational thinking, do you understand me?"

There was silence.

"Do you?"

Djamila finally said, "Yes."

"The plan has changed. It's actually a little cleaner now. I want you to listen very carefully. And then you will practice this new routine, over and over until you can do it in your sleep."

When he finished telling her of the new details, she said, "Like you say, it is easier. It is the way I would go to the Franklins' house."

"Exactly. But we have to account for everything. On *that* day, if the Franklins' routine varies for any reason, and it may, because presidents don't come to town every day, someone will be standing by. You remember what you have to say?"

"'A storm is coming,'" Djamila answered. "But I do not think it will be necessary."

"But if it *is* necessary, then it will be done." He said this sternly, in Arabic.

She hesitated, then asked, "And if the storm comes?"

"Then you will do what you were brought here to do. But if they catch up to you"—he paused—"you will have your reward. As a *fida'ya*."

Djamila smiled as she gazed at a point in the cloudy sky where a bit of the sun was easing through. No one had ever referred to her as a *fida'ya* before.

She was still staring at this spot when Captain Jack left.

He'd learned enough.

# 28

"I THOUGHT THE CASE WAS closed," Jackie Simpson said as she and Alex drove away from WFO in his car.

"I never said that."

"The Bureau found the drugs; you filed your report. You said you were going back to catching counterfeiters and standing post. I remember it pretty clearly because it's when you also gave me that fabulous career advice."

"I got a call from Anne Jeffries last night. She said the drugs were bullshit. She threatened to sue us."

"She's full of crap. And she can't sue us for doing our job. Hell, it's not like we planted the heroin in Johnson's house."

Alex glanced over at her. "But what if someone else did?"

She stared back at him skeptically. "Planted drugs? Why?"

"That's for us to find out. Right from the get-go this case hasn't made sense."

"It makes perfect sense if you accept the fact that Patrick Johnson made a ton of money dealing drugs; he was getting married and didn't see a way out."

"If he didn't see a way out, why did he agree to get married in the first place?"

"Maybe despite her dowdy looks, little Annie is Superwoman in bed and wouldn't give it up anymore without a ring on her finger. So he pops the question and then has second thoughts. He feels trapped and decides the only way out is to bite the bullet."

"You're joking, right?"

"You don't know a lot about women, do you?"

"Meaning what exactly?"

"Meaning that being only a man's lust repository gets a little old after a while. Women want permanent relationships of the diamond variety. Men want conquests."

"Thanks for stereotyping the entire human race; it was very informative."

"Well, here's another theory for you: Johnson was dealing drugs, but with his marriage he wanted to quit the business. It's not the sort of business you just walk away from. As a wedding gift his associates gave him a bullet instead of a toaster."

"On the island where he had his first date? How would they have known?"

"Maybe from Anne Jeffries, the lady who is now protesting so much that her sweetie was never involved in drugs."

"So she's lying to us?"

"She's either incredibly stupid or else she knew about the drugs."

"So if she had no problem with it, why would he kill himself?"

"Maybe he wanted to walk away from the business, but *she* didn't want him to."

Alex shook his head. "So now in cahoots with the druggies, she kills her fiancé?"

"It's as plausible as your theory."

"I don't think Anne Jeffries could tell the difference between a kilo of heroin and a box of sugar even if we shoved them down her throat."

"Whatever." Simpson folded her arms across her chest. "So where are we going?"

"Remember the two guys we met out at Roosevelt Island, Reinke and Peters? I called them. They've finished the handwriting analysis, and I thought we could go learn those results, get our note back and then snoop around."

She exclaimed, "Snoop around! Did you know that when the president goes to NIC, the Secret Service isn't even allowed on certain floors with him because our security clearances aren't high enough?"

"Yeah, I know. That still pisses me off," Alex said.

"So what do you expect to find out there?"

"As part of our investigation we need to know what Johnson did at NIC."

"What happened to the man who didn't want to screw up his last three years?"

Alex stopped the car at a red light and looked over at her. "If I'm afraid to screw up, then I should just turn in my badge right now. And since I'm not willing to do that . . ."

"And this wonderfully patriotic epiphany just hit you?"

"Actually, an old friend pointed it out to me last night."

The light turned green and they started off again. He glanced over at her, and that's when he suddenly noticed it, because she'd unbuttoned her jacket.

"That's a SIG .357."

She didn't look at him. "My other gun was a little heavy."

Alex also noted that she was not wearing her usual flashy breast pocket handkerchief.

They were passing through western Fairfax County on Route 7 when Simpson finally spoke again. "I had dinner with my father last night."

"And how is the good senator?"

"Enlightened," she answered tersely.

Alex wisely kept his mouth shut.

When they pulled up to the main security entrance at NIC, Alex surveyed with awe the sprawling complex that lay ahead.

"What the hell is NIC's budget?"

"It's classified, like ours," Simpson answered.

It took them nearly an hour to clear security, and even then, despite their protests, they had to turn over their weapons. The two were escorted through the halls by a pair of armed guards and an inquisitive Doberman that kept sniffing at Alex's pant leg.

"Let's not forget we're all on the same team, little fellow," Alex said jokingly to the dog.

The guards didn't even crack a smile.

The two Secret Service agents were deposited in a small room and told to wait. And they waited. And waited.

"Is it my imagination, or did we cross into a foreign country back there?" Alex said sourly as he balled up a piece of paper and missed a three-pointer aimed at the wastebasket.

"*You're* the one who wanted to come here," his partner snapped. "I've got a full caseload back at WFO that I could be working on to build *my* career."

Before Alex could answer, the door opened, and in walked Tyler Reinke followed closely by Warren Peters.

"Long time no see," Alex said as he made a protracted show of checking his watch. "I'm glad you two could finally make it."

"Sorry about the wait," Reinke said casually. He pulled out a piece of paper, and they all sat at the small table in the center of the room.

"The handwriting on the note matches Johnson's," Reinke said. "No doubt about it." He passed across the analysis for the Secret Service agents to examine.

"No surprise there," Alex said. "Where's the note?"

"In the lab."

"Okay." Alex waited, but neither of the men said anything. "I'll need it back."

"Right, fine," Peters said.

"It might take a little time," Reinke added.

"I was hoping you'd say that, because we wanted to look around Johnson's office and talk to some of his co-workers. Get a feel for the stuff he was working on."

The men looked at him blankly. "I'm afraid that's not possible," Peters said.

"Guys, this is a homicide investigation. I need a little cooperation."

"As far as cooperation goes, we ran the handwriting analysis for you. Besides, it looks pretty clear that the man committed suicide. That's the Bureau's conclusion too."

"Looks can be deceiving," Alex shot back. "And investigating a person's workplace is standard for this sort of case."

"Patrick Johnson's work area is restricted to the highest security clearance levels," Reinke said firmly. "No exceptions. Your clearances aren't good enough. I checked."

Alex leaned forward and eyed Reinke. "I guarded the president of the United States for five years. I worked on the Joint Anti-Terrorism Task Force while you were still banging cheerleaders in college. I've stood post at meetings of the Joint Chiefs where they talked about stuff this country is doing that would make both of you crap in your Brooks Brothers pants."

"Your security clearances aren't adequate," Reinke reiterated.

"Then we have a big problem," Alex said. "Because I've been assigned to investigate this case. Now, we can do this the easy way or the hard way."

"Meaning what?" Peters asked.

"Meaning I can get a warrant to search Johnson's workplace and talk to his colleagues, or you can just let me do it, security clearance *inadequacy* notwithstanding."

Reinke smiled and shook his head. "There's not a court in this country that would issue a search warrant for these premises."

"What, you're playing the national security card?" Alex said scornfully.

"Secret Service uses it all the time," Peters retorted.

"Not for something like this. And let me remind you that the Department of Homeland Security is my boss now, not wimp-ass Treasury."

"Right. And the director of Homeland Security reports to Carter Gray."

"Bullshit, they're both cabinet secretaries."

Simpson cut in. "Are you guys finished seeing whose penis is bigger? Because this is getting pretty stupid."

The door opened, and both Reinke and Peters shot to their feet.

Carter Gray stood there gazing at them. Alex watched in stunned silence as Gray walked over and gave Simpson a hug and a peck on the cheek.

"You're looking lovely as always, Jackie. How are things?"

"I've had better days," she answered, and then gave Alex a scowl before turning back to Gray. "This is my partner, Alex Ford."

Gray nodded. "Good to meet you, Alex."

"Thank you, sir."

Simpson said, "I had dinner with Dad last night."

"The senator needs to go deer hunting again with me. The last time I bagged a six-pointer. Haven't had a damn bit of luck since."

"I'll tell him."

"What can we do for you?"

She told him about wanting to look around Patrick Johnson's office.

"I told them they lacked the necessary security clearances, sir," Reinke interjected.

"I'm sure you did." Gray glanced at Simpson. "Come on, Jackie, I'll walk you down there myself." He looked back at Reinke and Peters. "That'll be all," he said tersely. The two men instantly fled the room.

As Gray led them down the hall, Alex whispered into Simpson's ear, "Jesus, you didn't tell me you knew Carter Gray."

"You never asked."

"So how do you know him?"

"He's my godfather."

# CHAPTER

## 29

Wʜɪʟᴇ Aʟᴇx ᴀɴᴅ Sɪᴍᴘsᴏɴ ᴡᴇʀᴇ trying to make some headway at NIC, Oliver Stone was playing chess in a park near the White House. His opponent, Thomas Jefferson Wyatt, known universally as T.J., was an old friend who had worked in the kitchen at the White House for almost forty years.

T.J. was a member of the congregation of United Methodist that owned Mt. Zion Cemetery. It was T.J. who helped Stone get the caretaker's job there.

Weather permitting, Stone and Wyatt would often play chess on Wyatt's day off. In fact, it was through chess that the men became friends.

Stone made a move without his usual deliberation, and the adverse result was swift as Wyatt captured his queen.

"You okay, Oliver?" Wyatt asked. "Not like you to make mistakes like that."

"Just some things on my mind, T.J." He sat back against the park bench and gazed keenly at his friend. "It looks like your current boss will be around for another four years."

Wyatt shrugged. "From the kitchen one president looks a lot like another, Republican or Democrat. They all eat. But don't get me wrong. He's doing an okay job. He treats us good, gives us respect. Gives respect to the Secret Service too; not all of them do, you know. You think you'd treat people willing to take a bullet for you pretty good." Wyatt shook his head. "Things I've seen on that score make you sick."

"Speaking of the Secret Service, I saw Agent Ford last night."

Wyatt brightened. "Now, that's a good man. I told you after Kitty died and I had pneumonia he came to my house to check on me almost every day he was in town."

"I remember."

Stone moved one of his bishops forward and said, "I saw Carter Gray land at the White House yesterday."

"Secret Service don't like that one bit. Chopper coming in should only be Marine One with the man on it and that's all."

"Carter Gray's status allows him to make his own rules."

Wyatt grinned, hunched forward and lowered his voice. "Got some scuttlebutt on him you'll get a kick out of."

Stone eased forward. Their chess matches sometimes included snatches of relatively innocuous gossip. White House domestic staff tended to have long tenures at the White House, and they were famous for both meticulous attention to their duties and, more important for the First Family, their discretion. It had taken Stone years to get Wyatt comfortable enough to discuss anything that happened at the White House, however trivial.

"The president asked Gray to go up to New York with him on 9/11, you know, for his big speech at the memorial site." Wyatt paused and looked around at a passerby.

"And?" asked Stone.

"And Gray flat turned him down."

"That's a little brazen, even for Gray."

"Well, you know what happened to his wife and daughter, right?"

"Yes." Stone had met Barbara Gray decades ago. She was an accomplished woman even back then, with a compassion that her husband had never possessed. Stone had instantly respected her, later faulting the lady only for her poor choice in husbands.

"Then the president asked Gray to go up with him to that town in Pennsylvania, the place that changed its name to Brennan."

"And is he?"

"You don't turn down the man twice, right?"

"No, you don't," Stone agreed.

Both men fell silent as Wyatt studied the board and then made his move, edging his rook toward Stone's knight.

While Stone considered his options, he said, "I see that Gray has some problems of his own to deal with. This fellow Patrick Johnson who was found dead on Roosevelt Island, he worked for NIC."

"Oh, yeah, that's been making the rounds at the big house."

"The president's concerned?"

"He and Gray are real tight. So dirt hits Gray, it's bound to splash on the president. The man's no dummy. The president's loyal, but he's not stupid." T.J. glanced around. "I'm not telling tales out of school. Everybody knows that."

"I'm sure NIC and the White House have been working the media hard, because there wasn't much in the morning news about it."

"I know the president's been ordering a lot of late-night snacks and coffee. Man's going into the homestretch on the election, and he doesn't want nothing to upset the applecart. And a dead body can upset a lot of things."

After their chess match was finished and Wyatt had left, Stone sat and thought for a bit. So Gray was going to Brennan, Pennsylvania? That was interesting. Stone had thought it a little gutsy of the town to pull a stunt like that, but apparently, it had paid off.

He was about to leave when he saw Adelphia walking toward him, carrying two cups of coffee. She sat down and handed him one. "Now we have the café and we *chat,*" she said firmly. "Unless you have *meeting* to go to," she added drolly.

"No, no, I don't, Adelphia. And thank you for the coffee." He paused and added, "How did you know I was here?"

"Like that is big secret. Where do you come when you have the game of chess? It is here you come, always it is. With that black man who works at White House."

"I didn't know I was that predictable in my movements," he said, his tone somewhat annoyed.

"Men, men are always predictable. Do you like your café?"

"Very nice." He paused and then commented, "You know, these aren't cheap, Adelphia."

"It is not like I drink the café a hundred times all of the days."

"But you have money?"

Adelphia eyed his new clothes. "So? And you, you have the money."

"I have a job. And my friends, they help me."

"It is no one that helps *me*. I work for money, all of it."

Stone was surprised that he'd never asked her this before. "What do you do?"

"I am seamstress for laundry place. I work when I want. They pay me good. And they give me good deal on room," she said. "And then I can buy the café when I want."

"It must be very rewarding to have such a skill," Stone said absently.

They stopped talking, and their gazes idly took in other people in the small park.

Adelphia finally broke the silence. "So your match of chess, you were victor?"

"No. My defeat was based on equal parts lack of concentration and my opponent's considerable skill."

"My father, he was very excellent at the chess. He was a, how you say . . ." She hesitated, obviously searching for the right words in English. "My father, he was a, how you say, *Wielki Mistrz*."

"A grand champion? No, you mean a grand *master*. That's very impressive."

She glanced at him sharply. "You speak Polish?"

"Just a little."

"You have been to Poland?"

"A very long time ago," he said, sipping his coffee and watching the breeze gently move the leaves on the trees overhead. "I take it that's where you're from?" he asked curiously. Adelphia had never spoken about her origins before.

"It was in Krakow that I was born, but then my family, they move to Bialystok. I was just a child, so I go too."

Stone had been to both those cities but had no intention of telling her that. "I really only know Warsaw, and, as I said, that was a long time ago. Probably before you were born."

"Ha, that is nice thing you say that. Even if it is a lie!" She put her coffee down on the bench and gazed at him. "It is very much younger you look, Oliver."

"Thanks to you and your wizardry with scissors and a razor."

"And your friends, do they not think so too?"

"My friends?" he said, glancing at her.

"I have seen them."

He looked at her again. "Well, they've all come to visit me at Lafayette Park."

"No, I mean at your *meetings* I have seen them."

He tried not to look concerned at her stunning words. "So you followed me to my *meetings*? I hope they weren't too boring." *What has she seen or heard?*

She looked coy and, as though she'd read his thoughts, said, "It might have been things I hear, or it might not."

"When was that?" he asked.

"So finally it is I have your attention." She edged closer to him and actually patted his hand. "Do not worry, Oliver, I am not spy. I see things but I do not hear. And the things I see, well, they stay with me always. Always they do."

"It's not like we have anything worth overhearing or seeing."

"It is truth you seek, Oliver?" she said, smiling. "Like your sign say, it is truth you want. I can tell. You are such a man who seeks this."

"I'm afraid as the years go by, my chances of actually finding it are fewer and fewer."

Adelphia suddenly glanced over at a person who was staggering through the park. Anyone who had been on the streets of Washington over the last ten years had probably seen this pitiable sight. He had short stubs of bone and skin where his arms should have been. His legs were so horribly twisted that it was a miracle he could even remain upright. He was usually half-naked, even in winter. He had no shoes on. His feet were scarred and covered with sores, the toes oddly bent. His eyes were largely vacant, and a steady current of spittle slipped down his face and onto his chest. As far as anyone knew, he could not even speak. A small pouch hung from a string around his neck. Written across his tattered shirt in childlike scrawl was one word: "Help."

Stone had given money to the man on numerous occasions and knew that he lived over a steam grate by the Treasury Department. He'd tried to help the man over the years, but his mind was simply too far gone. If any government agency had stepped in to help, Stone was unaware of it.

"My God, that man, that poor man. My heart, it bursts for his suffering," Adelphia said. She raced over to him, pulled out some dollars from her pocket and placed them in his pouch. He babbled something at her and then staggered off to another group nearby, who also immediately opened their pocketbooks and wallets to him.

As Adelphia was returning to her spot next to Stone, a large man stepped in front of her, blocking the way.

He said gruffly, "I don't look as shitty as that guy, but I'm hungry and I need a drink bad." His hair was ratty and in his face, but he wasn't dressed that shabbily. However, the stench coming off his body in waves was overpowering.

"It is no more I have," Adelphia answered in a frightened tone.

"You're lying!" He grabbed her arm and yanked Adelphia toward him. "Give me some damn money!"

Before Adelphia could even cry out, Stone was beside her.

"Let her go *now*!" Stone demanded.

The man was a good twenty-five years younger than Stone and far bigger. "Get out of here, old man. This doesn't concern you."

"This woman is my friend."

"I said get out of here!" He followed this with a vicious swing that caught Stone flush on the chin. He dropped to the ground, clutching his face.

"Oliver!" Adelphia screamed.

Other people in the park were yelling at the man now, and someone was running off, calling out for a policeman.

As Stone struggled to get to his feet, the man pulled a switchblade out of his pocket and pointed it at Adelphia. "Give me the money or I'll cut you bad, bitch."

Stone made a sudden lunge. The man let go of Adelphia and staggered back, dropping his knife. He fell to his knees, every muscle in his body trembling, and then he collapsed onto his back on the grass, writhing in agony.

Stone picked up the switchblade and then palmed the weapon in a very unusual way. He reached over and ripped open his assailant's collar, exposing the man's thick neck and throbbing arteries. For an instant it seemed that Stone was going to slice that neck open from ear to ear as the knifepoint edged very near a pulsing vein. There was a look in Oliver Stone's eyes that virtually no one who had known him over the last thirty-odd years had ever seen. Yet Stone abruptly stopped and gazed up at Adelphia, who stood there staring at him, her chest heaving. At that moment it was not clear which man she feared more.

"Oliver?" she said quietly. "Oliver?"

Stone dropped the knife on the ground, rose and wiped off his pants.

"My God, you are bleeding," Adelphia cried out. "Bleeding!"

"I'm fine," he said shakily as he dabbed at his bloody mouth with his sleeve. That was a lie. The blow had hurt him very much. His head was bursting, and he felt sick to his stomach. He picked at something in his mouth and yanked out a tooth the man's punch had loosened.

"You are no fine!" Adelphia insisted as she watched him.

A woman came running up to them. "The police are coming. Are you both okay?"

Stone turned to see a patrol car, its lights flashing, pull to a stop at the curb. He quickly turned to Adelphia. "I'm sure you can explain everything to the police." This came out a little garbled because his lip was swelling.

As he staggered off, she called out to him but he didn't turn around.

When the police came up and started asking her questions, all Adelphia could think about was what she had seen. Oliver Stone had dug his index finger into the man's side, near the rib cage. This simple move had caused a very large, angry man to drop to the ground, helpless.

And the way Stone held the knife had struck her deeply, for a very personal reason. Adelphia had seen a man grip a knife that way only once before, many years ago in Poland. The man had been a member of the KGB, who had come to forcibly take her uncle away for speaking out against the Soviets. She had never seen her uncle alive again. His gutted body had been found in an unused well in a village twenty miles away.

As Adelphia glanced around, she gasped.

Oliver Stone had disappeared.

# CHAPTER

## 30

"This is where Patrick Johnson worked," Carter Gray said, sweeping his hand across the room.

Alex slowly took it all in. The space was about half the size of a football field with a large open area in the middle and cubicles along the perimeter. Computers with flat screens were on every desktop and servers hummed in the background. Men and women dressed in business attire either sat at their desks totally focused on their work or else walked the halls speaking into phone headsets using cryptic jargon that not even Alex, with all his federal time behind him, could understand. The sense of urgency here was palpable.

As Gray led them over to a set of corner cubicles, Alex caught images of people's faces flashing across some of the computers, most of them Middle Eastern, with data, presumably about each person, flowing down one side of the screen. The thing he didn't see was a single scrap of paper.

"We *are* paperless," Gray said.

Alex was startled by this comment. *Has the man added mind reading to his repertoire?*

"At least the people working here are. I still like to feel the material in my hands." He stopped at one cubicle, larger than the rest, whose walls, instead of waist level, were six feet high.

"This is Johnson's office."

"I take it he was a supervisor of some sort," Simpson commented.

"Yes. His precise task was to oversee the work on our data files of all terrorist-related suspects. When we took over N-TAC, we combined that staff and their files with ours. It was an ideal fit. However, we, of course, didn't want to strip the Secret Service of all involvement. That's why Johnson and others here were joint employees."

Gray said this in a magnanimous tone. However, as Alex looked around the space, he thought to himself, *Nice but useless bone to throw our way, since we had no control over our "joint" employee.* His gaze came to rest on the only personal item in the office. It was a small framed photo of Anne Jeffries sitting on Johnson's desk. Alex noted that when the woman was all made up, she looked very pretty. He wondered if Anne Jeffries was meeting with a lawyer right now. A moment later another man joined them.

Tom Hemingway flashed a smile as he put out his hand to Alex. "Well, I guess my cover's blown, Agent Ford."

"I guess so," Alex said as he winced at the man's crushing grip.

Gray raised an eyebrow. "You two know each other?"

"Through Kate Adams, the DOJ lawyer I was working with, sir."

Simpson stepped forward. "I'm Jackie Simpson, Secret Service."

"Tom Hemingway."

"Nice to meet you, Tom." She gazed appreciatively at the handsome Hemingway until she caught Alex scowling at her.

"I was just showing them Patrick Johnson's office and explaining what he did for us," Gray said. "They're investigating his death on behalf of the Service."

"If you'd like, sir, I can take over from here. I know you have a meeting."

"Tom knows much more about computers than I do," Gray said. That wasn't exactly true, but Gray had never been one to boast of his strengths, because that very hubris often turned them into weaknesses.

"Don't forget to tell your father what I said, Jackie." Then Gray left them.

"So what exactly are you looking for?" Hemingway asked.

"Basically an understanding of what Johnson did here," Alex answered. "Secretary Gray said that he oversaw the data files on terrorist suspects."

"That's right, among other things. I guess the best way to describe it is that he and the other data supervisors are like senior air traffic controllers making sure all the pieces go together smoothly. The databases are constantly being updated with fresh intelligence. And we've streamlined things too. The FBI, DEA, Homeland Security, ATF, CIA, DIA and others each had its own database. There was a lot of overlap and wrong information and no way for one agency to thoroughly access another agency's files. That was one of the problems that led up to 9/11. Now it's *all* maintained here, but the other agencies have 24/7 access."

Alex spoke up. "Isn't that a little risky, putting everything in one place?"

"We have a backup center, of course," Hemingway said.

"Where is it?" Alex asked.

"I'm afraid that's classified."

*Well, I saw that one coming.*

"And keep in mind that our system didn't replace the Bureau's AFIS," said Hemingway, referring to the FBI's fingerprint identification system. "We're after terrorists, not pedophiles and bank robbers. We also bought several private firms that specialized in intelligence data mining and other areas of technological expertise."

"NIC bought private companies?" Alex said.

Hemingway nodded. "Government doesn't have to reinvent the wheel any more than the private sector. The software literally digs into trillions of bytes of information in numerous databases and builds patterns, suspect signatures and behavior and activity models that can be used in investigations. Our agents have handheld devices, like Palm-Pilots, that allow them instant access to these databases. With a single query they can access all relevant information about a subject. It's incredible stuff."

"How do you effectively oversee an operation this big with people constantly firing stuff at you?" Alex asked.

"When all the other agencies' files came over, it created quite a backlog to work through. And between you and me, there were some glitches, and the system actually crashed a couple of times. But it's all running smoothly now. It was Johnson's task and others here to oversee that and also to ensure the accuracy of the data input. It's very labor-intensive work."

"So not so speedy," Alex said.

"Speed is useless if the information is wrong," Hemingway countered. "While we try to keep everything as up-to-date and accurate as possible, perfection, of course, is not attainable."

"Could you show us some file examples?" Simpson asked.

"Sure." Hemingway sat down at Johnson's desk and put his hand in a biometric reader. Next he hit some keys on the computer, and a face appeared on the screen along with a fingerprint and other identifying data.

Alex was suddenly staring at himself, along with seemingly everything he'd ever done since coming out of his mother's womb.

"Underage drinking conviction," Simpson said, reading one of the sections.

"That was *supposed* to have been expunged from my record," Alex snapped.

"I'm sure it *was* expunged from the official record," Hemingway said. "How is your neck by the way? Looks like a nasty injury you suffered."

"You've got my *medical* records? What the hell happened to privacy?"

"You must've neglected to read the fine print on the Patriot Act." Hemingway hit some more keys and another search field came up. He said, "You go to the LEAP Bar a lot." He pointed at a list of credit card purchases from that pub. "I'm sure the presence of the lovely Kate Adams is a factor."

"So every time I use my credit card you know what I'm up to?"

"That's why I always pay in cash," Hemingway said smugly.

He typed in some more commands, and Jackie Simpson's photo, digitized fingerprint and basic information sheet came up. She pointed at one line. "That's wrong. I was born in Birmingham, not Atlanta."

Hemingway smiled. "See, not even NIC is infallible. I'll make sure it's corrected."

"Do you have any bad guys in there, or do you just spy on cops?" Alex asked.

Hemingway punched some more keys and another face sprang up. "His name is, was, Adnan al-Rimi. He was killed by another terrorist in Virginia. You can see that al-Rimi has been *confirmed* as deceased. That's what the little skull and crossbones symbol in the upper right-hand corner signifies. A little corny and I'm not sure who came up

with that idea, but it's pretty clear as to a person's current status."
Hemingway opened a drop-down window. "You can see the fingerprint image here. We were able to positively ID al-Rimi from his digital prints, which we had on file."

"Did Johnson have any information that would be valuable to
someone?"

"I think in broad terms everyone who works at NIC would have information that could be valuable to an enemy of this country, Agent
Ford. That's why we run background checks and perform a rigorous
vetting process."

"Can't do any better than that," Jackie Simpson said.

"But didn't Patrick Johnson's sudden *wealth* raise red flags here?"
Alex asked.

Hemingway looked chagrined. "It should have. Heads will roll for it."

"But not yours," Alex remarked.

"No, that wasn't my responsibility," Hemingway answered.

"Lucky you. So if the drugs weren't Johnson's source of income,
you're saying it's unlikely that he could have been selling secrets from
here?"

"Unlikely but not impossible. But the drugs *were* found at his
house."

"Do you mind if we talk to some of Johnson's co-workers?"

"I can arrange that, but I'm afraid your discussions will have to be
monitored."

"Wow, just like in prison, only we're the good guys," Alex said.

"We're the good guys *too*," Hemingway shot back.

An hour later, after they'd spoken to three of Johnson's colleagues,
Alex and Simpson learned that none of them really knew Johnson on a
personal level.

After they'd collected their guns, Hemingway escorted them out.
"Good luck," he said before the automatic doors shut behind them.

"Right, sure, thanks for all your help," Alex groused.

They walked back to the car while two army grunts toting M-16s
followed.

"Either one of you guys wanna hold my hand in case I suddenly go
berserk?" Alex asked before turning back around and marching on in
disgust.

"Well, that was a complete waste of time," Simpson said.

"So is ninety percent of investigative work. *You* should know that," Alex said heatedly.

"What are you so pissed about?"

"Are you telling me all that stuff in there didn't creep you out? Hell, I was half expecting a photo of when I lost my virginity to pop up."

"I've got nothing to hide. And why were you such an asshole with Tom?"

"I was an asshole with *Tom* because I don't happen to like the son of a bitch."

"Oh, well, I guess that explains your relationship with me."

Alex didn't bother to answer. But he did lay down rubber on NIC's pristine asphalt getting the hell out of Big Brother Town.

# CHAPTER

# 31

A FEW MINUTES AFTER ALEX AND Simpson had left, Hemingway passed Reinke and Peters in the hallway at NIC and gave a short nod of his head. Fifteen minutes later Hemingway drove out of NIC. Ten minutes after that, Reinke and Peters did the same.

They met at Tyson's II Galleria, a large upscale shopping mall, purchased coffees and walked along the concourses. They'd already used an antisurveillance device to ensure that none of them had been bugged, and each had taken great pains to make sure they hadn't been followed. A major rule of being a spy was to make certain your own agency wasn't spying on *you*.

"We tried to stop them from going through Johnson's office," Peters said. "But then Gray came in."

"I know," Hemingway replied. "That's why I went down there. The last thing I want is Carter Gray turning his attention to this."

"What about Ford and Simpson?"

"If they get too close, there are ways to deal with them," Hemingway said. "We found a print on the suicide note and ran it."

"Did you get a match?" Reinke asked.

"Yes."

"Who is it?" Peters asked.

"It's in your jacket pocket." Hemingway finished his coffee and threw away the cup. Peters pulled out the piece of paper Hemingway had slipped there at some point. He read the name: *Milton Farb*.

Hemingway explained, "He worked at NIH years ago as a computer systems expert but had some mental problems and popped up in some psych centers. He was in the phone book, so it wasn't hard tracking his address. I've e-mailed an encrypted version of his background file to you. Watch him, and he'll probably lead you to the others. But do nothing without checking with me first. If we can avoid killing them, we will." He walked off in one direction while Reinke and Peters headed off in the other with renewed energy.

Carter Gray returned to his office, made a few phone calls, including one to the White House, and then held a series of brief meetings. After that, Gray settled down for another task that would take him several hours. Whenever the president was traveling and Gray was unable to accompany or meet him on the road, they conducted a secure video conference call for the daily briefing. Gray typically spent a good deal of each day preparing for that call, but he knew that the salient points could be summed up very quickly.

"Mr. President, the world as we know it is going straight to hell, some of it due to our own actions, and there's little we can do about it. However, so long as we keep spending hundreds of billions of dollars on homeland security, I can reasonably guarantee that most Americans will be safe. However, all our expensive efforts can still be defeated by a small group of people with enough nerve, dumb luck and plutonium. Then all bets are off, and we could all very well be dead. Any questions, sir?"

Instead of preparing for the briefing with Brennan, though, Gray wanted to go for a drive. Unfortunately, he wasn't allowed to. As with the president, the secretary of intelligence was not allowed to drive himself; he was deemed too vital to the security of the nation to be behind the wheel of a car. However, what Gray really wanted to do was go fishing. Since he couldn't do that right now with a pole and bait, he decided to try another version of fishing, one at which he was also very skilled.

He typed in a request for a name on his laptop. Within five minutes he had the information he wanted. NIC personnel were nothing if not efficient.

It had been one of his most brilliant moves, Gray thought, centralizing all terrorist databases under NIC's control. While it made the system far more accurate, it also gave NIC the heads-up on other intelligence agencies' operations. If the CIA, for example, needed information on something, they would have to access one of the NIC databases and

Gray would instantly know what they were looking at. It had worked beautifully, allowing him to spy on his intelligence brethren under cover of bureaucratic efficiency.

He set up the images and data on split screens so he could view them all simultaneously. There were many men staring back at him. Almost all were Middle Eastern; they had all been duly recorded in the NIC database, complete with digital fingerprints, if available. And they were all dead, many at the hands of other terrorists. The skull and crossbones marker resting in the upper right-hand corner of each man's picture confirmed this fate. They included an engineer and chemist who were also expert bomb makers. Another, Adnan al-Rimi, was a courageous fighter with nerves that had never broken in the heat of battle. Six others lost their lives when an explosive went off in the van they were in. Whether it was accidental or intentional had never been determined. The crime scene had been horrific, with body *parts* instead of bodies to collect. Other than Muhammad al-Zawahiri, none of these men were on the "A-list" of terrorist suspects, but it was still fortunate for America that they were dead.

Gray had no way of knowing that the photos of al-Rimi and others had been altered subtly. They were not the pictures of the men who'd *actually* died either. They were a digitized combination of the real al-Rimi, for example, and the dead man identified as al-Rimi. This was done so that any "earlier" photos of the men still floating around would not look so different as to raise suspicion. It had taken time and considerable expertise. The result had been worth it, though. It was now virtually impossible to identify any of these Arabs from their photos in the NIC database.

The other brilliant stroke had been leaving no "faces" behind on the dead men to identify. What had been substituted in their entirety, of course, were the men's fingerprints, the forensic signature by which they'd been positively identified. Fingerprints never lied. Of course, in the digital age nothing was inviolate.

And yet with all that, Carter Gray's gut was telling him something was not right.

Gray clicked out of the file and decided to go for a walk around the NIC grounds. He was allowed to do that, he supposed.

As Gray strolled outside, he looked at the sky, following the flight of a Lufthansa 747 as it made its way into Dulles Airport, and his mind wandered to the past.

Early on in his career at the CIA Gray had been assigned to the CIA's ultrasecret and now abandoned training facility near Washington, Virginia, a bit over two hours west of D.C. The building, extremely well hidden within the surrounding forest, was known, in CIA parlance, as Area 51A, demonstrating that the Agency did, indeed, have a sense of humor. Unofficially, though, it had usually been referred to as Murder Mountain.

Long since closed down, NIC had recently moved to have it reopened as an interrogation facility for terrorist suspects. However, the Justice Department had gotten wind of the scheme, and the process had slowed down considerably. Then, after the cumulative effects of "Gitmo" Bay in Cuba, the disgrace of Abu Ghraib prison in Iraq, and the Salt Pit prison fiasco in Afghanistan, the plans to reopen the facility were on the verge of being nixed.

Gray was unconcerned, though. There were lots of other places *outside* the country that would serve the same purpose. Torture of prisoners was illegal under American and international laws. Gray had testified before many committees regarding compliance with this law by his intelligence community, lying to the Congress with virtually every word he spoke. However, did those great and pious legislators who neither knew one word of Arabic nor could even name the capitals of Oman or Turkmenistan without a staffer's help, really think that was how the world worked?

Intelligence was a filthy business where people lied and people died all the time. The fact that the U.S. president was right now contemplating the assassination of another country's elected officials was testament enough to how complicated the global politics were.

Gray returned to his office. He wanted to take another look at all these "dead men" who might somehow figure prominently in his future. God help America if they did.

# CHAPTER

## 32

A LEX E-MAILED HIS UPDATED report to Jerry Sykes as soon as he got back to WFO. Unlike his first filing, however, the response this time was very swift. The phone call didn't merely instruct him to go to Jerry Sykes' office, or even the SAIC's. He was ordered to report immediately to Secret Service headquarters and meet with none other than the director of the Secret Service.

Okay, Alex thought, this was probably not a good sign. It was close enough to WFO that Alex could walk, and he did. The time in the fresh air allowed him to ponder his future after the Service, which might be coming faster than he had envisioned, in fact about three years faster.

He had met the current director face-to-face only a couple times before. They'd been social occasions, and the few minutes of chitchat had been quite pleasant. Alex's gut was telling him that this encounter wouldn't be nearly as chummy.

A few minutes later he walked into the director's spacious office. Jerry Sykes was there, apparently trying to disappear into the sofa he was perched on, and, much to Alex's surprise, Jackie Simpson was sitting next to Sykes.

"You want to close the door, Ford?" Wayne Martin, the director of the Secret Service, said.

*Close the door.* That was definitely not a good sign. Alex obeyed this instruction and then sat and waited for Martin to start speaking. He was a large man who favored striped shirts with big cuff links. He'd worked his way up through the ranks and was one of the agents who tackled John Hinckley after his attempt to assassinate Reagan.

Martin was studying a file in front of him. Shooting a quick glance at it, Alex thought it appeared to be his Service history. Okay, this was *really* not looking good.

Martin closed the file, sat on the edge of his desk and said, "Agent Ford, I'll get right to it because, believe it or not, I've got a lot of things to do today."

"Yes, sir," Alex said automatically.

"I got a call from the president a little while ago. He was on Air Force One. The man was on his plane going to a string of campaign events, and he took the time to call me about *you*. That's why you're here today."

It was as though all the blood were evaporating from Alex's body. "The president called about *me,* sir?"

"Would you like to take a guess what about?"

Alex shot a glance at Sykes, who was studying the floor. Simpson was looking at him, but she didn't appear to be in a helpful mood.

"The Patrick Johnson case?" Alex could barely hear his own voice.

"*Bingo!*" Martin boomed, slamming a fist down on his desk and causing everybody to jump.

"Since you're batting a thousand, Ford, you care to take another guess as to what you *did* that prompted a call from the president of the United States?"

Alex had no saliva left in his mouth, but the man obviously wanted an answer. "I've been investigating the death of Patrick Johnson. That's what I was ordered to do."

Martin was shaking his head halfway through this answer. "The FBI is the lead investigative agency on the case. My understanding is that you were assigned to merely observe that investigation so as to protect the interests of this agency. And that our only connection to the deceased is that he was technically a joint employee of this agency and NIC. But in reality he was fully under NIC's control and jurisdiction. Do you disagree with that assessment?"

Alex didn't even bother to glance at Sykes. "No, sir."

"Good, I'm glad that we've got that established. Now, the FBI found drugs at Mr. Johnson's residence and is following up along those lines, which would tend to indicate that he was selling said drugs and generating considerable income from that endeavor. And consequently, his employment at NIC was not being considered as possibly connected to his death. Are you aware of this?"

"Yes, sir."

"Good again." Martin stood, and Alex braced for what was coming. He wasn't disappointed.

Martin erupted, "Now, with all that said, would you care to tell me what in the living hell you were thinking when you went out to NIC and questioned none other than Carter Gray about this matter?" This was conveyed in what could only be described as one long drill sergeant scream.

When Alex finally found his voice, he said, "I thought that to cover all the angles, going out to NIC was proper. They had run an analysis on a note for us and—"

"Did you or did you not interrogate Carter Gray?"

"I did *not,* sir. He showed up and offered to take us to Johnson's work space. Until then, I was merely speaking with two junior subordinates who were not being particularly cooperative."

"Did you threaten to seek a warrant to search the NIC premises?"

Alex's heart seemed to skip a beat. "That was just a routine jab at—"

Martin smacked his desktop again. "Did you!"

Sweat now christened Alex's face. "Yes, sir."

"Did you learn anything useful while you were there? Did you find a smoking gun? Did you find evidence to implicate Secretary Gray in some nefarious plot?"

Even though he well knew these were rhetorical questions, Alex felt compelled to answer the man. "We learned nothing that was particularly helpful to the investigation. But again, it was on Secretary Gray's initiative that he showed us around, sir. And it was only for a couple of minutes."

"Let me fill you in on the politics of our business, Ford. Secretary Gray didn't randomly run into you at NIC. He was alerted to your presence and purpose and came down to see you. He told the president that he felt compelled to do so because if word leaked out to the media that NIC was not being cooperative in a criminal investigation, it would reflect badly on him and his agency. As you know, Secretary Gray and the president are especially close. So things that reflect badly on NIC and Secretary Gray don't make the president happy. Are you following this?"

"Yes, sir."

"Are you also aware that under Secretary Gray's initiative a full internal investigation is being conducted at NIC with regards to the Johnson matter and that the FBI will be assisting in this?"

"No, sir, I was not aware of that."

Martin didn't appear to be listening now. He picked up a piece of paper from his desk. "According to your first report, you'd concluded that Mr. Johnson was probably a drug dealer, and you were going to let the FBI track that lead down. That was it. You filed that report last night. Now this morning you showed up at NIC asking a bunch of questions that were in clear contradiction to your initial conclusions. My question to you is, what happened between the time you filed the report last night and your going to NIC this morning that made you change your mind?"

By the way Martin was looking at him, it suddenly struck Alex that the man already knew the answer. He shot a glance at Simpson, who was now looking nervously down at her thick-heeled pumps. That's why she was here. *Oh, shit!*

He looked back at the director.

"I'm waiting for your answer," Martin said.

Alex cleared his throat, buying time. "Sir, they'd analyzed the handwriting on the note, and I wanted to get the results."

Martin gave Alex a look so scathing the agent could actually feel the swells of perspiration under his armpits.

"Don't ever bullshit me, son," Martin said in a very low, steady voice that was somehow far more threatening than the man's prior tirade. The director looked over at Simpson. "Agent Simpson informed us that you told her an *old friend* had convinced you to get up a head of steam on this case and go for it." He paused and said, "Who was that 'friend'?"

*Talk about a casual slip of the tongue coming back to crater your life.* Alex's mind was racing from how he was going to afford his mortgage after he was fired from the Service in disgrace, to how he could kill Jackie Simpson and not get the death penalty.

"I don't really recall that conversation with Agent Simpson, sir."

"It was *this* morning. I'm not sure the Service needs agents with memories that poor, so you want to load up and try again? Keep in mind that there are *two* careers in question here, and one of them is just starting out." He again shot a glance at Simpson.

"The identity of the person isn't important, sir. I'd already concluded that I was going to keep investigating the case because certain things didn't add up, that's all. It's solely my responsibility. Agent Simpson had nothing to do with my decision to go to NIC. She was merely doing what I told her to, and reluctantly at that. I'm prepared to take the full consequences for my actions."

"So you won't answer my question?"

"With all due respect, sir, if I thought it had the slightest bearing on this case, I would answer it."

"And you're not going to let me be the judge of that?"

For a lot of reasons Alex was not going to tell the director of the Secret Service that a man calling himself Oliver Stone, who sometimes occupied a tent across from the White House, and who'd been known to harbor a few conspiracy theories, was the "old friend" who had convinced him to keep investigating. It just didn't seem like a good idea right now.

Alex nervously licked his lips. "Again, with all due respect, it was said to me in confidence, and unlike some people, I don't break confidences." He didn't look at Simpson when he said this, but then he didn't really have to. "So you can just stop the buck right at me, sir."

The director sat in his chair and leaned back. "You've had a good, solid career at the Service, Ford."

"I'd like to think so." Alex felt his breath quicken as he sensed the axe coming.

"But it's the *end* of the career that people remember."

Alex almost started laughing because this was exactly what Stone had told him, for an entirely different reason, of course. "That's what I've heard, sir." He paused and said, "I'm assuming I'm being transferred to another field office." When the Service was ticked off at an agent, it usually sent that person to one of the least desirable field offices. Although, in this case, that might have been wishful thinking.

Disobeying a command from the director would probably result in his immediate expulsion from the Service.

"You just take the rest of the day off. Then starting tomorrow you're officially transferred out of WFO and back to presidential protection detail. Maybe standing post in some doorways will knock some sense into you. Quite frankly, I don't know what I'm going to do with you. Half of me wants to kick your ass right out of the Service this minute. But you've put in a lot of good years; it'd be a shame to see that go right in the crapper." He held up a finger. "And just so there's no miscommunication, you are not to go near the Patrick Johnson case in any way at all, even if your 'old friend' tells you otherwise. Is that clear?"

"Absolutely, sir."

"Now get the hell out of here."

# CHAPTER

# 33

Djamila gave the baby his bath while Lori Franklin played with the other two boys on the elaborate play set in the backyard. As she was dressing the little one afterward, Djamila watched the others from the nursery window. Lori Franklin didn't spend enough time with her children, at least in Djamila's estimation. Yet even the Iraqi woman had to admit that the time the mother did spend with her sons was real quality time. She read to them and drew with them and played games with them, spending patient hours with her three sons as they grew and changed every day. It was clear that Lori Franklin adored her boys. Now she was pushing the middle child on the swing while giving the oldest a piggyback ride. They all ended up chasing each other around the yard before collapsing in a pile. The peals of laughter reached all the way to Djamila, and, after a few seconds of fighting the urge, Djamila found herself laughing too at this heartwarming spectacle. Sons. She wanted many sons who would grow up tall and strong and take care of their mother when she grew old.

Djamila abruptly stopped laughing and turned away from the window. People should never take for granted what they had. Never! Especially Americans, who had everything.

Later, while Djamila and Franklin were preparing lunch, the latter closed the refrigerator door with a puzzled look.

"Djamila, there's *kosher* food in here."

Djamila wiped off her hands on a towel. "Yes, miss, I buy some at store. I use my money. It is for my meals here."

"Djamila, I don't care about that. We'll pay for your food. But you must know that kosher is, well, it's *Jewish* food."

"Yes, miss, this I know."

Franklin flashed a confused look. "Am I missing something here? A Muslim eating Jewish food?"

"Jews are people of the Book, in the Qur'an, I mean. As are Christians too, miss. And Jesus, he is recognized as a very important prophet of Islam, but he is not a god. There is only one God. And only Muhammad communicated the true word of God to the people. But David and Ibrahim, who you call Abraham, are important prophets too for Islam. We respect them for what they did. It was Ibrahim and his son Ishmael who built the Kaaba and established the practice of hajj, the pilgrimage to Mecca."

Franklin looked impatient. "Thanks for the theology lesson, but what does all that have to do with *food*?"

"Muslims must eat food that is deemed lawful, or *halal*, and avoid what is *haram*, or unlawful. These rules they come from the Qur'an and fatwas and other Islamic rulings. We cannot consume alcohol or eat the meat of pigs, dogs or monkeys or other animals that haven't died by human hand. We can only eat the meat of animals that have the cloven hoof and chew the cud and only fish that have the fin and scales, just like the Jews. The Jews, they prepare their food in ways acceptable to Muslims. As example, they drain all blood from the meat. Muslims, we cannot drink blood or have anything to do with blood in our food. And Jews do not kill the animal by boiling it or by electricity, although they do not declare three times, 'Allahu akbar,' that means God is great, when they slaughter the animal. But we Muslims recognize God by saying his name before we eat the food. And God will not let his people starve if they can't find *halal* food. You say God's name over the food, it is *halal*. Not all Muslims will eat the food of Jews, but if I cannot find *halal* food, I will eat the kosher."

Lori Franklin was frowning at her nanny. "Well, I'm afraid I don't understand that. I pick up a newspaper and pretty much can count on at least one story of Jews and Muslims killing each other somewhere. I know it's not all that simple, but you'd think if you eat their food and they're in *your* Bible, you could find *some* way to get along."

Djamila stiffened. "It is not about *food* that we differ. I could tell you much—"

"Yes, well, I really don't want to get into it. I have to meet George after lunch. He forgot his plane tickets for his flight tonight. Honestly, George can't remember anything. You'd think an investment banker would have a better memory."

After lunch was over and Lori Franklin had left, Djamila put the children into her van and drove to the park. On the ride over, her thoughts turned to her recent past.

She had known young men who'd trained with her in Pakistan that kept what they called journals of sacrifice, *their* sacrifice. The West, she knew, called them suicide diaries. She had read accounts in the papers of these diaries being found after the young men had died for Islam. Djamila had thought about what the last day of her life would look like. In her head she ran through what she would be thinking when the time came, how she would react. She had many questions and some doubts that troubled her. Would she be brave? She had imagined herself being noble and stoic, but was that unrealistic? Would she instantly be transported to paradise? Would anyone mourn her? And yet this also made her feel guilty, for her love of God should be enough; as it was for all Muslims.

Under normal circumstances it would have been unheard of for women to be deployed in terrorist cells with men, since there were strict rules and tribal customs forbidding unrelated men and women from being around each other. However, it had become quickly evident that Muslim men were almost always placed under heavy scrutiny in America, whereas Muslim women were given much more leeway. Thus, Muslim women were being engaged in much greater numbers now.

Djamila had grown close to one man she'd trained with. Ahmed was an Iranian, which instantly made her suspicious because there had never been harmony between Iran and her country. Yet he described a world in Tehran that was different from what she'd been told in Iraq.

"People want to be happy," he told her. "But they cannot be happy if they are not free. You can love and worship God, without other people telling you how to live every part of life." Then he went on to tell her that Iranian women could drive, vote and even hold seats in the Parliament. They were not forced to cover their entire face, just their hair and body, and they had started to wear cosmetics. He also told her that satellite dishes were being smuggled into the country in large numbers, and that, even more astonishing, men and women sat in cars while music played on the radio. If you knew where to go and the right things to say, you could get around the rules and the mullahs. You could have a chance to live life, if only for a little time, he had said. Djamila listened very intensely whenever he spoke of this.

He had also told Djamila that her name, which meant "beautiful" in Arabic, was most fitting to her. Most fitting, he'd said with respect and admiration, his gaze averted from hers. This comment had made her very happy. It had given her possibilities for a future that she had not thought realistic. However, he also spoke often of his coming death, even writing down in his diary the very day and hour that he planned on dying for God. But he would never show her the date he had chosen.

Djamila didn't know if he'd fulfilled that wish or not. She didn't know where he'd been sent. She would read the newspapers looking for his name or his picture telling of his death, but she'd never seen it. Djamila wondered if he ever read the newspapers looking for *her* picture and the account of *her* death.

He'd been a fledgling poet who had modest dreams of seeing his verses in print for other Arabs to read. His poems were filled with tragedy that Djamila knew came from years of violence and suffering in Iran. One of the last things he told her was, "When one has lost everything except one's life, it doesn't make that life more valuable, it only makes the *sacrifice* of that life more potent. To die for God, life could have no greater purpose." She would never forget those words. They gave her strength and her life meaning.

The Qur'an said that any man or woman who has led a righteous life while believing in God enters paradise without the slightest injustice. But Djamila had learned that the only way for a Muslim to be *guaranteed* passage into paradise was to die as a martyr during an Islamic holy war. If that was so, and Djamila prayed every day that it was true, then she would willingly make that sacrifice. The life after must be better. God would not let it be otherwise; she was certain of this.

Sometimes Djamila would imagine her poet joining her in paradise, where they could live in eternal peace. This thought was one of the very few that could still bring a smile to her lips. Yes, Djamila would like to see him again, very much. In life or death, it did not matter to her. It did not matter at all.

# 34

STONE WALKED BACK TO HIS cottage and cleaned himself up, putting ice on his face and resting while the swelling went down. Then he used his borrowed cell phone and contacted Reuben and Caleb. They scheduled a meeting for that night; he was unable to get hold of Milton.

After that, he tended to the cemetery and helped a couple of visitors find a grave they were looking for. Many years ago the church had documented the people interred here, but that list had been lost. Over the past two years Stone had checked every headstone and local records to re-create an accurate list. He'd also steeped himself in the history of Mt. Zion Cemetery and acted as an informal tour guide, narrating this history to groups that came by.

As he finished with the visitors and returned to work, he felt his face burn. And it wasn't from his recent injuries, but rather from embarrassment. It had been so stupid of him to do that particularly in front of Adelphia. He could still feel the weight of the knife in his hand. *So stupid.*

Later he decided to take the Metro to Milton's house. If his friend had been able to trace the car tag, Stone wanted to know. Plus, he wanted to make sure Milton was all right. The people they were dealing with could also run down a fingerprint as easily as Milton could.

He was walking down the street toward the Foggy Bottom subway station when he heard a horn sound behind him. He turned. It was Agent Ford. He pulled his Crown Vic to the curb and rolled down the window.

"Want a ride?" Alex suddenly noted his friend's injuries. "What the hell happened to you?"

"I fell."

"You okay?"

"My ego was bruised more than my face." Stone climbed into the car and Alex sped off.

Waiting for what he hoped was an acceptable period of time, Stone finally said, "I was thinking about our conversation last night. How's your investigation going?"

"It's going so well I've been busted back to protection detail."

"Agent Ford—"

"You know, Oliver, after all these years, you can probably call me Alex."

"I hope that my advice didn't get you in trouble, Alex."

"I'm a big boy. And you happened to be right. Only I didn't have all the facts straight, and now I'm paying the price."

"What facts?"

"Afraid I can't say. Where you heading, by the way?"

Stone told him. "I'm visiting some friends," he added.

"I hope they're the ones in high places. You can never have too many of those."

"I'm afraid I don't have *any* of those."

"Neither do I. But hell, it turns out my rookie partner—and I use the term 'partner' very loosely—it turns out she has some of those kinds of friends. In fact, she informed me today that her godfather is none other than Carter Gray."

Stone looked at him. "Who's your partner?"

"Jackie Simpson."

Stone stiffened. "Roger Simpson's daughter?"

"How'd you know that?"

"You mentioned friends in high places, and they don't come much higher than Roger Simpson. He worked at the CIA but that was decades ago."

"I didn't know about that, but I guess it explains his interest in intelligence."

Stone was staring out the window. "How old is the woman?"

"What, Jackie? Mid-thirties."

"And she's just starting out at the Secret Service?"

"She was a cop in Alabama before joining the Service."

"What's she like?"

"Well, she's pretty high on my shit list right now. The lady basically sold me down the river this morning."

"I mean what does she *look* like?"

"Why do you want to know?"

"Just curious," Stone said.

"She's petite, black hair, blue eyes, and has a big-time drawl when she's real pissed. She doesn't back down and says what's on her mind. No shrinking violet."

"I see. Attractive?"

"Why, you thinking about asking her out?" Alex said grinning.

"Old men are always curious about young women," Stone replied with a smile.

Ford shrugged. "She's pretty, if you get past the attitude."

*Mid-thirties,* thought Stone. *Black hair, blue eyes and an attitude.*

"Have you ever met Carter Gray?" Stone asked.

"I did today," Alex said.

"What was your opinion?"

"Pretty damn impressive."

"So is that why you got in trouble? You ran into Gray?"

"Let's just say I thought I'd be real smart and let the two NIC agents on the case run some analysis on the suicide note we found. That would give me an excuse to go there and poke around. Turns out I got sandbagged. I should've seen it coming."

Stone had not been listening to the last part. His attention had been captured by the part about NIC having the suicide note. *Were Milton's fingerprints on it?*

"Uh, were the two agents at NIC helpful?"

"Not particularly. You know, I hate spooks, I really do. I don't give a crap if you call them the National Intelligence Center, the Central Intelligence Agency, or the Defense Intelligence Agency, they wouldn't tell you the truth if their mother's life depended on it."

"No, they wouldn't," Stone said under his breath.

Halfway to his destination, Stone instructed Alex to let him off up ahead.

"I can take you all the way to where you're going, Oliver," he said. "The director gave me the rest of the day off to think about my sins."

"I really need to walk."

"Well, you should get that jaw checked out."

"I will."

As soon as Alex drove off, Stone pulled out his cell phone and called Milton. In one way it was disheartening to learn that the Secret Service agent was off the case, but at least he would not be in danger. Stone could not say the same about the rest of them.

Milton's voice interrupted these musings. "Hello?"

"Milton, where are you?"

"I'm at Chastity's."

"How long have you been there?"

"Since this morning, why?"

"When you left your house, did you notice anyone around?"

"No."

"Don't go back home. I want you to meet me somewhere else." Stone thought quickly. "Union Station. Can you be there in the next half hour or so?"

"I think so."

"I'll be standing by the bookstore. Were you able to run the car tag down?"

"That was no problem. I have his name and address. It's—"

"Tell me in person. And, Milton, I want you to listen very carefully. You need to make sure that no one is following you."

"What did you find out?" Milton asked nervously.

"I'll tell you when I see you. Oh, one more thing. Could you see what you can find on a Jackie Simpson, Senator Simpson's daughter? She's a Secret Service agent."

Stone clicked off and then called both Reuben and Caleb and updated them. After that, he set off for the nearest Metro station and a little while later stood at the entrance to the B. Dalton bookstore that occupied a large chunk of massive Union Station. While browsing through some books, Stone periodically checked the subway exit, where he assumed Milton would be coming out.

When Milton arrived from a different part of the train station, Stone looked at him questioningly.

"Chastity drove me," he explained. "What happened to your face?"

"It's not important. Is Chastity here?"

"No, I told her to go back home."

"Milton, are you absolutely certain you weren't followed?"

"Not with the way Chastity drives."

Stone led him over to a bagel shop located across from the bookstore. They bought coffees and then settled down at a table in the far corner.

Milton took out his cell phone and hit a button.

"Who are you calling?" Stone asked.

"No one. My cell phone has a recorder built in. I just remembered that I have to call Chastity later about something, and I'm leaving myself a reminder. The phone I gave you has the same capability. And it's also a camera." Milton spoke into the recorder and then put his phone away.

"What's the man's name?" Stone asked.

"Tyler Reinke. He lives out near Purcellville. I have the street address."

"I know the area. Did you find out where he works?"

"I checked everywhere I could get into, and I can get into quite a few places. But I didn't find anything on him."

"That might mean he does work at NIC. I don't think even *you* could hack them."

"It's possible."

"Did you find anything on Jackie Simpson?"

"Quite a bit. I printed it out for you." He slid a folder over to Stone.

He opened it and gazed at a laser printer picture of the woman. Alex had been right, thought Stone; the attitude was evident on her features. Her home address was in the file too. It was close to WFO. Stone wondered if she walked to work. He closed the file, put it away in his knapsack and told Milton about NIC having the suicide note and the possibility of his prints being on it.

Milton let out a deep breath. "I knew I shouldn't have touched that paper."

"Would you still be on the NIH database?"

"Probably. And the Secret Service printed me when I sent that stupid letter to Ronald Reagan. I was just so upset with all his budget cuts on mental health."

Stone hunched forward. "I wanted to have a meeting tonight at Caleb's condo to go over things, but now I'm not sure if that's safe."

"So where do we meet, then?"

Just then Stone's cell phone rang. It was Reuben and he was excited. He said, "I met an old buddy of mine for a beer. We fought together in Nam, and we joined Defense Intelligence at the same time. I heard he'd just retired from DIA, so I thought I'd have a drink with him and see if he'd open up a little about things. Well, he told me NIC had pissed everybody off by demanding that all terrorist files be turned over to NIC. Even the CIA's files were purged. Gray knew that if he controlled the flow of information, then he controlled everything else too."

"So all other intelligence agencies have to go to NIC for that information?"

"Yep. And that way NIC knows what everyone else is working on."

"But by law, NIC oversees all that anyway, Reuben."

"Hell, who cares what the law says? Do you really think the CIA's going to be absolutely truthful about what it's doing, Oliver?"

"No," Stone admitted. "Telling the truth would be counterintuitive for it as well as having no historical basis. Spies always lie."

"Is the meeting tonight still at Caleb's?" Reuben asked.

"I'm not sure that Caleb's . . ." Stone's voice trailed off. "Caleb?" he said slowly.

"Oliver?" Reuben said. "Are you still there?"

"Oliver? Are you all right?" Milton asked in a worried tone.

Stone spoke quickly. "Reuben, where are you?"

"At the disgusting shack I call my castle. Why?"

"Can you pick me up at Union Station and take me to my storage place?"

"Sure, but you didn't answer me. Is the meeting still at Caleb's?"

"No, I think instead . . ." Stone looked around. "We'll meet here at Union Station."

"Union Station," Reuben repeated. "That's not exactly private, Oliver."

"I didn't say we were *holding* our meeting here."

"You're not making much sense," Reuben said grumpily.

"I'll explain it all later. Just get here as quickly as you can. I'll be waiting out front." Stone clicked off and looked at Milton.

Milton said, "What are you going to your other place for?"

"There's something I need from there. Something that might finally make sense out of all this."

# 35

"No one seems to be home," Tyler Reinke said as he watched the front of Milton's home from the car outside. He glanced at a file on Milton Farb. "Threatening to poison President Reagan's jelly beans sort of tanks your career opportunities," Reinke added wryly. "That may be why they didn't come forward. Because of his record."

Peters said, "What I want to know is, what was he doing on Roosevelt Island in the middle of the night?"

"I say we wait until later and then go exploring. If he's in hiding, chances are he left something behind at his house to show us where he is."

"In the meantime I think we should take another trip to Georgetown. Somebody might have seen something that night that could be helpful," Peters said.

"And it might not hurt to take another look at the boat while we're there," Reinke added.

Captain Jack adjusted his hat and rubbed a finger against the yellow rose sticking out of his lapel as he surveyed the inside of his new property. The garage was large with three expansive work bays. However, the place was empty now except for one vehicle that was receiving the complete attention of his "mechanics." Ahmed, the Iranian, wiped his brow as he came up out of the oil pit cut into the floor of the garage.

"How's it coming?" Captain Jack asked.

"We're on schedule. Have you talked to the woman?"

"That piece is in place and ready," Captain Jack said. "And don't ask again, Ahmed," he added, looking stonily at the man. The Iranian nodded curtly and swung himself back down into the pit. Soon the sounds of power wrenches filled the space, and Captain Jack stepped out into the sunshine.

Ahmed waited a few more minutes, and then he reemerged from the pit, walked quickly to the worktable and slid out a long-bladed knife from an oily cloth that he'd hidden under some tools. He placed the knife under a piece of carpeting in the back of the vehicle and then popped the carpet back into place.

Outside, Captain Jack climbed into his Audi and drove to the apartment across from Mercy Hospital. One of the Afghans let him in.

"Are the weapons here?" Captain Jack asked.

"Carried them up piece by piece in paper grocery bags like you said to."

"Show me."

The man led him over to the large-screen TV set up in one corner of the room. Together they moved the TV out of the way, and the Afghan used a screwdriver to pry up the carpet, exposing the padding and subfloor. Here the subfloor had been cut away and replaced with plywood. Under the plywood Captain Jack could see that short lengths of rope had been attached to the floor joists in six-inch intervals. Lying on top of the ropes were two assembled sniper rifles with high-powered scopes.

"I've heard of the M-50s but I've never used one," Captain Jack said.

"It's got digital optics so no visible signature; it chambers the twenty-one-millimeter cartridge with environmental sensors built in, together with multithermal detection." The Afghan knelt down and pointed to one part of the rifle. "It's also got a neural feedback system that cancels muscle twitch."

"I never needed that to do the job," Captain Jack said matter-of-factly.

"And it's coated with advanced Camoflex so it blends in with its surroundings with a push of this button. Its barrel is nanotechnology-refined and can place a round at less than .00001 minute of angle at one thousand meters. Overkill for this job, but so what. We've also got a couple of MP-5s with about two thousand rounds. "

Early in his career Captain Jack had made the inexcusable error of inputting the barometric pressure *after* the adjustment for altitude had been made, the number typically given by weather forecasters. However, shooters needed the actual barometric pressure without regard to altitude adjustment. It had been a huge mistake because cold air was denser than warm, and the speed of sound was also lower in cold air, which was critical when one was chambering supersonic ammo. That mistake had caused his bullet to wound instead of kill, not an acceptable result when one was attempting to assassinate a head of state.

"Where have you hidden the ordnance?" he asked.

The Afghan went around to the back of the big-screen TV and unscrewed the rear panel. Neatly stacked inside were dozens of fully loaded MP-5 mags and boxes of M-50 rounds. "As you can see, we don't watch much TV," the Afghan said unnecessarily.

"How about the *other* two rifles and ordnance you'll be using? They're the most important of all."

"They're under the other floorboards. They're ready to go. We've practiced over fifty hours with them. Don't worry, we won't miss."

"The weather looks good for game day, but it can change quickly around here."

The Afghan shrugged. "It's not that difficult a shot at this distance. I've easily hit the target at three times this range at night *with* people shooting back."

Captain Jack knew this was not mere bravado on his part, which was one of the reasons the man was here in the first place.

"But you've never done it quite *this* way before," he said. "The range and flight path are a little different."

"Believe me, I know."

Captain Jack went into the bathroom and looked at his disguise in the mirror. He took off the hat and examined his thick hair shot through with gray and a mustache and short beard of the same coloring. He took off his tinted glasses, and blue eyes looked back at him. A small scar rested on the side of his nose, which was long and thick. In reality the beard and hair were fake. He was actually bald and clean-shaven with brown eyes and no scar, although his nose *was* long, but thin.

He put the hat and glasses back on. He'd disappeared many times in his life, sometimes while in the employ of others, including the government of the United States. Other times he'd been on his own, his shooting skill and nerve purchased by the highest bidder. But as he'd told Hemingway, his next disappearing act would be his last.

He drove out of town to the ceremonial grounds, barely ten minutes from downtown, and yet a lot could happen in ten minutes.

Captain Jack didn't stop at the grounds but instead drove past them slowly, eyeing certain landmarks he'd long since committed to memory. The ceremonial grounds were framed by white rail farm fencing with only one vehicle entry point and numerous pedestrian entrances. Six-foot-high brick columns framed the car entrance, and the motorcade would have to pass through there going in and out. The Beast would find it a tight squeeze.

He eyeballed the surrounding tree lines, guessing at the placement of the American countersnipers that would be posted along this perimeter. How many would there be? A dozen? Two dozen? It was hard to tell these days, even with the best intelligence. They would be wrapped in their camouflage suits, blending in with their surroundings so perfectly you would step on them before you ever saw them. Yes, his men would most certainly die on these hallowed grounds. At least it would be quick and painless. Supersonic long-range ordnance, particularly to the head, killed you faster than your brain could react. The *fedayeen's* death, however, would not be nearly as painless.

Captain Jack envisioned the motorcade coming in and the president exiting the Beast. He would wave, shake hands, pat some backs, give some hugs and then be escorted to the bullet- and bombproof podium as "Hail to the Chief" was played.

The reason the song was used when a U.S. president entered a room originated with President James Polk's wife, who was furious that her diminutive, homely husband was often totally ignored when making an entrance. Thus, Sarah Polk ordered that the song be played whenever her husband came into a room. All presidents since had followed this imperious woman's lead.

However, the origin of the song itself was even more amusing, at least to Captain Jack's thinking. Set to the words of Sir Walter Scott's epic poem *The Lady of the Lake*, it described the demise of a Scottish chieftain who was betrayed and then put to death by his archenemy, King James V. Ironically enough, the song that was used to herald the coming of the president of the United States actually chronicled the assassination of a head of state. In the last part of Canto Five, the poem summed up, in Captain Jack's opinion, a query that all would-be politicians should give serious thought to: "*O who would wish to be thy king?*"

"Not me," he muttered to himself. "Not me."

The ex–National Guardsman settled himself in the chair and looked at his new hand while the two men watched him carefully.

"Now that we've added the pouch, let's begin practicing the movements," the engineer said.

The American moved his hand and wrist as he had been shown, but nothing happened.

"It takes practice. Soon you will be an expert."

Two hours later they had made considerable progress. Taking a break, the men sat and talked. "So you were a truck driver?" the chemist asked.

The former soldier nodded, holding up his hook and fake hand. "Not an occupation you can really do with these because I also had to help unload the cargo."

"How long were you in Iraq before it happened?"

"Eighteen months. I only had four more months to pull, at least I thought. Then we got orders extending our tour another twenty-two months. Four years! Before all this happened I was married with a wife and family and holding my own in Detroit. The next thing I know, I'm scrambling to get the money to buy my own body armor and GPS because Uncle Sam didn't have the cash. Then a land mine outside of Mosul takes *both* my hands and a chunk of my chest. Four months in Walter Reed Hospital, and I get back home to find my wife's divorcing me, my job's long gone and I'm basically homeless." He paused and shook his head. "I did my tour during Persian Gulf One and sucked in all the shit Saddam was chucking at us. After my discharge from the army I joined the National Guard so I could at least have some income until I got back on my feet. I did my Guard duty and then resigned and started driving trucks. Then after all those years the army knocks on my door and tells me my Guard resignation was never 'officially' accepted. I told them not so politely to go to hell.

But they literally hauled me kicking and screaming away. Then a year and a half later boom, there go my hands and my life. My own country did that to me!"

"Now it's your turn to repay them," the engineer said.

"Yes. It is," the very ex–National Guardsman agreed as he flexed his hand.

Adnan al-Rimi strode through the hallways of Mercy Hospital, his observant gaze methodically taking in all details of his surroundings. A minute later he returned to the hospital's front entrance just as an elderly patient was wheeled in, a portable IV hooked to her arm.

Adnan stepped outside and breathed in the warm air. To the left of the hospital's front steps was a ramp for gurneys and wheelchair-bound patients. Al-Rimi walked down the steps to the sidewalk that ran in front of the hospital. There were fourteen steps. He turned and walked back up them, silently counting time as he did so. Seven seconds at a normal pace, perhaps half that if someone was running.

He went back inside the hospital, his hand sliding down to his sidearm. It was an old .38 revolver, a piece of American crap, as far as he was concerned. Yet that was the only weapon the security firm he worked for had to offer. It didn't really matter, he knew, but still, weapons were of paramount importance to Adnan. He had required them virtually his whole life simply to survive.

He walked back down to the nurse's station and stopped at the fourth tile over from the exact center of the station. Then he turned around and walked back toward the front entrance. Anyone watching him would just assume he was making his rounds. He counted off his paces in his head, nodding to a pair of nurses who walked by as he did so. Near the front entrance he turned right, counted his steps down this hallway, turned, pushed open the door to the exit stairs, counted his steps down two flights and found himself in the basement corridor on the west side of the hospital building. This corridor ran into another that carried him north and then emptied out into the rear exit area. A wide asphalt drive was located here that sloped upward to the main road running behind the hospital. Because of the grade and poor drainage, it often flooded here after even a moderate rain, which was another reason why everyone preferred entering through the front.

As he stood there, Adnan visualized several times a particular maneuver in his head. Finished, he went over to a pair of double doors,
unlocked them and stepped inside, closing the doors behind him. He
was now in the hospital's power room, which also housed the backup
generator. He'd been coached on the basics of this room by the security firm, in case there was an emergency. He'd supplemented that
coaching by reading the manuals for every piece of equipment in the
room. There was only one that he was really interested in. It sat on a
wall across from the generator. He opened the box with another key
on his chain and studied the controls inside. It wouldn't be difficult to
rig it, he decided.

He locked up the power room and went back inside the hospital to
continue his rounds. He would do this every day, until *the* day came.

A little while later Adnan's shift ended, and he changed out of his
uniform in the hospital's locker room and rode his bicycle to his apartment about two miles away. He prepared a meal of flat bread, dates,
fava beans, olives and a piece of *halal* meat that he cooked on the
stovetop in his tiny kitchen.

Adnan's family had raised livestock and grown dates in Saudi Arabia, no small feat in a country with only 1 percent of its land arable,
but they had suffered great hardship. After his father's death the al-
Rimis fled to Iraq, where they grew wheat and raised goats. Adnan, as
the eldest son, became the family's patriarch. He began butchering
meat in accordance with Islamic law so it was *halal*, and the additional
monies that this endeavor provided had been very welcome.

Adnan sat in his apartment staring out the window and cradling a
cup of tea, his mind drifting back to that time. Goats, lambs, chickens
and cattle had met their end at the point of his very sharp knife. These
animals had to be slaughtered from their necks while Adnan spoke
God's name. Adnan never struck the spinal cord while doing his
butchering, for two reasons: It was less painful to the animal, and it allowed convulsive motions to remain, which hastened the drainage of
blood, as required by Islamic law. Under that law no animal could witness the death of another, and the animals had to be well fed and
rested. It was a far cry from the mass killings of the "stun and stick"
method used by American slaughterhouses. Yes, the Americans were
the best at killing lots of things quickly, Adnan thought.

As he sipped his tea, Adnan reflected still more on his past. He fought in the decade-long Iran-Iraq war where Muslim slaughtered Muslim by the thousands in some of the fiercest hand-to-hand fighting history had ever seen. After that conflict was over, Adnan's life returned to normal. He married, raised a family and did his best to avoid giving the megalomaniac Saddam Hussein or his minions cause to harm him or his family.

Then 9/11 happened, Afghanistan was invaded and the Taliban quickly fell. Personally, Adnan had no problem with any of that. America had been attacked and it had struck back. Adnan, like most Iraqis, did not support the Taliban. Life went on in Iraq. And even with the international embargo on his country Adnan was able to earn a modest living. And then, the U.S. declared war on Iraq. Like all his countrymen, Adnan waited with dread for the bombs and missiles to start falling. He sent his family away to safety, but he remained behind because it was his adopted country and was about to be attacked by another nation.

When the American planes came, Adnan watched in silent horror as Baghdad became one continuous fireball. The Americans called it collateral damage, but to Adnan these were men, women and children blown apart in their homes. And then the American tanks and troops came. There had never been any doubt in Adnan's mind as to the outcome. The Americans were simply too powerful. They could kill you from a thousand miles away with their weapons. All Adnan had ever had to fight with was his gun, his knife and his bare hands. And it was said that the U.S. had missiles that could take off from America and vaporize the entire Middle East minutes later. This terrified Adnan. There was no way to beat such a devil.

Still, after Hussein had been toppled, there was hope. Yet that hope quickly turned to despair as violence and death took hold and civil society simply disappeared. And when the American presence truly became an "occupation," Adnan felt his duty was clear. So he fought against them, killing his fellow citizens in the process, an act that sickened him but one that he somehow rationalized away. He had killed Iranians during the war between the two countries. He had killed Arabs and Americans in Iraq. He had slaughtered animals using his knife. It seemed to Adnan that his whole life had been consumed with taking the lives of others.

And now his own life was the only one left. His wife and children were dead. His parents, brothers and sisters were all gone too. It was only Adnan still here on earth while his family resided in paradise.

And here he was in the United States in the palm of his enemy. This would be his last stand, his final act of a life spent attacking and being attacked. Adnan was tired; he'd lived eighty years in only half that time. His body and mind could not endure much more.

He finished his tea but continued to look out the window as a group of children ran around the playground of the apartment complex. There were black children and white children and brown children playing together. At that age, differences in color and culture meant nothing to them. Yet, unfortunately, that would change when they became adults, Adnan knew. It always did.

# 36

"YOU WANTED TO SEE ME, SIR?" Tom Hemingway asked as he walked into Carter Gray's office. This space was rumored to be the only square inch of the NIC facility that was not under electronic surveillance.

Sitting behind his desk, Gray motioned Hemingway in. "Shut the door, Tom."

For a half an hour the two men discussed various geopolitical events coming up, the state of several world crises and Hemingway's take on some key developments in ongoing intelligence operations in the Middle and Far East. Then the conversation turned to other matters.

"The Secret Service agents who were out here today?" Gray said.

"I fully cooperated with them, sir, at least NIC's version of full cooperation. I hope I did the right thing extricating you like that."

"You did. The agents they were meeting with initially that I spoke with?"

"Warren Peters and Tyler Reinke. Both good men. They were assigned to represent NIC's interests during the investigation. I believe they were processing some evidence found at the scene for the Secret Service."

"I spoke to the president about Ford and Simpson. I don't think they'll be back."

"I understand that Simpson is your goddaughter?"

"Yes. Jackie is Roger Simpson's only child. I was honored when he asked me to be Jackie's godfather, although I'm not sure if I've been a good one."

"She looks like she's done all right for herself."

"I love her like a daughter." Gray looked a bit embarrassed by his words and quickly cleared his throat. "An internal audit is being conducted over Patrick Johnson's death. The FBI will be involved."

Hemingway nodded. "I think it's a good move. I can't believe there's anything to it, but we have to cover the bases."

Gray eyed him closely. "And why don't you think there's anything to it, Tom?"

"A house and cars he couldn't afford? Drugs found in the house? Seems straightforward. It's not the first time it's happened."

"It's the first time it's happened *here*," Gray said. "Did you know Johnson well?"

"As well as I knew any of the data supervisors. By all accounts he was excellent at his job."

"How did he strike you?"

Hemingway thought about this. "From my limited contact he was a man whose ambitions outstripped his opportunities."

"A keen insight for someone you admittedly didn't know all that well."

"That assessment could apply to half the people here. Quite frankly, they want to be you. But they never will and it bothers them."

Gray sat back in his chair. "I've taken a good look at Johnson's file. There was nothing in there to indicate that he would be turned. Do you agree?"

Hemingway nodded.

"But then again, the same could be said of virtually all the people who have been turned against this country. It has more to do with psychology than bank accounts."

"There are others here who knew Johnson better than I did."

"I've spoken with them," Gray said. "I've also spoken with his fiancée. She believes the drug business is absolute garbage."

"Well, it's not surprising that she'd defend him."

"Tom, I recall that the centralization of all intelligence databases was completed four months ago. Is that correct?"

"Yes, with the proviso that we only recently completed integration of the Transportation Safety Administration's files from their Screening, Coordination and Operations Office. That was due to some legal hang-ups with Homeland Security, among others."

"Any more significant glitches in the system?"

"No. And as I'm sure you also recall, the TSA piece was fairly substantial. It had the Secure Flight, Registered Traveler and the US VISIT programs among others. The US VISIT program was particularly sensitive for us because it contained detailed backgrounds, digital fingerprints and photos of foreign travelers. However, the ACLU had a field day with that one, screaming profiling and big brother to every court that would entertain them. But it belonged here and we eventually got it. Before, this data was scattered over a dozen departments with no workable integration, incredible overlap and duplication, with the result that much of it was worthless."

"Well, that failure was one of the chief reasons 9/11 happened," Gray said.

"Speaking of, I understand the president asked you to attend the memorial event in New York tomorrow."

"The office grapevine; it's better than any spy network devised. Yes, he did and yes, I declined. As always, I prefer to hold a very private ceremony honoring those who lost their lives that day."

"I also heard that you're going up to Brennan, Pennsylvania."

Gray nodded, opened his desk drawer and pulled out a book.

"How well up are you on your Bible, Tom?"

Hemingway was accustomed to swift changes in direction with Gray. "I've read the King James Version. Along with the Qur'an, the Talmud and the Book of Mormon."

"Good. What's the one similarity you find in all of them?"

"Violence," he answered promptly. "People talk about the Qur'an inciting violence. They have nothing on the Christians. If I recall correctly, Deuteronomy was particularly full of fire and brimstone. Thou shalt smite this and that dead."

"At least it's consistent. And yet the Qur'an instructs its followers not to take their own lives, which does not reconcile with the concept of a suicide bomber. Indeed, it doesn't promise paradise, but rather warns of condemnation in hell for taking one's own life."

"The Qur'an says this when the death is *outside* the cause of Allah; it doesn't apply to those who die *for* the cause. And there are enough references to killing the unbelievers in the Qur'an, and also in writings and local laws and customs subsequent to the Qur'an that it's possible to justify that killing oneself and unbelievers at the same time is authorized. And for those who die in the cause, it says they don't really die, nor should their loved ones grieve for them. That's a distinction between Islam and Christianity."

"Correct. But there's also another great similarity between the two religions."

"What's that, sir?"

Gray put away his Bible. "The *resurrection* of the *dead*."

# CHAPTER

# 37

THE SPACIOUS HOUSE THAT Captain Jack had rented in the suburbs of Brennan was set far off the main road with no other residences nearby. It also had a large home theater, a facility he was taking advantage of right now.

Captain Jack placed the DVD that Hemingway had given him in the player but did not turn it on yet, as the men who'd come here today took their seats. None of them were eating popcorn; no refreshments at all had been passed around. It was not that sort of movie night.

Captain Jack took a minute to survey his crew. They were good, capable men. They had been hardened by a life that had not included many moments of happiness or things that others took for granted, such as food, clean water, a bed and a life free from constant persecution and threat of violent death. Assembled here were his bomb makers and engineers, his shooters, his snipers, his *fedayeen*, his mechanics, his inside people and his wheelmen. Djamila was not here, however. Her mission was completely separate. And quite frankly, Captain Jack didn't know how the males would react to a woman being such a critical part of the operation. Only a few of his company knew of her involvement, and the American knew it was best to keep it that way.

The men's appearances had all changed. Hair cut or grown longer. Beards shaved off. Weight gained or lost. They all wore Western-style clothes. Some sported glasses, others had dyed their hair. While none of their "real" images remained on the NIC database, the operation was too important to become slack with the small but important details. Altered NIC photos notwithstanding, they might still be recognized by American intelligence operatives who'd seen them in the flesh years ago.

He walked to the front of the room and addressed them all by name as a sign of respect and camaraderie. He asked for progress reports, and each man reported back succinctly and knowledgeably.

Captain Jack, Tom Hemingway and a third person had handpicked these men from a pool provided to them by this third party, a man they both trusted. They had not chosen the most violent and zealous Muslims among the group. Ironically, restraint was the quality they'd required above all.

The 9/11 hijackers had come from varied backgrounds. Fourteen of the fifteen hijackers who accompanied the four "pilots" on the jets were from Saudi Arabia. They were from middle-class families that were not particularly active either politically or in the Muslim faith. And yet these young men left their good homes and families, trained with Al Qaeda, became steeped in the practice of radical Islam and jihad and carried out their orders with military precision, no doubt with the hope of riding that flight path to paradise. The 9/11 hijackers had not had to make any decisions for themselves; all had been planned out. The situation developing in Brennan was far different. Each man would have a great deal of input in what would happen.

Thus, Hemingway and Captain Jack had sought out older, reasonably educated men who had once led normal lives. These men had not trained with Al Qaeda. They had not given their lives over to jihad for reasons typically associated with that mind-frame. And while several had had run-ins with American and European law enforcement, and their fingerprints and photos had been taken, necessitating the cover-up at NIC, none were at the level where their photos were plastered in newspapers everywhere. The youngest of them was thirty, the oldest fifty-two, and the average age was forty-one. These men, while they had experience with killing, were not eager in taking someone's life. Every one of them had lost at least three immediate family members in wars and other conflicts over the years. Indeed, a half dozen had lost their entire families to such violence. They had volunteered for this mission for reasons other than those typically assumed to be at the core of the Middle Eastern terrorist mind. Indeed, all of these men considered themselves soldiers, not terrorists. That was the composition of the "holy warrior" Tom Hemingway had insisted on.

"Remember this," Captain Jack told his men. "While we sit here planning this operation, in another room somewhere, there will be far more people planning how to stop us. They are excellent at what they do, so we have to be better than excellent. We have to be perfect." He paused, making eye contact with each of them. "One mistake along the chain brings the whole thing crashing down. This is understood?"

All the men nodded in silent agreement.

Captain Jack went over the ceremony details again. The army of Secret Service and local police would have voluminous notebooks containing all the prep work for the president's visit. Captain Jack and his team could afford no such luxury. One page lost could have catastrophic results. Thus, all details had to be memorized. To be absolutely clear, Captain Jack changed from Arabic to English and back again, depending on the subtlety of what he was trying to communicate.

"Before the president ever sets foot here, a Secret Service advance team will arrive in Brennan to begin their planning for the event along with the most elaborate and secure motorcade in the world. Typically, the motorcade consists of twenty-seven vehicles including local police escorts, a 'Road Runner' communications van, a press vehicle, VIP van, an ambulance, a SWAT vehicle carrying a counterassault team inside, and two 'Beasts.' One will carry the president and in the other, Secret Service agents. All roads leading from the airport to the dedication grounds in Brennan will be thoroughly checked and, on the day of the visit, sealed off.

"At the dedication grounds the president will enter from the right of the stage and exit in the same direction. When he's speaking, he will be behind a bulletproof and bombproof glass podium known as the Blue Goose. Countersnipers will be positioned all along the perimeter tree line. When the president moves, he will be surrounded at all times by a wall of agents, hip and flank. Wherever the man is, is known as the kill zone, and the Secret Service takes that concept very, very seriously. The crowd will be very large, thus magnetometers will be set up at all pedestrian entrance points to the dedication grounds. We have the exact same magnetometers that will be used by the Secret Service and have tested them on the highest detection level." He paused and added, "Shooters, you can pass through these points without fear.

"You must keep in mind that the Service will key on personal demeanors—namely, persons not fitting in, not participating in the ceremony, and those not relating to others in the crowd. Because you are Middle Eastern, they will give you extra scrutiny. They have an entire database on assassins that takes profiling down to the most insignificant detail. As you know, your photos are no longer on file with the Americans, and your appearances have been greatly altered, so risk of identification is very low. But that is no reason to be careless. Thus, your dress and behavior at the ceremony will be dictated to you, and you will adhere to every single detail, without exception. When you enter those grounds, you will look like doctors, lawyers, teachers, tradesmen, shopkeepers, respectable citizens in your adopted country." Captain Jack paused and eyed each man.

"The video I'm about to show you will illustrate quite vividly how seriously the Secret Service takes its mission."

He hit a button on the remote he was holding, and the screen jumped to life. Tom Hemingway had provided his colleague with a publicly available video on the Secret Service and their general protection techniques, rare footage of assassination attempts and, rarer still, a video of Secret Service agents training at their Beltsville, Maryland, facility. Beltsville was where agents learned to do J-turns with their cars, nail targets with their guns, and also practiced protection techniques over and over until fragile thought was taken out of the process and resolute muscle memory took its place.

The men watched mesmerized as footage was shown of attempts on the lives of Gerald Ford and Ronald Reagan. The assassination of John Kennedy was not included on the DVD. Presidents no longer rode around in open cars. And every mistake that had been made in Dallas that day by the Secret Service and overzealous politicians had been long since corrected.

"You see," Captain Jack commented, "that the agent's actions are the same in each instance. The president is completely shielded and almost bodily carried away from the scene with the utmost speed. In Reagan's case he's shoved into the presidential limo and is gone within seconds. On 9/11 when it seemed a plane was heading for the White House, the Secret Service evacuated the vice president from his office there; it is said his feet never touched the ground until he was safely away. Speed. Keep that in mind. It is built into their training and thus their psyches. Acting in practiced routines without wasting time thinking. Nothing can override that impulse. And the most important impulse they have is to save the president's life. They will sacrifice anything for that, including their own lives. We can count on that with certainty. We cannot possibly match them in firepower, manpower, training or technology. But we *can* understand the psychology of who and what they are and use it to our full advantage. Indeed, other than the element of surprise, that is the *only* advantage we have. And it will be enough if we are *perfect* on that day."

He went through this part of the video again, breaking it down like game film, frame by frame, as his men committed all of this to memory. Questions were numerous, which the American always took as a good sign.

Next up on the screen was a diagram of the ceremonial grounds. Captain Jack, using a laser pointer, went grid by grid, pointing out general strategic items, entry and exit points and the positions of the Beast and other pertinent vehicles in the motorcade. "Note that the presidential limo is always parked at a spot with a completely unobstructed exit point. That is critical to our plans."

He then assigned numbers to each of his men who would be on the ceremonial grounds that day and pointed out corresponding numbers on the screen that indicated each man's position there. Next he pointed out the ambulance. "Above all, this vehicle must be disabled. All you men who are responsible for this, you must ensure that it is done."

The next frame showed a slender white-haired man wearing glasses. Captain Jack said, "The president travels with his personal physician, this man here, Dr. Edward Bellamy. He will be on the podium with the president. He must be taken out first. He must be, without fail."

The next frame showed a simulation of the rope line.

Captain Jack put his finger on the screen, using it to trace the rope very slowly and carefully, as though he were a surgeon making a precise incision into flesh. "This is the Secret Service's worst nightmare. If it were up to them, they would never allow it, but it's the lifeblood of a politician to shake hands and kiss babies," Captain Jack explained. "It's here, on the rope line, where he is most vulnerable. Yet it's also a double-edged sword, because it is precisely here where the bodyguards are at their absolute highest alert."

The next image on the screen was that of the ex–National Guardsman who had been given a new hand by Captain Jack's men. He was in full-dress uniform. It was a slightly older photo and thus showed him with two hooks where his hands should have been.

Captain Jack said, "We will have no electronic communications capability at the dedication grounds because the Service will crisscross the area with jammers and interceptors. Thus, everything will be done the old-fashioned way, through eyes and ears." He pointed to the man on the screen. "This is the person who you will key off. He will be wearing this exact uniform. But there will be others there with uniforms on, so you must not make a mistake. Each of you will receive a copy of this DVD and a portable DVD player. You must study it for four hours each day so that you can memorize his every feature and every other detail I am showing you tonight. However, this man you must spot early and never lose sight of where he is. The organizers of the event have arranged that all disabled American soldiers will be up front on the rope line as a way to honor them. It is very good of the town fathers to do this. And it certainly aids our plan."

He looked at the engineer and chemist in the group who'd supplied the ex–National Guardsman with his new hand. "It has been confirmed that the desired effect will take less than two minutes." The men nodded and Captain Jack continued. "When that happens, the pattern becomes immediately this." He snapped his fingers as he talked. "Shooter sequence 1. Then fedayeen A and B. Then shooter sequence 2, followed by fedayeen C and D. Then shooter sequence 3. Then the final *fida'ya*. And then shooter sequence 4. As you know, each sequence has precise targets. If one target is not hit during its sequence, the next sequence must add that to its responsibilities. Every target must be struck, no exceptions. All agents will be wearing the latest-generation body armor, as will most of the police, so place your shots accordingly. Is this understood?"

He stopped and scrutinized each of them again, something he planned to do constantly tonight. One by one they nodded at him. He repeated the attack sequence again and again and then had each man repeat it to him exactly, also confirming what sequence they were in.

"Because of the limited range of your weapons, you'll see on the position grid that each shooter is located no more than two rows back from the rope line, and in most cases only one row back. You will arrive at the event in assigned shifts and early enough to make your way to those spots."

Captain Jack stopped talking and looked at his men for a long minute. What he was about to say next was, in many ways, the heart of the matter. "Each of you must realize that as soon as you fire your weapon, you almost certainly will be killed by the countersnipers. The proximity of the crowd will afford you some protection but probably not enough. Our information is that the countersnipers will be using the standard Remington 700 series bolt-action sniper rifle with .308 rounds. The American sharpshooters you will be facing can place a shot within a ten-inch circle at over a thousand yards."

There was a murmur of appreciation around the room at the skill of their opponents. It was an interesting reaction in the face of what he was telling them. He couldn't allow them to choose between life and death when the time came. Captain Jack simply wanted them to act, just as the Secret Service trained their people. And each man had to understand that the forfeit of his life was the price to be expected for being a part of this historic day for Islam.

"As you know, the bullets that hit you will instantly carry you to paradise. You will have more than earned such a reward." He said this part to them in Arabic.

Captain Jack now looked at each of the fedayeen. He had given them that title as one of honor. The Arabic term was *fida'i* and originally meant "adventurer." Now it usually referred to Arab guerrilla fighters or to "men of sacrifice." It was likely that all of Captain Jack's men on the ceremonial grounds would perish, and thus they should have all been called by that title. However, some of Captain Jack's men would unquestionably die. And thus their colleagues had not begrudged them being referred to as the fedayeen during the course of this mission.

After the briefing Captain Jack led them downstairs to a room that had been soundproofed by its former owner and used as a recording studio. That was another reason Captain Jack had leased the house, although the weapons they would be using wouldn't be making that much noise. Here a firing range had been set up, and the men were given their guns and ordnance. For the next two hours they practiced on their targets, with Captain Jack throwing in unexpected disruptions via sound and video equipment, because it would be complete chaos when the real firing started.

Although Adnan al-Rimi would not be at the dedication grounds, he'd attended this meeting because he was a man who insisted on knowing everything that had to do with a mission. He had fought side by side with Captain Jack in the Middle East, and the American trusted Adnan as well as he trusted anyone.

Adnan was standing behind the Iranian named Ahmed, who lived in the apartment with the two Afghans, across from Mercy Hospital, and was working on the vehicle at the garage. Ahmed wouldn't be at the dedication grounds either but, like Adnan, he had insisted on attending the meeting tonight. Ahmed kept muttering to himself. Something he said caught Adnan's attention but the Iraqi didn't show surprise. He spoke to Adnan in Arabic.

"My language is Farsi," Ahmed answered. "If you wish to speak to me, do it in Farsi, Adnan."

Adnan didn't answer him. He didn't like the young man commanding him to speak "his" language. Iranians, Adnan had long ago concluded, were a very different breed of Muslims. He moved away from the younger man. However, his gaze continually returned to him, and his ear to the Iranian's angry words.

A half hour after the last of his men had left, Captain Jack drove to downtown Pittsburgh. The man he was meeting was waiting for him in the lobby of the city's priciest hotel. The gentleman looked a little jet-lagged after the long flight. They rode the elevator to a suite overlooking the city skyline.

Though the man was fluent in English, he opened the conversation in his native Korean. Captain Jack answered him, in Korean.

As Captain Jack chatted with his North Korean colleague, he thought of a quote from a man he much admired. "Know your enemy and know yourself; in a hundred battles you will never be in peril." The Chinese general Sun Tzu had written those words in a book titled *The Art of War*. Though centuries old, the advice still held true today.

# CHAPTER

# 38

Sᴛᴏɴᴇ ᴀɴᴅ Mɪʟᴛᴏɴ ʜᴀᴅ ᴛᴏ look twice as the motorcycle pulled to a stop in front of them at Union Station. Reuben lifted up his goggles and rubbed his bloodshot eyes.

"Reuben, what happened to your pickup truck?" an amazed Stone asked.

"Found this baby in a junkyard, if you can believe it. Spent the last year fixing it up."

"What is it?" Stone asked.

"It's a 1928 Indian Chief motorcycle with sidecar," Milton answered promptly.

"How the hell did you know that?" Reuben said, glaring at him.

"I read about it in an article six and a half years ago in *Antique Motorcycle Magazine* while I was waiting at the dentist. I was there for a crown prep."

"A crown prep?" Reuben asked.

"Yes, it involves isolation with rubber sheeting and drilling to shave off the enamel, which leaves a post of dentin approximately two millimeters in diameter, but without exposing the nerve. The permanent crown is made of porcelain. It's quite nice. See?" He opened his mouth and showed them.

Reuben said impatiently, "Thank you for the bloody dental lesson, *Dr*. Farb."

"Oh, there's hardly any blood, Reuben," replied Milton, who'd entirely missed the sarcasm in his friend's remark.

Reuben sighed and then proudly ran his gaze over the pin-striped candy-apple-red motorcycle with attached sidecar. "A thousand cc power plant, rebuilt transmission and magneto. The sidecar's not authentic; it's a fiberglass replica, but it doesn't rust and it's a lot lighter. I got most of the parts off eBay, and a friend of mine had some extra cowhide leather that I used to reupholster the sidecar seat. And it's a left-mount sidecar, which is pretty damn rare. One in this condition would sell for north of twenty grand, and I've only got about a tenth of that in it. Not that I'm thinking about selling, mind you, but you never know."

He held out a black crash helmet to Stone that had goggles attached.

"Where exactly do I ride?" Stone asked.

"In the sidecar, of course. What the hell do you think it's for? A damn flowerpot?"

Stone put on the helmet and adjusted the goggles, then opened the small door, stepped into the sidecar and sat down. It was a very cramped space for the tall man.

Reuben said, "Okay, let's go."

"Wait a minute!" Stone exclaimed. "Is there anything I should know about the motorcycle?"

"Yeah, if the wheel on the sidecar goes off the ground, you can start praying."

Reuben hit the kick-starter and the motor caught. He revved it a couple of times, waved good-bye to Milton, and they sailed away from Union Station.

Reuben steered the motorcycle west on Constitution Avenue. They cut past the Vietnam Veterans Memorial, where war veteran Reuben gave a respectful salute to the wall, looped around the Lincoln Memorial and passed over Memorial Bridge, which carried them into Virginia. From there they headed south on the George Washington Parkway, which was referred to locally as the GW Parkway. As they raced along, they drew curious stares from people in vehicles they passed.

Stone found that if he angled his legs just so, he could nearly stretch them fully out. He sat back and gazed over at the Potomac River on his left, where a powerboat had just passed two crew teams racing each other. The sun was warming, the breeze inviting and refreshing, and for a few moments Stone allowed his mind a respite from the many dangers that lay ahead for the Camel Club.

Reuben pointed to a road sign and shouted over the whine of the engine. "Remember for years that sign read 'Lady Bird Johnson *Memorial* Park'?"

"Yes. Until someone informed them she wasn't dead," Stone called back. "And named it after LBJ, who *is*."

"I love the efficiency of our government," Reuben cried. "Only took them about a decade or so to get it right. It's a good thing I don't pay taxes, or I'd be really ticked off."

They both watched as a jet lifted off the runway at Reagan National Airport heading north and then did a long bank and eventually turned in the southerly direction they were traveling. A few minutes later they entered the official city limits of Old Town Alexandria, one of the most historic places in the country. It boasted not one, but two boyhood homes of Confederate general Robert E. Lee, as well as Christ Church, where the posterior of none other than George Washington had graced the pews. The town was chock-full of wealth, ancient but beautifully restored homes, rumpled cobblestone streets, wonderful shopping and eclectic restaurants, a vibrant outdoor life and an inviting waterfront area. It also was home to the federal bankruptcy court.

As they passed the court, Reuben said, "Damn place. Been through there twice."

"Caleb knows people who can help you with your money. And I'm sure Chastity could provide valuable services to you too."

"I'm certain sweet Chastity could service my needs, but then Milton would be really mad at me," Reuben called out with a roguish wink. "And I don't need help with the money I *have*, Oliver, I just need help with getting *more* of it."

He turned left, and they pulled down a side street heading toward the river until it dead-ended at Union Street. Reuben found a parking space, and Stone extricated himself from the sidecar with some difficulty.

"What the hell happened to your face?" asked Reuben, who'd obviously just noticed these injuries.

"I fell."

"Where?"

"In the park. I was playing chess with T.J., and then I was having coffee with Adelphia. I tripped over a tree root when we were leaving."

Reuben grabbed his friend by the shoulder. "Adelphia! Oliver, that woman is mental. You're lucky she didn't drop a lethal Mickey in your java. Mark my words, one night she's going to follow you to your cottage and slit your throat." He paused and then added in a low voice, "Or worse, try and seduce you." Reuben shivered, apparently at the thought of Adelphia as a seductress.

They walked past Union Street Pub and then crossed the street and headed toward a shop near the corner. The sign above the door read: "Libri Quattuor Sententiarum."

"Where the hell did that come from?" Reuben asked, pointing at this plaque. "I know I haven't been here in a while, but didn't this place used to be called Doug's Books?"

"That name wasn't attracting the desired upscale clientele, so they changed it."

"Li-bri Quat-tuor Senten-tiarum? That's real catchy! What does it mean?"

"It's Latin for 'Four Books of Sentences.' It was a twelfth-century manuscript by Peter Lombard that was cut up and bound around the 1526 edition of St. Thomas Aquinas' lectures on the Epistles of Paul. Some scholars consider the Aquinas work to be the world's rarest book. An even earlier work that was bound around that one might be even more special. Hence, it's a very appropriate name for a rare book shop."

"I'm impressed, Oliver. I didn't even know you spoke Latin."

"I don't. Caleb told me about it. In fact, it was his idea to rename the shop. As you know, I introduced him to the shop's owner. I thought it would be productive, given Caleb's expertise with rare books. At first he simply advised on a few things, but now Caleb has an ownership interest in the place."

They went inside the shop accompanied by the jangle of a bell attached to the arched, solid-oak door. Inside, the walls were equal parts exposed brick and ancient stone with worm-eaten wooden beams overhead. Tasteful oil paintings hung on the walls, and ornate bookshelves and massive armoires were bulging with ancient tomes that were all carefully labeled and housed behind glass doors.

In a separate room a pretty young woman was standing behind a small coffee bar making drinks for some thirsty customers. A sign on the wall asked customers not to enter the rare book area with their beverages.

A small, balding man came out from the back dressed in a blue blazer, slacks and a white turtleneck, his arms outstretched and a smile on his tanned face. "Welcome, welcome to Libri Quattuor Sententiarum," he announced, the words rolling adroitly off his tongue. Then he stopped and eyed Reuben and looked at Stone.

"Oliver?"

Stone put out his hand. "Hello, Douglas. You remember Reuben Rhodes."

"Douglas," Reuben muttered under his breath. "What happened to 'Doug'?"

Douglas gave Stone a prolonged hug and shook Reuben's hand. "Oliver, you look, well, you look very different. Nice but different. I like the new style. No, I love it. Muy chic. *Bellissimo!*"

"Thank you. Caleb says that things are going well here."

Douglas took Stone by the elbow and led them over to a quiet corner.

"Caleb is a jewel, a treasure, a miracle."

"And here I was thinking he was just a print geek," Reuben said with a smirk.

Douglas continued enthusiastically. "I can't thank you enough, Oliver, for introducing Caleb to me. Business is booming. Booming! I started out selling porno comic books out of my car trunk, and now look at me. I have a condo in Old Town, a thirty-foot sailboat, a vacation house at Dewey Beach and even a 401(k) plan."

"All through the power of the written word," Stone said. "Remarkable."

"Do you still sell the porn stuff?" Reuben wanted to know.

"Uh, Douglas, I need to look at my *things,* in the space Caleb arranged for me to use," Stone said quietly.

Douglas' face paled and he swallowed nervously. "Oh, of course, of course. Go right ahead. And if you want anything, just ask. In fact, we have some very fine cappuccino and wonderful scones today. It's on the house, as always."

"Thank you. Thank you very much."

Douglas hugged Stone again and then hurried off to help a woman who'd entered the shop dressed in a full-length fur coat despite the balmy weather.

Reuben looked around at all the books. "Most of these writers probably died penniless, and he's buying condos and boats and 401(k)s off their sweat."

Stone didn't answer. He opened a small door set off to the side of the shop's entryway and led the way down a narrow staircase that emptied into the basement area. He headed along a short corridor and through an old wooden door marked "Authorized Personnel Only." He closed the door behind them and turned left down another hall. Then Stone took an old-fashioned key from his pocket and used it to open an arched door at the end of this hall, and they entered a small room that was paneled in very old wood. He flicked on a light and went over to a large fireplace that sat against one wall. While Reuben watched, Stone knelt down, reached his hand up into the inside of the fireplace and pulled on a small piece of metal attached to a short wire hanging there. There was an audible click, and a panel of the wall next to the fireplace swung open.

"Gotta love those priest's holes," Reuben said as he gripped the exposed panel and swung it all the way open.

Inside was a room about eight feet deep and six feet wide and tall enough for even Reuben to easily stand up in. Stone pulled a small penlight from his pocket and stepped in. Bookshelves lined all three walls. On each of these shelves were neatly stacked journals and notebooks, a few locked metal boxes and numerous cardboard boxes taped shut.

While Stone looked through the journals and notebooks, Reuben had a sudden thought. "How come you don't keep all this stuff at your cottage?"

"This place has an alarm system. All I have guarding my cottage are dead people."

"Well, how can you be sure that old *Douglas* doesn't come down here and poke through your stuff when you're not here?"

Stone kept examining the journals as he talked. "I told him that I'd booby-trapped this room and that no one other than myself could open it safely without threat of instant death."

"And you think he believed you?"

"It doesn't really matter. He has no personal courage, so he'll never find out for sure. Plus, at my suggestion Caleb let some hints drop to Douglas that I used to be a homicidal maniac before my release from a hospital for the criminally insane solely on a technicality. I think that's why he hugs me every time he sees me. Either he wants to stay on my good side or he's checking for weapons. Ah, here we are."

Stone pulled out an old leather-bound journal and opened it. The book was filled with newspaper clippings carefully glued to the pages. He read through it as Reuben waited impatiently. Finally, Stone closed the journal and then pulled out two other large books on a shelf. Behind these books was a leather case about eighteen inches square in size. Stone put this in his knapsack along with the journal.

On the way out Reuben got three scones from the attractive young lady in black.

"I'm Reuben," he said, towering over her and holding in his belly.

"Good for you," she said curtly before hurrying off.

"I think that young babe in there was rather taken with me," Reuben said proudly as they got back to the motorcycle.

"Yes, I suppose she ran off like that to tell all her friends," Stone replied.

# CHAPTER

## 39

It took Alex Ford about an hour to decide what to wear on his night out with Kate Adams. It was a humbling and embarrassing sixty minutes as he realized how long it'd been since he'd gone on a real date. He finally decided on a blue blazer, white collared shirt and khaki pants with loafers on his big feet. He combed down his hair, shaved off his five o'clock shadow, dressed, chewed a couple of breath mints and decided the big, somewhat weathered lug staring back at him in the mirror would just have to do.

D.C. traffic had reached the critical stage where there was no good time or direction to be driving, and Alex was afraid he was going to be late. However, he lucked out after skirting an accident on Interstate 66 that left a clear field ahead. He took the Key Bridge exit, crossed the Potomac, hooked a right onto M Street and soon found himself cruising up 31st Street in posh Georgetown. It was a place named after a British king, and certain elements of the area retained that regal dignity that some might equate to outright snobbery. However, on the main shopping drag of M Street and Wisconsin Avenue, the tone was decidedly funky and modern with gaggles of underdressed kids crowding the narrow sidewalks yakking on their cell phones and checking each other out. Yet in the upper regions of Georgetown where Alex was heading lived famous families with enormous financial portfolios and nary a tattoo or body piercing in sight.

As Alex passed one stately mansion after another, he started growing more nervous. He had guarded some incredibly powerful people over the years, but the Service prided itself as being an elite agency with a blue-collar nature. Alex was solidly in that mold and much preferred the lunch counter at the local IHOP to a three-star restaurant in Paris. Well, there was no going back now, he told himself.

The road he was on dead-ended at R Street near the massive Dumbarton Oaks mansion. Alex hung a left and continued on down R until he found the place.

"Okay, she wasn't kidding about the mansion status," Alex said as he stared up at the brick and slate-roofed behemoth. He pulled into the circular driveway, got out and looked around. The grounds were formal with the bushes all cut to the same height and shape and the late summer blooms presented in all their colorful and symmetrical glory. The moss was growing lushly around the stone slabs that led to an arched wooden door that accessed the backyard. Or with palaces such as this it was probably referred to as the rear grounds, Alex thought.

He checked his watch and found he was about ten minutes early. Maybe Kate wasn't even here yet. He was about to drive around the block to kill some time when he heard a lilting voice calling out to him.

"Yoo-hoo, are you the Secret Service man?" He turned and spotted a small, stooped woman scurrying toward him, a basket of cut flowers hooked over one arm. She had on a wide-brimmed sun hat with white cottony hair poking out, beige canvas pants and an untucked long-sleeved jeans shirt; large black sunglasses covered most of her face. She seemed shrunken with time, and he put her age at around mid-eighties or so.

"Ma'am?"

"You *are* tall *and* cute. Are you armed too? With Kate you better be."

Alex glanced around, briefly wondering if Kate was playing a joke on him and this odd woman had been hired as part of the gag. He didn't see anyone and turned back to the woman. "I'm Alex Ford."

"Are you one of *those* Fords?"

"Sorry, afraid there's no trust fund in my future."

She took off her glove, stuck it in her pants pocket and put out her hand. He shook it but then she didn't let go. She pulled him toward the house. "Kate isn't ready yet. Come on in, have a drink and let's talk, Alex."

Alex allowed himself to be led along by the woman because,

frankly, he didn't know what else to do. She smelled of strong cooking spices and even stronger hair spray.

When they reached the house and went inside, she finally let go of his hand and said, "Where are my manners, I'm Lucille Whitney-Houseman."

"Are you one of *those* Whitney-Housemans?" Alex said, with a grin.

She took off her glasses and smiled back coquettishly. "My father, Ira Whitney, didn't found the meatpacking industry, he just made a fortune off it. My dear husband, Bernie, may you rest in peace," she added, looking at the ceiling and crossing herself, "now, his family made their money in whiskey and not all of it legally. And Bernie was a prosecutor before he became a federal judge. It made for some interesting family gatherings, I can tell you."

She led him into a vast living room and motioned for him to sit down on a large sofa placed against one wall. She put the flowers in a cut crystal vase and turned to him.

"Now, speaking of whiskey, name your poison." She went over to a small cabinet and opened it. Inside was a fairly complete bar.

"Well, Mrs. . . . uh, do you go by both names?"

"Just call me Lucky. Everybody does because lucky I've been, my whole life."

"I'll have a glass of club soda, Lucky."

She turned and looked at him sternly. "I know how to make lots of cocktails, young man, but club soda ain't one of them," she said in a scolding tone.

"Oh, uh, rum and Coke, then."

"I'll make it Jack and Coke, honey, with the emphasis on the Jack."

She brought him the drink and sat down next to him with her own glass. She held it up. "A Gibson. I fell in love with them after I saw Cary Grant order one on that train in *North by Northwest.* Cheers!"

They tapped glasses and Alex took a sip of his. He coughed. It tasted like she'd let the Jack run solo. He looked around the living room. It was about the size of his entire house and with far nicer furniture.

"So you've known Kate long?" he asked.

"About seven years, although she's only lived with me for three. She's wonderful. Smart as a whip, beautiful, a real pistol, but then, I'm not telling you anything you don't already know. Plus, she makes the best buttery nipples I've ever tasted."

Alex nearly choked on his drink. "Excuse me?"

"Don't get all excited, honey, it's a specialty drink. Baileys and butterscotch schnapps. She *is* a bartender, after all."

"Oh, right."

"So are you one of the agents who guard the president?"

"Actually, starting tomorrow, I am," Alex said.

"I've known every president since Harry Truman," she said wistfully. "I voted Republican for thirty years and then Democratic for about twenty, but now I'm old enough to know better, so I'm an Independent. But I loved Ronnie Reagan. What a charmer. He and I danced at one of the balls. But of all the presidents I've known I have to confess that I liked Jimmy Carter best. He was a good, decent man; a real gentleman, even if he did lust in his heart. And you can't say that about all of them, can you?"

"No, I guess you can't. So you know President Brennan, then?"

"We've met, but he wouldn't know me from Eve. I've long since passed my usefulness in the political arena. Although in my prime I had some sway. Georgetown was the place to be for all that. Kate Graham, Evangeline Bruce, Pamela Harrington, Lorraine Cooper, I knew them all. The dinner parties we had. The national policy we came up with sitting around drinking and smoking, although the ladies were often separated from the gentlemen. But not always." She lowered her voice and looked at him with raised pencil-thin eyebrows that looked painted on. "Because the *sex* we had, oh, my Lord. But not any orgies or anything like that, honey. I mean you're talking about government people, public servants, and it's hard to get up early and work those long hours after sex orgies. It takes it out of you, it really does."

Alex suddenly realized his mouth had opened wider and wider as he listened to her. He quickly closed it. "So, uh, Kate lives in the carriage house?"

"I've wanted her to move in here—the place has eight bedrooms, after all—but she won't. She likes her space, all women do. And she can come and go as she wants." She patted his leg. "So this is your first date with her. That's sweet. Where're you going?"

"I'm not sure. Kate picked the place."

She gripped his hand again and looked directly into his eyes. "Okay, honey, let me give you some advice. Even the modern woman likes the man to take charge every once in a while. So next time *you* pick the place. Be decisive about it. Women hate men who can't make up their minds."

"Okay, but how do I know when *else* she wants me to take charge?"

"Oh, you won't. You'll just screw it up like every other man does."

Alex cleared his throat. "So does she date a lot?"

"Okay, you want the 411 on Kate, don't you, honey? Well, Kate only brings someone around every few months. Nobody's stuck yet but don't let that discourage you. She usually brings home some fancy-pants lawyer, lobbyist or big-shot government type. Now, you're the first man with a gun she's brought here," she added in an encouraging tone. "You *are* packing heat, aren't you?" she asked hopefully.

"Would that be a good thing?"

"Honey, all civilized women throw their underwear at dangerous men. We just can't help ourselves."

He grinned, opened his coat and showed her his gun.

She clapped her hands together. "Oh, that is so thrilling."

"Hey, Lucky, get away from my man."

They both turned around and saw a smiling Kate Adams standing in the doorway leading into the next room. She had on a pleated black skirt that ended midthigh, a white blouse open at the neck and sandals. Alex realized he'd never seen her legs before; she always wore pants at the bar. She gave Lucky a hug and a kiss on the cheek.

"I have been entertaining your beau while you made yourself beautiful, my dear," Lucky said. "Not that it takes that much effort for you. Oh, it's just not fair, Kate. Not even the best plastic surgeon in the world could give me your cheekbones."

"You liar. The men were always gaga over Lucky Whitney. And they still are."

Lucky smiled at Alex and said in a very coy tone, "Well, I have to admit, this young man did show me his *piece,* Kate. I bet you haven't had that pleasure yet."

Kate looked surprised. "His piece? No, I haven't seen it yet."

His expression one of horror, Alex jumped up so fast he spilled some of his drink on the couch. "My gun! I showed her my gun."

"That's right, that's what he called it. His *gun*," Lucky said, smiling impishly. "Now, where are you two going for dinner?"

"Nathan's," Kate answered.

Lucky raised her eyebrows. "Nathan's?" She gave Alex a thumbs-up. "That's where she takes the ones with real potential."

# CHAPTER

## 40

"Reuben," Stone called out from his perch in the sidecar. "We have some time yet. Can we stop in at Arlington Cemetery?"

Reuben looked over at the nation's most hallowed burial place for its military dead and nodded.

A few minutes later they passed through the visitors' entrance and walked past the Women in Military Service Memorial. They paused for a moment near the Kennedy graves, Arlington's biggest visitor draw, with the changing of the guard at the Tombs of the Unknowns a close second.

Continuing on, Reuben stopped and gazed at a stretch of grass near Arlington House. It had once been Robert E. Lee's home but had been confiscated by the federal government after Lee had chosen to lead the Confederate army against the Union.

"Isn't that where you found me, stoned outta my head?"

Stone looked at the spot. "It was a long time ago, Reuben. You pulled yourself out of it. You fought off your demons."

"I couldn't have done it without you, Oliver." He paused and looked around at all the white tombstones. "I was just so damn pissed off. I lost half my company from Nam to Agent Orange, and the army wouldn't even admit they'd done it. And then the same thing happened with the Persian Gulf syndrome. I just wanted to come here and scream, make somebody listen."

"It's probably best that you passed out when you did. The secretary of defense was here that day; it might've gotten ugly."

Reuben gazed curiously at his friend. "You know, I never asked you what you were doing at the cemetery that day."

"Just like everyone else, I was there to pay my respects."

Stone stopped at one area and silently counted down the rows of white headstones until he came to one near the middle. He stood, his arms folded across his chest, while the setting sun burned down into the horizon. Reuben checked his watch but seemed reluctant to interrupt his friend.

Stone's solitude was finally halted by a group of men passing nearby. He watched as they headed toward the newest expansion of Arlington Cemetery and one that was not yet completed. It was the 9/11 memorial site that abutted the grounds of the cemetery. The site included a signature monument to the lives that were lost at the Pentagon, and a memorial grove.

Stone stiffened when he saw who was in the center of the wall of armed security. Reuben glanced over too.

"Carter Gray," Reuben muttered.

"Here to see his wife, I would assume," Stone said quietly. "Before the crowds come tomorrow."

Carter Gray stopped at the gravesite of his wife, Barbara, knelt on the ground and placed a small bouquet of flowers on the recessed earth. Technically, the anniversary of his wife's death was tomorrow, but the cemetery would be filled that day, and, as Stone had deduced, the man had no desire to share his grief with a mass of strangers.

Gray rose and stared down at where his wife's body lay, while his security detail kept a respectful distance away.

Barbara Gray had retired from the army as a brigadier general after a distinguished career in which she set many firsts for women in the military. Barbara Gray had also been one of the most vocal advocates for members of the World War II–era WASPs, or Women's Air Force Service Pilots, to be eligible to receive burial at Arlington with *full* military honors, something denied to them because they were summarily disbanded after the war. In June of 2002 a new regulation allowed a number of women's military groups, including the WASPs, to at least be buried with the more limited *funeral*, instead of full, military honors. Unfortunately, Barbara Gray had not lived to see it happen.

On the morning of September 11, 2001, Barbara Gray, then a civilian consultant, was meeting at the Pentagon on a project with two members of the army when the American Airlines flight slammed into the building, obliterating the room she was in. As an appalling foot-note to this tragedy, the Grays' daughter, Maggie, a government lawyer, had just arrived at the Pentagon to meet her mother. Her body was virtually cremated in the initial explosion.

As Carter Gray stood there looking at his wife's grave, the image of that morning cut deeply into him. And then the waves of guilt fol-lowed, for he should have been in that building too. Gray was sup-posed to meet his wife and daughter at the Pentagon before they all headed out on a long-planned family vacation. He'd been caught in traffic and was running about twenty minutes late. By the time he got to the Pentagon, his family was gone.

As he finally pulled his gaze from the consecrated ground, Gray looked around and spotted the two men staring back at him from a dis-tance. He didn't recognize the large man, but there was something fa-miliar about the other. Then he watched as the two men turned and walked off. Gray lingered by his wife's grave for another ten minutes, and then, his curiosity getting the better of him, he headed to the spot where the two men had been standing. He realized this section of graves was familiar to him. He started looking at the headstones, his gaze mov-ing swiftly down the neat rows of markers, until he stopped at one.

The next moment his security staff was hustling after Gray as he rushed down the walkway. As he drew closer to the exit, he stopped and bent over, sucking in huge amounts of air as his security team circled him, asking if he was all right. He didn't answer them. He didn't even hear them.

The name on the grave marker that had caused his pell-mell rush was pinballing around his mind. There was no body in the casket under that marker, Gray well knew. It was all a sham, all part of a cover-up. Yet the name on the marker wasn't a fraud. It was a real man who, it was thought, had died in the defense of his country.

"John Carr." Gray said the name, one he had not uttered for decades. *John Carr.* The most accomplished killer Carter Gray had ever seen.

Nathan's wasn't that crowded yet, and Alex Ford and Kate Adams were seated at a table in a corner near the bar area and had ordered some drinks.

"Lucky's a real pistol," Alex said. "How'd you hook up with her?"

"Before I went to Justice, I was in private practice. I handled the trusts and estates work when her husband died. We became friends, and she eventually asked me to come live with her. I said no at first, but she kept asking, and Mr. Right had failed miserably to show up at my door in the meantime. I pay rent for the carriage house," she added quickly. "Lucky's a very interesting person. She's someone who's been everywhere, knows everybody. But she's lonely too. Old age doesn't go down well with someone like her. She's so alive, and she wants to do everything she used to do; but she really can't anymore."

"From what I saw she's doing a pretty damn good job of trying," he replied. "So why'd you jump to the government side?"

"Nothing too original. I got burned out on the billable hour treadmill. And you're not going to change the world doing T and E law."

"So what do you do at Justice to change the world?"

"I'm into a fairly new thing actually. After Gitmo Bay and treatment of POWs at Abu Ghraib, the Salt Pit and other places, Justice formed a new group to enforce the civil rights of prisoners deemed to be of a highly political nature as well as foreign combatants, and to investigate any crimes against those class of persons."

"Well, judging from what I read in the papers, you must keep pretty busy."

"The U.S. overall has an excellent record when it comes to treatment of POWs and persons listed as foreign combatants, but the longer the war against terrorism goes on, the more tempting it is for our guys to stoop to the other side's level. After all, they're only human, and they might come to view the person sitting across from them as someone not worthy of any rights at all."

"But that doesn't excuse them breaking the law."

"No, it doesn't. And that's where people like me come in. I've been to the various war zones six times in the last two years. Unfortunately, it's not getting much better."

"It looks like Carter Gray has started counterpunching well."

Kate sat back and sipped on the glass of red wine she'd ordered. "I have mixed feelings about that. I feel for him personally and his loss on 9/11. I think that's the only reason he came back into the government sector. But I'm not convinced it was a good thing. "

"What do you mean?" Alex asked.

"I know he's gotten extraordinary results. I wonder if he employs extraordinary means to achieve them. For example, we've had real problems with rendition."

"I've heard that's quite a political football."

"It's no wonder with the way the procedure works. Suspected terrorists are transferred from the U.S. to other countries or vice versa without any legal processing or access by the International Red Cross. When we transfer prisoners out to other countries, verbal assurances are first required from the receiving country that the transferees won't be subjected to torture. Well, the problem is there's no way to verify that torture doesn't occur. And in fact, it seems clear that the torture often *does* happen. On top of that, because such torture in the U.S. is illegal, some think NIC and CIA are actively involved in rendering prisoners to other countries so that torture can be used as a tool to get useful information. They'll even get the receiving country to trump up charges against a suspect so he can be jailed, interrogated and often tortured. That's against everything that America stands for."

"Well, after seeing the place firsthand, I believe NIC is capable of pretty much anything."

"So I take it your looking into that man's death isn't going all that well?"

Alex hesitated and then decided it wouldn't hurt to come clean. He told her about his uncomfortable "chat" with the director of the Secret Service and about being busted back to protection detail.

"I'm so sorry, Alex." She reached over and touched his hand.

"Hey, I set myself up for it. Gray plays in the big leagues, and having your own partner rat you out doesn't help. I guess I was outclassed." He took a drink of his cocktail. "Your martinis are much better," he said, smiling.

She clinked her glass against his. "I knew I liked you."

His expression grew serious. "I should've stuck to my original plan: with three years to go to finish off my twenty, put it on cruise control and don't rock the boat."

"You don't strike me as a 'cruising' sort of person," Kate replied.

He shrugged. "Look, let's cut the shoptalk. Tell me more about yourself. That's what first dates are for."

She sat back and picked at a piece of bread in front of her. "Well, I'm an only child. My parents live in Colorado. They'll tell you we're descended from the Massachusetts Adamses, but I'm not sure I buy that. My dream was to be a world class gymnast. And I worked my guts out for it. Then I grew six inches in one year, and there went that dream. Right after high school I decided I wanted to be a croupier in Vegas. Don't ask why, I just did. I enrolled in a course, passed with flying colors and took off for Sin City. But it didn't last too long. I had a teeny problem with drunken high rollers thinking they could grab my butt whenever they wanted. After a few of them lost teeth, the casino suggested I head back East. When I started college, I decided to bartend to pay for it, and then I continued pouring drinks when I went to law school. At least with that occupation you have solid wood between you and the resident animals. And as you deduced earlier, I also play the piano. I earned money teaching it to help pay for school. I don't need to keep bartending, but honestly I like to. It's an outlet for me and you meet a lot of fascinating people at the LEAP bar."

"Gymnast, croupier, bartender, piano-playing defender of truth and justice. That's pretty damn impressive."

"Sometimes I think it's far more dysfunctional than it is impressive. So how about you?"

"Nothing too exciting. I grew up in Ohio. Youngest of four and the only son. My dad was an auto parts salesman by day, but by night he was the second coming of Johnny Cash."

"Really?"

"Well, he wanted to be anyway. I think he had the largest collection of Cash memorabilia outside of Nashville. Always dressed in black, played a wicked acoustical guitar, pretty good pipes. I learned guitar so I could play with him. We even went out on the road together, playing some of the best hole-in-the-walls in the Ohio Valley. We weren't great but we weren't bad either. It was a blast. Then his four-pack-a-day habit caught up to him. The lung cancer took him in six months. My mom lives in a retirement village in Florida. My sisters are scattered around the country."

"So what made you want to play the human shield?"

Alex took another drink and his look became somber. "I saw the Zapruder film clip of Kennedy's assassination when I was twelve years old. I remembered thinking that something like that should never happen again. I'll never forget the image of Agent Clint Hill jumping on the limo, pushing Mrs. Kennedy back into her seat. A lot of people at the time thought she was part of the conspiracy to kill the president, or else condemned her because they thought she was just trying to get away from all the blood on her, even if it was her husband's. What she was actually doing was trying to retrieve the piece of her husband's head that had gotten blown off."

He finished his drink before continuing. "I met Clint Hill at a Secret Service function. He was an old guy by then. Everybody wanted to shake his hand. I told him how honored I was to meet him. He was the only guy to react when it happened. He helped Mrs. Kennedy, and he put his body between her and whoever was shooting at them. I told him if the time came, I hoped I did as well as he'd done. You know what he said to me?"

He looked up to see her gaze directly on him; Kate Adams seemed to be holding her breath. "What did he say?" she prompted.

"He said, 'Son, you don't want to be like me. Because I lost my president.'"

There was a long silence and finally Alex broke it. "I can't believe that I'm sitting here dishing out this depressing crap. I'm not really like that."

"With the day you had I'm surprised you didn't bag tonight."

"Kate, the thought of going out with you tonight was the *only* thing that got me through today."

Alex looked a little surprised at the frankness of his words and quickly looked down, studying the exterior of his remaining martini olive.

Kate reached out and touched his hand. "I'm going to further embarrass you," she said, "by telling you that's the nicest thing anyone's ever said to me."

The conversation turned to more innocuous subjects, and time sped by. As they were leaving, Alex muttered an expletive under his breath.

Coming in the door were Senator and Mrs. Roger Simpson and their daughter, Jackie.

Alex tried to duck by but Jackie spotted him.

"Hello, Alex," she said.

"Agent Simpson," Alex replied curtly.

"These are my parents."

Roger Simpson and his wife looked like twins: very tall and fair-haired. They towered over their petite, dark-haired daughter.

"Senator. Mrs. Simpson," Alex said, nodding at them both. Roger Simpson glared back at him so menacingly that Alex was convinced Jackie must have told him the whole story in her own biased way.

"This is Kate Adams."

"Pleasure to meet you both," Kate said.

"Well, take care, Agent Simpson. I doubt I'll be seeing you around." He walked out with Adams trailing him.

As soon as they were outside, Alex blurted out, "Can you believe, of all the restaurants in this damn town—"

He broke off when Jackie Simpson popped out of Nathan's.

"Alex, can we talk for just a minute?" She glanced anxiously at Kate. "Privately?"

"I'm pretty damn certain we have nothing to say to each other," he shot back.

"It'll just take a minute. Please?"

Alex looked at Kate, who shrugged and moved down the street a bit, studying the clothing in a shop window.

Simpson drew closer. "Look, I know you're upset as hell at me. And you think I ratted you out."

"Well, you're batting a thousand so far."

"It didn't happen like that. As soon as Carter Gray left us, he must've called my dad. Even before he called the president. My father called and gave it to me up one side and down the other. He said I couldn't let some maverick wreck my career before it even got started."

"How did the director find out about my 'old friend'?"

Simpson looked miserable. "I know, that was stupid. My father can be overwhelming. He ground it out of me." She sighed. "My dad's one of the most accomplished people you'll ever meet. And my mother was a Miss Alabama, which makes her a saint down there. So being a simple detective didn't cut it with them. They wanted me to go into business or politics. I put my foot down and said I was a cop. But they kept pushing for me to go on to a bigger pond. Just to get them off my back, I joined the Service. Dad pulled strings so I got assigned to

WFO. His dream is for me to be the first female director of the Service. All I ever wanted to be was a good cop. But for them that wasn't enough."

"So are you going to do what your parents want your whole life?"

"It's not that easy. He's a man that's used to people obeying him. " She paused and looked up at him. "But that's *my* problem. I just wanted you to know that I'm really sorry for what happened. And I hope I get a chance to make it up to you."

She turned and walked back inside before he could reply.

When Kate rejoined him, he explained the gist of the conversation. After he'd finished, Alex added, "Just when you think you have somebody pegged and you're justified in hating her guts, she pulls a fast one and complicates things." He glanced across the street and his features brightened. "Please tell me you'd like to go get some ice cream."

She looked over at the shop across the street. "Okay, but I have to warn you I'm a minimum two-scoop sort of girl and I *don't* share."

"My kind of woman."

# 41

At Union Station Stone and Reuben found Caleb and Milton in the B. Dalton Bookstore. Caleb was poring over a Dickens masterpiece, while Milton was firmly entrenched in the computer magazine section.

Stone and Reuben rounded up the pair, and they all boarded the Metro, taking it to the Smithsonian station, where they rode the escalator up to the Mall.

"Keep your eyes and ears open," Stone cautioned.

They took a stroll past the major monuments as tourists flocked around taking pictures and videos of all the sights. The Camel Club eventually reached FDR Park, where the FDR Memorial, a fairly recent addition to the Mall, was located. It covered a large area of ground and was made up of various statuary depicting significant symbols from FDR's reign as America's only four-term president. Stone led his friends over to a secluded section that was shielded from wandering tourists by a Depression-era breadline immortalized in bronze.

After he'd glanced around for a few moments, Stone shook his head in dissatisfaction and led them back to the subway, which they rode to Foggy Bottom. They exited and started walking. At 27th and Q Streets, NW, Stone stopped. Staring back at them was the entrance for Mt. Zion Cemetery, where Stone was the caretaker.

"Oh, no, Oliver," Reuben complained. "Not another bloody cemetery."

"The dead don't eavesdrop," Stone replied curtly as he opened the gates.

Stone led them into his cottage, where the others looked at him expectantly.

"I've done some research that I believe is critical to our investigation into Patrick Johnson's murder. Thus, I hereby call this special meeting of the Camel Club to order. I propose that we discuss the topic of the recent spate of terrorists killing each other. Do I have a second?"

"I second," Caleb said automatically, though he glanced curiously at the others.

"All in favor say aye."

The ayes carried the motion, and Stone opened the large journal he'd brought from the rare book shop.

"Over the last eighteen months there have been numerous instances where terrorists have allegedly killed each other. I found this to be so interesting that I started keeping all the articles I could find on the subject. The last such incident involved a man named Adnan al-Rimi."

"I read about that," Milton said. "But why do you say *allegedly*?"

"In each instance the dead man's face was fully or partially obliterated, either by gunshots or explosives. They had to be identified by their fingerprints, DNA and whatever else was available."

Reuben spoke up. "But that's just normal procedure, Oliver. When I was at DIA, we did that too, although we didn't have DNA tests back then."

"And we know from Reuben that NIC now controls all terrorist-related information." Stone added, "The same information databases which Patrick Johnson helped oversee were used to identify all these dead terrorists." He paused. "Now, what if Mr. Johnson were rigging that database somehow?"

After a long silence Milton was the first to speak. "Do you mean he might have been *manipulating* data somehow?"

"Let me put it more bluntly," Stone replied. "What if he substituted on the NIC database the prints of the men found dead in place of the fingerprints of the terrorists the authorities thought had been killed?"

Caleb looked horrified. "Are you suggesting that someone like Adnan al-Rimi isn't actually dead, but as far as American intelligence is concerned—"

"He *is* dead," Stone finished for him. "His past has been wiped clean. He could go anywhere and do anything he wanted to do."

"Like a sterilized weapon," Reuben interjected.

"Precisely."

"But wait a minute, Oliver," Reuben said. "There are safeguards in place. If I remember correctly, at DIA no file alteration was allowed unless certain steps were followed."

Stone looked over at Caleb. "They have a similar procedure at the Library of Congress Rare Books Division. For obvious reasons the person buying the books can't input them into the database, and the converse is also true. That's actually what made me think of this possibility. But what if you had both people in your pocket: the gatherer of the intelligence and the one assigned to put that data in the system? And what if one of them was senior? Perhaps *very* senior."

Reuben finally sputtered. "Are you suggesting that Carter Gray is involved in this? Come on, whatever else you say about Gray, I don't think you can reasonably question his loyalty to this country."

"I'm not saying it's an easy answer, Reuben," Stone replied. "But if not Gray, then perhaps someone else who's been turned."

"Now, that's more likely," Reuben conceded.

Milton spoke up. "Well, if this is all true, why was Johnson killed?"

Stone answered. "If the two men we saw kill Patrick Johnson are with NIC, then it seems to me—given his extravagant lifestyle on a modest government paycheck—that two things might have happened. One, whoever hired him to alter the files was afraid his newfound wealth would lead to an investigation, so they killed him and planted the drugs. Or else Johnson might have gotten greedy, asked for more money and they killed him instead."

"So what do we do now?" Milton asked.

"Staying alive would be my priority," Reuben answered. "Because if Oliver is right, there's going to be a lot of powerful folks looking to make sure we're dead."

"And Milton's identity and home have no doubt already been compromised," Stone said. "As for the men after us, I propose that we turn the tables on them."

"How?" Caleb asked.

Stone closed his notebook. "We have the home address of Tyler Reinke. I suggest we follow up on that."

"You want us to go marching right into the man's crosshairs?" Reuben exclaimed.

"No. But there's no reason why we can't put him in *our* crosshairs."

*       *       *

Ice cream in hand, Alex and Kate strolled down to the Georgetown waterfront near the spot where hundreds of years ago George Mason operated a ferry. Kate pointed out three boulders that were barely visible in the center of the river north of the Key Bridge and across from Georgetown University.

She said, "That's Three Sisters Island. Legend has it three nuns drowned at that spot when their boat overturned. And then the boulders sprung up to symbolize their deaths and warn others."

"The Potomac's current *is* deceptively calm," Alex added. "Not that anyone would want to swim in it these days. When it rains hard, you usually get some sewer overflow."

"When they built Interstate 66, they were also going to build a spur off it that included a bridge across the river at that point. They were going to call it the Three Sisters Bridge, but there were so many weird construction accidents they finally gave up. Some said it was the ghosts of the nuns."

"You believe in stuff like that?" Alex asked.

"Stranger things have happened. I mean look at some of the conspiracy theorists in this town. Most are probably crazy, but some of them turn out to be right."

"I know a guy who falls into the category. His name's Oliver Stone. The guy's flat-out brilliant, if a couple paces off the sidewalk of life."

"Oliver Stone? You're kidding."

"Not his real name, of course. I think it's just his little joke aimed at people who believe he's a quack. One of the most interesting things about him is he has no past, at least that I can find." Alex smiled. "Maybe he's been on the run all these years."

"Sounds like a man Lucky would like to meet."

"So does she still throw her underwear at dangerous men?"

"What?" a surprised Kate asked.

"Never mind." Alex ate a spoonful of ice cream and looked over at Roosevelt Island. Adams followed his gaze.

She finally said, "So would you care to talk about it? Bartenders are great listeners."

Alex motioned her to join him on a bench near the riverfront.

He said, "Okay, here's what's bugging me. The guy swims to the island and shoots himself. Does that sound likely?"

"Well, it *was* the island where he and his fiancée went on their first date."

"Right. But why *swim* to the island? Why not just drive to it or walk? There's a footbridge that crosses over the parkway and empties right into the parking lot of the island. And so does a bike trail. Then you jump the gate, go over to the island, get stoned and blow your brains out without schlepping through the Potomac. They found his car a good ways upriver, which means it was a long swim, in street clothes and shoes and carrying a pistol in a plastic baggie. It's not like the guy was Mark Spitz or Michael Phelps."

"But his prints were on the gun," Kate retorted.

"Forcing someone's hand around a gun and pulling the trigger isn't that easy or smart to do," Alex conceded. "The last thing you want is to put a gun in somebody's hand that you're trying to kill. But what if you got him drunk first?"

Alex pointed to his feet. "And the bottoms of his shoes bothered me."

"How so?"

"They had dirt on them as you'd expect from walking through the brush, but there wasn't any dirt on the ground around him. You'd think that some of that red clay would've ended up on the stone pavers around him. And his clothes were too clean. If you'd hiked around that island, you'd have twigs and leaves stuck all over your clothes. There was nothing like that on him. And if he had swum to the island, he would've had to trek through that bramble to get to the main trail."

"That doesn't make a lot of sense," Kate admitted.

"And the suicide note in his pocket? It was barely damp and the ink hadn't run."

"He probably carried it in the same plastic bag he used for the gun."

"Then why not leave it in the baggie? Why pull it out and put it in a soaking-wet pocket that might cause the ink to run and the message to be lost? And while Johnson was wet when he was found, if he'd really swum all that way I would've expected him to be soggier and grimier than we found him. I mean the Potomac can get pretty foul around here."

"But he *was* wet."

"Yeah, but if you wanted it to seem like someone had swum all that way, what would you do?"

Kate thought for a moment. "Dunk him in the water."

"Right, you'd dunk him in the water. And then there's motivation. No one I talked to knew anything about Johnson dealing drugs. Hell, his fiancée was so ticked she threatened to sue me for even suggesting it might be true!"

"Like I always said, Secret Service doesn't miss the details."

"But come on, it's not like we're inherently better than the FBI with this stuff. They should've seen it too. I think there's a lot of pressure from up top to put this to rest the easy way."

"If someone brought him to the island and they didn't want to use a car for fear of being seen, what would they do?"

As they were talking, they saw a police boat slowly pass.

Alex and Kate looked at each other and said together, "A boat!"

"That's not something that's easy to hide," Alex said slowly.

Kate looked up and down the waterfront. "I'm game if you are."

They threw their ice cream containers in the trash and headed down to the water.

It took them a solid hour, but they finally found it when Kate spotted a tip of the bow sticking out from the drainage ditch.

"Good eyes," Alex complimented.

She slipped off her sandals and Alex his shoes and socks. He rolled up his pants, and they scrambled down there as a couple of passersby watched curiously. Alex ran his gaze over the old wooden rowboat, stopping at one point and putting his face very near the hull. "That looks like a bullet hole."

"And that could be blood," Kate said, pointing to a small dark patch near the gunwale.

"Which doesn't make a lot of sense, unless they killed Johnson in the boat and then took him to the island. It was foggy that night, so I guess it could've been done without anyone seeing."

"So what do you do with all this?" Kate asked.

Alex rose and pondered this. "I'd like to see if the blood matches Patrick Johnson's or if it's someone else's. But if the director finds out I've been poking around this case again, I'm going to end up in a brand-new Service outpost in Siberia. That is, if he doesn't kill me with his bare hands."

"I can nose around," Kate offered.

"No. I don't want you anywhere near this. Some of the thoughts going through my head are downright scary. For now we'll just have to leave it alone."

# CHAPTER

## 42

Cₐₚₜₐᵢₙ Jₐcₖ ₗₒₒₖₑd ₐₜ ₜₕₑ note that had just been delivered. The message was coded but he'd memorized the key and quickly deciphered it. It was hardly good news:

> Gray met with me today. He accessed some files, but I can't find out which ones because he put an override on. He mentioned the resurrection of the dead to me personally. I discovered he made the same statement to other senior people here. He's obviously fishing, to see who would jump at the bait. That's why I sent this by courier. Go ahead with plans. I will hold down this end. Communicate via Charlie One from now on.

The problem with trying to communicate in this day and age was that it was virtually impossible to do so in secret if you used modern technology. Spy satellites were everywhere, and faxes, computers, cell and hard-line phones and e-mails were all potentially monitored. It was no wonder terrorists had resorted to couriers and handwritten messages. Ironic, that modern surveillance technology was driving them all back to the Stone Age. Charlie One was simple to use: coded messages on paper delivered by a trusted messenger, with the paper destroyed after being read.

The Secret Service advance team would be arriving in Brennan very soon. Shortly after that, the president would fly into Pittsburgh on Air Force One, and the most heavily guarded motorcade in history would make its way to Brennan. There they would be confronted by what some would consider a ragtag army of mostly forty-something men and one young woman. Yet Captain Jack would bet on his crew. He took his lighter and burned the letter to ash.

After she'd said her final prayer of the day, Djamila stood in front of her bathroom mirror and studied her features. Today was her twenty-fourth birthday; however, she thought she looked older than that; the last few years had not been kind to her. There had never been enough food and not enough clean water, and there were far too many nights of sleeping without a roof over her head. And bullets and bombs dropping all around you aged you faster than anything else. At least she now had enough to eat. America *was* the land of abundance, she'd often been told. They had so much, she thought, and it was hardly fair. It was said that there were homeless people here and children who went hungry, but she didn't believe that. It couldn't be possible. That was just American propaganda to make people pity them! Djamila swore in Arabic at this thought. Pity *them?*

She was twenty-four years old, alone and halfway around the world from where she belonged. Her family was all gone. Murdered. She felt the lump in her throat growing. And a moment later she was choking back the tears. She quickly wet a towel and put it over her face, letting the cool fabric dry the tears.

Recovered, she grabbed her purse and van keys and shut the door to her apartment, being careful to make sure it was securely locked.

She had been told that there would always be one of Captain Jack's men watching her van wherever it was parked. They could not afford to let the vehicle be stolen. There was not time to get another one like it.

Captain Jack was a strange man, she thought. An American who spoke fluent Arabic was not common. He seemed to know the customs and history of the Islamic world better than some Muslims. Djamila had been instructed that whatever he told her to do she *must* obey. It had not seemed right at first, taking orders from an American. Yet, after meeting him in person, there was an aura of authority around the man that she couldn't deny.

Driving her van around the area in the evening had become a ritual for Djamila. It was as much to unwind after a long day of playing nanny to three energetic boys as it was to commit to memory the various roads and shortcuts necessary to her task. She drove into downtown Brennan and passed by Mercy Hospital. Adnan al-Rimi was not on duty, but Djamila wouldn't have known him if she saw him. In the same vein she had no reason to look to the right and eye the apartment where, at that moment, a pair of camouflaged M-50 sniper rifles were trained on the hospital as part of a practice round.

Her path took her by the auto repair shop. Out of habit she drove down the alley past a set of overhead doors situated there, their windows painted black. Her route on that day would take her through the southern tip of the downtown area, and then she would head west on the main road leading out of Brennan. In thirty minutes' time her part would be over. She prayed to God that his wisdom and courage would guide her.

She continued her trek and soon passed by the ceremonial grounds. All she knew was that the president of this country would be speaking here before a very large crowd. Other than that, the grassy piece of earth meant little to her.

Her travels had taken her past the home of George and Lori Franklin, her employers. It was a very pretty home, if you liked the traditional architecture of America. But what Djamila enjoyed best about the Franklins' home was the backyard. It was full of green grass to run across and trees for climbing and places to hide when she was playing games with the boys. Having grown up in a desert climate, Djamila had to admit that America was a very beautiful country. At least on the outside.

Djamila's route back to her apartment took her past the Franklins' house once more. As the van glided by, Djamila instinctively looked to the upper dormer windows where the three boys slept in two rooms. She had found herself becoming more and more attached to them. They were fine children who would no doubt grow up as haters of Islam, of all that she believed in. If she could only have them for real, she would teach them the truths; she would show them the real light of her faith and her world. They might find that the differences between them were far outweighed by their similarities. Djamila pulled the van to a stop as she thought about this. For so long she had been told that America and Islam were not capable of being reconciled. And yes, that must be true. *They are destroying my country,* she reminded herself. They are a violent nation with an unbeatable army. They took what they wanted, whether it was oil or lives. And yet as she gazed around the peaceful neighborhood all that was hard to imagine. Very hard.

Alex looked around the interior of Kate Adams' home and liked very much what he was seeing. Things weren't too orderly, and there was clutter here and there. Alex himself was no neatnik and doubted he could long stand the company of someone who was. And there were books everywhere too, which was also a good thing. Never a reader in school, Alex had made up for that with a vengeance when he joined the Service. Long plane flights allowed for plenty of time spent between the pages. And she obviously wasn't a snooty, highbrowed reader. While many literary classics were tucked on shelves, Alex noted a healthy dose of commercial-grade fiction there as well.

Family photos dotted tables and walls, and he took his time looking at Kate Adams as she evolved from a gangling, shy young girl into a lovely, confident woman.

In one corner of the room that took up most of the first floor sat a black baby grand piano.

When she came back downstairs from her bedroom, Kate had changed into jeans, a sweater, and was barefoot.

"Sorry," she said, "I start to implode after a day in a dress and shoes."

"Don't let the thousand-dollar suits and impeccable grooming fool you, I'm a jeans-and-T-shirt kind of guy myself."

She laughed. "Beer?"

"Always a good chaser to mocha mint ice cream."

She pulled two Coronas from the fridge, cut up limes, and they sat on the couch that looked out onto the rear grounds.

She curled her legs up under her. "So what's your next move?"

He shrugged. "Not sure. Officially, I'm on White House protection detail, and I should be thankful for that. I mean it's not like I did anything wrong during the investigation. But I sat in the director's office and refused a direct order from him to reveal the name of someone. I still can't believe I did that."

"So was the old friend you told me about Oliver Stone?"

He shot Kate a glance that answered the question for her. "How the hell did you figure that out?"

"You're not the only person in the room with deductive powers."

"Apparently not." He took a swig of beer and sat back against the cushions. "Like I said, I think at this point my hands are tied. How can I even tell them about finding the boat without revealing that I was doing the very thing the director ordered me not to do? If he finds out, I'm history. I can't risk that."

"I see your dilemma." She brushed against his shoulder as she set her beer down on the coffee table. That simple touch was like an electric spark shot through Alex's body.

Kate sat down in front of the piano and started playing a piece that he recognized as *Rhapsody on a Theme of Paganini*. It was clear that the woman was a highly skilled pianist. After a couple of minutes he joined her on the bench and started tapping out a side melody.

She said, "That's Ray Charles. I thought you were a guitar player."

"My old man said if you start with piano you can play pretty much anything."

"Wasn't Clint Eastwood a piano-playing Secret Service agent in the movie *In the Line of Fire*?"

"Yep, with Rene Russo sitting next to him."

"Sorry, I'm no Rene Russo."

"I'm no Clint Eastwood. And FYI, Rene Russo has nothing on you."

"Liar."

"I'm not the kind of guy to take my clothes off on a first date like Eastwood. Sorry," he added with a grin.

She smirked at him. "Pity."

"But that rule doesn't necessarily hold for the second date."

"Oh, you're that confident there'll be a second one?"

"Come on, I'm packing heat. I'm a lock, according to Lucky."

He ran his fingers across the keys until they touched hers.

The kiss that followed made the electrical spark Alex had felt before seem like a faint tickle.

She kissed him one more time and then stood. "I know this is probably unfair, but I think your first-date rule is a good one." She said this only halfheartedly, but then glanced away. "You don't give it away the first night, because they might not be back the second."

He put his hand on her shoulder. "I'll be back any night you want me, Kate."

"How about tomorrow?" She added, "If I can wait that long."

Alex fired up his old Cherokee and drove off, his spirits soaring. He pulled off down the street, turned back onto 31st and started the long, winding descent into the main drag of Georgetown. His first hint of trouble was when he tapped the brakes and they didn't respond. His second hint of coming disaster was when he punched them again and they sank to the floor. And he was rapidly gathering speed as the descent angle steepened. On top of that, there were parked cars on both sides of the street and the asphalt here curved like a damn serpent.

He fought the wheel and also tried to downshift to slow his momentum, neither of which did much. And then the headlights of another car cut through the darkness coming toward him.

"Oh, shit!" He cut the wheel hard to the right, and the Cherokee slid between two parked cars, where a sturdy tree did what the brakes couldn't. The impact deployed the air bag, briefly stunning him. Alex pushed the bag away, undid his seat belt and staggered out of the car. He could taste blood on his lips, and his face was burning, probably from the air bag's hot gas.

He sat on the curb, trying to catch his breath and also trying not to be sick as the mocha mint ice cream and Corona ratcheted up his throat.

The next thing he knew, someone was kneeling beside him. Alex started to say that he was okay when he froze. The hard, cold object was flush against his neck. His arm instinctively shot out and smashed into the person's knee, buckling it.

The man yelled out in pain, but as Alex tried to get up, a searing blow caught him across the head. Then he heard footsteps running away and a car squeal off. Moments later he understood the hasty retreat as other car lights appeared and people were surrounding him.

"Are you all right?" they were asking him over and over.

Alex could still feel the icy touch of the gun barrel against his neck. Then a thought hit him. His brakes!

Alex pushed the people away and, ignoring the pain in his head, grabbed a flashlight out of the Cherokee and shone the light under his left front wheel well. It was all covered with brake fluid. Someone had tampered with his truck. Yet the only place they could've done that was at Kate's. *Kate!*

He reached in his pocket for his cell phone. It wasn't there. He threw open the door to the wrecked Cherokee. His cell phone was on the floorboard, broken in half from the force of the collision. He screamed in fury. By now the people who'd come to his aid were backing away, their expressions fearful in the face of his bizarre behavior.

Then one of them spotted it as he wheeled around and his jacket flew open. This person yelled, "He's got a gun!" On this they all scattered like frightened pigeons.

He started running after them. "I need your phone! Your phone!" he yelled. But they were already gone.

Alex turned and started sprinting back up 31st Street. The blood was dripping down his shirt from his scalp wound, and his arms and legs felt disconnected from his body, but on he raced, up the steep incline until he felt his lungs would burst. He hit R Street and turned left, redoubling his speed, finding a reserve of energy and another gear he never knew he had. As the house came into view, he pulled out his gun.

He slowed and crouched low as he slipped into the yard. The main house was dark. He made his way quietly to the garden gate leading to the backyard and the carriage house. The gate was locked, so he clambered over the fence. His feet touched the grass on the other side, and Alex squatted down to reconnoiter the area and catch his breath. His head was pounding, and his ears were ringing so badly he didn't know if he could even hear. He moved, crouching, through the cover of the bushes toward the carriage house. There was a light on upstairs. He took several deep breaths, forcing himself to stay calm as he gripped his SIG.

He inched forward, his eyes scanning the grounds through the bushes. *If someone is out there drawing a bead . . .* Then a light came on in the first floor of the carriage house. Alex watched through a window as Kate came into his line of sight. Her hair was pulled back in a ponytail. She was still barefoot but now wore only a long T-shirt. He inched forward some more as his gaze veered from Kate to the outside of the carriage house to the line of bulky Leland cypresses that surrounded the rear grounds. If Alex were sniping, that's the spot he would have chosen.

He took one more calming breath and went into pure protection mode. This meant his gaze was steady and moved in and out in grids, with Kate representing the center of his protection "bubble." It was rumored that when Secret Service agents went into this groove, they could actually count the beats of a hummingbird's wings. That was ridiculous, of course, but all Alex wanted to do was prevent the lady from being hurt. All he wanted to do was see the gun before it fired. He'd had all those years of training to do this very thing. *Please, God, let it be enough.*

And that's when he spotted it: across the yard and to the right, behind a giant rhododendron, the almost invisible glint of a rifle's optics. He didn't hesitate. He brought his gun up and fired. It was a long shot for a handgun, but he didn't care if he hit the shooter. He just wanted to drive him away.

He placed the shot directly behind the optics. As soon as he fired, the rifle barrel fully appeared, jerking upward and discharging. A split second later Alex put six more bullets into the same area. Next he heard Kate scream. Then the rifle disappeared, and he heard feet running hard away. Damn, he'd missed, but accomplished his goal just the same. *Still, the bastard had gotten off a shot!*

Alex sprinted for the carriage house. Bursting through the door, he heard Kate scream again. She stopped when she saw him. He rushed to her, grabbed her around the waist and pushed her to the floor, his body shielding hers.

"Stay down, there's a shooter out there," he said into her ear. He wriggled forward on his belly and punched the light switch, plunging the carriage house into darkness. Then he crawled back to her.

"Are you all right?" he asked frantically. "You're not shot?"

"No," she whispered back. Then she felt his face. "My God, are you bleeding?"

"I'm not shot. Someone used my head as an anvil."

"Who did it?"

"Don't know." He caught his breath and leaned his back against the stove, his gaze on the door, his hand clenched around his pistol. Kate crawled forward, reached up and pulled a roll of paper towels off the counter.

"Kate," he said harshly, "stay the hell down. The guy could still be out there."

"You're bleeding," she said firmly. She reached up again and ran some water over a wad of the towels. She cleaned his face off and examined the lump on his head. "I can't believe it didn't knock you out."

"Fear is a great antidote to unconsciousness."

"I didn't even hear your truck drive up."

"My Cherokee was put out of commission. Brake line cut. I had quite the roller-coaster ride down 31st."

"Then how'd you get back here?"

"I ran."

She looked astonished. "You ran! All that way?"

"I figured the only place they could've tampered with my brakes was at your place. I . . . I had to get back here. I had to make sure you were okay!" This came out in one long breathless purge of his emotions.

She stopped cleaning the blood off him even as her mouth started trembling. Then Kate wrapped her arms around him, her face nestled against his neck. Alex put an arm around her.

*What a hell of a first date!*

# CHAPTER

## 43

THE CAMEL CLUB HAD WALKED back to Foggy Bottom and ridden the Metro to Union Station, where they had some late dinner at the food court in the lower level and talked things over. Afterward, they went to the train station's parking garage to pick up their vehicles. Stone elected to ride in the sidecar with Reuben. He turned to Caleb and Milton, who were getting into the Malibu.

"All right, you two can go to your condo, Caleb. I believe you'll be safe there, but please keep vigilant."

"Wait a minute," Caleb said sharply. "Where are you and Reuben going?"

Stone hesitated. "I'll just have Reuben drop me back at my cottage."

Caleb scrutinized his friend. "You're lying! You're going out to Purcellville, where that man lives."

"Tyler Reinke," Milton stated, glaring at Stone.

"You're going out there," Caleb continued. "And you don't want us along because you're afraid we might get in the way."

"Consider, Caleb, that you and Milton don't really have any experience at this sort of thing. Whereas Reuben and—"

"I don't care," Caleb snapped. "We're going."

"I'm afraid I can't allow that," Stone replied evenly. "If we're discovered, he'd have all four of us instead of simply two."

Caleb said with dignity, "Can't allow it! We *are* adults, Oliver. And full members of the Camel Club. And if you don't agree to let us go, I'll follow right behind you blowing my horn the whole way, and let me tell you, my car's horn sounds like a damn cannon going off!"

"And I've already located his house on my computer using Map-Quest," Milton said. "It's very difficult to find without precise directions, which I happen to have in my pocket."

Stone looked at Caleb, Milton and finally Reuben, who shrugged.

"All for one and one for all," Reuben said.

Stone finally nodded, albeit grudgingly.

"Shouldn't we just take my car, then?" Caleb said.

"No," Stone replied as he eyed the motorcycle. "I've actually grown fond of riding in this contraption, and it also might come in useful tonight."

They headed west, picking up Route 7 in Virginia heading northwest, passing very close to NIC headquarters as they zipped through Leesburg. A sign at one of the intersections indicated the direction and proximity of the intelligence center. It had always amazed Stone that there were actually *signs* to NSA, CIA and other highly sensitive places. Yet, he supposed, they had visitors too. Still, it certainly put a crimp in the "secret" part of the business.

Reinke's place was very, very rural. They wound up and down back roads for a half hour after leaving Route 7, when Milton finally saw the route sign they wanted. He motioned for Caleb to pull off to the side of the road. Reuben slid in behind them, and he and Stone climbed off the motorcycle and joined them in the car.

Milton said, "His house is two-tenths of a mile up that road. I did a cross search of other addresses up there. There aren't any. His house is the only one."

"Bloody isolated," Reuben said, looking around nervously.

Stone commented, "Murderers are notorious for wanting their privacy."

"So what's the plan?" Caleb asked.

"I want you and Milton to remain in the car—"

"Oliver!" Caleb argued immediately.

"Just hear me out, Caleb. I want you and Milton to remain in the car, but first we're going to drive up the road and see if anyone's home. If they are, we leave. If not, you and Milton will come back here and serve as our lookout. This is the only road in or out, correct, Milton?"

"Yes."

"We'll communicate by cell phone. If you see anyone coming, call us immediately and we'll take the necessary actions."

"What are you going to do?" Caleb asked. "Break into the man's house?"

"You know, Oliver, he's probably got an alarm system," Reuben ventured.

"I would be surprised if he didn't."

"So how do we get in, then?" Reuben asked.

"Let me worry about that."

The house was indeed dark and presumably empty, since there was no car visible and the house didn't have a garage. While Milton and Caleb stood guard in a hidden location near the entrance to the road, Reuben and Stone drove up on the Indian, parking it in a clump of trees behind the house and making their way on foot.

It was a two-story old clapboard with chipping white paint. Stone led Reuben to the rear. The door here was solid, but there was a window next to it. Stone peered through the window and motioned Reuben to look too.

A greenish glow emanated from a new-looking object on the wall opposite the door.

"He's got a security system, all right," Reuben muttered. "Now what?"

Stone didn't answer him. He peered closer at the screen. "We'll have to assume he has motion detectors. That complicates things."

Suddenly, something flew at them from the inside of the house accompanied by twin slashes of emerald. It hit the window and bounced off. Both men leaped back, and Reuben was already turned to run when Stone called out to him.

"It's all right, Reuben," Stone said. "Mr. Reinke has a cat."

His chest heaving, Reuben staggered back up to the window and looked through it. Peering back up at him was a black tabby with a white chest and huge luminous green eyes. The room they were looking into was the kitchen. And the cat had apparently launched itself from the countertop when it noticed their presence.

"Damn cat. I bet it's a female," Reuben said, grimacing.

"Why do you say that?"

"Because women have always tried to give me heart attacks, that's why!"

"Actually, the presence of the animal simplifies things greatly," Stone said.

"How the hell do you figure that?"

"Security systems with motion detectors do not cohabit very well with cats."

Reuben snapped his fingers. "Pet corridors where the motion doesn't hit."

"Exactly." Stone was pulling something from his pocket. It was the black leather case he had taken from his secret room. He unzipped it. Inside was a first-class burglary kit.

Reuben stared at these felonious instruments and then looked up at his friend and said, "I don't want to know."

The window to the kitchen was opened within ten seconds.

"How'd you figure the window wasn't wired to the security system?"

"Wired windows *and* a motion detector is a bit of overkill," Stone replied. "And a house this old has plaster walls which are very difficult to run wire through. I doubt our Mr. Reinke could justify the price. And I checked for a *wireless* security pod on the window before I jimmied it."

"Okay," Reuben demanded. "I *do* want to know. How the hell do you know about stuff like wireless window security pods?"

Stone glanced at him with an innocent expression. "The library *is* open to the public, Reuben."

They climbed inside and the cat met them immediately, rubbing up against their legs and waiting patiently to be stroked.

"All right, before we enter any room, we need to find the motion detector. Then I'll send the cat across the room and we'll follow its lead," Stone said. "Be prepared to crawl on your belly."

"Great! I might as well be back in Nam," Reuben groused.

A half hour before Stone and Reuben broke into Tyler Reinke's house, the back door of Milton's place was forced open and Warren Peters and Tyler Reinke slipped inside and shut the door behind them. It had not been that easy, since Milton had six locks on every door, and all the windows were nailed shut, something the fire marshal doubtless would've disapproved of. They had already checked the power box going into the house for any signs of a security system and had found none.

Reinke was limping from where Alex Ford had punched him in the knee. And there was a bullet hole in Warren Peters' coat sleeve where one of the Secret Service agent's shots had almost found its mark. They'd stumbled upon the two when they went to Georgetown for another look at the boat, only to find that Ford and Adams had beaten them to it.

Both men were furious about their failure to kill the pair, and it was fortunate indeed for Milton Farb that he wasn't at home right now.

The two men pulled out their flashlights and started searching. Farb's place wasn't that large, but it was filled with books and expensive computer and video equipment for his Web design business. Also located there was the one thing Reinke and Peters hadn't counted on: a wireless infrared surveillance system that looked like overhead track lighting. Located in each room, it was now recording their movements, and had also sounded a silent alarm to a security firm that Milton had hired because of several previous burglaries. The system ran off a regular household outlet with a battery backup. He'd stopped using a loud alarm because in his neighborhood the police took their time coming and the alerted thieves had always been long gone before their arrival.

As the pair searched the house, their amazement grew with each new discovery.

"This guy's a freaking nutcase," Peters said as they explored the kitchen. The canned goods in the pantry were all neatly labeled and placed in excruciatingly precise order. The utensils hung from a rack on the wall arranged from largest to smallest. The pots and pans were organized the same way on a large rack over the stove. Even the oven mitts were lined up with precision, as were all the dishes in the cupboards. The place was a monument to fastidiousness of the most zealous kind.

When they went upstairs and poked around Milton's bedroom and closet area, it was more of the same.

Reinke came out of the master bathroom shaking his head. "You're not going to believe this. This bozo has torn off each sheet of the toilet paper and stacked them in a wicker box beside the toilet with instructions on disposal. I mean what do you do with toilet paper except flush it!"

In the bedroom closet Peters said, "Yeah, well, come in here and tell me who puts their *socks* on hangers?"

A moment later they were both staring at the socks and the tri-folded underwear and shirts that all hung on wooden hangers in precise order, with the shirts fully buttoned, including the cuffs. And they were organized by season. The men weren't guessing at this, as Milton had helpfully posted pictures depicting winter, summer, spring and fall.

Finding nothing useful in the master bedroom, the two NIC men slipped into the other room upstairs that had been fitted out as an office. They both were immediately drawn to Milton's desk, where every item there was laid at right angles to its neighbor.

And finally in this house of perfect order they found something that they could actually use. It was in a box marked "Receipts," on a shelf behind Milton's desk, and the receipts, they quickly determined, were divided by both month and product. From the box, Reinke plucked out a credit card slip that had a name on it.

"Chastity Hayes," Reinke read. "Want to bet that's his girlfriend?"

"If a guy like that can *have* a girlfriend."

Each probably thinking the same thing, they shone their lights on the wall of Milton's office. The pictures there were arranged in a very elaborate configuration that Peters recognized first. "It's a double helix. DNA. This guy is a total freak."

Reinke's light flickered across one picture and then came back to it.

"Love, Chastity," Reinke read at the bottom of the picture, which showed Chastity in a revealing bathing suit and blowing a kiss to the photographer, presumably Milton.

"That's his girlfriend?" a stunned Reinke said as he eyed a picture of Milton next to the one with Chastity in her bikini. "How the hell does a geek like that get a chick like *that*?"

"Nurturing instinct," Peters answered promptly. "Some women love to play mother."

Peters pulled out an electronic device that looked like a larger version of a BlackBerry and typed in the name Chastity Hayes. A minute later three possibilities came up. Restricting his search to the Washington, D.C., area, Peters found Chastity Hayes, accountant and the owner of a house in Chevy Chase, Maryland. In addition it revealed her educational, medical, employment and financial history. As Peters ran his gaze down the info pouring over his tiny screen, Reinke pointed a finger at one line. "She was in a psych hospital for a while. I bet you she's OCD like Farb."

"At least we know where she lives. And if Farb isn't here" — Peters glanced once more at the photo of the lovely Chastity — "chances are he's there. Because that's where I'd be sleeping if I were him."

The noise in the back of the house froze them both. They were footsteps. And then they heard a groan and a thudding sound.

They pulled their guns and moved in the direction of those noises.

When they reached the kitchen, they saw it. The man was on the floor, unconscious. They both started when they saw the uniform.

"Rental cop," Reinke said finally. "We must've tripped some alarm."

"Yeah, but who the hell knocked him out?"

They looked around nervously.

"Let's get out of here," Reinke whispered.

They slipped out the back of the house and soon reached their car a block over.

"Do we hit the chick tonight?" Peters asked.

"No, you don't," a voice said causing both of them to jump.

They turned and saw Tom Hemingway rising from the backseat. He did not look very happy.

"You've had a singularly unproductive night," he began ominously.

"You followed us here?" Peters asked in a small voice that broke slightly.

"After your last report of screwing up, what exactly did you expect me to do?"

"So you did the rental cop. Is he dead?" Reinke asked.

Hemingway ignored him. "Let me impress upon both of you once more the seriousness of what we're trying to accomplish here. I have an army working their asses off just north of here doing far more than either of you have been asked to do. And unlike them, you two are being paid very well. And they've made no mistakes whatsoever. " He stared at them so intensely that both men held their breaths. "Maybe what happened tonight was just a string of bad luck. But going forward, I will make no more allowances for bad luck."

"What do you want us to do now?" Reinke asked nervously.

"Go home and get some rest. You'll need it." He held out his hand. "Give me the receipt with the woman's name on it."

"How did you—," Reinke began.

However, Hemingway looked at him with such disdain that Reinke closed his mouth and passed the paper over. In a few seconds Hemingway had disappeared.

Both men sat back in their car seats and let out deep breaths.

Peters said, "That guy scares the complete and total shit out of me."

Reinke nodded. "He was a legend at CIA. Even the drug guys in Colombia were scared to death of him. Nobody ever saw him coming in or going out." He paused. "I've watched him working out at the gym at NIC. He looks like he's carved out of granite, and he's quick as a cat. *And* he's destroyed two seventy-five-pound body bags with just his hands. They won't even let him use his legs on the heavy bags anymore because he was breaking them with just one kick."

"So what now?" Peters asked.

"You heard the man. We get some rest. After three close shaves tonight we don't need a fourth. You can crash at my place."

# CHAPTER

## 44

AFTER WHAT HE'D SEEN AT Arlington Cemetery, Gray had gone directly to CIA headquarters at Langley. Inside this facility was a room that only current and former CIA directors were allowed to enter. Each director could access documents and other materials that pertained to missions he was involved in while at the Agency. They were held in vaults that contained large safe-deposit-style boxes. Because of the secrets housed here, it was the most heavily guarded room at Langley.

Gray put his hand on a biometric reader in front of the vault door that was labeled with his name. The door slid open and Gray entered, taking out his keys. He knew exactly the box he wanted: number 10.

He unlocked it and drew out the contents, sat down and spread the materials out on a desk kept in the vault.

The file he was perusing was officially marked "J.C." Those two initials could stand for many things, including Jesus Christ. However, they didn't refer to the Son of God, but were simply the initials of a remarkable flesh-and-blood man named John Carr.

As Gray read through the exploits of Carr's career at the CIA, his head continued to shake in absolute amazement at what the man had accomplished. And survived! Although it could be argued that the world was a more dangerous place now, it was not appreciably more perilous currently than when John Carr worked for the Agency.

As Gray came to the last pages of John Carr's career at Langley, it ended, the way it had meant to end, with burial at Arlington Cemetery with full military honors, although John Carr had not technically worked for the army for years and had not died in a uniform. After that, his entire past had been wiped clean from every record in the United States. Gray had seen to that personally based on orders from the highest level at the CIA.

And though John Carr wasn't buried in that grave, he was still supposed to be dead. The initial hit on him killed only his wife. But there had been another attempt deemed successful, though no body had been recovered; it was presumably in the bellies of fish in the middle of the ocean. Perhaps Gray was simply jumping to conclusions. The man he'd seen was thin and seemingly frail. Could that be the mighty John Carr? The years could take their toll, but still, with a man like Carr, Gray figured age would simply bounce off him. Yet the man *had* been standing directly in front of the grave marked for John Carr. And hadn't he managed to disappear, much like the legendary Carr made a career out of doing?

Gray's pulse accelerated as he thought how close he'd possibly been to a man who'd been betrayed by his country. And not just any man, but a man who, in his time, was the perfect killing machine for the United States government. Until, that is, he became a liability, as such men often did.

Carter Gray put away the box and left the room of old secrets with a curious emotion filling his chest. Carter Gray feared a dead man who, inexplicably, might still be among the living.

Later, back at his home, Gray lit the candles in his bedroom as he kept glancing at the photos on his mantel. In a few minutes it would be midnight, and September 11 would be with him again. He sat in the chair next to his bed and opened his Bible. Carter Gray had been baptized a Catholic, had dutifully performed his first Communion at age seven and his Confirmation at age thirteen and had even been an altar boy. Since reaching adulthood, however, he had never once set foot inside a church unless it was for some political function. With his occupation, religion had never seemed to be that relevant. However, his wife *had* been a devout Catholic, and their daughter, Maggie, had been raised in that faith.

Now, with both of them gone, Gray had taken up reading the Bible. It wasn't for his salvation, but as a way of picking up the banner for his fallen family, although, he had to admit, the words did give him some level of comfort. Tonight he read out loud some passages from Corinthians and another from Leviticus and then ventured into the Psalms. It was now well past midnight, and he knelt down in front of the photos and performed his prayers, although they were more akin to conversations with his dead family. He almost always broke down and cried during this ritual. The tears felt deserved and, in a sense, were healing. Yet, as he sat back in his chair with his Bible, Gray's thoughts returned once more to a burial plot with an empty coffin. *Is John Carr dead or alive?*

Tom Hemingway returned to his apartment, the receipt with the name Chastity Hayes safely in his pocket. He made his usual tea and drank it barefoot, standing by the window looking out onto the Capitol grounds. A lot had happened in the last twenty-four hours and none of it positive from his perspective.

His pathetic duo of Reinke and Peters had missed two targets tonight, and now Alex Ford and Kate Adams would no doubt go straight to their respective agencies and demand that full investigations move forward. Added to that was the fact that Carter Gray was talking about the resurrection of the dead. In Hemingway's mind that was a clear reference to all the terrorists supposedly killed by their colleagues. That had prompted Hemingway's hurried message to Captain Jack.

He turned from the window and looked at a portrait on the wall. It was a very good likeness of his father, the Honorable Franklin T. Hemingway, ambassador to some of the most difficult territories in the world of diplomacy. And his last post proved to be too violent even for him. A bullet in China ended the career of a man who had devoted his life to cobbling peace where none seemed possible.

The son had not followed the father's footsteps principally because Tom Hemingway didn't believe he possessed the necessary skills and qualities that went into a successful statesman. And back then he was an angry young man. While that fury had diminished over the years, it had never entirely gone away. Why should it? At his funeral it was said by many distinguished voices from all over the world that Franklin Hemingway would be sorely missed as a global peacemaker. Hemingway still felt the loss of his mentor as strongly this minute as he had felt it the day an assassin's bullet ended his father's life. For him, time lessened nothing. It only intensified the sense of agony he'd carried with him since learning that precious, valiant heart had stopped beating.

# CHAPTER

## 45

Tʏʟᴇʀ Rᴇɪɴᴋᴇ's ʜᴏᴍᴇ ᴡᴀs ᴠᴇʀʏ sparsely furnished. Reuben and Stone crawled on their bellies to each room, hoping for anything that could be useful, but came away disappointed each time. They passed the front door where another alarm code pad was mounted and slithered up the stairs after the fat tabby.

When they reached the bedroom, something caught Reuben's eye.

"Our Mr. Reinke is a chopper pilot." He picked up the only picture on the nightstand. In it Tyler Reinke was at the controls of a sleek black helicopter.

"Any insignias on it?" Stone asked as he searched other parts of the room.

"Nope." Reuben put the picture back down after using a corner of the bedspread to wipe off any fingerprints.

Stone had rummaged around in the closet and came out carrying a small box.

"Financial records," he said in response to Reuben's questioning look.

He took out a stack and started going through them, scanning each page.

"Anything of interest?"

Stone held up one page. "It seems this account is set up under a false name, although the address matches the house we're in. However, I'm afraid I have little experience with financial portfolios."

"Let me take a look." Reuben spent some time going over the statements and some handwritten notes also contained in the batch. "It looks like Reinke, if this *is* his account statement, has recently bought an enormous long-put option on margin."

"Long-put option on margin? What's that?"

"Margin means he's borrowed money to purchase his position and he has the option to sell the position at a certain level. According to these handwritten notes, he's essentially betting the farm that the S&P will take a dive. So it's like sell low and buy back high. That's not what you usually want, but in this case you can make enormous amounts of money doing that very thing. And the amount at risk is far more than someone would make off a government salary. That's why it's on margin."

"I had no idea you knew so much about finances."

"Hey, a guy likes to take a plunge every now and then. And I don't plan on working on that damn loading dock until I croak, I can tell you that."

"But how would he know that it's going down? It's one thing to have inside info on one stock, but the whole market?" Stone thought for a moment. "But then again, the financial markets almost always drop in the face of an unforeseen catastrophe."

"What, like an earthquake?" Reuben said.

"But also with man-made catastrophes. On 9/11 I recall they had to close the stock market and calm everyone down. Left to its own devices, the market would've plunged. It still went down when it reopened after 9/11. Unscrupulous people with advance knowledge could've made a fortune."

"So maybe Reinke knows of a coming catastrophe?" Reuben said nervously.

"Or else he's helping create one," Stone replied.

As soon as they saw the car approaching from their hiding place off the road, Milton got on his cell phone and called Reuben. Well, he attempted to call, but no ringing sound came. He looked at his cell phone and his heart sank.

Caleb glanced at him as the headlights crept closer.

"Call them!"

"There's no signal strength."

"What!"

"There's no signal strength here. It must be a bad cell zone. I can't get through."

Caleb pointed at the oncoming car. "That is very likely a murderer in there."

"Caleb, there's nothing I can do."

"Damn these high-tech abominations," Caleb said angrily. "They never work when you really need them to."

The other car turned off the road and headed to Reinke's house.

"That's Tyler Reinke's car. I recognized it," Caleb said.

"I know, I did too," a panicked Milton added. "What are we going to do?"

Caleb started the car. "Well, I'm certainly not going to let them kill Oliver and Reuben while we just sit here with useless *technology*. Hold on!"

Milton braced himself as Caleb hit the gas and the Malibu sprang forward.

They squealed back onto the road, where Caleb floored it and took the turn toward Reinke's house just barely on four wheels.

As the Malibu flew forward, Caleb hit the horn. He hadn't been joking before to Stone. It was very loud, like a shriek and a train whistle rolled into one.

Reinke glanced over his shoulder at the Malibu as it raced by honking its horn.

He looked at Peters and muttered, "Stupid high school kids joyriding. Happens all the time around here."

Inside Reinke's house, both Stone and Reuben raced to the front bedroom window when they heard the car horn. That's when they saw the headlights turn into the drive.

"Oh, shit, that's Reinke," Reuben said.

"And his friend," Stone added as the two men climbed out of the car. Then he glanced at the Malibu disappearing down the street. "I told them to *call* us, not race around sounding like a banshee," Stone said irritably.

They hurtled downstairs, and then in the nick of time Stone remembered and grabbed Reuben by the shirt an instant before he would've stepped into the infrared arc of the motion detector mounted by the front door. They crawled forward as they heard the front door being unlocked. They hit the kitchen as the front door opened and the beeps

started to sound. They were getting off the floor as they heard someone punching in the code and the beeps stopped.

"Okay," Stone whispered. "The alarm's off, so we can open the back
door."

Reuben did so as quietly as possible, even as they heard a set of footsteps coming their way. They bolted out of the house, shutting the
door behind them, and turned the corner of the house.

And ran right into Warren Peters, who was pulling a trash can back
behind the house.

"What the hell—" was as far as Peters got before Reuben's massive
fist sent the NIC man flying head over heels backward. Stone and
Reuben ran for the motorcycle. They were on it and Reuben had kick-
started the bike to life when Reinke, hearing all the commotion, came
flying out of the house.

He spotted Stone and Reuben, and his hand went inside his jacket as
he ran forward. He had a clear line to shoot. What he didn't count on
was a rusted Malibu going partially airborne driven by a crazed rare
book specialist with a terrified OCD genius counting madly in the
copilot's seat.

"Holy mother of God!" Milton screamed as Reinke went flying .
across the windshield, rolled off and landed in a heap in the grass.
Then Milton resumed his ritual counting.

Peters had staggered to his feet by this time. However, Caleb, his
mind and body seemingly possessed by the spirit of a youthful dare-
devil, rammed the Malibu into reverse, put the gas pedal to the floor
and sped backward, the wheels spitting gravel like machine-gun bullets.

Peters screamed as the car bore down on him. He got off one shot
and dove out of the way. He was coming up for another attempt when
the motorcycle flew past him. As Reuben drove, Stone was sitting on
the lip of the sidecar swinging his helmet by the strap. It caught Peters
on the side of the head, and he went down for the count.

It was a full ten minutes before Peters and Reinke began to stir. By the
time they had regained consciousness, the Camel Club was long gone.

# CHAPTER

## 46

THE AUTHORITIES' RESPONSE TO what had happened to Alex Ford and Kate Adams was not exactly encouraging. According to the police the brake line seemed to have popped all by itself. Not unusual for a vehicle that old, the police said. And there was no evidence of any shooter at Kate Adams' home, other than what Alex had said he'd seen and heard. Two of his bullets were found embedded in the fence behind where he shot. No other slugs were recovered.

It was the next morning, and Alex was sitting in Jerry Sykes' office listening to the official version of last night's event.

Sykes stopped pacing and looked at him. "The people who tried to help you after your 'accident' reported you were acting in a bizarre manner and then you took off running. Alex, all this crap just isn't like you. Is there something going on in your life you want to talk about?"

"Absolutely nothing other than someone wanting me dead," Alex said stonily.

Sykes dropped into his chair and picked up a mug of coffee. "Why in the hell would anyone want you dead?"

"Some guy put a freaking gun to my head, Jerry. I didn't take the time to ask him why."

"And nobody saw this guy except you. So again, I'm asking you what happened between yesterday and today to make somebody want you dead?"

Alex hesitated. He wanted to tell Sykes about the discovery of the boat but figured that admitting he'd disobeyed another order from the director would be the end of his career.

"I've got a lot of years of damn good service behind me. Why all of a sudden would I start making this sort of crap up?"

"You put your finger on it. You've put in a lot of years. The director cut you a break yesterday. He could've canned your ass on the spot. Hell, I probably would've if I'd been in his shoes. Don't blow a gift from the top, Alex. You're not getting another one."

"Fine, but can you at least put someone on Kate Adams' house? I didn't imagine that optics reflection."

Sykes sat back. "I'll call the D.C. police and ask them to have a car make some extra rounds. But that's all. And consider *that* a gift." Sykes looked at his watch. "I've got a meeting, and I think you have a post to stand."

"Right. In the White House," Alex said wearily.

"No, actually *outside*. You'll have to work your way back inside the place."

The Camel Club held a hasty meeting at Caleb's condo early that morning. The first order of business was to congratulate the esteemed librarian and gutsy wheelman on his bravery. They had to wait a bit for that, however, as Caleb was in the bathroom still throwing up after realizing just how close he'd come to dying.

When Caleb finally emerged from the toilet Stone said, "I would like the official record to reflect that Caleb Shaw has earned the deepest thanks of the entire Camel Club membership for his extraordinary bravery and ingenuity."

A pale but smiling Caleb shook each of their hands. "I'm not sure what came over me. I just knew that I had to do something. I've never been that scared since I was given the honor of handling Tocqueville's *De la Démocratie en Amérique* in its original paper wrappers."

Reuben gave a fake tremble. "Handling a Tocqueville! Gives *me* the piss shivers just thinking about it."

"However, we have to assume that Reinke and his partner have now 'made' us, so to speak," Stone warned.

"I'm not so sure. I took my license plates off while we were watching the road," Caleb said as they all stared at him in surprise. "After Milton got their license plate and ran it so easily, I was terrified they'd do the same if they saw mine," he explained.

Just then Milton's cell phone buzzed.

"Yes?" he said. He listened for a bit and then clicked off and looked at the others. "Someone broke into my house and knocked out the security guard who responded to the silent alarm."

"Was anything taken?" Stone asked.

"Doesn't appear to be. However, I have surveillance devices disguised as track lighting throughout the place. The security company doesn't know about that."

"It would be very interesting to see who broke in," Stone remarked.

"I have to go there to check it. The DVD recorder's hidden behind my refrigerator."

"We'll have to chance it," Stone said. "If it was Reinke and his colleague, it might give us the leverage we need."

Reuben put a big arm around Caleb. "Well, if those two show up again, they're going down for the count. Right, Killer?"

His first day back on presidential protection detail was a little awkward for Alex Ford. Everyone seemed to know that this reassignment was a demotion for the veteran agent. Still, they were cordial and professional with him. There was one good thing about being assigned to exterior White House duty: Alex could patrol Lafayette Park.

However, Stone wasn't there, but Adelphia was. She was hovering in the middle of the park, shooting glances in the direction of Stone's tent.

"Hello, Adelphia," Alex said politely. "I was just looking for Oliver."

To his surprise, Adelphia's response was to burst into tears. That was something Alex had never seen the woman do before.

"Adelphia, what's the matter?"

She just covered her face with her hands.

Alex moved over to her. "Adelphia, what is it? Are you hurt? Or sick?"

She shook her head, then took a deep breath and uncovered her face. "It is all right," she said. "It is fine."

Alex led her over to a bench. "You're obviously not fine. Now, tell me what's wrong. Maybe I can help."

Adelphia took a series of replenishing breaths and then looked over at Stone's tent again. "I no lie to you. *I* am fine, Agent Fort."

"It's Ford, but if you're all right—" Then he followed her gaze to Stone's tent. "Has something happened to Oliver?" he asked quickly.

"I not know that."

"I don't understand. Then why are you crying?"

She stared at him in a way she never had before. It wasn't her usual distrustful and surly expression. It was one of hopelessness. "He trusts you. Oliver has said this to me, he say Agent Fort is good man."

"I like and respect Oliver too." He paused and then added, "His face was bruised the last time I saw him. Does it have something to do with that?"

Adelphia nodded and told him of the encounter in the park. "He took this finger," she said, holding up her middle finger, "and he poke it in the man's side. And this giant of a man, he fall like baby." She drew a deep, troubled breath. "And then Oliver, he pick up the knife and he hold it in a way"—she shuddered—"he hold it like he know well the knife. And I think he will cut the man's neck open, like this." She made a slashing motion with her hand and then stopped. She stared at Alex with an expression of both sadness and relief. "But he did not. He no cut the man. He leave when police come. Oliver no like police."

"And you haven't seen him since?"

She shook her head, and Alex sat back against the bench letting this all sink in.

"Hey, Ford," a voice called out. Alex looked over at his supervisor.

"You wanna come back and join the party, if it's not too much trouble?" the man said curtly.

Alex jumped up. Before leaving he turned to Adelphia. "If you see Oliver, tell him I want to talk to him."

Adelphia didn't look very enthused about that.

"I won't tell him you told me anything. I promise. I just need to see him."

She finally nodded and he raced off.

Work in Brennan for the president's visit had accelerated, and Captain Jack was kept very busy. The vehicle being constructed in the garage was right on schedule, and the various wheelmen were ready. He hadn't visited the snipers' nest again. He didn't want to risk being seen going to the apartment too often. Captain Jack had spent time with al-Rimi and his colleague at the hospital while the two were off duty. There were no problems there.

He had met once more with Djamila late last night after she had made her nightly rounds of Brennan. He was still a bit concerned about her emotional makeup, but there was no time to substitute now. He reinforced the notion of how important her work was to the whole project. About how many men would be sacrificing their lives and how that sacrifice would be for naught if she failed.

He would hold two more meetings before game day, one tonight, before the Secret Service advance team arrived in the morning. And, as with the last group meeting, he would afterward meet with his North Korean counterpart to go over necessary details.

However, Carter Gray was on the prowl. Actually, Captain Jack was a little surprised it had taken the old man this long to become suspicious. They had used every connection they had in the Muslim world to set up this operation. But Hemingway's plan was, in Captian Jack's mind, an ultimately futile exercise, although Tom Hemingway simply refused to see that. To Captain Jack's thinking, Hemingway's chief problem was he still believed in the good in people. That logic was inherently flawed, Captain Jack knew, because the people who really mattered didn't possess any goodness. With every mission he'd ever carried out, Captain Jack always allowed for contingencies, and this time was no exception. Following his old maxim had once again led him down the right path. It really was all about the *money*.

In the rental space on the outskirts of town the engineer and chemist were going over again the workings of the prosthetic hand with the ex–National Guardsman.

He had gotten the maneuverings of the device down very well. They watched as he put his new hand through a series of grips, waves and other exercises. Then he executed the water bag implement flawlessly. Before leaving he thanked them both.

Afterward, the men packed up a duffel bag and headed into town, where they ran errands at a half dozen businesses along the town's center. At each place they left a little present. These presents would further help lay a place in history for Brennan, Pennsylvania, although certainly not one the townspeople would have wanted.

# CHAPTER

## 47

Alex found out later that day he'd been assigned to the advance team for the Brennan event. This thoroughly ticked him off, because it meant time away from Kate. However, it wasn't as if he could complain. He was barely hanging on to his Service pension as it was. Indeed, Alex sensed that he'd be sent to every bump-in-the-road campaign outpost Brennan was targeting on his reelection charge across America. He'd be a zombie by the time it was over.

He and Kate met at a restaurant in Dupont Circle. She'd rebounded well from the frightening events of the previous night and was now determined to get to the truth. That spunk drew both admiration and terror from Alex.

"I understand how you feel, Kate, but don't get carried away. These guys have guns, and they're obviously not afraid to use them."

"More reason to get them off the streets," she said determinedly. "So when do you leave for Brennan?"

"Crack of dawn. It's a short flight but there's a lot to do. Advance teams do the heavy lifting that keeps the president safe. But it's killing me that I won't be around here in case you need me."

She put her hand over his. "Well, for what it's worth, I thought you were pretty damn terrific last night."

Right as she said these words, their young waiter stopped by with their meals and overheard them. Obviously misinterpreting the import of her words, he gave Alex a wink and a smile.

As they ate, Kate asked, "So any new developments?"

"Just one." He told her about his conversation with Adelphia about Stone.

"You said Stone didn't have a past that you could find. And yet based on what Adelphia saw, he definitely *has* a past, maybe a pretty interesting one."

Alex nodded and then looked thoughtful. "What do you say after we eat we take a little stroll over to 16th and Pennsylvania?"

"I hear that's a really nice place. Think you can get me in?"

"Right now I'm not sure they'd let *me* in. But I was talking about the 16th and Pennsylvania on the *other* side of the street."

Forty-five minutes later the two arrived at Lafayette Park.

"Doesn't look like he's there," Alex observed as he stared at Stone's darkened tent. This was confirmed moments later when they opened the tent and saw it was empty.

"So you have another address for the man?" Kate asked.

"Actually, I do."

Twenty minutes later Alex pulled his car to the curb outside Mt. Zion Cemetery.

A light was on in the caretaker's cottage.

"He lives here?" Kate asked. "At a cemetery?"

"What'd you expect? A penthouse near the MCI Center?"

The gate to the cemetery was locked, but Alex boosted Kate over and then scaled the fence, landing next to her.

When he answered their knock, Stone couldn't hide his surprise. "Alex?" he said, and then glanced curiously at Alex's companion.

"Hello, Oliver, this is my friend Kate Adams. She's a lawyer at Justice and the best bartender anyone could want."

"Ms. Adams, it's very nice to meet you," Stone said, shaking her hand. He looked questioningly at Alex again.

"We just thought we'd drop by to see you," Alex said.

"I see. Well, please come in." Stone didn't ask how Alex knew where he lived.

He let them into the cottage and then poured out some coffee he'd made while they looked around. Kate leafed through a book she pulled from the shelf. "Have you read all these, Oliver?" she asked.

"Yes," he said, "though most of them not more than twice, I'm afraid. Unfortunately, there's never enough time to read as much as one would want."

She eyed Alex. "Solzhenitsyn. No lightweight stuff."

"I think I read the Cliffs Notes on him in college," Alex said.

She held out the book. "Yeah, but in Russian?"

Stone came out of the kitchen carrying two cups of coffee.

"I like your home, Oliver," she said. "It's how I'd envision a college professor's place to look."

"Yes, untidy, dusty, rumpled and full of old books." Stone glanced at Alex. "I understand you're on the advance team to Brennan, Pennsylvania?"

Alex gaped. "How the hell did you know that?"

"White House detail can often be very tedious, and people pass the time by talking shop. And voices carry amazingly there, if one is actually listening, which I'm afraid that few people really do anymore."

Kate smiled at Stone as they all sat down in chairs around the fireplace. "Alex said you were quite extraordinary, Oliver, and I've found I can thoroughly rely on his opinion of people."

"Well, Ms. Adams, I can assure you that Alex is truly special."

"Please call me Kate."

"Yeah, and if I get any more *special*," Alex said, "I'll be pumping gas for a living." He glanced at Stone. "Your face looks like it's healing."

"It was nothing to begin with. A little ice. I've suffered worse."

"Really? Care to talk about it?" Alex said.

"You would find such a discussion terribly boring, I'm afraid."

"Try me," Alex said pointedly.

A voice reached them from the street. They all got up and went to the door. There was Adelphia standing outside the locked gates calling to Stone.

"Adelphia?" Stone quickly went and let her in.

After they had settled back around the fireplace, Stone introduced Adelphia to Kate Adams.

Kate put out her hand but Adelphia simply nodded at her. The woman had obviously not planned on Stone having any company.

"I didn't know you knew where I lived, Adelphia," Stone said.

"You know where I live, it work both way," she snapped.

Suitably rebuked, Stone sat back in his chair and stared at his hands.

"Oliver was just telling us that his face is much better," Alex said quickly, giving the woman what he hoped would be a clear segue into her concerns.

However, Adelphia said nothing, and there was another awkward silence until Kate remarked, "I actually knew one of the attorneys from the ACLU who worked on your relocation case in Lafayette Park. He said it was a tough battle."

"I believe the Secret Service were very aggressive in not wanting us back for security purposes," Stone agreed.

Adelphia suddenly broke in. "But then the rights of people, they win out. People here have good rights. That is why this country is great country."

Stone nodded in agreement.

"Yes," Adelphia continued. "My friend Oliver, he has sign. It say 'I want truth.'"

"Don't we all," Kate said with a smile.

"But sometime truth, it must come from inside a person," Adelphia said forcefully as she touched her chest. "One who asks for truth, they too must be truthful, is this not so?" She looked around the group as she said this.

Stone was clearly uncomfortable with the direction of the conversation. He responded slowly, "The truth comes in many different shapes. But sometimes even when the truth is staring someone in the face, he fails to see it." He abruptly stood. "Now, if you'll excuse me, I actually have someplace I have to be."

"It's pretty late, Oliver," Alex said.

"Yes, it is late, and I hadn't anticipated visitors tonight."

His meaning was clear. They all stood and hurriedly walked out with mumbled good-byes.

Alex and Kate gave Adelphia a lift back to her apartment.

From the backseat she said, "He is in trouble. I know that this is true."

"What makes you so sure?" Alex asked.

"He come by the park today with his friend, the giant one. He on a motorcycle. Riding in a sidecar." She added this last in a tone implying that doing such was a criminal act.

"A giant man? Oh, you mean Reuben," Alex clarified.

"Yes, Reuben. I no like him much. He has, how you say, the shifty pants."

"You mean shifty eyes," Alex corrected.

"No, I mean the shifty *pants*!"

"It's okay, Adelphia," Kate said, "I know exactly what you mean."

Adelphia shot her an appreciative look.

"But you still haven't told us why you think he's in trouble," Alex said.

"It is everything. He is not same. Something troubles him much. I try to talk to him, but he will not speak. He will not!"

Alex looked at her, puzzled by the intensity of her response, and his suspicions were suddenly engaged. "Adelphia, is there something else you want to tell us?"

She looked terrified for an instant and then assumed an expression of deep offense. "What do you say? That I lie!"

"No, that's not what I meant."

"I am no liar. I try to do good, that is all."

"I'm not—"

She cut him off. "I no talk any more. I no tell you more lies!"

They were stopped at a light. She jerked open the door, got out and stalked off.

"Adelphia," Alex called after her.

Kate said, "Better let her cool off awhile. She'll come around soon enough."

"I don't have time for that. I leave tomorrow morning."

"And tomorrow is when I start my vacation."

"What? When did that happen?"

"After last night I needed some time off, so I'm taking a week. Maybe I'll come up to see you in Brennan. I hear it's a real happening place."

"It's probably a cow pasture where a president happened to be born."

"And maybe I'll have some time to check out your Mr. Stone and his friends."

He looked at her in alarm. "Kate, I don't think that's a great idea."

"Or I can start trying to find the people who wanted us dead. It's your call."

He put up his hands in mock surrender. "Okay, okay. Go after Oliver Stone and company. Damn, talk about the lesser of two evils."

"Aye, aye, sir," she said, giving him a salute.

# 48

THE SECRET SERVICE ADVANCE team touched down in Pittsburgh at seven A.M., and the equivalent of a small army rolled off the planes and headed directly to Brennan. The president traveled hundreds of times each year. And at least several days before he got to a particular location the Secret Service sent a regiment of agents who would spend collectively thousands of hours checking every conceivable detail to ensure that the trip would be uneventful from a security standpoint.

Since the president had numerous trips planned on his campaign and would hop from one state to another, there were multiple advance teams out in the field, which had stretched the Service's manpower. Normally, an advance team would have a full week to do its work, but because of the number of events President Brennan had booked on the campaign, the Service had had to prioritize. Events deemed lower risk were allotted less advance time. With higher-risk events the Service had its usual week to prepare. The Brennan, Pennsylvania, event had been deemed low risk for a number of factors. Of course, what that meant for Alex Ford and the rest of the advance team was that they would have to cram a week's worth of work into a few days.

The Service set up shop at the largest hotel in Brennan, taking over an entire floor. It had been renamed the Sir James, in honor of the president's first name. That had caused about ten minutes of funny one-liners from the field agents, until their leaders came within earshot. One room became the communications center and was consequently stripped of all furniture and completely debugged. From this point until the Service left there'd be no room service or maids allowed there.

That afternoon the Service met with members of the local police forces. As Alex watched, the lead advance agent faced the cadre of law enforcement officers while briefing books were handed out.

"Just remember," he warned. "In another room near here there may be a group of people planning to do the exact opposite of what we're trying to accomplish."

Alex had heard this spiel many times, but as he looked around the room, he couldn't believe that many of those present were buying the line. Still, Alex, with all his experience, discounted nothing. Secret Service agents were paranoid by nature. While Brennan didn't look like a potential trouble spot, no one had expected Bobby Kennedy to be shot in the kitchen of a hotel. James Garfield bought it at a train station; William McKinley went down at a rope line after having been shot by a man who wrapped his revolver inside a "bandage"; Lincoln was gunned down in a theater and JFK in his open limo. *Not on my watch*, Alex kept telling himself.

*Not on my watch.*

Potential motorcade routes from the airport to the ceremonial grounds were discussed, and possible trouble spots with each were considered. Then the group broke into smaller units, and Alex found himself asking the usual questions of the local law enforcement. Had gun sales peaked? Were any police uniforms missing? Were there any local threats against the president? What were the locations of the nearest hospitals and potential safe houses?

After that, they drove out to the site. Alex walked the ceremonial grounds and helped establish sniper posts. He eyed the area, locating what the Service referred to as the assassin's funnel. You had to think like a killer. Where, how and when could the person be expected to strike?

The stage was finished, and a work crew was putting the finishing touches on lighting and sound and the two giant TV screens that would allow the crowd to see the president up close, at least digitally.

To Alex's experienced eye the place looked reasonably doable from a protection point of view. The single entry and exit for vehicular traffic was both bad and good for obvious reasons. Still, the president wouldn't be here that long. Two hours tops.

As Alex drove back into Brennan, he looked around the small town.

It had long been a Service myth that the best time to rob a bank was when the president was in town, because every cop within twenty miles would be watching him and not the townspeople's money. Alex had a feeling that adage would be pretty accurate here. There were no cops anywhere.

Back in his hotel room Alex decided to go for a run. He'd gone through college on a track scholarship, and, despite his neck injury, he ran whenever he could. It was one of the few things keeping him from feeling totally washed up physically. He hit the main street and headed east, passed the hospital and then turned left and picked up his pace as he headed north. A van passed him. He had no reason to look over and didn't. He wouldn't have recognized the woman anyway. Nor did Djamila look in his direction as she drove by with the three boys in the back.

Next Alex passed an auto repair facility with its blacked-out windows. Hidden behind them was a lot of work going on as a new vehicle was fashioned. If Alex had been aware of the plot, he would've charged into the garage and arrested everyone there. But he wasn't aware, so he just kept jogging. Indeed, the downtown area of Brennan held little interest for Alex because the president would never be coming here. The ceremony at the dedication grounds would constitute the entire program.

After he had showered back at his hotel room, Alex went to volunteer for another chunk of work that night. Might as well do all he could to get back into the Service's good graces.

While Alex was working away up in Brennan, Kate was busy too. She'd risen very early that day and eaten breakfast with Lucky. She asked the older woman a favor, which Lucky quickly granted.

After that, Kate had gone to the carriage house, sat down at her small desk and planned out her attack on Oliver Stone. Alex had said that he had run Stone's prints through all the usual databases and come up with zilch. To Kate, that could only mean one of two things: Either the man had never held a position requiring a fingerprint check or else his identity had been erased from those databases so completely that whoever Oliver Stone really was had ceased to exist. She wrote down some possible lines of inquiries and then mapped out her strategy in the same manner she would a legal case. Satisfied, she quickly showered and headed out.

A little later she parked as close to Mt. Zion Cemetery as she could and then waited. It was only seven-thirty in the morning, but as she watched, Stone emerged from his cottage and headed off down the street. Kate ducked down in her car so he couldn't see her. When he was almost out of sight, a surprising thing happened. Adelphia came out from behind some parked cars on Q Street and started following Stone. Kate thought for a moment and then put the car in gear. She quickly caught up to Adelphia and rolled down her window.

At first Adelphia pretended not to know who she was, but Kate persisted and Adelphia finally said self-consciously, "Oh, yes, it is you I know now." Then she cast an anxious glance in Stone's direction. He was almost out of sight.

"Do you have somewhere to go?" Kate asked, following her gaze.

"It is nowhere I have to go," Adelphia said curtly. "I am free to do nothing."

"Then how about I buy you a cup of coffee? Alex told me that you like coffee."

"It is my own café I can buy. I earn living. I no need charity."

"I was just being friendly. Friends do that, you know. Like when Oliver helped you in the park when that man attacked you."

Adelphia looked at her suspiciously. "How is all this you know?"

"Adelphia, you're not the only one worried about Oliver. Alex is too. And I'm trying to help him while he's out of town. Now, please come and have a cup of coffee with me. Please."

"Why you help Agent Fort?" she asked suspiciously.

"Woman to woman? Because I care about him. Just like I know you care about Oliver."

At these words Adelphia looked once more in the direction of Stone, started to sniffle a little, got in the car and allowed Kate to buy her coffee at a nearby Starbucks.

"So what is it that you do?" Adelphia said.

"I work for the Department of Justice."

"So that is what you do? Make the justice?"

"I'd like to think so. At least I try."

"In my country, for years—no, for decades—we have no justice. We have Soviets telling us what to do. Whether we can breathe air or not, they tell us. It is hell."

"I'm sure it was awful."

"Then I come to this country, get job, have good life."

Kate hesitated but then couldn't help herself. "So how'd you end up in Lafayette Park?"

At first Adelphia got an obstinate look on her face, but that dissolved quickly. Her voice trembling, she said, "No one ask me that before. Just you now. All these years and just you now ask me this."

"I realize you don't know me very well, and you don't have to answer."

"It is good thing. I no want to talk about it. I no want to."

They both sipped their coffees for a bit longer. Finally, Adelphia said, "You right. I worry sick about Oliver. He a troubled man. I know this."

"And how do you know?"

Adelphia reached in her sleeve and drew out a handkerchief to wipe her eyes. "I watch the TV the other night. I never watch the TV. I never read the newspapers. Do you know why I never do these things?" Kate shook her head. "Because they are lies. Filled with lies they are."

"But you said you *did* see the TV."

"Yes, the news, it is on. And then I see it."

"What did you see?"

Adelphia suddenly looked frightened, as though she had said far too much. "No, it is not thing I can say. It is not right for me to say. You are lawyer. You work for government. I no want to get Oliver in trouble."

"Adelphia, do you think Oliver did something wrong?"

"No! No, it is not this I think. I tell you, he is good man."

"Okay, then he has nothing to worry about from the government. Or me."

Still, Adelphia didn't say anything.

"Adelphia, if you're really concerned about Oliver, let me help. You can't follow him everywhere to make sure he's okay."

Finally, Adelphia sighed and patted Kate's hand. "It is right what you say. I will tell." Marshaling herself, she said, "On TV I see that there is body of a man found on that island in river."

"Roosevelt Island?" Kate said quickly.

"That is one."

"But what does that have to do with Oliver?"

"Well, you see . . . I want to take the café with Oliver, but he has meeting to go to."

"Meeting, what sort of meeting?"

"Ah, that is what I say. What sort of meeting in middle of night? But off he go. Now, me, I am angry with this. Meeting and no café? So I pretend to go away, but I see him get in cab. And I get in cab too. I have money, I too can take cab."

"Of course, of course," Kate said. "What happened next?"

"I follow him to Georgetown. He get out, so I get out. He walk to river. I walk to river. And then I see his friends he meet with. I see what they do."

"What!" Kate said it so loudly that she startled Adelphia.

"They get in old boat and they row out to island, that is what they do."

"And then what did you do?"

"I take cab and go back. I not wait for them. And I not *swim* to island. I go back in cab. I get my café, and I see Agent Fort when he come by for Oliver." Adelphia started to tear up. "And then I see TV and dead man."

"And you're sure it was the same night?"

"They say on TV. It is same night."

"Adelphia, you say you don't believe that Oliver did anything wrong. And yet you saw them row out to that island, and then a man was killed there."

"They say he killed by gun. Oliver no has gun."

"You can't be sure of that. And what about the others? His friends?"

Adelphia laughed. "I know these men. Except for the big one, they are little frightened mice. One, he work at library. He love books. He has brought me some. The other one, he checks things."

"Checks things?"

"You know he counts and hums and whistles and grunts. I know not what it was, but Oliver say it to me. He call it OD, something like that."

"OCD?"

"That is it."

"Do you know their names? The friends?"

"Oh, yes, this I know. The bookman, his name is Caleb Shaw. Sometime he dress in old clothes. Oliver say it is hobby. I say little bookman he is crazy."

"And the others?"

"The counting one, he is Milton Farb. He is smart that one. He tell me things about the world I not know."

"And you mentioned the 'big one'?"

"Yes. *Shifty* pants. His name is Reuben, Reuben Rhodes. Rhodes like in Greece is how I remember."

"So what do you think happened on that island? If none of them killed the man?"

"Do you not know?" Adelphia said breathlessly. She lowered her voice and said, "It is they see who did it. They *see* killer."

Kate sat back against the bench. Her first thought was she had to tell Alex about all this. But then she wondered if that would be wise. Doubtless his first reaction would be to come back. That would get him in even more trouble with the Service. And she didn't know if anything Adelphia was telling her was true. She had a sudden thought.

"Adelphia, would you mind coming with me to look at something?"

"Where?" Adelphia asked suspiciously.

"It's nearby. I promise it won't take long."

Adelphia reluctantly agreed, and they drove to a parking lot near the Georgetown waterfront.

Kate said, "Can you describe this boat you saw them in?"

"It was long, about twelve feet maybe. And old. It all rotted. They take it from old junkyard down that way," she added, pointing south.

Kate led her over to the river wall. "I want you to stay here." She slipped down some rocks located to the side of the seawall and reached the drainage port. "If you lean over a little, I think you can see it all right." She pulled some brush out of the way, exposing the bow as Adelphia leaned over.

"Is this the boat you saw them in?"

"Yes, that is boat."

*Oh, my God.*

# CHAPTER

## 49

Oliver Stone waited outside the high-rise condo building, watching well-dressed people emerge from the building and head off, probably to work, given the number of briefcases he saw. And then she came out. Jackie Simpson carried only a small purse over her shoulder. She didn't look at Stone as she passed by. He waited a suitable time and followed her. His strides were long and hers short, so he had to constantly slow down. A couple of times he thought about approaching her, but both times something happened which had never happened to him before: He lost his nerve. However, when she stopped to buy a newspaper from a box, she spilled her change. He rushed to help her, laying the coins in her outstretched palm. His breath quickened when he saw it, but he merely smiled when she thanked him and walked off.

When she arrived at WFO, he stopped and watched her go in the building.

Petite, olive complexion and an attitude. He'd known a woman just like that once.

He turned and headed to a Metro station. He had a very important meeting to go to. Emerging from the subway at an agreed-upon spot, he found the other members of the club waiting for him.

They had decided that the safest way for Milton to retrieve his record of the break-in was to be escorted to his house by the security firm that had responded to the silent alarm. Arrangements were made, and Milton, followed at a discreet distance by the rest of the Camel Club in Caleb's Malibu, met two guards near his home, and the three men went in together.

About thirty minutes later Milton joined up with his friends, and they sat in Caleb's car.

Stone said, "Did you get it?"

Milton nodded and slipped a DVD out of his knapsack. "It was activated, so presumably there's something on it."

He popped it in his laptop, and a minute later they were looking at the darkened interior of Milton's house.

"There!" Stone said, pointing at a man coming around the corner.

"That's Reinke," Caleb exclaimed.

"And there's his confederate," Reuben added. "The one you nailed with the helmet, Oliver."

They continued to watch, seeing the pair move stealthily from room to room.

"My God, Milton," Reuben said sarcastically. "You're quite the Messy Marvin at home, aren't you?"

"What's he pulling out of that bin?" Caleb asked.

Milton ran that part again. "That looks like my receipt box, but I can't see what the paper is."

"Look, there's the security guard," Stone said.

They watched as the man advanced, and then something flew out of the darkness at him and he crumpled.

"What the hell was that?" Reuben asked.

"A man in a mask," Stone said. "At least one of them had the good sense to burglarize the place without showing his face."

"But it wasn't Reinke and the other guy," Milton said.

"Which clearly means there's someone else," Stone said slowly. "But this tape gives us the leverage that we—" He was cut off by the buzzing of Milton's cell phone.

Milton answered, "Oh, hi, Chastity." Then his expression changed in a hurry. "What! Oh, my God! What are you talking abou—"

Stone ripped the phone from his friend. "Chastity!"

However, it was a man's voice on the line.

"I think under the circumstances that we can call it even right now. So long as you don't act, neither will we."

The phone went dead.

Stone looked at the panicked Milton, who had tears welling into his eyes. "I'm sorry, Milton."

*      *      *

Kate had spent the next morning and afternoon researching Milton Farb, Reuben Rhodes and Caleb Shaw. She'd also gone on Google and found some material on Milton and his *Jeopardy!* stint. However, Oliver Stone remained an enigma. Kate was certain of one thing: She believed the men had seen who killed Patrick Johnson. The bullet hole and blood on the boat seemed to indicate that they'd almost lost their lives as well.

Armed with her newfound knowledge, she went back to Mt. Zion Cemetery that afternoon and was fortunate to find Stone working in the grounds.

"Hello, Oliver. Kate Adams. We met briefly the other night."

"I remember," he said curtly.

"Are you okay? You look worried."

"Nothing too important."

"Well, as you know, Alex is out of town, and I hope you don't think it's too forward of me, but I'd like to invite you to dinner tonight."

"To dinner?" Stone looked at her as though she were speaking a language he was not familiar with.

"At my house. Well, not exactly my house, I live in the carriage house. It's actually Lucille Whitney-Houseman's home, in Georgetown. Do you know her?"

"I'm afraid I haven't had the pleasure," he said distractedly.

"And I wanted to invite Adelphia and your other friends."

Stone threw some weeds in a garbage bag. "That's very nice, but I'm afraid—" He stopped and looked at her sharply. "What other friends?"

"You know. Reuben Rhodes, Caleb Shaw and Milton Farb. I'm starting to collect rare books, and I think Caleb will be fascinating to talk to. And I'm a huge fan of *Jeopardy!*, though I don't think I saw Milton when he was on. And Reuben's work at DIA all those years ago, how could that not be enthralling? And then, of course, there's *you*." She let that comment hang for a long moment. "I'm sure it'll be a wonderfully interesting dinner. They used to have them in Georgetown all the time, or so Lucky—that's Mrs. Whitney-Houseman—tells me."

Kate said this all in one long surge, hoping to overwhelm Stone into accepting if only because his curiosity had to be piqued by now.

He said nothing for about a minute as he knelt on the ground, apparently dissecting all she had said. "I've found that when one takes the time to learn that much about someone, there's usually a reason for the interest that's not readily apparent to everyone."

"I wouldn't disagree with that," she answered.

"However, I'm not sure tonight is good for us. We've had, well, we've had some bad news very recently."

"I'm sorry to hear that. Alex and I had some bad things happen too. Some people tried to kill us. Funny, it was right after we discovered an old boat hidden in a storm drain in Georgetown that looked like it had a bullet hole in it and also some blood."

"I see." Stone's calm response to what must've been a stunning revelation only increased her esteem for the man, along with her curiosity. "Well, then perhaps we *should* have dinner. I can contact my friends."

"Around seven will be great. Do you need the address?"

"Yes. Mrs. Whitney-Houseman no doubt resides in circles where the common masses do not often tread."

She told him the address. "Now, I'll just pop over to invite Adelphia. I'm sure she can catch a ride with you and your friends."

"Kate, I really don't think that's a good idea."

"Oh, I think it's a great idea," she said firmly.

"And why is that?" he asked.

"Because, Oliver, you strike me as someone who needs all the friends he can get right now."

Caleb, Milton and Adelphia arrived at Lucky's manse in the Malibu, its tailpipe smoking and its springs creaking from the strenuous activities at Reinke's place. Reuben and Stone pulled up behind them on the Indian motorcycle.

Kate had been watching for them and opened the ornately carved front door.

"Nice bike," she said to Reuben, who wore a frayed leather jacket, wrinkled khaki pants, collared shirt and his usual moccasins. However, for the dinner he'd wrapped a blue kerchief around his neck as a cravat.

Reuben ran his gaze appreciatively over the young woman's figure. She was dressed in black slacks and matching pumps with a white blouse and a small string of pearls around her neck. Her blond hair was done up in a bun that showed off her long, slender neck.

"I'll take you for a spin sometime," he said. "That sidecar has seen some action, let me tell you."

Adelphia nodded stiffly at her hostess as she passed into the house. Milton followed her. He was dressed in an immaculate green blazer and striped tie, his slacks perfectly creased. He held out a small bouquet of flowers he'd brought.

"It's Milton, right? Well, thank you very much, they're beautiful." Even as she said this, Adams saw tears forming in the man's eyes.

Next came Caleb, who'd decided not to wear his Abe Lincoln outfit after Stone had spoken with him, something to the effect of not wanting their hostesses to think he was dangerously insane. However, in an act of subtle defiance he *had* worn his fat pocket watch and chain.

"Nice to meet you, Caleb," Kate said pleasantly. "Go right in."

Oliver Stone brought up the rear. He was dressed in some of his new clothes and was holding his motorcycle helmet in one hand. "Would you care to give me a preview of the agenda?"

She looked at him with a twinkle. "But that would take all the fun away."

"This isn't a fun business we find ourselves in."

"I agree. But I think you'll find the evening informative."

Lucky met them with a pitcher of sangria. As she scuttled around talking and pouring, it was clear that the old woman was in her element. Sufficiently refreshed, they passed a pleasant hour before dinner was served.

Reuben and Caleb ate heartily. Stone, Milton and Adelphia merely picked at their meals. Coffee was served in the library. Cigars were offered by Lucky but only Reuben lit up. "I like to see a man smoke," she said as she sat next to Reuben and patted his big shoulder. "Now, you look to me to be a man who packs heat."

As Reuben stared at her quizzically, the conversation, craftily guided by Kate, turned to intelligence circles.

"I tell you what," Reuben said, "the best security in the world can be defeated by a rumbling stomach."

"How's that?" Kate asked.

"Just this. I knew before anyone else the exact time the bombings of Afghanistan and Iraq were going to start."

"Were you with DIA back then?"

"Hell no, they'd long since kicked my butt out. I knew because I was the dispatcher for Domino's. Each time, the pizza order for the Pentagon spiked right before the bombs started falling. So yours truly knew before the likes of Dan Rather or Tom Brokaw or probably even the president."

While Reuben had been talking, Caleb was making the rounds of the books on the massive shelves, with Lucky as his guide.

Caleb's face brightened with each new discovery. "Oh, that's quite a good copy of *Moby-Dick*. And a *Hound of the Baskervilles*, first English edition. Very nice. And over there, is that Jefferson's *Notes on the State of Virginia* from 1785? Yes, it is. We have one in our collection. Lucky, you really should let me get you acid-free boxes for these, computer-cut to the book's exact dimensions."

Lucky was hanging on Caleb's every word. "Oh, acid-free boxes cut by computer, how terribly exciting. Would you, Caleb?"

"It would be my honor."

Reuben helped himself to more coffee spiked with a little something from a flask he pulled from his coat pocket. "Yeah, you'll find brother Caleb a real dynamo in the excitement department."

"Lucky," Kate said finally, "we're going to head out to the carriage house. I need to talk over some things with my friends."

"All right, dear," she said, patting Caleb's arm. "But first they have to promise to come back."

Reuben immediately raised his glass. "Lucky, you couldn't keep me away with a squad of Special Forces."

Kate led them outside and over to the carriage house, where they settled down around a table on the large sofa and two wing chairs.

"I'm assuming you've told them of our discussion and the discovery of the boat?" Kate said in a businesslike tone to Stone.

"I have," he answered, casting a glance in Adelphia's direction. "And for some reason you believe that we were in that boat and on the island?"

"I don't believe, I know. Now I want to know how much you saw."

"There's no evidence that we saw anything," he replied evenly. "Even if Adelphia has told you that she followed us to the river and watched us head to the island, that doesn't mean we were witness to that man's death."

"But I believe you saw everything. And I think whoever killed Patrick Johnson discovered your presence, and you had to make a run for it. That would explain the bullet hole in the boat and the blood. What I can't understand is why you didn't simply go to the police and tell them what you saw."

"Easy enough for you to say," Reuben interjected. "They'd believe *you*. But look at us, we're a scruffy bunch with questionable pedigrees."

"So you're admitting you did witness the murder?"

Caleb started to speak but Stone broke in. "We're not admitting anything."

Kate said, "Oliver, I'm just trying to help you. And don't forget, someone tried to kill Alex and me after we found the boat."

Reuben shot Stone a puzzled look. "Oliver, you didn't tell us that."

Milton blurted out, "But what about Chastity? They've kidnapped Chastity!"

They all stared at him as tears fell down his twitching cheeks.

"If someone's been kidnapped," Kate said, "the police should be notified immediately."

"It's not quite that simple," Caleb said, glancing at Stone, whose gaze was on the floor. "We really can't go to the police."

Kate looked at Stone. "Oliver," she said quietly, "as a team we might be able to do something."

"Hell yes, we could," Reuben said. "She's official, being with DOJ, and our sorry asses can only get things second- and third-hand."

"It *is* time to work together," Caleb chimed in.

Stone still said nothing.

Reuben put down his cigar "Okay, since our exalted leader is uncharacteristically mute, I hereby call a special meeting of the Camel Club to order. And I move that we tell Kate here everything. Do I have a second?"

"Second," Caleb said immediately.

"All in favor," Reuben said, his gaze on Stone.

The ayes carried.

Reuben said, "The Camel Club has spoken."

"*What* is the Camel Club?" a puzzled Kate asked.

"Let me do the honors," Stone finally said.

# 50

"You did what!" Alex yelled into his cell phone. He had been sitting in his hotel room the next morning just strapping on his gun when Kate called.

"See, that's why I waited until this morning to call you," she said. "Because I knew you'd be upset."

"What the hell did you expect me to do? Say, 'Good job, Kate, and I'm really glad you're not a corpse'?"

"I *told* you I was going to check into Oliver Stone and his friends, and you said it was okay."

"But I didn't know they were eyewitnesses to Johnson's murder, which was the very thing I told you to stay away from in the first place!"

"Well, I didn't know they were connected either. So just hear me out. I've got a lot to tell you." She spoke for several minutes, relaying what Stone had told her last night.

When she finished, Alex shook his head incredulously. "Okay, okay. Let me get this straight. They saw the murder and didn't go to the police because they were afraid the police would think they were involved?"

"I don't believe Oliver likes the police very much. Maybe it's to do with his past."

"And on top of that, they traced one of the murderers, went to his house and were almost killed?"

"Yes."

"And while they were 'burglarizing' the killer's house, Milton Farb's home was broken into by these same guys, and they got them on film doing it?"

"But Milton's girlfriend's been kidnapped by these people, and so they can't go to the police about that either."

"But they didn't tell you the names of the murderers?"

"I think they only know one of their names."

"But they have them on film. Did you recognize them?"

"They haven't shown me the film."

"Why the hell not?"

"They want to show it to you first."

"Great, but I'm a four-hour drive away with work out the gazoo, and the president will be here tomorrow."

"They won't budge on that, Alex. I tried. They'll only show it to you. I mean come on. I work for the Justice Department, and they don't know me. It was a real effort for them to tell me as much as they have. Oliver trusts you, not me."

Alex rubbed his hair, cupped the phone under his chin and finished putting on his holster. "Okay, so do you have a plan?"

"Well, I was thinking we could come up to see you tomorrow."

"Tomorrow! Tomorrow POTUS is here. And he takes precedence over everything, Kate, you know that."

"I know. But I wanted you to meet with the Camel Club—"

"The what?"

"Oh, I'm sorry. That's what Oliver and his friends refer to themselves as, the Camel Club. It's sort of a conspiracy watchdog organization they've been running for years. Do you know they were the ones who first got on to the scandal with the defense secretary years ago? You remember, right? He was taking kickbacks for directing government contracts to certain vendors? The Camel Club discovered that through a scrap of information they got from an assistant chef at the White House. It's really amazing stuff, Alex."

Alex lay back on his bed and closed his eyes. "An assistant White House chef is spying on the secretary of defense for something called the *Camel Club*? This is a joke, right? Please tell me this is a joke, Kate."

"Forget that. It's not important."

Alex jumped up. "Not important!"

"Alex, will you please listen to me? They've done some incredible investigative work on this case. They really have."

Alex managed to calm down. "Okay, you all come up here and then what?"

"We attend the ceremony, and after that we all sit down, and they can show you the film and tell you the man's name. Then we can go from there."

"Meaning I take all this to the Secret Service?"

"Right. With a name and these guys on film, we have solid stuff. And we have to get Chastity back. Milton is heartbroken."

"Who the hell is Chastity?"

"Oh, I'm sorry, that's Milton's girlfriend. She's the one who was kidnapped."

"The FBI handles kidnappings. And every second that goes by the odds are she won't be found alive."

"These aren't ordinary kidnappers. They have a lot more at stake. They've called and let Milton talk to her for a few seconds every couple of hours, to show she's alive. I don't think they'll harm Chastity, for now anyway. Things are at a stalemate."

"And how exactly does Patrick Johnson tie into all this?"

"Well, they were sort of vague on that. I'm sure they'll explain it more fully to you. From the little they've told me, I think they actually have it figured out."

Alex let out a long breath. He had a day crammed with final preparations ahead of him. He should be totally focused on his work as a Secret Service agent. And yet now he knew the main thing occupying his mind would be the Camel Club. *God help me.*

"Alex, are you there?"

"I'm here," he snapped.

"So what do you think? Can we come up?"

Alex actually glanced at his gun, wondering for a fleeting second if it wouldn't just be easier to end it right now.

"Alex!"

"Yeah, okay. Come on up."

"And can we bring Adelphia? She's been really worried about Oliver."

Alex finally exploded. "Oh, sure, Kate, bring Adelphia. And bring the freaking Monkey and Giraffe Club too. And while you're at it, why the hell don't you pop over to the White House and snatch the president. I bet he'd get a real *kick* out of all this. And he'll probably give you a ride up here on Air Force One. And be sure and give him my name so he knows exactly whose *ass* he'll be reaming out when he gets here!"

Kate's voice was irritatingly calm. "Okay, I'm hanging up now. We'll see you tomorrow."

The phone went dead, and Alex plopped back on the bed just as someone knocked on his door.

"Ford, time to hit it. Let's go." It was his squad leader. "Ford, you ready?" he said again more loudly.

Alex jumped up and opened the door. His squad leader stared back at him. "You okay?"

"Never better," Alex said.

Darkness was gathering as Tom Hemingway walked through the streets of a small town an hour outside of Frankfurt, Germany. He passed through the charming shopping district, alongside a Gothic-style cathedral, ducked down a side street and entered an apartment building. He took the lift three flights up, rapped on the door of the fourth flat down the hall and was told to enter.

There were no lights on, and yet Hemingway almost instantly focused on one corner of the room that was almost completely dark.

"I see your sixth sense has not failed you, Tom," the man said as he stepped forward with a smile. An Arab, he was not dressed in a *djellaba* but in a two-piece business suit, although he wore a turban around his head. He motioned for Hemingway to sit in a chair next to a small table. The man sat across from him. Hemingway sensed the presence of others but said nothing about this.

The Arab sat back and rested his hands on the arms of his chair. "Your father was an excellent man and a great friend of mine for nearly thirty years. He knew us; he took the time to learn our language, religion and cultures. No one does that today unfortunately."

"He was special," Hemingway agreed. "Very special."

The man took a small cup of water off the table between them and drank from it. He offered one to Hemingway but he declined. The Arab handed a piece of paper over to Hemingway. "As agreed," the

Arab said. Hemingway put the document away in his pocket without looking at it.

"I'm sure you put a great deal of thought into it," Hemingway said.

"I have been thinking about these things my whole life."

"You will ensure that no one claims responsibility?"

The Arab nodded. "It is done. I take it that my people have been satisfactory to work with?"

"It is a testament to their loyalty to you that they have done everything asked of them without question."

"What happened was not solely for your benefit. Al-Zawahiri, and others like him, they'd been seduced by your country. They had lost their ties to Islam." He paused. "You are confident about tomorrow?"

"Yes."

"Attacking a superpower, that is something never to be done lightly."

"Superpowers are still made up of people."

The Arab shook his head. "We are *very* different people, different in ways your country refuses to recognize."

"The more we're different, perhaps the more we're the same. We all want peace."

"Excuse me for saying so, but that is your Buddhist bullshit talking." The man took another sip of water. "America spends more on its military than all other countries in the world *combined*. No country does this for protection, for peace, only aggression. Your president can push one button, and the Arab world disappears in a mushroom cloud."

"We have no reason to do that. Great strides have been made in the Middle East. Democracies are replacing dictatorships."

"Yes, replacing dictatorships that *America* helped foster and support. And yet, in most cases, the democracies coming to power hate America more than the dictators they replaced. You went into Iraq not understanding its history or its culture. America seemed amazed that Great Britain took a land called Mesopotamia and artificially created a country it called Iraq. And that its population is composed of Shiites and Sunnis and Kurds and dozens of other groups that are not known to get along with one another. Did you really think you would waltz in and save the Iraqis and everything would be peaceful?" He held up his hand. "And one cannot 'bomb' people into a democracy. That comes from the ground up, not the sky down. Muslims going to the voting booths pass the bomb craters that took their families. Do you think the possibility of having an American-style democracy will ever make them forget who killed their husbands, wives and children?"

"*My* country needs to recognize that there are many ways to be free. I fear that we still see the only way to resolve things is *our* way."

The Arab took another sip of water. "It is a nice sentiment, Tom, but not one, I think, that is shared by your leaders. Mighty God could vanquish your army with one sweep of his hand. Yet we *mortal* Arabs simply cannot beat you militarily with all your money and weapons. And we see American *businesses* and American *pipelines* marching behind the great American armies. You say your goal is a free world. Well, Africa has more dictators than the Middle East, and the genocide there is far worse. Yet I see no American tanks blasting their way through that land. But, of course, the Middle East has far more *oil*. Do not think we poor desert savages aren't aware that America's goals are less than altruistic, Tom. At least allow us that courtesy."

"Freedom *is* a good thing, my friend. And America is the world's most free country."

"Really? A country that had *slaves* for two hundred and fifty years and kept the black man de facto enslaved for a hundred more? But I have also seen your style of freedom personally. Over fifty years ago Iran had a *democratically* elected prime minister who had the effrontery to nationalize the petroleum industry. American oil companies were hardly pleased. So your CIA helped overthrow the government and reinstall the puppet shah. His pathetic love of Western ways led to the Iranian revolution, and all hope for *real* democracy ended there. America has played these games all over the globe, from Chile to Pakistan. The Western world's policies have led directly to the slaughter of countless millions across the world." He paused and studied Hemingway closely. "So if the new government in Iraq is not to America's liking?"

"And yet I know that you believe in freedom," Hemingway said quietly. "As a young boy I sat and listened to you and my father discuss such things."

"It is true that I have fought my whole life for certain freedoms that are in keeping with the word of God. I see clearly the benefits of people having a strong voice in their lives. I do not agree with how Muslim women are treated in some Arab countries. And it sickens me to see grand palaces rising next to mud huts. The Muslim world has many problems, and we need to address them. Yet is it really freedom when someone *else* tells you what you should be seeking? And why doesn't it work both ways, Tom? America represents less than five percent of the earth's population yet consumes *one-quarter* of its energy. Poor nations cannot get the energy they need, and their citizens suffer and die because America takes so much. So should these countries *invade* the great energy *dictator* America and make it use less oil and gas? Would the U.S. like that?"

"If you feel that way, can I ask why you're helping me?"

The man shrugged. "It is simple. For every American killed, hundreds of Arabs die. Arab suicide bombers are now slaughtering their *brethren* by the thousands. We are weakening ourselves with every new explosion and playing right into the hands of the United States." He paused and took another sip of water. "The Western press is fixated on suicide bombers killing themselves so that they can enter paradise. But God says that to *save* lives is a great thing. To save one life is to save *many*. Do we have to be slaughtered to enter paradise? Why can't Muslims enjoy a peaceful life on earth, believe in God and serve him and enter paradise that way? In the Western world the young ones grow up in peace. Do *our* children not deserve that right?"

"Of course they do," Hemingway said.

"Your country is asking the impossible, you know this. Before the 1970s energy crisis America did not care about the Middle East, other than the Arab versus Israeli issue. Then 9/11 happened and you attacked the Taliban. I have no issue with that. In your place I would have done the same thing. Yet the goal you seek now, turning the entire Middle East into a democracy overnight, is madness. You ask us to do in *years* what it took you *centuries* to accomplish." He paused. "And it is not simply a question of Islam against the West. For thousands of years Arab nations developed customs and cultures inextricably tied to a desert climate with few natural resources, often with the law of the tribe as their base, and the men as their leaders. For a very long time America had no problem with that. And now they do, of course and thus, according to you, we must change. Immediately. So far a hundred thousand Iraqis have died and the country is in chaos. I cannot applaud the progress, Tom. I really can't."

"I can only do my best. If it doesn't work, what will have been lost?"

"Many good lives, that is what will be lost, Tom," the Arab said sternly.

"And that is no different than what's happening right now," Hemingway replied.

"You have an answer for everything. Just like your father. It was in Beijing that he was killed?"

Hemingway nodded.

"Surely not the Chinese, though. They're vicious but hardly stupid."

Hemingway shrugged. "I have my suspicions. Officially, it was never solved."

"It is interesting about the Chinese, Tom. They will one day replace America as the world's largest economy. They have an army *ten times* the size of yours, and it is growing stronger and more technologically advanced every day. They have the capability to hit the United States with nuclear weapons. They kill and enslave millions of their own people, and yet you call them friends, while America crushes the Arab world under the pretense of freeing us. Do you know what we Arabs say? We say, go and 'free' your friends, the Chinese. But America does not do this. Why? Because the Chinese will not fight back with rifles and car bombs as we Muslims are forced to. Thus, you leave them alone. And you call them friends."

"My father didn't think of them as all that friendly actually."

"A wise man. He has gone on to a better world now."

"I'm an atheist. So I'm not sure where he's gone on to."

The Arab stared at him in sadness. "It is an insult to yourself not to believe in God, Tom."

"I believe in myself."

"But when your physical being ceases to exist, where does that leave you?" The Arab paused and said, "With nothing."

"It is *my* freedom to make that choice," Hemingway said firmly.

The Arab rose from his chair. "Good-bye, Tom, and good luck. We will not see each other again."

A few minutes later Hemingway was walking along the sidewalk back to his rental car. He looked at the sheet of paper his friend had given him, translating the Arabic in his head. The man *had* thought things out very carefully.

Hemingway was on a flight out of Frankfurt that night and would be in New York eight hours later. He looked at the clear sky and wondered if there were as many gods as there were stars. According to some religions, there might be. The answers really didn't matter to him. No god had ever answered his prayers. To Hemingway that was more than adequate proof that there was no such being.

Several thousand miles away across the Atlantic, Captain Jack gazed up at the same sky and also pondered the events of the next day. Everything was done and only awaited the arrival of James Brennan and company. As a last measure all laptops used by the members of his operation had been destroyed. There would be no more movie chat room discussions. He would actually miss them.

Later that evening Captain Jack drove into the parking lot of Pittsburgh International Airport. He dropped off his car and headed for the terminal. His official itinerary was fairly straightforward: Pittsburgh to Chicago O'Hare; O'Hare to Honolulu; and Honolulu to American Samoa, where a puddle jumper would take him to his precious island.

His work in Brennan was done. He would not stay for the actual mission. That would be a little too tight even for him. And yet while his work here was finished, in other respects it was just beginning. And now it was time to activate his contingency plan. His partnership with Tom Hemingway was officially over, though the latter didn't know it. *It was fun while it lasted, Tom.* He now worked for the North Koreans.

Captain Jack checked in for his flight but kept his bag, which was small enough to carry on. He went to a bar to have a drink. Afterward, he hit the restroom. From there he wandered the airport and then headed to the security lines. Yet instead of going through security he exited the airport, went to a different parking lot and picked up a car waiting for him there. He headed south.

*          *          *

Djamila sat at the kitchen table in her apartment and wrote the date and time of her death in her journal. She wondered how accurate she would be. If she did die tomorrow, her journal would be found. Perhaps they would publish it in the paper, along with her full name, which she wrote next to her time of death. Then, for some reason, she erased it. Would there be a possibility that she would survive tomorrow?

She stood by the open window and looked out, letting the gentle breeze wash over her, and smelled air that held the fragrance of cut grass, a relatively new sensation for her. It was quiet, peaceful here. No bombs or gunfire. She could see people walking together, talking. An old man sat on the front steps of the building smoking a cigarette and drinking a beer. She could hear the peals of laughter of children from the small playground nearby. Djamila was young with her whole life ahead of her. Yet she slowly closed the window and drew herself back into the dark shadows of her apartment.

"Do not let me fail you," she quietly asked God. "Do not let me fail you."

Barely twenty minutes from Djamila's apartment, Adnan al-Rimi had just completed his last prayer of the day. As Djamila had, he'd lingered over his words with God too.

He rolled up his prayer rug and put it away. Adnan only performed his prayers twice a day, at dawn and in the evening. He was a reluctant follower of Ramadan, his belly had been empty for too many years to starve it. Over the years he'd had the occasional cigarette and alcoholic drink. He had never made the pilgrimage to Mecca because he couldn't afford the trip. And yet he considered himself a faithful Muslim because he worked hard, helped others in need, never cheated, never lied. But he had killed. He had killed in the name of God, to defend Islam, to protect his way of life. Sometimes it seemed his entire existence consisted of three elements: working, praying and fighting. He had worked hard to ensure that his children would not have to fight, would not have to blow themselves and others up to prove a point. But his children were all dead. The violence had reached them despite their father's attempt to keep them safe.

Now Adnan had only one more task ahead of him.

With his eyes shut, Adnan paced off the dimensions of the hospital corridor in his apartment. He went down the hall, turned right, went fourteen paces down and moved right, opened the door and simulated going down eight steps, hitting a landing, turning and going down eight more, down the hall and reaching the exit door. Then he did it again. And again.

Afterward, Adnan removed his shirt and looked at his body in the bathroom mirror. Though his physique was still impressive, there was a frailty beneath the muscle that more resembled an old man than someone in the prime of life. The numerous external injuries he'd suffered over the years had healed. Inside, though, the scars were permanent.

He sat on his bed and withdrew from his wallet ten photos that he arranged in front of him. They were crumpled, faded reminders of his family. He lingered over each, recalling moments of peace and love. And horror. As when his father had been beheaded by the Saudis, for what amounted to a misdemeanor. It usually took two whacks with the sword to behead someone. Yet Adnan's father had a very thick neck, and it had taken three strokes to sever it, an event eight-year-old Adnan had been forced to watch. Few people could have gone through these memories without shedding at least a few tears; however, Adnan's eyes remained dry. And yet his fingers trembled as he kissed the fading images of his dead children.

A few minutes later Adnan put on his coat and left his apartment. The bike ride into downtown Brennan went quickly. He chained his bicycle to a rack and started walking. His path took him in front of Mercy Hospital, where he briefly glanced at his place of employment, at least until tomorrow. Then his gaze darted to the apartment building across the street where he knew the two Afghans were checking and rechecking their weapons, because they were methodical and obsessive men, as all good snipers had to be.

Adnan continued walking, turned down one street and then another and finally slipped into an alley. He rapped twice on the door. He heard nothing. Then he called out in Farsi. Footsteps approached, and he heard Ahmed's voice answer in Farsi.

"What is it you want, Adnan?"

"To talk."

"I am busy."

"Everything should be done, Ahmed. Is there a problem?"

The door opened and Ahmed scowled at him. "I have no problems," Ahmed said, but he stepped back for Adnan to enter the garage.

"I thought it wise to go over things one more time," Adnan said as he sat on a stool next to the workbench. His gaze took in the vehicle that would play such an important role the next day. He nodded at it. "It looks good, Ahmed. You have done well."

"Tomorrow will see whether we have done well or not," Ahmed answered.

He and Adnan spent twenty minutes going over their assigned tasks.

"I am not worried about us," Ahmed said sullenly. "It is this woman who troubles me. Who is she? What is her training?"

"That is not your concern," Adnan answered. "If she was picked for this, she will do her job well."

"Women are only good for having babies and to cook and clean."

"You are living in the past, my friend," Adnan said.

"The Muslim past was glorious. We had the best of everything."

"The world has moved past us, Ahmed. For Muslims to be truly great again we must move with it. Show the world what we can do. And we can do much."

Ahmed spat on the floor. "That is what I think of the world. They can just leave us alone."

"We will see after tomorrow who is right."

Ahmed slowly shook his head. "You trust in things too much. You trust the American who leads us too much."

"He may be an American, but he is brave and knows what he is doing." He gazed sternly at the Iranian.

"I will do *my* job," Ahmed finally said.

"Yes, you will," Adnan answered as he rose to leave. "Because I will be right there to ensure that you do."

"You think I need an *Iraqi* babysitting me," Ahmed said fiercely.

"Tomorrow we are not Iraqi or Iranian or Afghani," Adnan replied. "We are all Muslims, following God."

"Do not question my faith, Adnan," Ahmed said in a dangerous tone.

"I question nothing. Only God has the right to question the souls of his people." Adnan went to the door but then turned back. "I will see you tomorrow, Ahmed."

"I will see you in paradise," Ahmed answered.

# CHAPTER

## 51

At one o'clock in the afternoon Air Force One touched down at Pittsburgh International Airport. All other air traffic had been diverted from the area, as it would be when Air Force One took off again later. The long line of cars was ready to go. In a presidential motorcade there was a basic rule that one risked ignoring at his peril: When the president's behind touched his seat in the Beast, the motorcade left. And if you didn't have your ride yet in one of the other vehicles when this occurred, you weren't going to the party.

The road the presidential motorcade took had long since been closed off by the Secret Service, and motorists sat in foul moods staring at the Beast and the other twenty-six cars sailing by. In the presidential limo with Brennan was his wife, his chief of staff, the governor of Pennsylvania and Carter Gray.

When the motorcade pulled into the dedication grounds, they were already filled with more than ten thousand people waving banners and signs to show their support for the town and its namesake. National media trucks were parked outside the fence, and perfectly coiffed anchormen and -women stood next to far younger and hipper but equally well coiffed news candy types from the cooler cable networks. Collectively, they would broadcast the event to the nation and the world, although with various spins of their own; the younger voices were predictably far more cynical about the entire proceedings.

Alex Ford was positioned near the stage but then moved behind a roped-off area and toward the motorcade as it pulled into the fenced grounds. He stiffened for an instant as he saw Kate, Adelphia and the Camel Club in the crowd, about midway back but working their way forward. Kate waved to show she'd seen him. He didn't wave back but did nod his head a bare inch at her, and then he returned to trying to spot potential trouble. In a crowd this large and boisterous that was nearly impossible. However, the magnetometers had been set up at all pedestrian entrance points, which had given the Service some comfort. Alex took a moment to gaze at the tree line where he knew the snipers were positioned, although he couldn't see them. If it comes to it, don't miss, guys, he said under his breath.

When the president appeared, he was boxed in on all sides by the A-team protection detail that formed a wall of Kevlar and flesh around him. Alex knew these agents; they were a rock-solid crew.

The president stepped onto the stage and shook some important hands while his wife, the governor, the chief of staff and Gray took their seats behind the podium. Brennan joined them a minute later.

The event started off right on schedule. The mayor and some local dignitaries spoke and attempted to outdo one another when it came to extolling their president and their town. Then the governor rambled on a bit longer than the schedule had dictated, which caused the chief of staff to start frowning and tapping her high heel. Air Force One's next stop was a fund-raiser in Los Angeles that was far more important—at least in her mind—than the renaming of this small if ambitious Pennsylvania town in her boss's honor.

Alex continued scanning the crowds. He noted a number of military personnel in the front row, near the rope line. He could see from their uniforms that most were regular army. A number of them were missing arms and legs, probably from their tours of duty in the Middle East. There were a couple of National Guardsmen, including one with a hook for a left hand. Alex shook his head in commiseration for their sacrifice. Brennan would certainly go down and see these soldiers after he had spoken. He'd always been good about that.

As Alex's gaze swept across the thousands of faces, he noted quite a few Middle Easterners. They were dressed much like everyone else around them. They carried signs and sported "Reelect Brennan" buttons and appeared to be just like the rest of the happy, proud and patriotic crowd. However, Alex had no way of knowing that some of these people were not happy or proud or patriotic.

Captain Jack's men were organized in various pockets throughout the crowd so that their fire would cover maximum ground in front of the podium area. They'd all already keyed on the hook-handed National Guardsman. It had been easy after that, since the man stayed planted at the rope line waiting his turn with the president.

Indeed, they were all waiting for James Brennan.

At about the time Air Force One had been making its final approach into Pittsburgh a sleek black chopper was taking off from a helipad in downtown New York City and heading south. Next to the pilot sat another man dressed in a flight suit. In one of the seats in back was Tom Hemingway. In his hand he held a portable television set that he was watching intently. The crowds in Brennan were very large, and the grounds were already packed. That was what worried Hemingway most of all. *The crowd.*

He checked his watch and told the pilot to hit it. The chopper shot across the Manhattan cityscape.

For the past two hours Djamila had been on an outing with the children. As she pulled the van into the Franklins' driveway, her plan was to make them all a quick lunch and then it would be time to go. As she opened the door, carrying the baby on her hip with the two toddlers in her wake, she received a shock so paralyzing that she almost dropped the baby.

Lori Franklin was talking on the phone in the foyer, still dressed in her tennis outfit, although she was barefoot. She smiled at Djamila and motioned that she would be done with the call in a minute.

When she clicked off, Djamila immediately said, "Miss, I not expect you home. You say you at club for tennis and then lunch there."

Franklin dropped to her knees and gave her sons big hugs as they rushed to her. Then she took the baby from Djamila.

"I know, Djamila, but I changed my mind. I was talking with some of my friends from the club, and they're going to the dedication today. So I decided to go too." She bent down and said to her two oldest boys, "And you're going too."

Djamila drew in a sharp breath. "You take them?"

Franklin stood and waved the baby's dimpled fist with her hand. "And this little guy." She cooed to the baby. "You wanna see the president? You wanna?" She looked at Djamila. "It'll be fun. And it's not like the president comes to town every day."

"You go to dedication?" Djamila said in a soft, disbelieving voice.

"Well, I voted for him, even if George thinks he's an idiot. That's between you and me," she added.

"But, miss, there will be large crowd there. I read in papers. Do you think it good to take the boys? They are so small and—"

"I know, I thought that too. But then I realized it would be such a wonderful experience for them, even if they don't remember it. When they grow up, the boys can say they were there. Now I'm going to grab a quick shower. I thought we could get lunch beforehand—"

"We?" Djamila said. "You want *me* to come?"

"Well, of course, I'll need help with the strollers and the rest of their stuff. And you're right about the crowds, so I'll need an extra pair of eyes and hands to make sure the boys don't get lost."

"But I have much to do here," Djamila said dully, as if this moment she cared about housework.

"Don't be silly. This will be a wonderful experience for you too, Djamila. You'll see firsthand what really makes this country so great. You know, we might even get to meet the president. George will eat his heart out even if he says he doesn't like Brennan."

Franklin went upstairs to shower and change. Djamila sat down in a chair to steady herself. The oldest boy tugged on her shirt, asking her to come to the playroom with them. At first Djamila resisted but finally she went. As she heard the shower start in Franklin's bathroom, she knew that she needed some time to think.

She put the baby in the playpen and spent some time with the older boys. Then she went to the bathroom and ran some cold water over her face. The shower was still running upstairs. Djamila knew that Franklin didn't take quick showers.

Finally, Djamila knew there was no way around it. She went to get her purse.

"A storm is coming," she said to herself, practicing it before she had to say it for real on her cell phone. It was four simple words and then her problem would be over, and still her skin tingled. It would perhaps not be such a good resolution for Lori Franklin, who had picked today of all days to do something with her sons.

When she saw it, her heart nearly stopped. Her purse was turned upside down on the floor. She'd stupidly left it on the chair and forgotten to move it to higher ground. She dropped to her knees and searched through the objects strewn there. Her cell phone! Where was her cell phone?

She raced to the playroom and found the oldest boy, Timmy, the one who had made a habit of taking things from her purse until she started putting it out of reach. She grabbed up the boy and tried to say in as calm a voice as she could manage, "Where is Nana's phone, Timmy, you naughty boy. You take Nana's phone again?"

The boy nodded and smiled, obviously pleased with himself.

"Okay, you naughty boy, you take Nana to her phone. Nana needs her phone. You show me, okay?"

Only he clearly didn't remember where he'd put it. They searched for ten minutes as the boy led her to one spot and then another. With each failure Djamila's spirits dropped lower and lower. And then she heard it: The shower stopped. She looked at her watch. She had to leave very soon, or she would be off schedule. Her mind raced. Then she had the solution: She could use the Franklins' phone to call her cell phone and the ringing sound would tell her where it was. She punched in the number as she walked around the house. However, she heard nothing. Timmy must have hit the silent button on her phone when he'd taken it. She had another thought. She would simply make the calls using the Franklins' telephone. She started to dial and then realized that would not work. The man on the other end of the phone would not answer. This person, she had been told, would only take the call if Djamila's name and number came up on the caller ID screen. She ran to the front window and looked out. Could she see him? Could she signal to him? But she saw no one. No one. She was all alone.

She heard feet moving around upstairs. She ran back into the kitchen and opened one of the drawers. Djamila slid out a steak knife and quietly made her way upstairs, where she knocked softly on Franklin's door.

"Yes?"

"Miss?"

"You can come in."

She opened the door, closed and locked it behind her. Then she saw that Franklin was wrapped in a towel and was putting an assortment of clothes on her bed.

She glanced up at Djamila. "I should've given myself more time to pick out something. Are the boys ready?"

"Miss?"

"Yes?"

"Miss, I really think it better that you go alone. The boys, they stay with me."

"Nonsense, Djamila," Franklin replied. "We'll all go. Now, do you think the green or the blue?" She held up each outfit.

"The blue," Djamila said distractedly.

"I thought so too. Now for the shoes."

Franklin stepped into her closet and looked through her shoes.

"Miss, I really think it better you go alone."

Franklin stepped out of the closet, a look of mild annoyance on her face. "Djamila, I can't force *you* to go, but the boys and I are going." She crossed her arms and eyed her nanny harshly. "Tell me, do you have a problem seeing our president, is that it?"

"No, that is not—"

"I know there's a lot of tension between America and your part of the world, but that doesn't mean you can't show respect for our leader. After all, you came here. You have a lot of opportunity here. And what really gets me upset are people coming to this country, making money and then complaining and whining about how bad we are. If people hate us so much, they can go back where they came from!"

"Miss, I no hate this country, even with all it has done to my people, I do not hate." Djamila instantly knew she had made a mistake.

"What the hell have we done to Saudi Arabia? *My* country has spent a lot of time and money on the Middle East, trying to make it free, and what do we have to show for it? Just more pain, misery *and* tax increases." Franklin took a deep, calming breath. "Listen, I don't like to argue like this, Djamila. I really don't. I just thought it would be fun to have a nice lunch and go to this event. When we get there, if the crowd's too big and it feels too uncomfortable, then we'll just leave, okay? Now, would you please make sure the boys are ready? I'll be down in about twenty minutes." Franklin turned and went back into her closet.

Djamila withdrew the steak knife from her pocket, summoning the courage to do what she had to. She took a step forward and then froze. Franklin had abruptly come back out of the closet and was staring at Djamila openmouthed.

"Djamila?" she said fearfully as she glanced from the knife to her nanny.

The expression on the other woman's face revealed to Franklin all she needed to know.

"Oh, my God." Franklin tried to close the closet doors so Djamila could not reach her, but Djamila was too quick. She grabbed Franklin's hair and pressed the knife against her neck.

Lori Franklin started sobbing hysterically. "Why are you doing this?" she shrieked. "You're going to hurt my babies. I'll kill you if you touch them!"

"I no hurt your sons, I swear this!"

"Then why are you doing this?"

"You not going to see president!" Djamila snarled back. "Get on the floor. Now, or you will not live to see your sons grow up." She pushed the blade edge against Franklin's neck.

Trembling, Franklin lay on the floor on her stomach. "Don't you touch my babies!"

Djamila reached over and ripped the phone line out of the wall and used it to tie up Franklin, binding her hands to her feet such that she could not even move. Then she tore a piece of the sheet from the bed and gagged her with it.

Just as she completed this, there was a tapping on the bedroom door, and she heard Timmy's voice asking quietly, "Mama? Nana?"

As Franklin tried to call out through her gag, Djamila said as calmly as she could, "It is all right, Timmy. I be right there. You go back with your brothers."

She waited until she heard the patter of his retreating feet and then looked down at Franklin. Djamila pulled a small vial from her pocket, poured some of the liquid from the vial onto a corner of the towel and pressed it flush against Franklin's nose and mouth.

The American thrashed and gagged and then slipped into unconsciousness.

Djamila dragged the sedated woman into the closet and shut the door behind her.

She went downstairs, readied the boys and loaded them into her van. Now that events had started, Djamila didn't think. She simply did exactly as she had practiced.

A minute after she'd driven away, the Franklins' downstairs phone rang. And rang.

George Franklin hung up the phone in his office. He tried his wife's cell phone. When there was no answer there, he tried Djamila's number. Inside one of the pot drawers in the kitchen Djamila's phone flashed but made no noise. Timmy *had* accidentally hit the silent key when he'd hidden it in there.

George Franklin put his phone back down. He wasn't worried; he was just annoyed. This wasn't the first time he'd been unable to track down his wife, although Djamila usually answered her phone. He had wanted his wife to bring him something he needed and that he'd left at the house. If he didn't get ahold of someone soon, he'd just have to go get it himself. He turned his attention back to some papers on his desk.

# CHAPTER

# 52

Brennan finished his speech and accepted a symbolic town key from the mayor while the crowd cheered. A couple of minutes later, waving and smiling, the president made his way down the steps, where he was enclosed immediately by a wall of agents.

About twenty yards away Alex stood near the Beast and scanned the crowd, which was certainly the largest this area had ever seen.

Before the president hit the first members of the rope line, the senior agent posted there said, "All right, folks, just like we talked about earlier, all hands out where we can see them."

Brennan headed to the soldiers first: some disabled regular army men, a couple of marines, a young woman in dress blues and some National Guardsmen. He shook hands, said thank you to the soldiers, smiled and kept walking while photos were taken. He bent down to shake the hand of the soldier in a wheelchair even as his Secret Service agents held on to his jacket, their gazes moving at whipsaw speed to each person within touching or shooting distance of the man. And then the president stepped in front of the disabled National Guardsman.

Brennan put out his hand, and the man shook it firmly with his prosthetic. The feel of the artificial hand caused Brennan, who'd obviously not noted it wasn't a real hand, to look slightly puzzled, but only for a second. He felt the moisture on his hand and subtly rubbed it against his other to wipe it off. He thanked the man for his service to his country, and the guardsman saluted his commander in chief with his other hand, or hook, rather. The president looked mildly surprised at this too, but then moved on, saying his sound bites to the fans on the rope line and shaking hands with another National Guardsman, two older men, a young woman and then an elderly lady who gave him a kiss.

While this was going on, the First Lady, accompanied by the governor and the chief of staff, was making her way slowly down the steps of the stage, stopping to wave and chat along the way. Gray had also risen from his seat and was absently scanning the crowd. He looked like a man who would rather have been anywhere except here. And then he abruptly stopped his random gazing as his eyes locked on Oliver Stone in the crowd, although Stone wasn't aware of this.

Gray started to say something, but the words never got out of his mouth.

The agent to the left of the president noted it first. Brennan was not looking well. Sweat had appeared on his forehead. Then he clutched his head, and next he ominously pressed the palm of his hand to his chest.

"Sir?" the agent said.

"I'm . . . ," Brennan said, and then stopped, his breath coming quickly. He looked panicked.

The agent immediately spoke into his wrist mike and, using Brennan's code name, said, "Ravensclaw's ill. Repeat, Raven—"

The agent didn't get any further because he was suddenly on the ground. Six other agents and five policemen around the president were also falling as the first wave of shots started.

"Guns!" screamed a dozen different agents, and the Secret Service switched directly to emergency response mode.

The crowd panicked and started to run in all directions trying to get away from the violence exploding all around them.

Four of the Arab shooters were killed seconds after they had fired by the countersnipers at the tree lines. They were miraculous shots considering the pandemonium that had flashed in front of their long-range scopes.

Next three fedayeen rushed forward with the crowd toward the motorcade, each lighting a match and pressing it against a small pack concealed under their coats. An instant later the trio was fully ablaze. One threw himself under the ambulance, and it became engulfed in flames. People raced away fearing an imminent explosion as the fire neared the gas tank.

A dozen agents sprinted forward and hurled themselves against the wall of the crowd, forming a protective perimeter around the president, who'd slumped to the ground, looking very pale. Five more of these agents went down with the second wave of fire. The remaining agents grabbed the president and carried him to the Beast, moving so fast and in synchronization that it appeared they were bound together as some elaborate mechanical insect. Yet two more agents were hit as the second firing sequence continued. They fell next to the prostrate form of Edward Bellamy, the president's personal physician, who'd been hit in the first volley of fire.

By the time the agents reached the Beast with the president, there were only two left standing. A cadre of police went to reinforce them. But a third wave of fire dropped almost all of them. The rest of the police were trying to control the crowd, which was climbing fences, rushing out of all the exits and screaming in terror as husbands grabbed wives and parents carried children as fast as they could from the nightmare scene.

Three more shooters dropped, their heads punctured by the federal countersnipers, who were now moving toward the president, but their progress was greatly impeded by the turbulent mob of citizens who only wanted to get away.

The second wave of fedayeen had commenced their attack, and more of the vehicles in the motorcade were now ablaze.

Carter Gray stood transfixed on the stage. Gone was his momentary astonishment at seeing Oliver Stone in the crowd, replaced by the horror he was witnessing right now. The president's wife was screaming to her husband, but her cries were lost in the noise of the crowd. Surrounding her, Gray and the chief of staff were three Secret Service agents, guns out. The unfortunate governor had stepped off the stage and gotten swept away by a crowd that was now almost as dangerous as the shooters or men on fire. Thousands of people were pushing against the stage in their panic to escape, and the supports holding it up were starting to groan under their collective pressure.

During the course of the speech Kate, Adelphia and the Camel Club had kept edging forward so that at the conclusion of Brennan's remarks they were only two rows back from the rope line. It was here that Reuben Rhodes was standing next to one of the first shooters. Yet he hadn't noted anything until the shot went off because his attention was on the giant TV screens showing the president shaking hands. When he did see what was happening, Reuben instinctively yelled, "Gun." And then he grabbed the man's arm and wrestled the weapon away. A moment later the man was killed as a supersonic round smashed into his head. Reuben dropped the gun and grabbed Adelphia's and Kate's hands and pulled them away. They and the rest of the Camel Club started to frantically push their way to the fence.

"Come on," Stone cried. "Just a little farther."

Kate looked behind her, up near the Beast. She was trying to spot Alex, to make sure he was all right. And then she was being shoved forward and had to turn back around.

Alex had reacted with the first wave of shots, his body operating on muscle memory. Pistol out, he pushed through to the small knot of agents now carrying the limp form of the president to the Beast. Alex instantly took the place of one agent who was hit. They reached the Beast and thrust the president inside. Two agents followed. The agent assigned to drive the Beast opened the driver's door and was about to jump in when he took a round and slumped to the grass.

Alex instinctively raced to the driver side, grabbed the keys from the front seat, started the car and hit the gas and horn simultaneously. Fortunately, much of the crowd had fled away from the motorcade and toward the other side of the grounds where there were more exits. Yet there were still people running everywhere. For an instant Alex had a sliver of an opening and he darted through it. Through the exit the enormous engine of the Beast responded when Alex smashed his size 13 shoe to the floor, and the limo hit the parking lot and tore across it toward the road. Alex weaved in and out of streams of people running for their cars. He clipped the front end of a truck but kept going.

Back at the dedication grounds other cars in the motorcade started up and began to race after the Beast. An instant before the first car in the line, a state trooper vehicle, reached the exit, the last fedayeen set himself ablaze and threw himself onto the windshield. The troopers jumped from their cruiser before it totally ignited in flames. Wedged right against the narrow entry and exit point to the dedication grounds, the fireball effectively blocked the rest of the motorcade from getting out. Normally, the remaining cars would have smashed through the fenced-in area, but they were stopped from doing so by the thousands of fleeing people.

At least the Beast had gotten away. At least the president was safe, thought one struck agent before he lapsed into unconsciousness.

The two agents in the back of the limo were examining Brennan.

"Get the hell to the hospital. I think he's having a damn heart attack," one cried out.

Brennan was writhing in pain, clutching his chest and his arm.

"Dr. Bellamy?" Alex asked.

"Shot."

*And the ambulance has been blown up.* Alex eyed the rearview mirror. There was no one back there. The twenty-seven-car motorcade had been reduced to one. He concentrated on the road ahead. Mercy Hospital was only ten minutes from here. Alex planned to make it in five. He prayed the president could hang on.

# 53

THE BLACK CHOPPER SOARED over the Pennsylvania landscape. Tom Hemingway gave precise landing coordinates to the pilot even as he watched what was happening at the dedication on his satellite TV. Even though everything was going just as he had planned it, Hemingway still felt an immense pressure in his chest as the events unfolded in real time. Even with all the thought he had given this, all the planning, all the thousands of times he had visualized these very same events happening in his mind, the reality was far more powerful, far more overwhelming. He finally turned off the TV. He simply couldn't watch any more.

Djamila raced through the streets of downtown Brennan, turned left and then hung an immediate right. She then eased into the narrow alley as the kids chortled and laughed in the backseat. She eyed them quickly, then stopped and hit her brakes. She'd almost missed it.

The overhead doors flew up and the man motioned her in. Djamila swung the van into the garage and the doors were pulled back down.

A half-block up the street from Mercy Hospital a tractor-trailer pulled out from an alleyway, tried to make a turn heading west, and the engine mysteriously died. The driver got out and opened the hood. The truck was effectively blocking the street in both directions.

A few blocks away on the same street in the other direction, the Beast made the turn onto the road on two wheels, and then Alex floored it. He could've used at least one damn police cruiser to clear his way, but apparently, there weren't any left. However, Alex presumed roadblocks were being set up on all streets leading in and out of

Brennan as no doubt an entire army of law enforcement descended on the area.

The Beast flashed by a street corner behind which rose the antique Brennan water tower emblazoned with the Stars and Stripes. At this section of the street a work zone had been set up only a half hour before by a pair of men dressed in the brown uniforms worn by town workers. The orange cones and tape effectively cordoned off the sidewalks and directed pedestrians to a detour down another side street. No one knew what work was to be performed, but the few people left in town followed the directive. As soon as the Beast cleared the area, two explosive charges set into the water tower's front supporting legs detonated. The tower buckled and then fell directly across the street and burst open, disgorging about twelve thousand gallons of filthy water that still remained in it. Now this end of the street was as effectively walled off as the other.

Ten seconds later, up and down the avenue, smoke started pouring out of businesses, causing people to flee and fire alarms to be pulled. This was the result of the smoke bombs hidden in these establishments earlier by the Arab chemist and engineer. The few souls who had chosen not to attend the dedication were soon out in the streets wandering around in a panic.

Alex skidded the Beast to a stop directly in front of Mercy Hospital. The rear passenger doors flew open, and the two agents burst out carrying the president. They had barely reached the first step leading to the hospital when they were both hit and went down. The president collapsed to the sidewalk and lay there next to the Beast.

"Son of a bitch!" Alex screamed into his mike as he scrambled out of the car on the passenger side. "Snipers at the hospital! Snipers at the hospital! We've been set up. Repeat, we have been set up! Agents down! Agents down. Ravensclaw—" He paused. "Ravensclaw's...," he began again, but didn't finish because he didn't know what the hell to say about Ravensclaw.

He was frantically trying to spot the muzzle flashes. Alex knew he had to get Brennan inside the hospital. His gaze surveyed the street level and then darted upward. That's when he saw it: six flights up, apartment building directly across the street. No optics signature, but twin muzzle flashes, a deuce of snipers.

Alex pulled his gun even as he felt slugs slam into the tires of the Beast. As soon as the holes were formed, however, the punctures closed up again as the self-healing tires did their thing. Rounds hit the limo front, back and on the side. One hit the glass but did not damage it. The Beast could survive a lot more than they were throwing at it. But the president of the United States was lying on the sidewalk, apparently dying. *Protect the man, the symbol, the office.* And Alex Ford was the only agent still standing who could uphold that mantra of the Secret Service. Yet as soon as Alex started up the hospital steps with the president, they'd be an easy target for the snipers who'd taken the high ground. Yet Brennan was breathing, his heart was still beating. That's all Alex cared about right now. *Not on my watch, sir. Not on my watch.*

He gripped the man under the shoulders, braced himself and then pulled. The president was now fully protected behind the steel and polycarbonate wall of the Beast.

"You're gonna be okay, sir," he said as calmly as he could.

"I'm . . . dying . . . ," the president managed to mutter back between moans.

Even with the Beast shielding them, Alex instinctively put his body between Brennan and the snipers. Millimeter by millimeter he edged his head over the rear of the Beast. He ducked back down when a shot sailed his way. He immediately sent back a few rounds with his SIG, but he wasn't going to waste ammo; it'd take a miracle shot to even nick one of the bastards at this distance and trajectory.

When he glanced toward the hospital, he saw a security guard and shouted, "Get down! Get down! Snipers across the street."

The man immediately ducked back inside. Then two seconds later he burst out firing at the upper floors of the apartment building, hurtled down the steps and rolled to a landing next to Alex as gunfire hit all around them.

"Damn!" Alex said. "You got some kind of death wish?"

"Is this the president?" Adnan al-Rimi asked breathlessly, nodding at the prostrate Brennan.

"Yeah. And we need to get him in there fast," Alex said, pointing with his gun at the hospital. "Because the next closest hospital's in Pittsburgh and he needs help *now*."

"Are you the only security?" Adnan asked in an incredulous tone.

Alex nodded grimly. "Looks that way."

"We saw on TV what happened."

Alex glanced at the man. "You the only security here?" Adnan nodded. "What kind of gun you have?"

"Piece-of-shit .38."

"Great." The president moaned loudly and Alex quickly said, "What's your name?"

Adnan answered, "Farid Shah."

"Okay, Farid, I'm hereby deputizing you."

Alex opened the rear door of the Beast, pressed a button on the panel on the back of the passenger chair, and it came down. Behind it was a cache of weapons, including a shotgun, an MP-5 machine gun and a sniper rifle. Alex pulled out the MP-5 and grabbed an extra mag for it. He turned back to his newly deputized colleague.

"Farid, you look like a pretty strong guy."

"I am very strong."

"Good. You think you can lift the president and carry him up those steps and into the hospital?"

Adnan nodded. "Easily."

"Okay, when I count to three, you're gonna do just that. I'm gonna put this gun here on two-shot bursts. That'll give you maybe ten seconds to get up those steps. And, Farid?"

"Yes?"

"You gotta do one thing for me, man."

"What?"

"I'm going to be between you and the president and the snipers. To get to you, they gotta kill me first." Alex paused and swallowed hard. "But if I go down, and I probably will, they're gonna have to go through *you* to get *him*. That means you gotta carry him in front of you so that at all times there is a body between the president and the snipers, you got that?" Adnan said nothing. "You got it!" Alex snapped.

"Yes!"

"Good luck." Alex waited for him to pick the president up. Then he turned and said, "Okay, one . . . two . . . *three!*"

Alex jumped up and opened fire, sweeping the two windows where he'd seen the muzzle flashes with his MP-5.

He wanted desperately to glance back and see the rental cop's progress, but that wasn't an option. Finally, his mag empty, he pulled his pistol and emptied that too. As shots rained at him, he dropped back down, reloaded and turned. He expected to see that the pair was safely in the hospital. But they weren't. In fact, the rental cop seemed to be taking his time getting up the steps, as though he were in no need of . . .

"Shit!" Alex screamed. He lined up the man's broad back in his gun sight.

"Hold it!"

The man instantly turned, and Brennan was now between him and Alex. Adnan backed slowly toward the hospital as Alex tried desperately to find an opening for a kill shot that had absolutely no chance of hitting the president. Unfortunately, there was no such opening, and the pair disappeared into the hospital.

Alex screamed into his wrist mic. "They've got the president. Repeat, they have abducted Ravensclaw at the hospital. We need to shut the whole damn town down."

Alex was just about to sprint up the steps, fully expecting to be gunned down, when good luck finally landed on his side. Police reinforcements appeared on the scene. Alex waited another minute as the lawmen engaged the snipers and then raced up the steps to Mercy Hospital. With gunshots splattering all around him he launched himself through the glass doors, shattering them in the process.

A split second later he heard a bomb go off inside the hospital.

# CHAPTER

# 54

Rᴇᴜʙᴇɴ ʟɪғᴛᴇᴅ Kᴀᴛᴇ ᴀɴᴅ Adelphia over the fence and then joined the other Camel Club members there. As terrified people ran screaming past them, they took a moment to catch their breaths and collect their wits.

"My God," a very pale Kate said, looking around frantically for Alex Ford.

"It is horrible," Adelphia moaned. "It is like Poland and Soviets."

Stone was surveying the dedication grounds where the bodies of the fallen lay. The grass was red with the blood of the gunmen. The federal countersnipers had control of the situation and were now securing the area, moving from body to body, ensuring that the Arab terrorists were actually dead. However, even from the perimeter Stone could see that there was no life left in the lumps of flesh on the ground.

Every one of Captain Jack's men lay dead; many of the fedayeen were burned beyond recognition.

They could all hear sirens in the distance. A few minutes later a fire engine appeared on the scene followed by several others. They quickly attacked the blazing cars with their hoses, and black smoke billowed into the air.

Stone continued to watch as the wreckage of the police cruiser was cleared so that the presidential motorcade, at least what was left of it, could start streaming out. Mrs. Brennan and the chief of staff were swept into the second Beast and whisked away. The bruised and battered governor of Pennsylvania had been recovered and driven off in a van.

Stone felt a big hand on his shoulder and turned to find Reuben staring at him.

"We should probably get the hell out of here," he said. "Damn cops might start shooting stragglers and ask questions later."

Stone looked puzzled. "Reuben, you grabbed one of the gunmen's weapons. Did you notice anything unusual about it?"

Reuben thought for a moment. "Well, I didn't want to hold on to it too long, or else my head would've probably been exploding too. But now that you mention it, it did feel kind of funny. Lighter than I would've thought." He looked at Stone. "Why'd you ask that?"

Stone didn't answer. He looked again at all the dead Arabs.

Seconds after Adnan had entered the hospital, he placed Brennan, who was still moaning continuously, on a gurney that he'd left just inside the front door. The gunfight outside had driven everyone inside the hospital away from the front entrance. Adnan saw a group of nurses, doctors and aides staring fearfully at him from farther down the hallway.

"What's going on?" one of the doctors shouted as he edged forward.

Adnan didn't respond to this query, but he did nod at the man who'd just appeared next to him. It was the hospital's newest staff physician who'd earlier expressed concern about the need for security guards at Mercy Hospital.

"A wounded man," the doctor called out. "I'll take care of him."

"Stay away from the front doors," Adnan warned. "People are shooting."

The doctor pulled a syringe from his pocket, uncapped it and injected the president in his arm; Brennan slipped into unconsciousness. Then the doctor placed a sheet over the president and strapped him to the gurney and pushed it down the side hallway. He got on the elevator there and took it down one floor to the basement. Adnan waited until this had happened and then turned back to the group of hospital personnel.

"Hey!" another doctor yelled at Adnan. "Who was that man on the gurney?" They now all started moving toward him.

Adnan reached inside his jacket, pulled out a gas mask, put it on and started walking toward the oncoming group. Then he pulled from his pocket what looked to be a grenade and held it up.

"Look out," one of the nurses screamed as the group turned and ran in the other direction.

"Call the police," another doctor yelled as she scrambled away.

An instant later Adnan reached the fourth tile across from the center of the nurse's station and threw the cylinder against the wall. It exploded, and the hall was immediately filled with thick smoke that was driven in all directions by the hospital's air circulation system. A split second before the smoke bomb went off, Adnan heard glass shattering, but he couldn't see the source. He couldn't know this was Alex Ford throwing himself through the glass doors, but the Arab knew he had to hurry. He turned back toward the front of the hospital and counted off his steps, navigating in the dark solely through memory from his constant practice. As he neared the front entrance, Adnan felt something bump his leg, but he kept going.

An instant later the timed explosive device he'd placed in the hospital's electrical room went off. All power to the hospital was now gone; everything went dark.

Adnan made his turn, walked down the passageway, stopped at the exit door, opened it and went through. He grabbed a long metal bar that he'd earlier hidden behind a steam pipe and wedged it through the closed door's push bar. Then he began to run.

As soon as the bomb went off and smoke filled the halls, Alex dropped to the floor and slithered forward on his belly. It was like being far underwater, and the fumes were making him gag. Then he bumped into something, and that something was flesh and bone. He made a grab for it, but then it was gone. He swiveled around and started heading the other way, following the sounds of the footsteps. They were measured, steady. How the hell could anyone be walking so calmly through this crap? And then it suddenly dawned on him: because that person had a mask. And the steady tread? The person was leading himself through the smoke by counting steps. Alex had practiced that very same tactic in the dark at the Secret Service's Beltsville training facility.

Alex crawled forward as fast as he could. The footsteps suddenly grew fainter and he redoubled his efforts, whipping his body back and forth like a serpent closing in on its prey. Thankfully, the footfalls picked up again. He hit another hallway, turned and belly-crawled down it. He heard a door open and then close. He slithered faster, pushing himself to the right and feeling for the wall. When his hand hit metal, he reached up and grabbed the handle, but the door refused to open. He pulled his gun and shot at the door at waist level. One of the slugs hit the push bar, collapsing it, and the metal pole bar Adnan had wedged there fell free. He wrenched open the door and flung himself through. The smoke wasn't as bad in here, but the power to the hospital had obviously gone out because there was no light.

Alex rose, found the handrail and made his way down the steps, slipping and sliding along the way. He missed an entire step and ended up in a heap at the bottom of the first flight of stairs. Bruised and bleeding, he picked himself up and kept going by using the rail the rest of the way down. His panic increasing, Alex started taking the steps two at a time before reaching the bottom and hustling down the hall. He burst out of the exit door right as Adnan was getting in the ambulance that was parked there. Alex suspected the president was in the back.

He didn't even cry out a warning. Alex just opened fire, hitting Adnan in the arm. Adnan fired back, and Alex had to throw himself to the side, where he lost his footing and tumbled down a set of concrete stairs. He rose, got off another shot and took a round in return, right in his ribs, fired by Ahmed, who'd emerged from the driver side of the ambulance. Luckily, Ahmed's small-caliber ordnance had zero chance of penetrating the latest-stage Kevlar that all Secret Service agents wore on protective detail. Still, it felt like Muhammad Ali had nailed him with his best punch, and Alex slumped down in pain just as another shot fired by Adnan, burned through the skin of his left arm.

The ambulance sped off, its sirens screaming, as Alex faltered after it on legs that were nearly dead. His chest killing him, his arm bleeding profusely and his lungs full of smoke, Alex finally dropped to his knees and fired at the ambulance, emptying his mag but failing to stop it. Then, he tried his wrist mic but it didn't work. He realized the bullet that hit his arm must've also severed the wiring to his comm pack. The last thing he remembered before passing out was one final sight of the ambulance, and then it was gone.

And so was the president.

*On his watch.*

## 55

GEORGE FRANKLIN PULLED HIS car into the driveway. He had come from the other side of Brennan, opposite where the ceremonial grounds were located, and he hadn't had his radio on.

"Lori?" he called out. "Djamila?" He plunked his keys on the kitchen island and went through the house calling out again. He opened the door to the garage and was puzzled to see his wife's convertible and the big Navigator SUV parked there.

Had they all gone out in Djamila's van?

"Lori? Boys?"

He went upstairs, starting to become a little uneasy. When he opened the door to his bedroom, that unease turned to panic as he saw the phone lying on the floor, along with a torn-up sheet.

"Lori honey?"

He heard a sound from the closet. He rushed over and ripped the doors open and saw his bound wife. Lori's eyes were not focusing well, but she did seem to be looking at him. He raced to her side and pulled her gag off.

"My God, Lori, what happened? Who did this?" he said frantically. She mouthed the name but he couldn't hear it.

"Who?"

She said softly, "Djamila. She has the boys." And then Lori Franklin started sobbing as her husband held her.

The ambulance raced into the garage, and the doors shut behind it. Adnan and Ahmed jumped out of the ambulance, opened the back door and unloaded the president.

Djamila had already opened the back of the van and was standing next to the rear passenger door where she was trying to keep the boys calm. They were all upset, but fortunately, they were also too young to free themselves from their car seats.

Now Djamila raced to the rear of the van and pushed the button that was hidden in a crevice inside the interior there. The floor lifted up, revealing a compartment. It was lead- and copper-lined and cut into two shapes: one of a man in a fetal position and the other of a small cylindrical object. The shape of the man conformed to the measurements of President James Brennan, with an inch all around to spare.

Djamila stared at the young man who had stepped back to let the doctor, Adnan and the other man present lift Brennan from the gurney.

"Ahmed?" she said unbelievingly.

He looked at her.

"Ahmed. It is me, Djamila." It was Ahmed, her Iranian poet; the one who had written down the exact date and time of his death, the young man who had given her so much good advice and also the young man she hoped to share paradise with.

However, there was now a look in his eyes that Djamila could not remember ever having seen, even when he was in his full oratorical fury. It frightened her.

"I do not know you," he said bitterly. "Do not talk to me, woman."

Djamila took a step back from him, her heart crushed at this response.

As Brennan was being transferred from the gurney to the van, Ahmed took a step toward the ambulance. Djamila saw him slip his hand inside the back of the ambulance but could not see what he was doing.

When he walked over to the others, Djamila came forward again.

"Ahmed, we were at the camps together in Pakistan. You must remember me."

This time Ahmed didn't bother to answer.

Djamila screamed as she saw a knife appear in Ahmed's hand, its point aimed right at the president's neck.

Adnan was faster and he slammed into Ahmed, knocking him down.

"You fool!" Ahmed screamed, getting to his feet as Adnan pointed his gun at him. "Do you realize who we have here?" He gestured to Brennan. "This is the American president. The king of evil. He has destroyed everything we have."

"You will not kill him," Adnan said.

"Listen to me," Ahmed shouted. "We will never have this chance again. Can you not see that? The Americans will keep killing. They will kill us all with their tanks and planes. But *we* can kill *him*. That will destroy America."

"No!" Adnan said fiercely.

"Why!" Ahmed cried. "Because of the plan?" he said derisively. "A plan devised by who, an American. We take orders from Americans, Adnan, do you not see that? This is all a plot. To kill us. I knew that. I have always known that. But now, now we take our revenge." He held his knife up in the air. "We do it now."

"I do not wish to kill you, Ahmed, but I will."

"Then kill me!"

Ahmed rushed forward and Adnan fired.

Djamila screamed as Ahmed slumped to the floor of the garage with a single shot to the center of his chest. Adnan put the gun back in his holster and pushed Ahmed's body out of the way. The tears slipped down Djamila's cheek as she stared at her dead poet.

The other men now worked away calmly, as though a cockroach had been killed in front of them instead of a man. Brennan was placed in the compartment, an oxygen tank in the other cutout space. The doctor fitted a mask over Brennan's face and turned on the feed line.

Adnan closed the compartment and turned to the sobbing Djamila.

"He *did* know me," she said haltingly between sobs. "That was my Ahmed."

Adnan's response was a hard slap to her face. This startled Djamila so badly that she stopped crying.

"Now get in your van," Adnan said firmly, "and do your job."

Without another word Djamila did exactly as he said. The garage door flew back up, and the van raced out.

Adnan looked at the other two men and nodded at Ahmed's body. They picked it up and placed it in the oil pit while Adnan wrapped up his bleeding arm where Alex had shot him.

Adnan had suspected that Ahmed would try something. He'd been keeping a close watch on him ever since they loaded the president into the ambulance. Still, it had been a close call.

Seconds later the three climbed into the ambulance, where Adnan became the patient, with the doctor presiding over him and the third man driving. This was the original plan of escape and would have also included Ahmed.

Despite this cover, however, Adnan knew they'd been seen at the hospital, and now he had a gunshot wound. They would not make it through the roadblocks. Yet they would make a fine decoy. And then very soon after that it would be over. Adnan gazed at the doctor, a man of fifty, and understood from his look that he knew this to be the case too. Adnan closed his eyes and held his wounded arm. The pain was not bad; he'd had far worse. It was just one more scar to add to what he already had. However, this time Adnan sensed it would be the last scar for him. He had no plans to rot in an American jail or let the Americans electrocute him like some animal.

After the apartment building had been cleared except for the snipers, the lawmen had launched multiple RPGs into the sixth-floor apartment. Only then were the two gunmen finally silenced after the most intensive gun battle Pennsylvania had seen since Gettysburg. When the apartment was stormed, the shooters were both found dead, but only after having fired all of their M-50 ammo and thousands of rounds from their overheated machine guns, which were now both sizzling to the touch.

The hospital was evacuated, and Alex Ford was discovered lying bleeding on the asphalt. When he was revived, he told them what he'd seen, and an APB went out on the ambulance.

Djamila ran into a roadblock barely five minutes outside of Brennan. There were three cars in front of her, and the police were making people get out of their vehicles.

She glanced back at the boys. The baby had fallen asleep, but the other two boys were still crying hard, and Djamila too felt tears sliding down her cheeks again.

Ahmed said he did not know her. He had told her not to talk to him. Ahmed had been killed right in front of her. He had tried to stab the man. He'd gone against the plan and been killed for that. And yet what hurt her most of all were his words: "I do not know you." His hatred had consumed him, crushing the poet's heart in its grip. That was the only way Djamila could make herself understand what had happened.

She was brought back from these thoughts by a tapping on her window. It was the police. She rolled down her window, and the howls of the children reached the ears of the officers.

"Damn, lady, are those kids okay?"

"They are scared," Djamila said, launching into her prepared speech. "I am scared too. There are sirens and police and people running and screaming. I have just come from downtown, and people they are screaming everywhere. It is mad; the world has gone mad. I take children to their home. I am nanny," she added, probably unnecessarily. She started to sob, which made the kids cry even harder. This woke the baby up, and he added his powerful lungs to the crisis.

"Okay, okay," the officer said. "We'll make this real fast." He nodded to his men. They looked through the van and underneath it. They were searching inches from where the president lay unconscious. However, he might as well have been invisible, and the police were quite anxious to move on to another car. From the putrid smells coming from the backseat, all three boys had gone to the bathroom.

The officers slammed the doors shut. "Good luck," one of them said to Djamila, and waved her on.

A minute later, after repeated attempts, George Franklin finally got through on the flooded 911 line and reported what had happened, giving a description of Djamila, the boys and the van. However, Djamila was on the way to her rendezvous spot long before this message was relayed to the field.

Ten minutes later the black chopper soared over the devastated dedication grounds and landed in the parking lot. One of the doors opened, and Tom Hemingway stepped out and hustled over to Carter Gray, who stood talking to some federal agents.

Hemingway said, "My God, sir, we were on our way back from New York when we heard. Is the president still alive?"

Gray's eyes had regained their focus and his mind its priorities. "The president, we have just learned, has been kidnapped," Gray said. "I need to get back to Washington as soon as possible."

A minute later the chopper lifted into the air and headed south.

# CHAPTER

# 56

Djamila slowly drove back from the rendezvous point toward the Franklins' house. The transfer of the president from her van to his final transportation out of the area had gone very smoothly, taking barely a minute. She had the radio on to drown out the sounds of the boys from the back and also to find out what the news stations were reporting. The airwaves were filled with the breaking events, although the commentators were not making much sense. There were reports of many dead, but right now it seemed that the country, which had been watching the event on TV, was focusing on the fact that the president had been rushed to the hospital. They would soon find the truth far different.

So engrossed was Djamila in her thoughts that she failed to notice the police cruiser closing in on her from behind. She finally looked in the rearview mirror when the flashing roof lights caught her attention. She could hear a loud voice coming from one of the cars as the police talked to her through their PA system.

"Pull the van over and get out immediately!"

She didn't pull the van over, and she had no intention of getting out immediately. Instead, she accelerated slightly.

In the lead cruiser the officers eyed each other. "Looks like she's still got the kids in there with her."

The other cop nodded. "We can box her in and try to talk her out."

"Yeah, but if she doesn't come out? Call in a sniper unit, pronto."

"I don't think there's any left. Hell, we haven't had a single murder here in over four years, and in one day we have an attack on the president and some crazy nanny kidnapping her employer's kids."

A half mile farther up the road another police cruiser blocked the way. Djamila saw this and pulled off the asphalt and drove across the grass. The cruisers were about to follow but then stopped as Djamila turned the van around so it was facing back toward the road. She unfastened her seat belt and climbed into the backseat.

"What the hell's she doing?" one of the cops said. "You think she's gonna hurt those kids?"

"Who knows? What's the status of the sniper?"

"I took it as a really bad sign when the dispatcher laughed when I asked for one."

"There's no way we can chance a shot with those kids in there."

"So what do we do?"

"Look! The side door of the van's opening."

They watched as an arm appeared and the baby was set on the ground still in its car seat. Next the two older boys were likewise deposited on the ground.

"I don't get this," the cop in the passenger seat said.

"If she makes one move to run them over, you take out her tires and I'll try for a head shot through the windshield," the other replied.

The men climbed out of their cruiser; one had his pistol out, the other held a pump shotgun.

However, Djamila had no intention of hurting the children. She glanced at them each in turn as she settled back in the driver's seat. She even waved to the oldest boy.

"Bye-bye, Timmy," she said through the window. "Bye-bye, you naughty little boy."

"Nana," was all the tearful boy said back as he waved his hand at her.

As much as Djamila had disliked Lori Franklin, she was relieved she hadn't had to kill the woman. Children needed their mothers. Yes, children needed their mothers.

She took a moment to write something down on a piece of paper that she pulled from her purse. She folded it carefully and then gripped it in her hand.

She put the van in gear, started rolling forward and pulled back onto the road.

Another police cruiser had joined the hunt now. Djamila headed toward the two policemen who were standing outside their cruiser.

"Stop the car!" one of them said over his portable PA.

Djamila didn't stop. She accelerated.

"Stop the car now or we'll open fire!" Both officers aimed their weapons. One cruiser closed in on the rear of the van while the other cruiser broke off and got the boys safely in their car.

"Shoot the tires out," one of the cops said as Djamila bore down on them.

They both fired and took out the front tires. Still, Djamila kept coming. She gunned the motor, and the van hobbled along at a fair clip on the shredded wheels.

"Stop the van!" the cop yelled again through his PA.

The cops behind the van shot out Djamila's rear tires, and still she rolled on. The van was weaving and lurching but was still headed directly for the two policemen.

"She's crazy!" one of the cops cried out. "She's gonna run us down."

"Stop the car! Now!" the cop shouted again. "Or we will open fire on you!"

Inside the van, Djamila didn't even hear him. She was chanting over and over in Arabic, "I bear witness that there is no God but God." For an instant, as she hurtled forward, her thoughts careened to a young man named Ahmed who didn't know her, despite having captured her heart. Ahmed, her poet, who was dead, and surely now in paradise.

Djamila thought of the Prophet Muhammad climbing the *miraj*, or ladder, that fateful night, until he reached the Farthest Mosque, the hallowed "seventh heaven." It was the promised paradise and it would be so beautiful. Far better than anything here on earth.

She pushed the gas pedal to the floor, and the crippled van shot forward.

The shotgun and pistol roared together. The van's windshield exploded inward.

The vehicle immediately weaved off the road onto the grass and hit a tree.

The van's horn started blaring. The cops rushed over to it and cautiously opened the driver's door. Djamila's bloodied head was resting against the steering wheel, her eyes open but no longer seeing. As the officers stepped back, a piece of paper floated out of the van. One of them stooped and picked it up.

"What's it say?" the other asked. "Suicide note?"

He looked at it, shrugged and handed it to his colleague. "I don't read Chinese."

It was actually Arabic. Djamila had written something down.

It was the date and exact time of her death.

# CHAPTER

# 57

Carter Gray said nothing in the chopper ride back to Washington. Hemingway didn't attempt to break into the man's thoughts; he had quite enough of his own.

They landed at NIC, and Gray climbed out of the chopper.

"Do you want to go home, sir?" Hemingway asked.

Gray looked at him incredulously. "The president is missing. I have work to do."

He walked into NIC headquarters as the chopper lifted off again. Hemingway spoke into his headset to the pilot.

Tyler Reinke confirmed this command and they headed west.

Hemingway glanced down at the floor of the chopper. In the cargo hold a foot under him, President James Brennan was sleeping peacefully.

Within a few hours even the most remote parts of the world knew at least some of the details of what had happened in the small town of Brennan, Pennsylvania.

The Secret Service had immediately implemented its continuity of government plan, securing all persons in the chain of command down to the secretary of state. The vice president, Ben Hamilton, had assumed the duties of the chief executive in accordance with the Twenty-fifth Amendment of the U.S. Constitution, the first time it had been invoked in response to a kidnapped president.

And the newly installed acting president was not a happy man.

Hamilton had verbally eviscerated the director of the Secret Service. Next he'd summoned the heads of every intelligence agency to the White House and took them to task for having been so totally oblivious to an operation that had clearly taken enormous planning and manpower. It was well known that the VP had presidential aspirations. He obviously thought that, aside from the damage the kidnapping had caused the country, it was probably not beneficial to him to assume the top spot in this way.

Then he ordered Carter Gray to come to the Oval Office that night. By all accounts, Gray handled the tirade thrown his way in stride. When Hamilton finished, Gray calmly asked him if he could now go about the business of finding the president and returning him safely. His new boss's response, according to the sources who'd heard it through the very thick walls, was not printable in any newspaper.

At Kate's invitation Adelphia and the Camel Club reconvened back at her carriage house on their return from Brennan. Adelphia still carried a horrified look. Kate gave her some water and a cold cloth, but the woman just sat there staring down at her hands and slowly shaking her head.

Kate said, "Alex is okay, but I haven't been able to see him, only talk to him on the phone for a few minutes."

"I'm sure he's being debriefed," Reuben replied. "He was right in the middle of it all. He might've seen something that could help."

"What did we all see that might be useful?" Stone asked.

"A lot of shooting, people dying and cars on fire," Caleb listed.

"And the president being carried away," Milton added.

"But there was something wrong with him before that," Caleb said. "I saw it on the big TV. He was clutching his chest."

"Heart attack?" Reuben suggested.

"Possibly," Stone said.

"Well, it was Arabs shooting," Reuben added. "I grabbed one of their guns before the man got shot."

"It was definitely a coordinated attack," Stone commented. "Even with all the chaos, that was clear to see. Shooters and then men setting themselves on fire, and then more shooters. In structured bursts of directed fire."

"At least the presidential limo was able to get away," Kate added. "Even if the president ended up being kidnapped."

"Yes, but the perpetrators probably intended that the limo escape,"

Stone said. "After cutting it off from the rest of the motorcade." He looked over at Milton, who was frantically typing away on his laptop. "Anything new, Milton?"

"Only that the president is confirmed missing, and there was a tremendous gun battle outside of Mercy Hospital in Brennan."

"Mercy Hospital," Stone said thoughtfully. "If the president was ill, they must've taken him to the hospital. That would have been standard procedure."

"And they set fire to the ambulance," Kate said.

"Also part of the plan," Stone replied.

Caleb looked at all of them. "So what now?"

"We really need to talk to Alex. He needs to look at that film," Kate said.

"I'm sure he's pretty busy right now," Reuben commented.

"I'll go and see him as soon as he's home," Kate said. "I know he'll want to help."

Stone, however, didn't look nearly as confident as she did.

At Secret Service headquarters the crisis room was abuzz. Although the FBI was officially handling the investigation, the Service was not about to back down on this case.

Alex Ford, his arm bandaged, his bruised ribs wrapped with tape and his lungs still feeling like they'd been charcoaled, had been debriefed for the tenth time and was, in turn, being caught up on recent developments.

"We've got the hospital security guard," said the Secret Service's director, Wayne Martin. "The two other men in the ambulance were killed after a gun battle, but we got the bastard."

"And the president?" Alex asked anxiously.

Martin said, "No sign of him. We think he was transferred to another vehicle. A woman named Djamila Saelem may have been involved. She worked as a nanny for a couple named Franklin. She tied up Mrs. Franklin and took the kids. Later she released the kids but was killed by the responding officers when she tried to run them down."

"What's the connection to the president?" another agent asked.

"We think she used the kids to get through the roadblocks. A nanny with three screaming babies is not really high on the suspect list."

"I'm still not getting it," the same agent commented.

"When the officers inspected the van she was driving, a secret compartment was found in the rear. It was copper- and lead-lined with an outline of a man's body roughly the size of the president's cut into it, plus space for an oxygen tank that was later recovered. Mrs. Franklin said the nanny was highly upset when she was told that Mrs. Franklin had changed her plans and was going to the dedication event with her sons. That would've thrown a big monkey wrench in their plan, so Franklin had to be taken out."

"Has he talked?" Alex asked. "The security guard, I mean."

"The FBI has taken over that line of inquiry," Martin said bitterly. "But his prints were run through the system and came back with zip."

"Sir, that guy is no rookie. I can't believe this is his first op," Alex said.

Martin said, "Agreed, but I guess he never got caught before."

Alex then asked the question he'd been dreading. "How many are dead, sir?"

Martin looked at him strangely. "Counting the dedication grounds and what happened in town, twenty-one terrorists were killed."

"I mean what about our guys?"

Martin glanced around the room at the other men and women there. "This is not public knowledge, and it won't be until we can figure out what the hell's going on." He paused. "We had no casualties."

Alex jumped up and looked at the man. "What the hell are you talking about? Guys were dropping all over the place. I was there. I saw them, damn it. Is this some kind of bullshit political spin? Because if it is, it stinks!"

"Just hold on, Ford," Martin said. "I know you're on heavy meds for the pain, but you don't talk to me that way, son."

Alex took a deep breath and sat back down. "Sir, we had casualties."

"Our guys *were* shot, over twenty-five of them, plus about fifteen uniforms. And Dr. Bellamy." Martin paused. "But they were shot with *tranquilizer* darts. They've all recovered. That's why the shooters were able to get their weapons through the magnetometers. The guns and darts were made of composite materials with no metal." He paused and then said, "None of what I'm telling you leaves this room."

All the agents in the room looked at one another. Alex said slowly, "Tranquilizer guns? They weren't firing tranquilizer darts at the hospital. Those were real bullets."

"The snipers fired darts into the two other agents we found there. Then they held off the reinforcements with real ammo. However, despite having the high ground and one of the best sniper rifles on the market, they didn't hit one damn person with live ammo. Eyewitnesses said the snipers only shot in the *vicinity* of our guys. They put up walls of fire in front of the hospital to keep our people away. That seems clear now. They apparently never took a kill shot, although our guys said there were plenty of opportunities for them to do so. I don't claim to understand it, but those are the facts right now."

Alex touched his wounded arm. "They used live ammo on me."

"Congratulations, you were the only one. I guess they didn't anticipate you being able to get into the hospital and mess up their plans."

"I obviously didn't mess them up enough."

Martin eyed him closely. "You did as much as any agent could've."

Alex didn't acknowledge this compliment.

Martin continued. "The plan obviously was to funnel the president to the hospital without his normal security contingent. They knew our procedures and methodology well, and used them against us. We think the fact they didn't harm any of the security forces may bode well for the president. They could have killed him easily."

"So they'll hold him for ransom, and not just money," another agent said.

"That's the probable scenario," Martin conceded. "God only knows what they're going to ask for."

"But why go to all the trouble of *not* killing us, sir?" Alex asked in exasperation. "I mean that's what these guys do, they kill. Look at 9/11, the USS *Cole*, Grand Central. And they were slaughtered in the process. It makes no sense."

"Agreed, it makes no sense. We seem to be in new territory here." Martin picked up a remote and pointed it at a large-screen plasma TV hanging from the wall. "We just got this video feed in. I want everyone to sit here and watch this thing. Anybody sees something that strikes 'em funny, sound off."

The TV came to life, and Alex watched as the horrific events at Brennan unfolded.

They viewed it three times, and while a few agents had some comments, nothing jumped out at them. It was clear that the terrorists had been very organized and very disciplined.

"They took the ambulance out and Dr. Bellamy too so we'd have to take the president directly to the hospital for treatment," Martin said. "Then they used a tractor-trailer and a downed water tower to block off reinforcements. Pretty damn clever. Lucky we weren't facing these guys when Reagan got shot. He got to the hospital with a handful of guys. Somebody waiting there would've had a pretty easy target. Which means we're going to have to change how we do things from now on."

"But the president *was* looking ill," Alex said. "I remember seeing him grab at his chest. When we got to the hospital, he told me he was dying. I checked his pulse. It seemed okay but I'm no doctor."

"The hospital staff said a doctor at the hospital injected him with something and he went unconscious," Martin added.

"They couldn't just count on him becoming ill and going to Mercy Hospital," Alex said. "They had to make that happen at the ceremony."

"Right, but we don't know how they did it."

Another agent spoke up. "Maybe he was hit with a dart that made him sick."

"That's possible. And the dart guns don't make a lot of noise, but no one saw a gun until the first volley of fire took place. We've gone over that film a hundred times. At no time does the president flinch or otherwise show that he's been shot with anything. Even with a dart gun you're going to have a physical reaction upon impact."

At that moment Jerry Sykes came in holding a paper. "This just in, sir."

Martin read it and then looked up at his crew. "The hospital in Brennan has reported five people who came to the hospital complaining of respiratory problems and heart attack symptoms. They sent us a rundown of the people's descriptions and other details. They're all being treated, but tests show there's nothing wrong with them."

"Some sort of biological agent might've been released in the air," Sykes suggested.

"And only hit the president and a few others? That's a mighty ineffective agent," Martin said skeptically.

Alex's gaze was on the TV screen. "Were the five people who went to the hospital a National Guardsman, two older men, a young woman and an elderly woman?"

Martin looked up from the file. "How in the hell did you know that?"

In response, Alex pointed to the screen. "Back up and run that sequence in slow motion."

They all watched as Brennan started shaking hands along the rope line.

"Okay, stop right there," Alex cried out.

Martin froze the playback.

"Look at the man's hand," Alex said, pointing to the National Guardsman's prosthetic device.

"It's a fake hand, Ford," Sykes said. "A couple of the agents on the line noticed it."

"Right, I saw him too," Alex said. "He shakes with his right hand, which is artificial. And you'll see Brennan shaking five more hands before he went down. Now roll the tape."

The National Guardsman saluted the president.

"Stop it right there," Alex said. "See, he saluted with his left hand. Or left hook. One hand and one hook?"

"So maybe he's waiting to get the other one done," Martin said impatiently.

"But why shake with your right and salute with your left?"

Sykes said, "I'm left-handed, but most people are right-handed. So I always shake with my right, but I sometimes salute with my left. So what?"

Martin said, "Okay, anybody else see anything?"

Alex kept studying the hand. "Can you zoom in on the guy's hand?"

Martin and Sykes looked at him crossly.

"Just humor me, guys," Alex said. "It's not like anybody else here is spotting anything."

Martin hit the zoom button until the prosthetic hand nearly filled the screen.

"Check that out," Alex said, pointing.

"Check *what* out?" Martin exclaimed.

"The moisture on the guy's palm."

Sykes looked at Alex quizzically. "That's sweat. It was a warm day, Alex."

"Right. It *was* a warm day. But artificial hands don't *sweat*."

"Holy shit!" Martin yelled as he stared at the screen.

As the men were leaving a little later, Martin stopped Alex.

"Ford, you have nothing to be ashamed of. You're a damn hero actually."

"You don't really believe that," Alex said. "And neither do I."

# CHAPTER

# 58

TWENTY-FOUR HOURS HAD passed, and a panicked America continued to wait for word on its missing president. The National Guardsman's address had been tracked down, but he was long gone by the time they got there. The other sickened people at the hospital were found to be suffering from a powerful synthetic hallucinogen that was absorbed through the skin. Tests showed that it caused heart-attack-like symptoms, partial paralysis and feelings of imminent doom. The hospital had to call in CIA scientists and technicians to help identify the substance. The CIA quickly informed everyone that *it* had never used the drug on anyone, but the enemies of America certainly had, the bastards. The good news, however, was that the drug was not fatal, and its effects could be counteracted quite easily by existing medications. It appeared the substance had been transferred when the infected president shook hands with five more people standing in the rope line.

Another body had been found in a garage in downtown Brennan. Alex identified the man as the one driving the ambulance at the hospital. The garage was owned by an American businessman; however, no trace of him could be found. The ballistics report showed that the bullet removed from the dead man was fired from the same gun that had wounded Alex. The bullet had glanced off the Secret Service agent's arm and embedded itself in a wooden railing. That coupled with the proximity of the garage to the hospital indicated strongly that the switch from the ambulance to Djamila Saelem's van had taken place at the garage. The president had obviously been transferred from the van to something else, perhaps another vehicle, and then slipped out of the area.

Acting President Hamilton had spoken several times to the American people to reassure them that the country was stable and its leadership running smoothly, and that whoever had done this terrible thing would be severely punished. He demanded that whatever terrorist group had kidnapped James Brennan return him at once, unharmed, or the United States' retaliation for the brutal act would be nothing short of annihilation for both the perpetrators and any countries aiding them.

However, the kidnapping had clearly stunned the United States. The financial markets had plummeted; people were afraid to leave their homes; the country had come to a standstill. It didn't help matters that some Muslim extremists were calling upon the kidnappers to kill Brennan if he wasn't already dead and show his body to the world.

The armed forces and the Strategic Air Command (SAC) were at DEFCON level 2, only the second time SAC had been placed on that level, the other being the Cuban Missile Crisis in 1962. Even the events of 9/11 had only pushed the DEFCON level to 3. Military experts warned that depending on how things developed, the DEFCON level might very well go to 1, the highest. Then all bets were off.

The intelligence sector was doing all it could to identify the kidnappers. Diplomatic inquiries were also put out to all quarters. And the Pentagon was itching for a target on which to use its high-tech weaponry.

In a conversation with a senator on the Armed Services Committee, a three-star general said, "We're through dicking around with these people. No more boots on the ground for them to shoot at. Just missiles through the air. They can kiss their asses good-bye this time."

The senator did not disagree with him.

Already heightened tensions between the Islamic world and America were ratcheted ever higher. Although no terrorist organization had claimed responsibility, every slain terrorist in Brennan was an Arab. Astonishingly, their prints and other information had been run through NIC's vast, comprehensive system and nothing had come back. It was unthinkable that the U.S. intelligence community had not a single byte of information about any of these perpetrators, but that indeed seemed to be the case.

Right now most people were not concentrating on that anomaly.

They simply wanted their president back. And they wanted answers as to how this could have occurred in the first place.

Late in the evening on the day following the kidnapping Kate Adams knocked on the front door of Alex Ford's house in Manassas after having called him repeated times without success.

Kate heard the soulful tunes of a guitar coming from somewhere inside. Those sounds stopped, and she listened as footsteps grew closer to the door.

"Yeah?"

"Alex, it's Kate."

Alex opened the door. He was unshaven and his hair a mess. He was wearing torn jeans, a dirty T-shirt and no shoes. His eyes were bloodshot, and Kate smelled alcohol on his breath. He was holding a black acoustic guitar in his right hand.

"You never returned my calls. I was really worried," she said.

"Sorry, I've been busy," he said curtly.

She stared at the instrument in his hand and then at the bandage on his arm. "How can you be playing guitar with a gunshot wound in your arm?"

"Who needs a sling when you have Jack Daniel's?"

"Can I come in?"

He shrugged, stepped back and closed the door behind her.

"I'm surprised your house isn't surrounded by media trucks."

"They haven't released my name. I'm just the unidentified Secret Service agent who screwed up and let someone kidnap the president."

He led her into a small family room, and they sat down. The room had very little furniture. In fact, Kate thought, it was so barren that it almost looked like someone was either moving in or moving out. The only thing out of the ordinary was hundreds of shot glasses on one shelf.

"I have a shot glass from every place I visited while on protection detail." She turned to find his gaze on her. "Not much to show after all those years, is it?" he said.

There was an awkward silence until he said, "You want something to drink?"

"Nothing as strong as what you're having."

He rose and came back a minute later with a glass of Coke on ice.

"No Jack, right?" she said warily.

"Nope, I'm actually fresh out. Funny, I had a whole bottle yesterday."

"So that's the plan? Stay here and drink yourself to death while you play Johnny Cash ballads?"

"It's a plan," he said dully.

"Not a very good one."

"You have a better idea?"

"You promised to meet with Oliver and the others."

"Oh, right, the Camera Club," he said absently.

"No, the *Camel* Club."

"Whatever," he said, and started strumming on his guitar.

Kate glanced around the room, and her gaze came to rest on a photo. She picked it up. The man in the picture was very tall and lean with a weathered face and a huge black pompadour slicked back to an exaggerated degree. A cigarette dangled from his lips, and he was holding a guitar.

She glanced at Alex, who was watching her closely. "Your father?"

"The one and only Freddy 'Hot Rod' Ford," he said.

"He doesn't really look like Johnny Cash."

"I know. More like Hank Williams, Sr."

She put the photo back down and looked around.

"Not much of a life, is it?" he said.

Kate turned and saw Alex watching her.

"Being a Secret Service agent doesn't mix really well with a home life," he said.

She smiled. "Don't worry, I'm not after you for your money."

"Good thing."

She sat back down, sipped her Coke and said, "You need to meet with Oliver, Alex. Remember, a woman has been kidnapped."

"Then call in the FBI, although I think they're tied up on *another* kidnapping right now."

"They want you."

He pointed to himself. "Look at me, Kate. If your sister were missing, would you really want me handling the case?"

"Yes."

"Bullshit!"

"Please, Alex, will you meet with them?"

"No, I won't!"

"Why not!"

"I don't owe you or anyone else a damn explanation!"

She set down her glass and stood. "I'm sorry you feel that way." She turned to leave, but he put a hand on her shoulder and turned her back toward him.

"I screwed up, Kate," he said simply. "I didn't do my job."

"It wasn't your fault. They almost killed you."

"No, they suckered me like I was a rookie. This Middle Eastern security guard just *happens* to stroll out of the hospital? And he just offers to risk his life to help me, and I let the son of a bitch walk away with the president of the United States?"

"You didn't let him walk away. You figured out what they were up to."

"Yeah, about sixty seconds too late, and in my job that doesn't cut it." He leaned against the wall. "You remember what Clint Hill, Kennedy's Secret Service guy, told me?"

"That you didn't want to be like him. Because he'd lost his president."

"That's right," Alex said. "And now I know exactly what the man meant."

# CHAPTER

# 59

CARTER GRAY HAD BARELY SLEPT since Brennan disappeared, yet the NIC chief had little to show for his efforts. Thirty-six hours after the president had been kidnapped, he was sitting at a conference table at NIC. Across from him, shackled to a chair with two burly guards hovering nearby, was a man answering only to the name Farid Shah, which matched his official documents. Gray knew that it was all phony and had managed to wrest control of Shah from the FBI, based mainly on the fact that he had considerable dirt on the FBI director.

"Farid Shah from India," Gray said. "But you're not Indian."

"My father was Indian, my mother was Saudi. I took after her," the prisoner said quietly. His wounded arm was taped to his side. They were not going to allow him to wear a sling, since it would also make a very effective suicide tool.

"A Hindu marries a Muslim?"

"Out of a billion people you'd be surprised how much it happens."

"And how exactly did you get from India to America?"

"America, it's the land of opportunity," he answered vaguely.

"Are Muslims now recruiting Hindus as terrorists?"

"I am a practicing Muslim. I'm sure you've watched me perform my *salat* in my cell, haven't you?"

"You know, Mr. Shah, you look familiar to me."

"I've found that to most Americans all of us look alike."

"I'm not most Americans. And how exactly did you get your job as a security guard at the hospital?"

The prisoner looked down at his hands and said nothing.

"And who are these people?" Gray asked as he spread out the photos on the table. "Are these your family?" No reply.

"They were found in your apartment, so presumably, you know who they are. It's interesting. On the backs of each photo are dates written in Arabic. They appear to be the dates of birth and death and also some other information." Gray held up one photo of a teenage boy. "This says he was sixteen when he died. It also says he was killed during the Iran-Iraq war. Was he your brother? Which side of the war was he on? Which side were *you* on?"

Gray didn't wait for an answer that he knew wasn't coming. He picked up another photo, this one of a woman. "It says she was killed in what is written as the 'first American invasion of Iraq.' I'm assuming you're referring to Persian Gulf One, when *Iraq* invaded Kuwait and the United States came to Kuwait's aid. Was she your wife? Did you fight for Saddam Hussein?" Again, nothing.

Gray picked up one more picture, that of a teenage girl. He turned it around and read, "'Killed in second American invasion of Iraq.' Was this your daughter?" The prisoner was still studying his hands. "You've lost all these people, your family and friends in war and insurrection; Muslim against Muslim and then Muslim against American. Is that what this is all about?" Gray leaned in closer. "Is this all about revenge?"

Gray slowly collected the photos and nodded to the guards. As he rose to leave, Gray said to the prisoner, "I'll be back very soon. And then you *will* tell me everything."

The following morning, responding to news rumors, the nation was finally told that during the kidnapping of President Brennan the terrorists had used tranquilizer guns. These resulted in no deaths to any American, although numerous people suffered injuries when the crowd stampeded at the dedication ceremony. The confirmed killing of twenty-one Arabs had the world shaking its collective head. The *New York Times* headline put the issue succinctly: "Suicide Killers Who Kill Only Themselves?" A commentary in the *Washington Post* wondered if it was due to the fact that real guns would have been detected by the magnetometers. Yet no one could explain why the snipers at the hospital also used tranquilizer guns.

The *New York Post* put it most bluntly with its headline: "What in the Hell Is Going On?"

Violence was spreading into the streets across America and the world. Clearly, it was only a matter of time before something major happened.

On that very same morning the White House absorbed more stunning news. Each of the major American television networks had received a heads-up from Al Jazeera that it was about to release a ransom note from the kidnappers that had just been delivered to the Arab news network. There were stunning revelations contained in the note, representatives of Al Jazeera claimed. No one, not even the acting president, would be given an advance copy of the ransom demand. Apparently, the kidnappers wanted the government to find out at the same time as the rest of its citizenry.

Acting President Hamilton's response to this, if it had been on live TV, would've required a number of bleep-overs and an official FCC rebuke for on-air profanity. Yet what could he do? Hamilton assembled his cabinet, advisers and military commanders to watch the announcement.

"How the hell do we even know if these people *have* Brennan? This could all be a load of crap," the national security adviser warned.

"Exactly," the secretary of defense, Joe Decker, echoed. He was well respected as a cabinet member who did his homework and played the political games to the fullest. He also had the reputation of a man unafraid to pull the trigger when it came to unleashing America's military juggernaut. Decker had been an iron man in Brennan's administration, and Hamilton was relying heavily on him during this crisis.

Hamilton withdrew a slip of paper from his pocket. "This was forwarded to the White House a few minutes ago from the networks. It accompanied the demand letter."

"What is it, sir?" Decker asked.

"They say it's the nuclear codes that President Brennan was carrying with him. We'll need to confirm that they're accurate. Obviously, the codes are no longer valid."

Two minutes later, after a quick consultation and a confirming phone call, Defense Secretary Decker glumly looked around the room. "They're the ones."

The other men and women in the room stared downward, avoiding eye contact with each other. They were all thinking the same thing. Whatever the kidnappers were asking for would almost undoubtedly be something the U.S. could not agree to. And that, unfortunately, would seal the fate of James Brennan.

A grizzled news anchor appeared on the plasma screen mounted on the wall. Hamilton, putting words to the unspoken thoughts of those gathered around him, said, "I swear to God, if those bastards film the beheading of Jim Brennan, there won't be one building left standing over there."

The veteran news anchor appeared upset but quickly started reading. First, America and the rest of the world had to recognize Islam as a great religion and give it the respect it deserved. Second, for every dollar given by the U.S. to either Israel or Egypt a dollar had to be given to Palestine for economic development. Third, there must be a complete withdrawal of all allied troops from Iraq and Afghanistan, although U.N. troops could remain. Fourth, all allied military bases in Afghanistan must be removed. Fifth, all private foreign oil interests in the Middle East must be turned over to the country where such oil interests were located, including the oil pipeline running through Afghanistan. Sixth, any foreign businesses operating in the Middle East must be majority-owned by Arabs, and must reinvest all their profits in the region for the next two decades to help build infrastructure and create jobs. Seventh, there must be agreement by the United States and its allies that they would not invade another sovereign nation unless specifically attacked by that nation's military or unless there was credible evidence of such nation's support of a terrorist attack against the U.S. or its allies. Eighth, the United States must refrain from using its powerful military to reshape the world in its image and must respect the diverse cultures in the Middle East. Ninth, there must be an acknowledgment that many problems in the Middle East were the result of the West's misguided foreign policies and colonial exploitation, and that a widespread dialogue must be initiated on how best to move forward.

As this list was read off, the mood in the room at the White House darkened even more. A general exclaimed, "Same old crap! I'm a little disappointed they weren't more creative."

"We *can't* bow to blackmail," Hamilton said. He looked around the room for confirmation.

"Absolutely not," the NSA agreed.

"Clearly we can't," Secretary Decker added forcefully.

Around the table people started scribbling notes on the appropriate spin for this chain of events. Meanwhile, the generals and admirals huddled in a corner sketching out a military response.

The secretary of state, Andrea Mayes, spoke up. "Wait a minute, people. Damn it, let's not just write Jim Brennan off." She was a close friend of the kidnapped president.

The Pentagon group looked at her in utter disbelief.

One of them snapped, "Do you really believe that they're just going to hand him back to us?"

There were eruptions around the table; then a very loud voice boomed out. Everyone's attention was directed to Carter Gray, who sat at one end of the table. Though his aura of invincibility had been substantially damaged, he could still command respect.

"Perhaps," Gray said, motioning to the TV, "we should listen to the rest."

The room grew silent.

"This is a new section," the TV anchor said, holding the paper tightly. He cleared his throat and began reading. "Civilized countries that unilaterally spread their will with bullets and bombs are terrorists and have no right to deny other countries the same privilege. When you lead with the sword, you often die by it." The anchor paused again. "Now we come to the most bizarre part of this message, although, quite frankly, what has happened thus far is the most incredible series of events that I have seen in my thirty-two years of covering the news." He paused a third time, as though to give the moment the substantial gravitas it deserved.

"Damn it," Secretary Decker roared. "Just tell us, for God's sake!"

The anchor started reading again. "Whether or not these demands are met, one week from today President James Brennan will be released unharmed, left at a safe location, and the appropriate authorities will be contacted immediately to retrieve him. However, we ask the world to take these demands with the utmost seriousness if we are ever to truly have *Salaam*." The anchor added hastily, "That means 'peace' in Arabic."

The White House group simply stared at the TV, shock and awe all over their faces.

"What the hell did he just say?" Hamilton asked.

Gray answered in a clear voice, "He said that even if the demands are not met, President Brennan will be released unharmed."

"Bullshit!" Decker yelled. "Do they think we're all idiots?"

Gray thought, *No, I don't believe* they *think you're all idiots.*

"This is preposterous," Decker said angrily. "What I want to know is where they recruited the people to pull this off."

Gray looked at him disdainfully. "There are over one billion Muslims on this earth. Muslims follow their faith fervently and do what is asked of them without question. So do you really think that it would be that difficult to find fewer than two dozen of them willing to sacrifice their lives under these circumstances? Do you?" he asked again. "We're fighting a war against these people, Joe. If you don't even know your enemy, I respectfully suggest that the *Defense* Department is not the best fit for your capabilities."

"Where the hell do you get off—" Decker began, but Gray snapped, "The question we *should* be asking ourselves is, *who* planned the scheme? Because I seriously doubt it was any terrorist organization of which I'm aware. That means there's someone else out there. Someone else we have to find if we're to have any chance of getting the president back alive."

# CHAPTER

## 60

AFTER THE STUNNING DEMAND, Carter Gray had gone back to work with renewed purpose. The files at NIC contained no record of Farid Shah, so Gray had mulled where next to search. The FBI had its AFIS criminal files, yet Gray was almost certain the name Farid Shah would not be found there. One did not assume a false name with a criminal record attached to it. And as Gray had predicted, a search in the AFIS database also turned up negative.

Next Gray hopped a chopper to Brennan, Pennsylvania. A temporary morgue had been set up there, and Gray examined all of the bodies. The corpse of the doctor from Mercy Hospital looked familiar, but that was all. The problem was many of the photos NIC had in its terrorist files were anywhere from five to fifteen years old. People could change a lot in that amount of time. Gray then traveled to the dedication grounds, the garage, the hospital and finally the apartment building where the snipers had kept the police at bay. Nothing occurred to the NIC chief except his ability to marvel at the terrorists' intricate planning. Who had set this in motion? Who?

On the chopper ride home he pulled out the photos he'd taken from Shah's apartment. A sudden thought occurred to him. The chopper was redirected to Langley.

When he arrived, Gray gave the photos and also a mug shot of Farid Shah to the DCI and asked him to make immediate inquiries to try to identify any of them.

Late that evening, back at his office, Gray received a phone call from Langley.

They had turned up an Arab informant who thought he recognized one of the people in the photos. It was the young girl. She was the daughter of someone the informant had fought with in Iraq, first as part of an underground movement against Saddam Hussein and then against the American occupation. When the informant saw Shah's mug shot, he identified it immediately, although the man's appearance had changed drastically. He was the young girl's father.

"What was the father's name?" Gray asked impatiently.

"Adnan al-Rimi," the CIA director said. "But that can't be right. He's dead."

Gray acknowledged this, thanked the man and hung up. He immediately accessed the database, pulled up al-Rimi's file photo and compared that picture with the current mug shot of the man calling himself Farid Shah. Though there was some likeness, even allowing for shaved hair and beard and weight changes, it was not the same man.

Gray sat back in his chair and dropped the photo on his desk. NIC's database had been corrupted and photos and fingerprints altered. Patrick Johnson had been paid to do it and then killed. That all made sense now; yet where did it leave Carter Gray? He'd been fighting this whole damn war with flawed intelligence. It was far more than a disaster. It was the greatest professional setback Gray had ever experienced.

He walked outside and sat on the bench by the fountain. While Gray listened to the soothing water he stared up at the NIC facility, the greatest intelligence agency in the world. And right now he knew it was absolutely useless to him. This had been an inside job. His earlier suspicions about terrorists killing terrorists and then being "resurrected" had been confirmed. But who was the traitor? And how deep did the treachery go? Despite the vast resources at his disposal, Carter Gray was now very much alone.

Tom Hemingway sat on the concrete floor, his long legs folded under him. His eyes were closed and his pulse and breathing so slowed that it was not apparent at first glance that he was actually alive. When he rose, he moved fast down the hallway and entered another room. He unlocked a heavy door, passed through it, unlocked another one and went inside.

In a small enclosure, lying on a cot, her arms and legs chained to the wall, was Chastity Hayes. Her even breathing showed her to be asleep. Hemingway left Hayes and went to another room, where his other, far more important prisoner was also sleeping comfortably. Hemingway stood in the doorway and watched President Brennan for a while. And reflected on what had happened.

When everyone expected murderous violence, Hemingway had given the world restraint. When everyone anticipated that the stereotype of the fanatical Muslim would be repeated once more, he had thrown the world a curve of historic proportion. Yet it was not without precedent. Gandhi had changed an entire continent with nonviolence. Brutal segregationists in the American South had finally been beaten by sit-ins and peace marches. Turning the other cheek was Hemingway's "new" way. He had no idea if it would work, but it was clearly worth a chance. Because without it, all he saw was the inevitable destruction of two worlds that he cared so much about. He was apparently ignoring the fact that what happened in Pennsylvania had terrorized thousands and injured hundreds, some critically.

Hemingway had agonized over how much to tell the Arabs about the mission. Would they follow orders if they knew not one of their enemy would perish? Yet finally, Hemingway had decided that if he was asking them to die for this cause, they should die fully informed. It was the right thing to do. So the men in Brennan, Pennsylvania, sacrificed their lives with the knowledge that their foes were safe. It was one of the most courageous acts Hemingway had ever witnessed.

Hemingway checked his watch. There would be another message delivered to the world shortly. It involved *where* the president would be returned. And this would be just as stunning as the last message.

Kate met with the Camel Club at Oliver Stone's cottage and reported her failure with Alex Ford.

She said, "He blames himself for what happened to the president."

"Having come to know him well over the years, I can't say I'm surprised," Stone replied. "He's a proud man who takes his work very seriously."

"*Too* much pride is sometimes a bad thing," Kate said.

"Well, we're running out of time," Milton said. He had his computer on and pointed to the screen. "It's getting very ugly out there." They all crowded around him, staring at the news flashing across the computer. Milton said, "Even with the demand note saying they'll let

Brennan go, the violence is getting out of control. Muslims are being beaten and killed by mobs all over the world. And the Muslims are retaliating. Five Americans were ambushed in Kuwait and beheaded. And Iraq has become totally destabilized again."

Stone added, "And now even the more moderate Islamic elements are calling for the kidnappers holding Brennan to extract a heavy price for him from America."

"One group is calling for the kidnappers to demand nuclear weapons in exchange for his return," Caleb said. "My God, the whole world is collapsing. Why can't people just sit and read books and be nice to each other?"

Reuben raised a thick eyebrow at that naive comment. "The U.S. military is cocked and locked, just waiting for the word to go."

"This might cause an all-out war with the Islamic world," Caleb said.

"Some people might want war," Stone said. *Carter Gray might want that.*

"What if the president is released . . . ," Kate said.

"It might not matter," Stone replied. "With the world so divided, all it could take is one single catalyst to set the final battle in place."

"But if we can find out who did it?" Kate said.

"Us?" exclaimed Reuben. "We haven't got a bloody chance in hell of doing that."

"You're wrong, Reuben," Stone interjected sternly. They all looked at him. "Alex Ford once paid me a visit here; perhaps it's time the Camel Club reciprocated."

Carter Gray walked down the hallway of an isolated cell area at NIC. He nodded to the guards and the cell door slid open.

"Mr. al-Rimi," Gray said triumphantly. "Shall we talk?"

There was no response from the burly prisoner who was lying on his bed, the covers over his head. Gray motioned to the guards.

The two men grabbed al-Rimi by the shoulders and attempted to haul him up.

"Oh, shit!" one of the guards exclaimed.

They let go of al-Rimi, and he fell to the concrete floor.

Gray rushed in and stared at the body. Loose strands of medical tape were sticking out of his mouth. He had taken it from his wounded arm, balled it up and crammed it into his mouth, suffocating himself under the cover of his blanket. His body was already cold.

Gray looked up at the video camera hanging in the corner and screamed, "A man chokes himself to death on medical tape, and you saw *nothing*! You idiots!"

He threw the file into Adnan al-Rimi's cell. The photos cascaded over the body.

As he stalked off, the glazed eyes of the corpse seemed to follow each furious stride of the intelligence czar. If a dead man could've managed it, Adnan al-Rimi would certainly have been smiling.

A half hour later Gray's chopper landed at the White House. He was not looking forward to this meeting with Acting President Hamilton. He decided to get the worst of it out of the way up front. Gray and Hamilton had never been close. Hamilton was an old political sidekick of Brennan, and he had been openly cool to the close relationship Brennan had with his intelligence chief. And it was still a sore point with Hamilton that the president asked Gray and not him to attend the event in Brennan. And yet that event had radically altered their professional relationship, giving Hamilton the upper hand. Gray assumed his new boss would look for any opening to sack him, and the NIC chief didn't intend to give him such an opportunity.

He told Hamilton about a prisoner's suicide, but without informing him of al-Rimi's true identity. Gray intended to take that secret to his grave. "However, I think we're making progress, sir," he added.

Hamilton snapped, "How the hell do you figure that, Gray?" He held up an Islamic newspaper. "You read Arabic, don't you?"

Gray translated the headline out loud: "They Are Finally Paying for Their Sins."

Hamilton picked up another paper. "This one says, 'Maybe Islam *Can* Turn the Other Cheek.' That ran in a major Italian daily. And now, while our president is God knows where, the international press is intimating that this is somehow our fault." He held up a long slip of paper. "In the last twenty minutes I've been informed that a Muslim cabdriver was pulled out of his vehicle in broad daylight in New York City and beaten to death. And you know what? He'd served six years in the army. *Our* army! And two Halliburton executives were snatched out of their hotel in Riyadh; their gutted bodies were found in an alley a half mile away with 'Death to America' written across their naked bodies. And that's just the latest in about a dozen such incidents I've gotten today. The Pentagon's waiting for me to tell them to nuke somebody and my *intelligence* folks are anything but intelligent it seems. We don't have one damn lead as to where Jim Brennan is." He stared at Gray, obviously itching to hear the man's feeble response so he could pounce.

Ben Hamilton had seemingly aged four years in the brief time since the kidnapping. Gray had never known a president to come into the White House with dark hair and leave with anything less than gray. This was the most impossible occupation in history and, in the strange way the world worked, the most coveted.

Gray said, "Regardless of how this happened, and what the international media is saying about it, dogs don't change their spots. When the inevitable happens, we'll have the opening we need."

Hamilton slammed his fist down on his desk. "I *want* Jim Brennan back alive! Your previous work for this country means squat to me. This happened on your watch, and I hold you fully accountable for it. The United States has been humiliated by a bunch of damn Arabs. Unless the president is returned safe and sound, you will no longer head this country's intelligence community. Are we perfectly clear on that?"

"Absolutely," Gray replied impassively. He knew this to be baseless rhetoric. There was no possible way the acting president could afford to fire his intelligence chief during such a crisis. "But let me point out that there is not one demand of the kidnappers that this country can seriously consider, given our current foreign policies. And we can't wait one week for his release, not that I believe they will release him. The American people will not tolerate that. And the violence is only going to become worse in the meantime."

Hamilton snapped, "Well, then I guess you'll just have to find him on your own."

Gray studied the man keenly. He sensed exactly what his adversary was thinking; politicians were all too transparent. Ben Hamilton had wanted this job more than anything. He had patiently paid his dues, waiting for Brennan to serve his two terms before it was his turn to wear the American Crown. Now he had the throne, yet could he do the job? In Gray's mind it wasn't even a close call. Ben Hamilton didn't make even a worthy *vice* president.

The chief of staff suddenly burst into the room with a Secret Service agent hard on her heels. "Sir," she exclaimed. "This is just in from Al Jazeera. The kidnappers have disclosed the location where the president will be released."

"Where?" Gray snapped.

"Medina."

Hamilton exclaimed, "Medina! How in the hell did they get Brennan out of the country and to Saudi Arabia?"

"Private plane and private airport," Gray answered. "Not that difficult."

Hamilton's face flushed. "We spend billions on airport and border security, and they manage to sneak the damn president of the United States to the *Middle East*." He stared at Gray as though he meant to fire him right that instant.

Gray spoke quickly. "It makes sense. Medina is the second holiest city in the Muslim world behind Mecca."

Hamilton looked at his chief of staff. "Get in touch with the Saudis and tell them that Medina is going to be annexed by this country until we get Brennan back." He eyed Gray. "I want every military and intelligence resource we have in the area focused there."

"I'm on it, sir," Gray said, rising from his chair. He wanted to get out of the room as fast as he could.

*I serve at your pleasure*, Gray thought as he fled the Oval Office.

# CHAPTER

# 61

Captain Jack sat back in his chair and smiled with excellent reason. He had in his hand the password he needed to set his final plan into motion. Their captive had endured far more torture than had been anticipated, although his North Korean colleagues were very skilled at such exercises. Yet the man had finally broken; they all did eventually. Captain Jack read the Arabic words and smiled.

From a cloned phone that was not traceable to him he made one call. Speaking in fluent Arabic with well-honed inflections, he said what he needed to say and then used the precious password. This authenticated the source of Captain Jack's statement to the party on the other line, and it would be immediately relayed to the world.

Captain Jack clicked off the phone and used his lighter to burn the piece of paper. If Tom Hemingway thought he had stunned the world, wait until it heard what his old friend had to say.

Secretary of Defense Joe Decker stared across the desk at Acting President Hamilton. They had just been informed of the latest statement issued through Al Jazeera. And they were furious.

"It's our only choice, sir," Decker said. "We simply don't have the troops to deploy there, and frankly, even if we did, it might quickly turn into another Iraq. We have to avoid that at all costs. We can't afford it."

Andrea Mayes, the secretary of state, who'd been hovering in the back of the Oval Office, came forward. She was a tall, large-boned woman with graying hair. "What Secretary Decker is proposing is a direct violation of the Nonproliferation Treaty, sir. We can't do it."

"Yes, we can," Decker insisted.

"How?" Hamilton asked sternly.

"This country has made it clear that any use against it of weapons of mass destruction, biological, chemical or nuclear, would void the terms of the Nonproliferation Treaty with regard to the offending country."

"But Syria hasn't attacked us," Mayes exclaimed.

"The Sharia Group has just now claimed responsibility for kidnapping President Brennan. Sharia is based in and financed by Syria. Under the foreign policies outlined previously by this country, that means Syria *has* attacked us through the Sharia Group, and they used some chemical agent to abduct the president. And we have evidence that Syria has recently started up a WMD program. Now, even though Syria hasn't used WMDs against us yet, the U.S. has no obligation to simply sit here and be attacked. Coupled with the fact that they've kidnapped our president and are now throwing that fact in our faces more than justifies our position."

Mayes shook her head in disbelief. "Syria is not a threat to develop WMDs. They are a fractured nation of Kurds, Sunnis and religious minorities."

"They are no friend of this country," Decker shot back.

Mayes said, "They don't want the chaos and violence they see in Iraq. Who would? And they don't buy our democracy goal. We're giving money to Libya because it dropped its nuke program; it's still a dictatorship. Saudi Arabia is one of the world's worst offenders of human rights, and their record on women's rights is atrocious. And yet we allow them the status of one of our greatest allies. How can we expect other Arab nations to take us seriously with such inconsistency in our foreign policies?"

She drew a quick breath before continuing. "The public in Syria is very aware of its government's shortcomings and opposition groups are growing stronger there. The government repealed the death penalty for members of the Muslim Brotherhood. There are other positive signs pointing to freedom growing there, *without* a U.S. invasion. Their government *will* change but it will take time." Mayes stopped speaking and looked at the president. "That's what I've been telling Jim Brennan for four years. These things take time. We can't just uproot a thousand-year-old culture overnight."

Decker piped in, "Many of the dissident groups in Syria are leftist and communists. We don't want to go down *that* road again."

Hamilton looked at the director of Central Intelligence, who was sitting in front of the fireplace. "Are you on board with Joe's opinion, Allan?"

The director said, "It's not a slam dunk, but it's close enough."

"And there's no reason to waste time going to the U.N. or building a coalition, sir," Decker added quickly. "They have our president, and we need to get back in the driver's seat. And this will put us there. Fast! And we can and should do it all alone." Decker's eyes blazed. "Damn it, sir, with all due respect, we *are* the world's only superpower. I say we start acting like it."

"And Jim Brennan?" Hamilton asked.

"If he's still alive, and we all pray that he is, then this will probably be the only shot we have of getting him back."

Hamilton mulled this over and finally said, "Okay, gentlemen. Call the networks and get me airtime immediately. I'm going to inform the public about this." He turned to Decker. "God help us if we're wrong, Joe."

When Alex Ford opened his door, Adams and the Camel Club stared back at him.

"Oh, hell!" Alex began angrily.

Kate said, "Alex, please, we have to talk to you."

Reuben added, "It's bad, Agent Ford. Really bad."

Alex said, "What are you talking about?"

Stone answered, "There have been some major developments."

"What developments, Oliver?" Alex asked.

Kate cut in. "A terrorist organization has claimed responsibility for the kidnapping. We heard about it on the drive over here."

"The Sharia Group. It has clear ties to Syria," Stone said.

"Where's your TV?" Kate asked. "The president is coming on in two minutes."

Alex led them inside and turned on his TV set. Ben Hamilton appeared on the screen a few minutes later looking very grave. He summed up the situation to the country and then said, "America is a generous nation. We have always been a people that reach out to others in need.

We came to the aid of our friends during two world wars. Wars fought to keep the world free. There is no doubt that we are a good, honorable people who use our might benignly to spread freedom around the world. But we are also a nation that defends itself and strikes back when we have been attacked. Well, my fellow Americans, we *have* been attacked. And now the organization that has attacked us has shown itself. The Sharia Group has irrefutable ties to the nation of Syria, a country that has long been known to harbor terrorist groups operating against America and its allies." He paused. "All American government personnel in Syria have been airlifted out. All other Americans known to be in Syria have been given early warning to leave the country immediately.

"The Sharia Group's own ransom demand conceded that the United States has every right to defend itself when attacked and to also strike back against any nation that assisted in that attack. And America will *not* be dictated to by terrorists." Here Hamilton gave a long pause. "Thus, my fellow Americans, the decision has been made by me, as your commander in chief, after consultation with the secretary of defense and the Pentagon."

"Oh, shit," Alex and Kate blurted out together, for they knew what was coming.

"We now make *our* demand of the kidnappers." Hamilton paused again and squared his shoulders. "If President James H. Brennan is not returned to us safely within eight hours from this exact moment in time, I have instructed my military commanders to immediately thereafter launch a limited nuclear missile strike against Damascus, Syria. The only way in which Damascus will avoid such a fate is if our president is returned to his countrymen unharmed within the allotted time. If President Brennan is in Medina, then he can be turned over to the American embassy in Saudi Arabia, and the launch will be called off. I pray that the kidnappers will comply with our demand immediately. If not, may God have mercy on the people of Damascus. There will be no negotiations and no reprieves. Members of the Sharia Group, you said you would return our president to us unharmed. Do so in the time dictated by the United States, or Damascus will pay the price for your heinous crime." Hamilton paused again. "God bless you, my fellow Americans, and may God bless the United States."

As the president faded out, everyone in Alex's living room sat motionless in their chairs, holding their breaths. It was a scene doubtless replicated in a hundred million homes around America, and across the world.

An anguished Kate looked over at Alex. "This could be the beginning of the end."

"If it is, it is," Stone said calmly. "But it will do us no good to sit around waiting for the mushroom cloud to appear over Damascus."

"What the hell can we do, Oliver?" Alex asked.

"Find the president!" Stone snapped.

"How?" Alex shot back angrily. "He's in Medina."

"I don't believe that and I hope you don't either." He looked at Milton. "Show him the DVD."

Milton opened his laptop. "This is the video that was taken during the break-in at my house, Agent Ford."

"What the hell does this have to do with anything?" Alex shouted. "We are going to launch a nuclear missile in eight hours. Don't you understand that?"

"Look at the film, Alex," Kate pleaded.

Alex finally threw up his hands and plopped down on the floor in front of the laptop.

"Damn," he said a minute later. "That's Tyler Reinke and Warren Peters. They're from NIC."

"I thought they were NIC employees," Stone said.

"Why'd you think that?"

"Because they were also the ones who killed Patrick Johnson."

Alex sat back, stunned. "Why would they have killed Johnson?"

"Because he was altering files at NIC. Making people seem dead who weren't really dead. And I think someone was paying him a lot of money to do it, but Johnson got greedy or sloppy or both."

"Let me get this straight. Johnson was altering files at NIC to make some people appear dead who really weren't?"

Stone said, "We believe that these men were the ones used in Brennan, Pennsylvania. The newspapers said that not one of the Arabs killed there was in the NIC files. That is inconceivable. I think these men were human sterilized weapons, and they were used to kidnap President Brennan. When we searched Reinke's home, we discovered that he'd invested a lot of borrowed money in expectation of the stock market plummeting, which it has now."

"Are you saying this whole thing was about making money in the stock market?" Alex exclaimed.

"No, it's much deeper than that," Stone replied.

Alex looked at him. "Any idea who's behind it?"

"Someone high up at NIC," Stone ventured. "Higher than Reinke and Peters certainly."

"Let me take another look at that video," Alex said.

He watched once more as Reinke and then Peters appeared on the screen. Then he pointed at the image of the man in the black mask as he leveled the security guard. "He hit the guy pretty hard," Alex noted. "He had to check his pulse to make sure he hadn't killed him."

Reuben suddenly put a finger up to his lips and motioned toward the window. The blind was drawn but the window was open. They all had heard it now: footsteps.

Alex eyed Stone, and the pair quickly reached a silent agreement. Stone motioned to Reuben to join the Secret Service agent. While the group talked as though they were all still there, Alex pulled his gun and silently opened the front door. He went left while Reuben went to the right and around the side of the house toward the rear.

A minute later they all heard screams and a struggle, and then silence. Then the front door opened and Alex marched in. Behind him Reuben was carrying someone.

Jackie Simpson didn't look very happy.

# CHAPTER

# 62

"WHAT THE HELL ARE YOU DOING here, Jackie?" Alex demanded.

She glared at him. "I've been calling your house to see how you were doing, but you never called me back. So I came by tonight to see you, and I seem to have stumbled upon a conspiracy. What's going on, Alex?"

Stone had not taken his gaze off Simpson. "We're actually trying to figure out what's going on at NIC."

"I know, I heard that part. And that Reinke and Peters broke into someone's house." Simpson looked at Alex. "If you know something about the president being kidnapped, you have to take it to the Service. Alex, you could get into a lot of trouble for withholding that sort of information."

Stone cut in. "I don't believe that's a good idea."

Simpson stared at him contemptuously. "Who the hell are you?"

He held out his hand. "Oliver Stone."

"Pardon me?" she said incredulously.

"His name's Oliver Stone," Alex interjected. "And these are his friends, Reuben, Milton and Caleb. You've already met Kate Adams."

Stone said, "And you are Jackie Simpson, the only child of Senator Roger Simpson of Alabama, and the goddaughter of Carter Gray, the secretary of intelligence."

"Is that a problem?" she asked coolly.

"Not at all. But going to the authorities at this stage *would* be a huge mistake, Agent Simpson"

"Listen, *Oliver Stone* or whatever your real name is, I can do anything I damn well please. I'm a cop, okay, and—"

"And you're a very intelligent cop," Stone broke in, gazing at her. "And because you are, I'm sure that you've already considered the obvious."

Simpson rolled her eyes, but Stone continued to stare at her until she said, "And what might that be?"

"If we're right and NIC's files have been corrupted, the unfortunate result was that an army of terrorists was allowed to go to Brennan, Pennsylvania, and successfully kidnap the president. That does not bode well either for your godfather, who heads that agency, or your father, who oversees its operations as chairman of the Senate Intelligence Committee. I'm quite sure that you would not want to do anything to hurt them professionally. If you go to the authorities now, you could very well destroy both of their careers."

All eyes were on Jackie Simpson as she and Stone engaged in a protracted stare-down. Finally, Simpson broke off and looked at Alex for help.

"Alex, what the hell is going on? What am I supposed to do here?"

"We're trying to figure this all out, Jackie. Until we do, we can't say anything, to anybody."

Caleb looked at his watch. "We now have exactly seven hours and forty-one minutes to find Brennan and prevent a possible Armageddon."

"Well, everybody ought to cross their fingers and toes, then," Reuben said.

"Omigod!" Alex asserted. "Fingers!"

"What?" Kate exclaimed.

Alex snatched Milton's computer and replayed the DVD. "There," he said, pointing. "Right there, do you see that?"

They all looked confused because he wasn't pointing at Reinke or Peters. He was pointing at the man in the mask who'd knocked out the security guard.

Stone looked at him puzzled. "All I see is a man in a mask, Alex. What else is there to see?"

He froze the screen and pointed with his finger. "This."

They all squinted at the screen. Simpson said, "The security guard's neck?"

Alex said, "No, the right *hand* on that neck. He took his glove off to check the guard's pulse."

Reuben shrugged. "Right. So what?"

Alex looked exasperated. "Look at that hand. Tell me you don't recognize it."

Kate said, "Recognize a *hand*? Are you serious?"

"Like I told you before, Kate, hands are my specialty. And I recognize *that* hand. It's very distinctive with bolt-size knuckles, and fingers thicker than I've ever seen." He hit another button, and the picture zoomed in on the hand. "And the thumbnail has a black spot the shape of a triangle in the upper left-hand corner. When I saw that earlier, I thought it was some weird tattoo."

"Saw it earlier? What are you talking about? When did you see it earlier?"

"In the bar that night. When you introduced me to Tom Hemingway. And I saw it again when he met us at NIC."

Kate stared at him openmouthed and then glanced at the screen. "You're saying that's Tom Hemingway's hand?"

"There's no doubt about it. To me hands are as good as fingerprints, Kate."

Simpson said, "I think Alex is right. I believe that *is* Hemingway's hand."

Stone ventured, "So this Hemingway may have kidnapped the president? Why?"

"Who the hell knows!" Alex exclaimed. "But I think we might be able to figure out *where* they're holding him. And Kate might have the answer."

"Me!" Kate exclaimed. "How?"

"You mentioned that you and Hemingway were working on a project together."

"That's right."

"If I recall correctly, you said it involved an old building."

She said slowly, "Right, near Washington, Virginia. I think it used to be a CIA asset, but it's been abandoned a long time. NIC wanted to use it as an interrogation facility for foreign detainees, but with all the problems at Gitmo, Abu Ghraib and the Salt Pit, DOJ is nixing it. Why?"

"Because I think that's where they may be holding President Bren-nan. Tell me everything you recall about it."

"That won't be necessary," Stone said

They all looked at him. "Why not?" Alex asked.

"Because I know that building *very* well."

"Who *is* this guy!" Simpson exclaimed.

"Shut up, Jackie," Alex snapped. "Oliver, you really know where this place is?"

"There's only one old CIA building in that part of Virginia."

"Alex," Simpson protested, "you're not actually buying any of this, are you?"

Alex ignored her. "Can you get me there, Oliver?"

"Yes. But are you sure you want to go?"

"The president was kidnapped on my watch, so I have to do every-thing I can to get him back safely."

"It won't be easy. Not only is it well hidden, it's designed such that a very small force inside can hold back a very large force outside indefinitely."

"What the hell kind of place is it?" Reuben asked.

"It was a CIA training facility for very . . . special operatives."

Alex checked his watch. "Washington, Virginia. If we start now, we can be there in about two hours."

"Longer than that actually," Stone said. "The facility is a bit off the beaten path."

"Why can't we call in the FBI?" Milton asked.

Stone shook his head. "We have no idea how high the corruption goes. This fellow Hemingway may have spies everywhere who could tip him off."

"And we have no idea if the president is even there," Alex added. "It's just a hunch. We can't waste their time leading them on what might be a wild-goose chase. We're on a nuke missile countdown, for God's sake."

Kate said, "Well, I have a van. We can all go in that."

Alex looked at her. "Forget it. You're not coming, Kate!"

"Then you're not going," she snapped.

Stone interjected, "You can't go, Kate, and neither can Caleb and

Milton." They all looked at him and started to erupt in protest all over again, but he held up his hand. "This facility's unofficial name was Murder Mountain, and it's an apt title." He paused. "I'll take Alex and Reuben there, but no one else."

Alex added, "And three people might be able to get up there unnoticed."

"Four," Simpson said. They all turned to look at her. "Make that *four* people." She stared defiantly at Alex. "I'm a Secret Service agent too."

# CHAPTER

## 63

THE NUCLEAR-POWERED SUBMARINE *Tennessee* had been given the unenviable task of launching the missile strike against Damascus. The 560-foot-long, nearly 17,000-ton Ohio-class nuclear submarine was based in Kings Bay, Georgia, along with the rest of the Atlantic ballistic missile sub fleet. Ohio-class nuclear submarines were the most powerful weapons in the United States military. Using its full complement of multiple warhead missiles, just one sub could obliterate any *nation* on the face of the earth with a single strike.

The *Tennessee* was currently parked in the middle of the Atlantic Ocean hundreds of feet down, although it could have hit Damascus with one of its latest-generation Trident II D-5 missiles while sitting in its East Coast home port. Each D-5 cost nearly $30 million, stood forty-four feet long, weighed over sixty tons and had a maximum range of twelve thousand kilometers with a reduced payload. Capable of Mach 20, the D-5 was ten times faster than the Concorde, and no military jet in the world could come anywhere close to matching its speed.

Only a single D-5 would be launched at Damascus, yet that was misleading as to the actual firepower being unleashed. The long-range D-5 configuration contained *six* MK 5 independent reentry vehicles, each one carrying a W-88 475-kiloton thermonuclear warhead. By comparison a *single* W-88 warhead far exceeded the *combined* explosive power of every bomb used in every war in history, including the two atomic bombs dropped on Japan in World War II.

While the 155 sailors on board the *Tennessee* had been at sea for four weeks, the crew was well aware of current events. The sailors knew what they had been ordered to do, and every one of them intended to carry out that order to the letter, even if most of them harbored secret fears about what path this would lead the world down. They stared at their computer screens and went over again and again the launch procedures that might very well send the world into a titanic war. It was quite heady stuff for a group whose average age was twenty-two.

Meanwhile, in the first hour since Hamilton had appeared on TV, the Arab world had united fully behind its sister nation. Diplomats from Saudi Arabia, Jordan, Kuwait and Pakistan were desperately trying to convince America to change its mind. While the city of Damascus was being evacuated, military commanders and political leaders of other Muslim countries were conferencing on how best to respond if an American missile struck Syria. Middle Eastern terrorist organizations everywhere had called for an all-out jihad against the United States if Damascus was hit. Across much of the Middle East the leaders of these groups began planning their retaliations.

If a missile did strike Syria, the devastation would be far beyond anything the world had ever experienced before. Damascus was one of the most densely populated cities on the planet with over 6 million residents. It would only be possible for a minuscule percentage of its citizens to escape to safety in the allotted time. All others would simply disappear in the nuclear flashpoint as a mushroom cloud of radiation rose into the air before descending onto the oldest continuously inhabited city in the world.

Syria and the Sharia Group had immediately and vigorously disclaimed responsibility for the kidnapping. However, this explanation was not widely believed in Western circles. The Sharia Group had become far more active in terrorism over the last year. And the person making the call to Al Jazeera had used the complex password assigned to Sharia by the Arab network for authentication purposes. This password was constantly changed and was known only to a few highly placed leaders of the terrorist organization. Statements from the Sharia Group that one of its leaders who knew the current password had been missing for two weeks largely fell on deaf ears.

The United Nations had called on America to step down from its intention of launching a nuclear missile, and all other members of the

U.N. Security Council had reiterated this demand through emergency diplomatic channels.

To all these pleas the United States' reply was the same: It was all up to the kidnappers. All they had to do was return James Brennan unharmed, which was what they said they were going to do anyway, and the Syrians could live. The only difference was the U.S. was now dictating the timetable of the return of the president.

Israel was on the highest alert. Its leaders well knew that the country would be one of the first targets of an Islamic counterattack. And Syria was close enough to Israel that the issue of nuclear fallout caused the Israeli prime minister to contact Acting President Hamilton for clarification on the matter. Its vital Golan Heights water sources weren't that far from the target zone. The government in Beirut also contacted Washington, since Damascus was close to Lebanon's border. Washington's terse reply was the same to both countries: "Take all precautions you deem necessary."

Back at the White House, Acting President Hamilton sat in the Oval Office with Defense Secretary Decker, his military commanders, the National Security Council, Secretary of State Mayes and a few other members of his cabinet. Carter Gray was conspicuously absent from the group.

The momentous decision to launch nuclear weapons was clearly weighing on Hamilton; his skin pale and his face drawn, the man looked terminally ill. He sipped on bottled water to alleviate the acid burning through his stomach, while his generals and admirals conversed with each other in low voices.

Decker left one of these groups and walked over to Hamilton. "Sir, I understand the enormity of your decision, but I want you to know that we have more than enough capability to do this."

"I'm not worried about your hitting the damn city, Joe. I'm worried about what happens *after* that."

"Syria has been aiding terrorists for a long time. Damascus is full of former Baathist heavyweights just biding their time before attempting a coup in Iraq. It's well known that mosques in Damascus are recruiting stations for mujahideen. And Syrian militia are all over the Sunni Triangle in Iraq. It's time we drew a *hard* line in the sand with them. It's the same domino theory as spreading democracy in the Middle

East by starting with Iraq. We make an example of the Syrians, then everyone else follows suit."

"Yes, but what about the radiation fallout?" Hamilton asked.

"There will be some certainly. But where Damascus is situated, we believe that it will be somewhat contained."

Hamilton finished his water and threw the bottle in the wastebasket. "Fallout somewhat contained. I'm glad *you* believe that, Joe."

"Mr. President, you made the right decision. We could not allow this to happen without retaliation. That would empower these people to do even more. It has to stop. And deploying more troops would only stretch our military beyond the breaking point and allow the Syrians to successfully fight us guerrilla-style just like the Iraqis are doing. Besides, when they realize we're not bluffing, they'll release the president. We won't have to launch."

"I hope you're right." Hamilton stood and stared out the window. "How much time left?"

Decker instantly looked at his military aide.

"Six hours eleven minutes thirty-six seconds," the aide promptly replied as he studied the laptop in front of him.

"Any more word from the Sharia Group?" Hamilton asked.

"Only that they don't have the president," Andrea Mayes said. The secretary of state came over and stood next to her boss. "And what if they're telling the truth, Mr. President? What if they *don't* have him? Maybe someone is trying to lay the blame on Syria in hopes that we'd do exactly as we are doing."

Decker interjected, "I'll grant you that even though authentication passwords are changed by Al Jazeera regularly, there is the possibility that someone else might have gotten access to it. But the person calling in the information had intimate details of the kidnapping that only the perpetrators would've known. Any terrorist organization that pulled off something like this would want the world to know. Historically, their strategy has never been to lay the responsibility off on another group. The only difference is the Sharia Group never expected us to use the nuclear card. That's why they're backtracking now and disclaiming culpability. The bastards have him, all right!"

Hamilton stared at Decker. "But if they don't, and we level Damascus?" Hamilton shook his head, turned back around and stared into the darkness of an otherwise beautiful late summer night in Washington, D.C. From the streets of the city thousands of voices screamed back at him in protest. The chants of "No nukes" managed to pierce even the thick walls of the White House, as the citizens of the U.S. made their opinion very clear to their leadership. Yet once the nuclear threat had been made, it could not be withdrawn, Hamilton understood. Otherwise America's trillion-dollar nuclear arsenal would instantly become worthless.

Instead of going to the White House and participating in what he considered a useless "death watch" for 6 million Syrians who were on the precipice of extinction, Carter Gray had remained at NIC headquarters. He stopped at Patrick Johnson's empty cubicle and stared at the blank computer screen. *Glitches and computer crashes.* And presto, living, breathing terrorists were placed neatly into their digital graves. He sat in Johnson's chair and surveyed the room. The picture of his fiancée, Anne Jeffries, was still on the desk. He picked it up and studied it. A nice-looking woman, Gray thought. She would find someone else to spend her life with. Johnson, from what he'd determined, was highly competent at his job but possessed the personality of a slug. He had certainly not concocted this scheme. It truly was an unbelievable thought, Gray mused. Someone at America's premier intelligence agency had orchestrated the use of a group of supposedly dead Muslims to kidnap the president of the United States. And now the world was on the brink of global jihad.

Gray had had the databases checked thoroughly. There were no electronic tracks showing who might have altered the files. That was not surprising, considering Johnson's expertise and the fact that he helped create the database and spent his days troubleshooting the system. He well knew how to hide what he'd done. Yet who got him to do it in the first place and paid him well, judging by his expensive home and cars? And Gray pondered something else. *Where was the president?* It had to be somewhere relatively close by. Despite what he'd said to Hamilton on the subject, Gray did not believe for one moment that James Brennan was in Medina, Saudi Arabia. No Muslim would take a Christian there.

He thought back to the day Jackie Simpson and that other agent came to NIC. They were accompanied by two of his men. Reynolds? No, Reinke. The tall, lean one. The other one was shorter and thicker. Peters. That's right. Hemingway told him that they'd been assigned to look into the Johnson homicide. Gray picked up a phone and asked for the whereabouts of these two agents. The answer was surprising. They had not reported for duty tonight. He made another query. This surprised him even more, and then he wondered why he hadn't asked that particular question before now.

Gray was told that Tom Hemingway had assigned the pair to investigate the death of Patrick Johnson. At least Gray knew where Hemingway was. He'd been dispatched to the Middle East under deep cover soon after the kidnapping to see what he could find out. Hemingway had volunteered for the mission. Yet, there was no way to communicate with him. They had to wait for him to contact them. *Wait for him to contact them.*

Gray put his hand in the biometric reader on Johnson's desk, instantly giving him access to the dead man's computer. Gray typed in a command and the result was very swift. Tom Hemingway had accessed Johnson's computer. When Gray looked at the time stamp of when this occurred, he concluded it was when Hemingway met with Simpson and Alex. And yet something puzzled Gray greatly. Hemingway was not supposed to have access to Johnson's computer, or any of the other data supervisors'.

Gray slowly rose from the chair. He was too old for this job. He was not up to it anymore. The truth had been dancing in front of his eyes this whole time. Gray's next question was an obvious one. *Where?* The answer to that query came almost immediately.

Gray picked up the phone again and ordered his chopper readied immediately and then called up a team of his most loyal field operatives. He bolted from Johnson's office and jogged down the halls of NIC.

Gray didn't need fancy databases to guide him to the truth. His gut was screaming the answer at him, and his gut had rarely led him down the wrong path.

# CHAPTER

## 64

THEY WERE IN ALEX'S CROWN Vic heading southwest on Route 29. Alex and Stone were in the front while Simpson and Reuben rode in the back. Alex glanced sideways at his companion. Here the Secret Service agent was, heading toward a possible showdown with a man who masterminded the kidnapping of a United States president. His "rescue team" consisted of a rookie Secret Service agent and a big guy pushing sixty whom Adelphia called Shifty Pants. And then there was the man named Oliver Stone, who worked in a cemetery, leading them all to a place called Murder Mountain. And to top it off, if they failed, the world might very well be toast. Alex sighed. *We're all dead.*

About thirty-five minutes after they'd branched off from Route 29 onto Highway 211, they entered the small town of Washington, Virginia, the seat of Rappahannock County. From there, Stone gave intricate instructions and they rose into the mountains, soon leaving any semblance of civilization behind as asphalt roads turned to gravel and then to dirt. It was difficult to believe they were a little over two hours away from the nation's capital and not that far east of the confluence of busy Interstates 81 and 66.

Simpson said from the backseat, "So what is this Murder Mountain place?"

Stone glanced at her with a bemused expression and then looked out the windshield. "Take the next right, Alex, and then pull off the road."

"Road!" Alex said in frustration. "What road? I haven't seen a real road for about twenty miles. My suspension's shot."

They were in the midst of the mountains now, and the only thing that looked back at them from out of the darkness was thick forest.

Stone glanced back at Simpson. "As I said before, Murder Mountain was a training facility for special operatives of the CIA."

"I know that's what you said. What I want to know is, why do you call it Murder Mountain?"

"Well, the short answer to that is they weren't being trained to be nice to people."

Simpson snorted. "So you're saying a U.S. government agency was training murderers? Is that what you're saying?"

Stone pointed up ahead. "Pull the car over there, Alex. We're going to have to walk now."

Alex obeyed this instruction, unclipped his magnetized flashlight from the doorpost of the Crown Vic, went around to the trunk and started passing out equipment. This included guns and night-vision gear.

Reuben and Stone both handled their weapons expertly.

"Nam, three tours and then DIA," Reuben said in response to a curious look from Alex. "I know my way around a pistol."

"Good," Alex said. He looked at Stone, who was checking his weapon.

"You all right with that, Oliver?"

"I'm fine," Stone said quietly. Actually, he was terrified to have a gun in his hand after all these years.

"In case we get split up for any reason, everybody got a cell phone?" Alex asked.

"The signal probably won't work well up here," Reuben commented.

"And once we get inside the building, there won't be any transmission possible," Stone said. "The building was constructed with copper and lead shielding."

"Great," Alex said. "Okay, Oliver, lead the way."

They headed into the woods.

"Does anyone have a problem with caves?" Stone asked as he halted the group at an entrance into the side of the mountain.

"I have a *real* problem with getting lost and dying in one," Alex said.

"That won't happen, but it does get a little snug in places."

"How snug?" Reuben asked anxiously. "I'm not exactly a little guy."

"You'll be fine," Stone reassured his friend.

Alex stared into the pitch-black hole. "Is this the entrance to the building?"

"It's not one of the official entrances, but they'd be watching the official entrances, wouldn't they?" Stone replied. "Okay, stay close to me." He shone his light ahead and stepped inside.

Simpson was the last to enter, and she clearly wasn't very happy about this turn of events. She glanced around behind her, shivered and followed the others inside.

It took them some time to navigate the curving passageways. In two spots they had to clear debris that had fallen down and blocked the way, and in several other locations they had to crawl through. Above them the ceiling creaked and groaned, prompting them to hurry along faster.

They reached a shaft that had rough foot- and handholds carved into the rock. Stone went first. When he reached the top, he shone his light on a wall of black rock. However, when he tapped it, the wall was hollow. He felt along the wall, then carefully pushed on it until the section started giving way. Alex clambered up and helped him, and soon the wall had been pushed back.

They all scrambled through the opening.

The wall they had pushed out was wooden, but painted on the back side to look like rock. The other side of the wall, the one inside the building, had a shelf attached to it. Stone popped the wall back into place.

Stone whispered, "Now, I think it would be wise for everyone to have their guns ready. We don't know how close we might be to someone."

As they walked along, they looked around at the immensity of the place. And it was as though they had stepped back in time forty years. There were even ashtrays built into the stainless-steel walls.

A few moments later loud noises echoed from somewhere, causing all except Stone to point their weapons in all directions.

"It's only birds that have gotten in," he explained. "That happened in the old days too."

With those words Stone felt himself freeze. *The old days.* It sounded so innocuous, as though he were returning to his cherished alma mater for a reunion. This place had been his home for twelve months. A year of his life devoted 24/7 to learning the most precise and intricate ways to kill people. As a young man Oliver Stone had excelled in these surroundings and at that task. A Special Forces soldier, the transition to the CIA team had not been that difficult. He had traded one weapon for another, and his enemies became civilians who didn't even know they were under attack. As a young man his successes in the field had made him a legend in the special ops world. As an older man he found it all too horrible to contemplate. He couldn't believe that two such different men could inhabit the same body.

As they walked along, memories kept flooding back to Stone. Every new sighting, every fresh smell or distant sound, brought with it a recollection of past horrors. The others would all be looking to him to lead them, perhaps to save them. And yet he had never been trained to *save* anyone. The sweat broke over Stone's forehead. He had brought three people he cared much about to die here. On Murder Mountain.

Reinke and Peters had driven to Murder Mountain after they'd heard Sharia's claim that it had kidnapped Brennan, and then Acting President Hamilton's televised demand. They left their car in a clearing and sprinted toward the woods. Passing through a narrow cleft in the trees, they reached another open area. Here a mass of fallen rock lay along with overgrown bushes. Picking their way around this barrier, a door was revealed when Peters drew aside a curtain of kudzu. Murder Mountain had been built right into the rock.

Peters lifted a small metal cover on the door, revealing a button and loudspeaker.

"It's me and Tyler," he said, talking into the loudspeaker. "Things are out of control. Hurry!"

Reinke put the metal sheet back down and stepped back. As the massive door clicked open, three figures leaped from behind a pile of fallen rock. Tyler Reinke and Warren Peters dropped to the ground, their throats garroted. Captain Jack walked out from behind the rock and stood over them. He nodded approvingly. Reinke and Peters hadn't even been able to make a sound to warn their colleague inside.

A number of other men joined them and Captain Jack led them all into the building.

# CHAPTER

# 65

CAPTAIN JACK BROUGHT WITH him eleven North Koreans with well-earned reputations as killers of considerable skill and ruthlessness. It had been relatively easy to get them into the United States posing as South Koreans as part of a technology fact-finding program. Asians coming into the country didn't inspire near the scrutiny that Middle Easterners did.

However, despite his men's murderous abilities, Captain Jack was also well aware of Tom Hemingway's prowess, and he wisely chose to split up his crew keeping two men with him. Captain Jack had seen firsthand what Mr. Hemingway could do in a fight. Eight members of a Yemeni death squad had the misfortune of running into Hemingway while Captain Jack observed from a safe distance. It had been a slaughter. All eight Yemeni, each tough, hardened and armed, were dead within five minutes. Hemingway never even pulled his gun. He did it all with his hands and feet, moving with a speed, precision and power that Captain Jack—with all his world travels—had never before encountered.

By now Hemingway would realize that something was wrong, and he would be coming for them. Separating his men would allow Captain Jack to wear Hemingway down, to outflank and finally surround him. There would be no hand-to-hand fighting. They would simply pour bullets into Hemingway.

The ancient fluorescent lights overhead flickered and popped. Then a sudden flash of illumination caused Captain Jack and the North Koreans with him to cover their eyes.

The first thing Captain Jack saw when he drew his hand away from his eyes was a foot that seemed to come right out of the wall. There was a thud and a grunt, and he watched one of his men topple headfirst to the floor. An instant later the other North Korean was being propelled backward with such force that he collided with Captain Jack, and they both went down in a tangle of arms and legs. His own training kicked in, and Captain Jack went flat to the floor, whipped his pistol around and fired an arc of shots in the direction of his assailant at the same time he drew out another pistol with his free hand. When the mag on his first gun emptied, he poured another line of shots from the second pistol in the same direction. However, his bullet struck nothing except wall.

Captain Jack got to his feet, his hands working at the same time to reload his weapons as he struggled to catch his breath. Despite all his experience in killing people, the swiftness and ferocity of the attack had staggered him. He noticed that both his men were still down.

Captain Jack used his foot to turn over the North Korean who'd slammed into him. The man's throat had been crushed so flat that he could see the bumps of his spinal column poking through the skin. Captain Jack touched his own throat, knowing full well that Hemingway might have easily killed him too. He looked at the other North Korean. The man's nose had been crushed, its cartilage driven into his brain. It looked like he'd taken a cannonball flush in the face.

"Jesus Christ," Captain Jack muttered.

He called out nervously, "Tom?" Captain Jack paused and then called out again. "Tom? That was pretty impressive, dispatching two first-class warriors in a couple seconds." There was no answer. "Tom, I think you know why we're here. Let us have him, and we can all walk away. And if you're thinking you're going to get backup from Reinke and Peters, think again. You'll find them at the front door with their throats cut. So it's just you against all of us. You can't kill us all."

*I certainly hope you can't.*

Captain Jack jogged in the direction of his other men. He hoped to God Hemingway hadn't gotten to them yet. Despite his confident words, Captain Jack was now wishing he'd brought a lot more North Koreans with him.

In another room off the main corridor, Hemingway picked up a pair of crescent swords. He took a deep, meditative breath, turned and raced off. Murder Mountain would live up to its name tonight.

*       *       *

When the shouts of the men reached them, Alex and the others retreated into a room off the main hall.

"That wasn't Hemingway's voice," Simpson said.

"No, but whoever it is, he knows Hemingway's in here, and apparently, Tom just killed two of the guy's men," Alex said. "So if Hemingway is here, the president may be too."

Stone checked his watch. "We have a little more than four hours to find out for sure." He looked at each of them. "Okay, our best bet is to split up. That way if we're ambushed, they can't get all of us."

Stone drew Alex aside. "This place has a number of training rooms that you need to be aware of."

"Training rooms?" Alex asked nervously.

"There's a firing range, a situation room similar to the FBI's Hogan's Alley, a maze and rooms of 'truth' and 'patience.'"

"Truth and patience? What is this place, a damn monastery?"

Stone went on to explain that the training rooms were situated on either side of the main corridor, with two rooms on one side and three on the other. "You have to go through one room to get to the next, until you reach a set of stairs that lead to the lower-level holding cells. That's probably where the president is." Stone ended by saying, "Once you enter the training rooms, you have to go completely through them; there is no other exit."

"I'm beginning to think none of us are ever going to *exit* this place," Alex said gloomily.

Stone motioned behind them with his hand. "Because we came in through the storage area, which is closer to the start of the training rooms, that means we may actually be ahead of the man we heard, if he came in through the front entrance."

Alex fingered his night-vision goggles, but they were useless in the light. He glanced behind him but saw no one.

Stone said, "Reuben and I will take the three rooms to the left, you and Agent Simpson take the two on the right. The doors only open the one way. So once you go into a room, the doors lock behind you. You can't go back."

"Of course not," Alex replied sarcastically.

"Oh, Alex, I understand that Agent Simpson is a rookie agent, so, well . . . I feel responsible for everyone here, you see."

"I'll look after her, Oliver," Alex replied, gazing at his friend curiously.

"Thank you. Now, there are some things you need to know about the rooms you'll be going into. What I'm about to tell you, you need to follow to the letter. Understand?"

"You're the guy, Oliver. Just tell me and it's done."

After Stone had finished talking with Alex, he led Reuben down the hall and reached the first door that was located off a side corridor, where the two men ducked inside.

As they scanned the dimly lit room, Stone whispered to Reuben, "This is the firing range." This explanation was unnecessary as they gazed at the cubicles where the shooters would stand, and then at the other end where old, tattered targets with bullet-ridden paper silhouettes of men hung on the movable pulley system.

Stone said, "You go to the right and we'll meet in the middle. Once we've cleared the room, the door out to the next room is over there."

They parted, and Stone made his way cautiously down the left side of the firing range. He'd barely gone ten feet when the door to the firing range opened.

Stone immediately extinguished his light and crouched low, raised his pistol and forced himself to remain calm. It was nearly three decades since he had done this sort of thing. He looked up for an instant and thought he saw someone flit by, but it was difficult in the poor light to make out who. The last thing Stone wanted to do was shoot Reuben by mistake. And there was just enough light to make his night-vision goggles useless.

Footsteps crept closer, and Stone eased forward on his belly until he was at the very back of the firing range next to the targets. As the seconds passed by, Stone could feel a strange sensation overtaking him. Changes seemed to be taking place in his mind and body. His limbs were becoming fluid and his mind completely focused on survival. His entire existence was reduced to a fifty-by-fifty-square-foot badly lit firing range full of shadows, crevices, difficult shooting angles and hiding places. He moved a little farther to the left and touched something. He looked up and suddenly had an idea.

*       *       *

The man crouched as he moved to the right, a pistol in one hand and a throwing knife in the other. He thought he heard something but wasn't sure. He cautiously stepped into one of the firing range target paths.

Seconds passed.

And then the North Korean was startled by a scream. He turned and saw the thing flying at him. He fired and his bullets ripped through it.

Stone fired an inch above the man's muzzle flashes. There was a groan and the North Korean dropped to the floor. The "thing" that had flown at him was one of the paper targets. Stone had used a pull wire to initiate this diversion and screamed simultaneously, tricking the North Korean into firing and revealing his position.

Then there was a more prolonged silence until Stone heard Reuben's voice. "Oliver, are you okay?"

A few moments later Reuben and Stone stood over the body after making sure the room was empty. Stone shone his light on the body. There were two bullet holes within a centimeter of each other, dead center of the man's chest. Stone examined the man's features, clothing and weaponry. "North Korean," he deduced.

"What exactly did you do at the CIA?" Reuben asked as he looked at the twin bullet holes.

"I was officially called a *destabilizer*. It sounds far less offensive than what I actually was."

The machine-gun bullets ripped through the door to the firing range; Reuben and Stone threw themselves to the floor.

The door burst open and a second man flew inside, still firing.

Stone managed to kick a leg out and trip the man, sending him sprawling and his machine gun flying out of his hands.

Reuben pounced on the much smaller man.

"Got 'im, Oliver," Reuben cried out. Reuben wrapped his huge arms around the man and squeezed. "Not so tough without your gun." Then Reuben cried out in pain as the man smashed his heel on top of Reuben's foot. Reuben's grip loosened a bit, which was the only opening the man needed. Two blows slammed into Reuben's chin, then two more thunderous strikes knifed into his gut, and Reuben was on his knees gasping for air and spitting up blood. The man's hand raised, the blade in it held in a killing position. It descended toward the back of Reuben's neck.

The bullet hit him flush in the brain, and he dropped to his knees and then toppled to the floor.

Stone thrust the pistol back in his belt and ran over to his friend.

"Reuben?" he said shakily. "Reuben!"

"Damn, Oliver," Reuben said slowly through his busted mouth. He rose on trembling legs. The two men looked at each other.

"What the hell are we doing here, Oliver?" Reuben said, wiping the blood away. "We're way out of our league."

Stone looked down at his trembling hands and felt the pain in his leg where he'd tripped the man. He'd killed two men tonight after not having killed anyone for nearly thirty years. Despite his brief feelings of his old training coming back, this was *not* like riding a bicycle. It was less about physical training and youthful strength and more about a mind-set that said it was okay to kill another human being by any means possible and for any reason. Stone had once been such a man. He no longer was. And yet he was trapped in a building that would very likely be his and his friends' crypt if he didn't continue to summon his old homicidal instincts.

"I'm sorry for bringing you here, Reuben. I'm very sorry." Stone's voice cracked as he said this.

Reuben put a big hand around his friend. "Hell, Oliver, if we gotta die, I'd rather go with you than anybody else I know. But we have to get back. I mean what would Caleb and Milton do without us?"

Alex and Simpson were in a large, dark room that smelled distinctly foul. They had not heard the shots from the firing range because it was insulated for sound. Using his night-vision goggles Alex was able to see that there was a narrow elevated passageway leading across the room that was reachable by a set of metal steps.

He whispered to Simpson, "I'll go first, to make sure it's okay. But cover me close," he added.

"Why do you get to play hero?" she asked.

"Who says I'm playing hero? If I get in trouble, you better damn sure come bail me out, even if it means getting your ass shot up. Now, listen, when you go across that passageway, you stay right in the middle, okay? Do not step on the sides."

"Why, what'll happen?"

"I don't know and I don't want to find out. Oliver just told me to stay smack in the middle, and that's what we're going to do."

Alex made his way cautiously up the stairs and then walked across the catwalk staying right in the middle and keeping low. He reached the other side, saw the door to the other room and called back softly.

"Okay, it's clear, come on."

Simpson hurried after him. As soon as she reached him, the entry door to the room opened and closed. Alex and Simpson instantly crouched low.

Alex studied the situation and then tapped Simpson on the shoulder and motioned to the exit door behind them and then indicated he was staying behind. As Simpson started off, Alex crouched on the edge of the catwalk, his pistol pointed straight ahead. He glanced back at Simpson and nodded. She opened the door and eased through. However, she made a slight noise, and this caused the other person in the room to hurry up the steps and onto the catwalk. Alex stepped forward and, unfortunately, to the side of the passageway. He heard a click, and the floor under him disappeared. He plummeted downward and landed in knee-deep, sludgy water. He heard another splash farther down the tank. The other guy had apparently fallen in too. It was now so black in here that Alex couldn't even see himself, and his night-vision goggles had fallen off into the muck. Alex prayed his adversary didn't have night-vision equipment, or he was dead.

A shot was fired, and the bullet clanged off the side of the tank far too close to Alex's head. He crouched down, returned fire and then moved. He tried not to breathe in the stench of the shit he'd fallen into. The wound in his arm was hurting, his bruised ribs were aching like hell and his neck was on fire. Other than that, he was in great shape.

Alex had another problem besides these physical injuries. Because he was in knee-deep sludge, it was impossible to move without revealing his position. So Alex didn't move. The problem was neither did the other man. This was turning into a battle of the first one to move dies. And now it occurred to Alex: This was the "patience" room that Stone had mentioned. After some minutes of standing still Alex realized he needed another strategy. He slowly reached out until his fingers touched the metal sides of the tank. Then he drew out his flashlight.

Alex suddenly jerked his torso to the side, and the knife sailed by him, clanged against the sides of the tank and fell into the water with a small splash. Alex didn't fire his weapon, though, which was undoubtedly his opponent's hope.

He hefted the flashlight in his hand, reached up and placed it carefully against the metal side of the tank. Its magnetized side instantly clamped securely there. Next Alex ducked down, and, stretching his arm as far as it would go, he placed his index finger on the flashlight's power button. He readied his pistol, said a heartfelt prayer, pushed the button and whipped his hand back. The light blazed on, and a second later two shots hit it directly. Another instant and Alex's own gun rang, and he let out a sigh of relief as he heard the body hit the water. Then someone was scrambling past overhead. How was that possible? There was no floor anymore. Then someone *else* raced by.

Alex jumped as high as he could, trying to reach a handhold to pull himself out. Twice he missed and fell into the water. The third time he was on target, pulled himself up and managed to jerk himself along the handrail to the next door and through it.

# CHAPTER

# 66

STONE AND REUBEN LOOKED around what appeared to be a replica of famed Hogan's Alley in Quantico, which the FBI used to train its agents for real-life scenarios. The Secret Service had a similar setup at their Beltsville training facility. This room had mock buildings, a phone booth, sidewalks and an intersection complete with traffic light. An old black sedan with rotted tires was parked on the street. It was as though they had suddenly stepped back in time.

Standing on the street were a number of mannequins—a couple of men, three women and some children. The paint on their faces had faded, and they were very grimy, but they still looked remarkably lifelike. Reuben noted that there were bullet holes in the heads of all of them.

Stone led Reuben behind one of the buildings. There were wooden staircases here leading up to landings at each of the cutout windows.

"This is where we'd do our sniper work," Stone explained.

"Who were you training to kill?"

"You don't want to know that," Stone tersely answered before putting a finger up to his lips. Footsteps were heading their way. Stone pointed upward, toward one of the windows. They made their way quietly up and cautiously peered out.

Three North Koreans had entered the space. They moved as one welltrained unit, each taking turns covering the others as they searched the area.

Stone's and Reuben's fingers tightened on their pistol triggers. Stone eased forward and lined up a shot. The problem was the men were carrying MP-5 machine guns. If Stone and Reuben each took out one of

the North Koreans, that would leave one left and their position revealed. And even with two pistols between them, it would not be an
easy thing to beat an MP-5 in a pair of skilled hands.

"Holy shit!" Reuben exclaimed.

One of the North Koreans had just dropped to the ground with a
knife stuck in the side of his neck. The other two instantly fired in the
direction of where the knife had come. Then there was silence as the two
North Koreans hurriedly moved forward, taking up cover behind
the old car. With the backs of the North Koreans now to Stone and
Reuben, the two Camel Club members could have taken out both of
them. Yet when Reuben looked over questioningly, Stone shook his
head. He wanted to see how this played out before they committed
themselves.

One of the North Koreans drew an object from his jacket, pulled a
pin and tossed it in the direction of the knife thrower.

Even though the grenade was not heading in their direction, Stone
grabbed Reuben and pressed him to the floor of the landing they
were on.

The explosion rocked the small space. When the noise abated and
the smoke cleared somewhat, Stone and Reuben glanced up in time to
see the North Koreans moving forward. Stone would have waited: It
was still too smoky to see all that clearly.

An instant later, leaping out of this cover of smoke was a figure
dressed all in black from head to foot. He moved with such incredible
speed and agility that he appeared to be immune to the effects of grav-
ity. A pair of crescent swords flashed at his sides like wings.

Using the swords, he struck the machine guns, knocking them out
of the North Koreans' hands. When they reached for their pistols, the
swords sliced into their holsters, dropping them to the ground, where
their assailant kicked them away. All this occurred in one blindingly
fast series of motions.

Then the man stopped and stood between the pair of North Koreans. He very deliberately took off his black hood and placed the crescent swords on the floor.

Tom Hemingway eyed the men closely and then spoke to them in
Korean.

"What'd he say?"

"Basically to surrender or die," Stone answered, his gaze transfixed on the scene in front of them.

"Think they will?" Reuben whispered.

"No. They're North Koreans. Their tolerance for pain and suffering is beyond most people's comprehension." As Stone stared at Hemingway, he thought to himself, *And they're going to need every ounce of that tolerance right now.*

The North Koreans both assumed Tae Kwon Do stances. One made a quick feint with his foot that Hemingway didn't even bother to respond to. He spoke again to them in Korean. They both shook their heads. The other launched a kick at Hemingway, who grabbed the man by the foot with one hand and, with a thrust of his arm, sent him sailing backward. He spoke again in Korean.

"He said, 'I'm sorry to have to do this,' " Stone answered as Reuben looked at him questioningly.

Before they took another breath, Hemingway struck. His fist broke right through the feeble defense of one of his opponents and slammed directly into the man's chest. Moving so fast it was actually difficult to follow with the naked eye, Hemingway whirled and delivered a crushing kick to the side of the man's head.

Even from where they were hiding, Stone and Reuben could hear the snap of the man's neck.

The other man ran across the street toward the car with Hemingway on his heels. When he whirled around, Hemingway saw the knife and leaped. The man threw the knife and it sliced into Hemingway's arm, but he kept coming. The heel of his foot hit the North Korean directly on the chin, knocking him back against the car. Hemingway stopped and looked at the blood on his arm, then turned his attention back to the man.

"This ain't going to be pretty," Reuben said.

Hemingway's first strike killed the man. Stone could see this from where he was crouched. He had never seen a blow that hard thrown by a human being. It was more like the raw power of a grizzly bear.

And yet Hemingway did not let the North Korean fall. He held him up against the car and kept striking away, in the head, in the chest and in the abdomen. He was hitting him with such force and astonishing speed that when Hemingway finally let go and the man slumped to the ground, Stone and Reuben could see that the car door behind him had been caved in.

Hemingway stepped back and took a deep breath as he surveyed the three dead men. As he went to pick up his swords, Stone took out his pistol and drew a bead on the back of Hemingway's head. Suddenly, Hemingway stiffened, stood straight and slowly turned in the direction of where Stone and Reuben were hidden.

He stared up at the window. Although he couldn't possibly see them, it was clear that Hemingway was aware of their presence.

As Hemingway stood there, apparently waiting for the bullet to come, Stone lowered his gun. Hemingway waited a few seconds, and then, in a blink, he was gone.

Simpson ran as fast as she could but was hopelessly disoriented. She finally stopped and looked around. She was in a maze. "Alex?" she cried out.

"Jackie!"

She ran toward his voice.

"Jackie, they're in here somewhere. Watch yourself."

She instantly stopped and knelt down, listening. All she could hear at first was her breathing. Then the sounds of footsteps, stealthy footsteps. She backed down the corridor, away from them. She held her pistol up, ready to fire

"Jackie?"

"Down here," she called out.

Alex stuck his head around the corner and saw her. He quickly joined her.

She looked at his filthy clothes. "What the hell happened to you?"

He rubbed at the muck. "Don't ask. Just don't ever say I lack patience, or I'll deck you." He gazed behind him. "Two guys blew past me coming in here. Any sign of them?"

She shook her head. "So how do we get out of here?"

"It's as simple as checking the floor."

"What?"

Alex didn't answer. He walked down the corridor and stopped where it intersected with another. He got on his knees and looked at the floor. "Damn, how about that?"

Simpson hurried forward and joined him.

"See?" He was pointing at a small dot in a crevice in the floor that was barely visible.

"A red dot," Simpson said. "What does that tell us?"

"Which way to turn."

"How?"

"You must be a landlubber."

"Meaning what?"

"Meaning sailors know that red means port and port means left." He turned left down the corridor, and they walked along until they reached another intersection. There they found another dot. This one was green.

"Green means starboard and starboard means—"

"Right," Simpson finished for him.

They made their way through the corridor this way and soon found themselves at the end.

"Okay, how did you know about the dots?" Simpson demanded.

"Oliver told me."

"So he really was here," Simpson said slowly.

Alex stared at her. "I never doubted it." He looked up ahead at the door at the far end of the hall. "Oliver said we only had two rooms on this side. That means through that door—"

"Is the president."

"And Hemingway," Alex added grimly.

"He is a federal agent, Alex, which means he might be on our side."

"Jackie, listen to me. This guy is a traitor, and he can probably kill you with his pinkie. If you get a chance to shoot him, take it."

"Alex!"

"No bullshit, Jackie. Just do it. Now come on."

While Alex and Simpson were dashing through the maze, Stone and Reuben stepped into a room that had a hanging cage, chains on the wall, gurneys and trays of surgical instruments and what looked like an electric chair.

Stone stared at the latter device and drew a sharp breath. "They called this the room of truth. They used it to break you. The *truth* was they broke everybody eventually, me included." He pointed to the chair. "They used too much electricity on one man that I trained with, and his heart stopped. They told his family he went missing overseas during a mission. He's probably buried on Murder Mountain."

"We might be too," Reuben pointed out glumly.

"Let's get on to the next room," Stone said. "This one always made me sick."

They had just started toward the exit when the door they had come through burst open.

"Run!" Stone shouted, throwing gunfire at the North Korean who had swept into the room. He fired back, and Stone had to hurl himself behind the electric chair.

Gunfire erupted on all sides of the room. A minute later while Stone was reloading as fast as he could, he heard Reuben yell out, "I'm hit! Oliver, I'm hit."

"Reuben," called out Stone as two shots whizzed by his head. He returned fire and ducked down. A clattering sound came from the left as though someone had overturned a tray of instruments; then came more noises of things being tossed around. Stone made a quick decision. He pointed his pistol at the ceiling lights and shot them all out.

In the darkness Stone put on his night-vision goggles, his gaze peering desperately through the gauzy green world the goggles created.

Where was Reuben? Where was he? Finally, Stone saw him lying on the floor behind an overturned gurney, holding his side. There was no sign of the North Korean. Stone kept sweeping the room with his gaze, finally stopping on one corner. Here gurneys and other medical equipment had been hastily stacked, forming a wall. The person had to be behind there. And then Stone's gaze went upward, and he saw what had to be done. He laid on his back with his knees bent. He rested his gun between his knees and then clamped them together, which held the gun motionless. He lined up his target, exhaled all the air from his lungs and relaxed his muscles fully. It was as though all his training on how to kill someone had come effortlessly back to him, right when he needed it. *Should I thank God or Satan?*

In daylight the shot would've been simple. Looking into a world of green haze and knowing you had only one chance made the task far more complex.

He squeezed the trigger. The chain holding the cage, which rested right above where the North Korean was hiding, was cut neatly in two. And the one-ton cage fell.

Stone continued to watch, his pistol ready. What he saw next slightly sickened him, even though it had been his intent. The blood flowed under the gurneys and started pooling a few inches in front of this barrier.

Stone rose and made his way over to the corner. He cautiously peered over the wall of gurneys. Only a hand was visible from under the fallen cage. The man hadn't even had time to scream. In Stone's old world this would have been labeled a "perfect kill."

"Oliver!" Reuben called out.

Stone turned and raced across the room to where Reuben sat against the wall, clutching his side. The knife was still in him, and blood had spread down his shirt and onto the floor.

"Shit, bastard got a lucky toss in. I'll be okay. Had lots worse than this." Reuben's face, however, was ashen.

Stone ran to a set of shelves against the wall and threw them open. There were still bottles of ointment and tape and gauze stored there. He doubted the ointment would be any good, but the gauze and bandages were still in their sterilized wrappers. It would be cleaner than using Reuben's shirt. He grabbed the supplies and headed back over to Reuben.

After bandaging him up, Stone helped him through the door into the next room.

As soon as they left the room, the door leading into the room of truth opened. Captain Jack cautiously peered in. He took a minute to search the space and then found his man under the cage.

Captain Jack said, "Okay, perhaps it's time to live to fight another day. I'm sure the bloody North Koreans will understand." He turned to retreat through the steel door but found that it wouldn't open.

"I'd forgotten about that," he muttered. He stood there wondering what to do. He checked his watch. Soon it wouldn't matter.

# CHAPTER

## 67

STONE AND REUBEN REACHED the lower level of the facility at about the same time as Alex and Simpson.

"So that makes nine Chinese dead," Alex said after the two groups had compared notes.

"Actually, they're North Koreans," Stone corrected.

"North Koreans! What the hell are they doing involved in this?" Simpson asked.

Stone said, "I have no idea." He pointed with his gun down the hallway. "But I *do* know that down there are the cells that were used to house 'detainees' for interrogation during my time here. Presumably, that's where the president is."

Alex checked his watch. "We've got three hours left," he said urgently. "We've got to get the president, get out of here, grab a cell signal and call the Service. They'll contact the White House and stop the launch."

"Do you think there are any North Koreans left?" Simpson asked.

Alex said, "I saw two guys running past me when I was stuck in that tank. So—" He suddenly shouted, "Look out! Grenade!"

They scattered for cover as the object bounced down the stairs and landed near them. However, it wasn't a grenade. It was a flash-bang, a device that stunned a person by using ear-piercing sound and blinding light. Members of the FBI's hostage rescue team swore by its effectiveness. And it did its job this time. When it went off, all of them were instantly incapacitated.

Two North Koreans raced down the steps. They wore earplugs and so were unaffected by the sound of the explosion. They pointed their weapons at the helpless Alex and the others. Stone struggled to get to his feet, but he was so disoriented he couldn't manage it. Simpson's hands were over her ears, and she looked ready to pass out. Reuben lay crouched in the corner, clutching his side and breathing weakly.

One of the North Koreans shouted one word, in English this time. "Die!"

He moved his MP-5 shot selector to auto, and his hand slid to the trigger. He could empty his entire thirty-round mag in a few seconds.

And he would have too, if he'd still been alive. His spine snapped when the foot struck it from behind. He dropped to the floor. As he fell, his finger pushed back the trigger, and the machine gun emptied a few rounds right into the concrete floor. They ricocheted into the man, not that he felt them.

The other man tried to fire his gun at Hemingway, but Hemingway ripped the mag right off the stock, then crushed it against the man's skull and finished him off with a vector strike to the liver, rupturing it. The man dropped to the floor with a thud.

Then Hemingway was gone.

As the effects of the flash-bang wore off, Alex struggled to his feet and helped Simpson up. Stone did the same with Reuben.

"Where did Hemingway go?" Stone asked.

Alex pointed down the hall. "That way. Through that door. I saw him right before he disappeared. I'm not sure how, because my head was exploding at the same time."

They took a moment to eye the battered North Koreans.

"This guy is a freaking nightmare," Alex exclaimed.

"He just saved our lives," Simpson pointed out.

"Oh, yeah? Probably because he wants to kill us all by himself," Alex shot back. "So what I told you still goes. Shoot to kill the bastard."

Stone looked at his watch. "We're running out of time."

Hemingway stood alone at the end of the hall, the two cells holding the president and Chastity behind him. The prisoners were unconscious after he'd given them amnesic drugs with their dinner earlier. He didn't believe they'd want to have any memory of what had happened to them.

As the door opened at the other end of the hall, Hemingway receded into the shadows.

Alex stepped through the doorway with the others and called out, "Hemingway, we've come for the president."

Hemingway made not a sound.

"You might not know what's happened, Tom," Alex added. "The Sharia Group claimed responsibility for the kidnapping. Right this instant the United States has a nuke aimed at Damascus. It's going to launch in less than three hours unless the president is returned safely. That's what Reinke and Peters were probably coming to tell you."

Hemingway drew a quick breath but still said nothing.

"Tom, I'm being straight with you," Alex continued. "The whole world is about to go up in flames. Every Muslim army and every terrorist organization in the world is gathering to attack the United States. We're at DEFCON 1, Tom. DEFCON 1. You know what that means. Everything's ready to blow." Alex paused and then shouted, "We've got three hours, goddamn it, or six million people die!"

Finally, Hemingway stepped into the light.

"Why would the Sharia Group have claimed responsibility?" he asked warily.

"They didn't, so I did it for them," Captain Jack said as he darted through the doorway and pressed his gun against the side of Simpson's head. He took her pistol and trained it on the others. "Now, drop your weapons, or you'll get a nice view of this lady's brains."

The others hesitated for a moment, and then one by one Alex, Stone and the wounded Reuben dropped their guns.

"Damn, that's the guy we heard earlier," Reuben muttered to Stone, but his friend wasn't listening. He was looking very intently at Captain Jack.

As Captain Jack's gaze swept over them, it stopped and came back to Stone. Captain Jack's brow creased. Then his attention was drawn to Hemingway, who said, "I thought we had an agreement."

To Alex, Hemingway seemed coiled so tightly he looked as though he could have jumped clear into outer space.

"We did, Tom," Captain Jack said pleasantly. "But then I got a better offer from the North Koreans. I told you I was only in this for the money. That was fair warning to you, mate, and don't blame me if you didn't pick up on it."

Hemingway said, "Why? To start an American-Muslim war? What does that gain for North Korea?"

"I really don't care. They paid my price."

Alex said, "We're going to drop a nuclear bomb on Damascus."

Captain Jack looked at him disdainfully. "I worked for the Syrians for a while. They're just as bloodthirsty as anyone else. It's not like they don't deserve it."

"Six million people," Alex said. "Including women and children."

Captain Jack just shook his head wearily. "You're really not getting my point, are you?"

"You've got dead North Koreans all over the place," Hemingway said. "Do you really think your plan will work now?"

"I'll have time to clean that all up, Tom. There's an old mine shaft not too far from here. Perfect place to dump the bodies. Except for one. The world needs to see that one."

"Brennan?"

"Have to finish the job."

Stone spoke up. "So you're intending on killing all of us?"

Captain Jack looked at him. "You seem very familiar to me."

"You didn't answer my question."

"Yes, I plan to kill each of you." He glanced at Hemingway. "I did right by you, Tom. Look at what happened in Brennan. Worked to perfection."

"It doesn't work if the president ends up dead too," Hemingway said flatly. "I'm supposed to return him unharmed. That's what I said I was going to do."

"If it's money you want, the U.S. has a lot more than North Korea," Simpson said.

Captain Jack shook his head. "Even I'm not that greedy. And I seriously doubt I'd get paid. I mean you are the biggest debtor country in the world."

Captain Jack shot Hemingway with a glancing wound to the left leg. The man grimaced and dropped to his knees. Next Captain Jack shot him in the right arm.

"Stop, please!" Simpson screamed.

Captain Jack said, "I'm sorry to do this piecemeal, Tom, but I have no desire to have my neck crushed by you."

Hemingway said between gritted teeth, "You might want to reconsider your plan."

"Why's that?"

"Because the cell doors are booby-trapped."

"Then turn the devices off and open the doors."

Hemingway shook his head.

"Then I'll just start killing them one by one until you do."

"You're going to kill them anyway, so what does it matter?" Hemingway said.

"We'll just see how long you can take the screams. Your only weakness is you're just too damn civilized, Tom."

Stone managed to catch Hemingway's gaze and motioned with his eyes to something. Hemingway gave a barely perceptible nod.

Captain Jack pressed the gun tightly against Simpson's temple and said, "Good-bye, whoever you are."

"My name is John Carr," Stone said quietly as he stepped forward. "You were right, we *do* know each other."

Captain Jack lowered his pistol slightly. "John Carr," he said in amazement as he looked Stone up and down. "My God, John, the years haven't been kind to you."

"You were a bastard traitor back then, and I see you still are."

"I went out on my terms. I don't think you can say the same," Captain Jack sneered. His attention was fully on Stone now, so he didn't notice Hemingway edging toward the wall.

Stone took another step forward, blocking Captain Jack's line of sight to Hemingway. "Why don't you kill *me*? You were always second best, so it'd be a thrill for you to take out the top man, wouldn't it?"

"You're still one cocky bastard," Captain Jack growled.

"Unlike you, I earned the right to be. How did you screw up again? Oh, that's right, you used the wrong barometric reading and you missed your target. They had to send me in a year later to do it right. Face it, you were a second-rate bungler."

Captain Jack pointed his pistol at Stone's forehead. "I won't have to worry about barometric pressure this time."

Hemingway leaped and hit the light switch, plunging them into darkness. Captain Jack fired. There were screams and shouts and scuffling and finally one horrific cry and then the sound of a body falling.

The lights came back on, and Captain Jack was lying on the floor, his guns gone. Stone was standing over him, holding a knife covered in blood, fabric and skin. He'd taken it from the room of truth.

"You bastard!" Captain Jack groaned as he grabbed his lower calves where Stone had cut him, immobilizing the man.

Captain Jack screamed, "Why didn't you just kill me?"

"Because I didn't have to," Stone answered.

"Listen to me," Captain Jack gasped. "Ten million dollars to *each* of you if you kill Brennan." They all looked at him in disgust. "He's just a man," he screamed.

"If you don't shut up," Alex snapped, "*I'll* kill *you*."

Hemingway managed to lever himself up against the wall. "You have to take President Brennan and leave him at a certain spot, to finish this the right way."

Alex looked at him in disbelief. "I don't know what the hell your crazy motivations are, and I don't care. You've left the entire world on the brink of war. So the only thing I'm doing is taking the president back where he belongs. And on the way we're going to make a call and stop six million people from being incinerated because of what you did." He pointed his gun at Hemingway. "Now you either open the cell door or I'll kill you."

Hemingway struggled to his feet. "I'm not a traitor to my country, no matter what you or anyone else might think. I did this *for* my country. I did this for my *world*."

"Open the damn door!" Alex yelled. "Now!"

Hemingway took out a set of keys and unlocked one of the doors.

"I thought you said it was booby-trapped," Captain Jack snarled.

"I lied," Hemingway said.

Stone and Alex carried the unconscious president out and sat him up against a wall. They found Chastity and placed her on the floor next to him.

Alex pulled out his cell phone. "Damn it, I forgot there's no signal in here, so we need to get out of here to call Washington and—"

A man's voice interrupted. "I don't think that'll be necessary."

They all turned and stared at Carter Gray and six men holding machine guns.

# CHAPTER

# 68

"THANK GOD," SIMPSON SAID, stepping toward her godfather. However, Gray turned his attention to Hemingway.

"The president was in the chopper that you flew me home in, wasn't he?" Gray clearly didn't expect an answer, and Hemingway didn't provide one. "You corrupted *my* files, assembled an army of dead men and kidnapped the president." Gray shook his head.

"The president's fine, Carter," Simpson said. "He's just drugged."

Gray said, "Very good. Well, we'll take over from here." He motioned two of his men to go get the president.

"Wait!" Hemingway shouted. "He needs to be returned the way I planned! You can't let all those people in Pennsylvania die in vain. They sacrificed themselves for a better world."

Gray's face screwed up. "You are insane!" He calmed and turned to Stone.

"Hello, John. I can't tell you what a shock it's been finding out you're alive," Gray continued. He glanced over at Captain Jack lying on the floor still clutching his bloodied legs. "Two old friends I believed to be dead. Resurrection seems to be a theme of the twenty-first century."

"I wasn't ready to die on your timetable, Carter," Stone said.

Simpson looked between the two men. "What the hell are you talking about?"

Alex interjected. "Look, people, we're running out of time. We have to notify the White House that we have the president back. They'll stop the launch."

Gray ignored this and said, "Jackie, I want you to step over here with me."

"What?" she said. "Didn't you hear Alex? We have to stop the launch."

"When you and I leave here together, you are never to speak of anything you've seen or heard tonight. Do you understand?"

Simpson looked at the others. "I'm sure you can trust all of us not to reveal anything that would damage the country."

"I'm not worried about the others, Jackie, just you."

Stone looked at the woman. "You're the only one leaving here alive, Agent Simpson." He glanced at Gray. "And I believe that includes the president."

"What the hell are you talking about?" Simpson shouted. She looked at her godfather for reassurance, but the truth of what Stone had just said was instantly revealed in Gray's features. She pointed at the unconscious Brennan. "This is the president of the United States!"

Gray said, "I'm aware of that. And there's a man in the Oval Office right now who's *equally* capable of running the country, which, unfortunately, isn't saying much."

Simpson stared at the men with Gray. "He's going to kill the president. You have to stop him!"

"These men are all loyal only to me, otherwise they wouldn't be here," Gray answered.

She said pleadingly, "Six million people are going to die if we don't make the call to the White House, Carter."

"Six million *Syrians*," Gray countered. "Do you know how many terrorist activities dear old Syria supports? And they're the clearinghouse for virtually all the suicide bombers going into Iraq. We should have nuked the damn country years ago."

Simpson looked at her godfather. "You're insane."

"This is bigger than any one man, Jackie," Gray replied very calmly. "This is strictly a war of good versus evil, and we have to ensure that those two sides remain clearly defined. And to do so, sacrifices have to be made, for the good of all. Even the president is not above that. And to accomplish that the world has to believe that his kidnappers have killed him." He paused and added, "I'm sure your father would have no problem with any of this."

"Bullshit!" Simpson roared. "He'd be the first one to throw you in jail."

"Step over here with me, Jackie," Gray said with urgency. "Do it now."

Simpson didn't budge. "No. You're going to just have to kill me too."

"Please don't force me to make that decision."

Alex suddenly screamed out, "Gun!" He threw himself toward Brennan. But someone else was a little quicker.

The shot rang out, as people seemed to be moving in slow motion. There were screams and scuffling feet and the sound of metal hitting the floor. And then there was silence.

Jackie Simpson dropped first to her knees and then fell facedown on the cold cement floor. The bullet that would have hit Brennan was now embedded inside her heart. Gray screamed and stood over Captain Jack, who'd pulled a small pistol from his ankle holster and fired at the president. Yet Simpson had denied him his kill.

Alex knelt down and checked her pulse and then looked up and shook his head.

"Jackie!" Gray cried out as he looked at his dead goddaughter.

"Beth," a stunned Oliver Stone whispered as he stared down at the woman.

Alex, who'd been the only one close enough to hear, looked at Stone. *Beth?*

Gray pointed his gun at Captain Jack, but Stone's voice boomed out. "If you shoot him, you have no connection to the North Koreans' plot to kill the president."

Gray's finger remained on the trigger, but he didn't pull it.

Stone was visibly trembling and his eyes were tearing up as he said, "We're going to take the president to Medina. To the place Mr. Hemingway tells us to."

"That is *not* an option," Gray barked.

"It is your *only* option, Carter," Stone replied. "You can't let millions of innocent people die for no reason."

He whirled on Stone. "Innocent! Those devils took my family from me!" Gray shouted. "They took everything I ever cared about."

"And *my* country did the same to me," Stone answered.

Gray and Stone stared at each other while everyone looked on. Then Stone's gaze went to Simpson's body. "Just like you, I've now lost everything." His voice trembled.

Gray's gaze went from Simpson to Stone. "I can't possibly take the president to Medina. There isn't enough time."

"I believe the Medina Mr. Hemingway has in mind is far closer," Stone replied.

They all looked at Hemingway. "Do you have the chopper?" Hemingway asked Gray, who nodded. "Then you can make *my* Medina in less than two hours, well within the deadline."

"If I agree why can't I just call from the chopper and tell them I found him in whatever Medina you're talking about?" Gray rejoined.

"Unless you actually go to the place, you won't be able to answer all the questions about where he was found. The press and the country will want to know," Hemingway answered. "In great detail."

Stone looked at Gray. "You can even take credit for finding the president, Carter. You'll be a national hero."

"How exactly do I do that?" Gray retorted.

"You're a smart man, you'll figure it out on the chopper ride," Stone replied.

Gray snapped, "This man stays with me." He pointed at Captain Jack.

"I'm sure you'll be successful in getting every last morsel of information from him," Stone said confidently.

"And Hemingway too," Gray added.

"Let's go!" Alex barked.

As the others were heading out, Stone knelt down next to Simpson as Gray looked on. Stone touched the woman's hair and then put her still-warm hand in his. He turned the hand over and looked at the crescent scar on the palm. It appeared remarkably the same as it had when she cut her hand all those years ago. He saw the scar when he picked up her change on the street that day. Tears slid down his cheeks. They were the tears of his nightmare, of losing his daughter in a dream. And now for real, which was immeasurably worse. He kissed her on the cheek.

Stone looked up at Gray, who just stood there, hands dangling uselessly at his sides. "You *will* make sure that her body is returned for proper burial," Stone said firmly. Gray nodded dully. Then Stone walked past the man without another word.

Outside, they followed Gray's men to a nearby clearing where the chopper sat.

The pilot leaned out. "Where are we headed?"

"To Medina," Hemingway called out.

"What?" the pilot exclaimed.

"The address is in my shirt pocket," Hemingway said.

One of the guards pulled out the piece of paper and read it. He shot Hemingway a glance. Stone had read the paper over the man's shoulder. He'd been right.

Hemingway settled into his seat in the rear of the chopper. A split second later he head-butted the guard closest to him, shattering the man's nose and right cheek. Then Hemingway kicked the seat in front of him with such force that it tore loose from its base and the guard sitting in it was thrown forward. In another instant Hemingway was running, wounded leg and all, toward the woods.

Alex raced after Hemingway as fast he could while tree limbs, bushes and vines ripped at him. The guy had been shot in the damn leg, and Alex couldn't catch him? He heard a shout ahead and he increased his pace. He broke free of the trees and skidded to a stop just before he would have plummeted over the side. He was standing on the edge of a long fall. He couldn't see what was at the bottom, but as he stood there listening, Alex thought he heard a splash. As other guards raced up to join him, he pointed down into the abyss and shook his head.

Tom Hemingway was gone.

# CHAPTER

## 69

ACTING PRESIDENT BEN HAMILTON was watching the screen in the Oval Office as people hovered around. The film footage was grainy and jerky—all professional news-gathering services had already fled the country—yet clearly showed the complete chaos that now was Damascus. The roads were clogged with cars, the streets with desperate, terrified Syrians. It was reported that people were sprinting down the runway of the airport, trying to grab onto the last few planes that were taking off. Law and order had long since disappeared. People were merely trying to get away. And as the hours wound down and that hope vanished, things were turning very ugly.

Hamilton and his group watched the screen as parents ran down the streets carrying their children and screaming in terror while soldiers pushed through the panicked masses using bullhorns to tell the crowds to evacuate. Yet, with less than one hour left under the United States' deadline, none of these people were going to survive. There was a jarring video segment of looters being beaten to death by angry citizens. Hamilton watched until he saw a group of small children become separated from their families and then being trampled underneath the fleeing crowds.

"Turn the damn thing off," Hamilton ordered, and the screen instantly went dark.

Hamilton's desk was covered with official pleas from all over the world begging him not to pull the trigger. Millions of Americans across the country were out in the streets, some in support of Hamilton's decision, but most opposed. The White House switchboard had been overwhelmed.

Secretary of Defense Joe Decker sat down next to his commander in chief. Hamilton looked at him in desperation.

Perhaps sensing his boss's wavering, Decker said, "Sir, I know that this is more pressure than a person should have to endure. And I know what the world is telling you. But if we back down now, we will lose all credibility with these people, and if that happens, then we've already lost."

"I understand that, Joe," Hamilton said slowly.

"There's another development, sir."

Hamilton stared wearily at him. "What?"

"There're some very unusual atmospheric conditions occurring over the Atlantic right now. The navy reports that satellite communication with the *Tennessee* could well be compromised in a few minutes."

"If that's the case we shouldn't launch the missile."

Decker shook his head. "These conditions will have no effect on the launch. The D-5 has inertial guidance. It takes two star sightings after separation of the final rocket motor, then it'll maneuver to optimal location to deploy the warheads for free fall onto the target. The problem is only with maintaining contact with the sub."

"So what are you saying, Joe?" Hamilton asked.

"I'm strongly suggesting that we just get it over with before we lose contact."

"What? Launch now?" Hamilton checked his watch. "There's still fifty-two minutes left."

"And what difference will that possibly make, Mr. President? If they were going to release him, they would've done so by now. In fact, this just gives the other side more time to plan how to strike back at us. And if we don't do it now, the *Tennessee* might not be reachable."

"Can't we use another nuclear asset?"

"That sub is in the ideal place with the ideal ordnance to hit Damascus, and it's prepped and ready to go. Our other subs in the Atlantic would face the same communications problems in any event."

"Well, just tell the *Tennessee* to fire when the deadline ends unless they hear from us."

"It doesn't work that way with nukes, sir. For lots of reasons, it's only when we tell them to launch that they launch. They don't watch clocks. And we could scramble something else, but it likely would be past the deadline by the time it's ready. And if we don't fire the missile within the time frame we've set out, then we've lost all credibility, sir."

"So that's how it's going to be from now on? We hit them; they hit us. What? Until we're all gone?"

"With all due respect, sir, we have far more to hit them with than they do us. And I have every confidence that we will win in the end."

Hamilton glanced up to see all gazes in the room upon him. *May God have mercy on me.* He said, "Get in touch with the Syrians first. Give them one last chance." He put his head in his hands as everyone in the room looked down.

Suddenly, Andrea Mayes jumped up. "Wait! Please. Sir, why wouldn't they give him back if they had him? Why would they let millions of their own people die?"

Decker snapped, "Because they're terrorists. That's how they think. And according to their faith, all those people will go right to paradise. And let's not forget that they attacked *us*. They took *our* president. And right now he's almost certainly dead. We have no choice. We have to strike back in a way that will leave *no doubt* as to this country's resolve. Anything less will give them courage to escalate their attacks on us. And there's no better way to do that than with a nuclear weapon. Japan only surrendered after we dropped two on them. It ended up *saving* millions of lives."

He failed to mention that the atomic bombs dropped on Hiroshima and Nagasaki had also killed and maimed hundreds of thousands of Japanese civilians and left both cities radioactive for decades.

Hamilton looked away, and the secretary of state slumped back in her chair.

Decker grabbed a secure phone and ordered the final demand be made to the Syrians and Sharia immediately. A few minutes later he had his answer.

Hamilton looked up. "Well?"

"The sanitized version is that God will strike us down for the evil we're about to do," Decker replied. "So am I authorized to contact Command Authority, sir?"

Hamilton suddenly looked indecisive. Mayes seized on this to say, "Mr. President, *please* think about what you're about to do. If we annihilate Damascus there will *never* be peace. Never."

Decker moved in front of her. "Mr. President, we don't have peace *now*. And if you fail to carry through on your demand America will be robbed of all its power. To the world we will become a laughingstock, inept and emasculated. I know that you are not that kind of leader." He paused and added firmly, "We have to do this."

Hamilton rubbed his eyes, glanced at Mayes and then nodded at Decker. "Make the call."

Hamilton stood and gazed out the window while Decker picked up another phone and gave the order to the National Command Authority, which instantly relayed it to the *Tennessee*. The mighty Trident missile would launch shortly thereafter, accelerating out of the water's depths with such incomprehensible speed and force that a protective wall of gas would enclose it. As it passed through hundreds of feet of ocean depths, not even a single drop of water would touch its metal hide. At a cruising speed of fourteen thousand miles an hour, the Trident missile would hit Damascus less than thirty minutes after launch with the force of a thousand category 5 hurricanes all rolled into one. There would be nothing left.

At first the ringing phone didn't register. Then slowly, Hamilton looked up. It was *that* phone. He raced over and snatched it up.

"Yes?"

His face paled and he grabbed at his side. Most in the room thought he was about to have some sort of attack.

"They have him," he screamed to the room. "They have *Brennan*." He whirled on Decker. "Call off the launch. Call it off!"

Decker quickly spoke into the other phone and ordered the *Tennessee* to stand down. However, the secretary of defense suddenly paled. "What? That can't be."

Everyone's gaze was riveted on him.

Decker looked ashen-faced as he said, "The atmospheric conditions over the Atlantic have started disrupting satellite communications. The *Tennessee* acknowledged and confirmed the order to launch, but now Command Authority is having trouble contacting the sub again."

Hamilton shouted at Decker, "I knew we should have waited the full eight hours. You idiot!"

Andrea Mayes said shakily, "Oh, my God."

Hamilton grabbed the phone from Decker and roughly pushed the man out of the way. Into the phone he said, "This is Acting President Hamilton. You have to get in touch with that damn sub and tell them not to launch. I don't care how you do it, just do it." He held on to the edge of the Resolute Desk for support as his knees started to buckle and sweat glistened his brow.

A stricken-looking Decker stood holding his shoulder from where Hamilton had shoved him against the wall.

Hamilton yelled into the phone again, "Blow the goddamn sub out of the water if you have to." He shrieked, "Just stop it! Stop it!"

Seconds ticked by, and not one breath could be heard in the Oval Office, because every last person was holding theirs. Finally, Hamilton replaced the phone receiver in its cradle and sank to his knees. He looked very close to passing out now.

Hamilton slowly looked up at his subordinates. "They stopped the launch," he managed to say before staring directly at Decker. "With . . . one . . . damn . . . second to spare."

There were no cheers in the Oval Office; all of them were frozen.

However, somewhere underneath the Atlantic Ocean 155 American sailors screamed in relieved joy.

The safe return of President James Brennan at an abandoned warehouse on the outskirts of Medina, *Ohio,* rocked the world yet again. The more than fourteen thousand American military and special operatives deployed to Medina in Saudi Arabia slipped away as quietly as possible. In the president's pocket had been found a typed note that read simply: "From great sacrifice comes great opportunity."

Franklin Hemingway had penned those words thirty years earlier, and his son could think of no better message to leave with the leader of the free world.

Carter Gray was hailed as a national hero for figuring out where Brennan was going to be released. While somewhat vague on the details, Gray explained that it was a combination of hard work, reliable informants and a lot of luck. "However, the kidnappers were true to their word," he said. "Because the president *was* in Medina, only about seven thousand miles away from the one we thought it was."

Gray had spent an emotional night with Senator Simpson and his wife, comforting them on the loss of their only child. The official version of what had happened, and the only one her parents had received as well, was that Jackie was the victim of a deadly carjacking while driving along Interstate 81 very late at night. There were no suspects, and Gray knew there would never be an arrest. The only other development was the unexplained disappearance of three NIC agents. Gray would take care of that too.

On a positive note Captain Jack had talked. And talked and talked. Carter Gray now had quite a lot of ammo to use against North Korea.

James Brennan triumphantly returned to the White House as huge crowds surrounding the area cheered. He gave televised remarks to the nation, thanking Carter Gray for his exemplary work, having no idea that the man had seriously contemplated killing him and blaming it on the Syrians. Brennan also thanked his beleaguered vice president for a job well done. Finally, he expressed his gratitude to the American people for being stalwart and true throughout the crisis.

They would never know that a mere second had been the margin of error in the commencement of a worldwide apocalypse. His chief of staff stood by beaming. With the crisis over, her attention had returned fully to the election. The latest polls showed Brennan with a historically high eighty-six percent approval rating. Barring something catastrophic her candidate would easily win the election and have four more years to build his legacy.

Brennan received a full briefing on all that had happened, but no one could shed light on who'd kidnapped him. It now appeared clear that neither the Sharia Group nor Syria had had anything to do with the abduction. In the colder light of reason the Sharia Group had no assets in the United States capable of having orchestrated such a scheme. The body of one of the group's leaders had been found, and the man had obviously died of torture. And no one had explained how so many skilled Arabs could have infiltrated the United States with America's intelligence sector having no record of any of them.

Damascus was still in shambles, but not nearly as bad as it would have been if the Trident had hit it. The Syrians and the rest of the Middle East were still understandably shell-shocked, but it seemed that with the world so close to the abyss people were looking at things with a more cooperative eye. It remained to be seen if this mood had permanence, though.

Vice President Hamilton had taken some time off from his official duties. Coming within a second of being the first American president since Harry Truman to order the use of a nuclear bomb was more pressure than any person should have to bear, and it had taken its toll on the man. However, Hamilton was expected to make a full recovery.

Brennan had been astonished to learn that the kidnappers had died nearly to a man while intentionally not inflicting any casualties on the United States. While he was still contemplating this stunning news, the president watched a recording of one of his favorite political roundtable shows that had been broadcast while he was still missing. Each of the four pundits on the show concluded that what was going on was a trick of some sort.

"And if the president is delivered back safely?" the moderator asked.

All of the pundits said that that would be *another* trick of some sort.

"With what goal in mind?" the moderator asked. "They sacrificed over twenty people. They could have killed the president quite easily at any time. And if they return him safely, what have they gained?"

"You have to understand, these people will stop at nothing," one of the pundits declared. "First they tried killing us. But that didn't work. We fought back and are winning the war on terror. So they've clearly changed tactics."

"And now they're trying the ploy of *not* killing us?" the bewildered moderator asked.

"Precisely," the smug pundit answered.

Brennan had received a copy of the kidnappers' demands and spent a long time in his private quarters going over them. He also reviewed with horror the details of how close the U.S. had come to launching a nuclear strike against a nation that, it turned out, was innocent of the alleged wrongdoing. While Brennan praised his vice president publicly, he was shocked when he learned how quickly Hamilton had been persuaded to authorize the use of nuclear weapons and how close he'd come to launching one. Brennan was now thinking seriously of other VP candidates.

He held lengthy meetings with his various experts in Muslim affairs and other Western leaders and spent long hours with his wife and family. He went to church several times in one week, perhaps seeking divine advice for the secular problems of humankind.

Now that the president was safely back, the international press started to report more openly about the kidnappers' demands. Throughout the capitals of Europe, South America and Asia, people were actually focusing more on the *substance* of the demands, since, for once, they didn't have an accompanying pile of human bodies and rubble to overshadow them.

Finally, Brennan called a meeting of his cabinet, his National Security Council and his top military advisers. There he brought up his abductors' demands.

His national security adviser immediately protested. "Sir," the NSA said, "it's absurd. We can't comply with any of them. It's beyond preposterous."

Secretary of Defense Decker spoke up. "Mr. President, to even consider those demands is a sign of weakness on behalf of this country."

Brennan's response was terse. "We came within seconds of killing six million people on what turned out to be deeply flawed evidence."

"We didn't start this thing. And there's always risk involved," Decker countered.

Brennan stared the man down. "We are the world's sole remaining superpower. We have a nuclear arsenal capable of destroying the world. Even if others don't show restraint, *we* have to!"

The way Brennan was looking at Decker, it was clear a new secretary of defense would be joining a new vice president in Brennan's second administration.

Brennan pulled a slip of paper out of his pocket. It was the note that had been found on him after the kidnapping. He read it to himself. "From great sacrifice comes great opportunity." And as history had shown and Brennan well knew, great presidents were often created during such times.

He turned away from Joe Decker and his Pentagon folks and looked at Andrea Mayes, his secretary of state.

"I think it's time we got to work," President Brennan said.

# CHAPTER

# 70

Jacqueline Simpson was laid to rest in a private service at a cemetery in northern Virginia. In attendance were her grief-stricken parents, close family friends, political dignitaries, representatives of the Secret Service and her godfather, Carter Gray.

Nearby but hidden behind a copse of trees stood Oliver Stone, wearing a brand-new black suit and tie that his friends had purchased for him. As the minister spoke words of religious wisdom and comfort, Stone didn't hear them. His gaze was transfixed on the coffin that held his daughter, *Beth*. He didn't cry. He was having trouble deciding what he should feel. He was her father, but then again, he wasn't. He had had her for three years; the Simpsons for the rest of her life. Simply from a time standpoint, he had little claim to be here. And yet he could not have stayed away.

When the ceremony was over and all the others had left, Stone emerged from his hiding place and walked down to the burial spot. The cemetery workers were about to lower the coffin into the hole in the ground, but Stone asked them to wait.

"Are you family?" one asked him.

"Yes," he answered. "I'm family."

For twenty long minutes Stone knelt in front of the coffin, with one of his hands resting on its smooth, polished surface.

He finally rose on shaky legs, bent over and kissed the coffin, placing a single flower on top. It was a daisy.

"Good-bye, Beth," he said quietly. "I love you."

\*      \*      \*

The Camel Club, Alex and Kate met at Stone's cottage the following day. Reuben had been treated for his wounds, and the doctors had taken care of a couple of bothersome kidney stones at the same time. Chastity was fully recovered from her ordeal, something she had absolutely no memory of.

Alex brought with him the newspaper account of Jackie Simpson's death. "She was a damn hero, and all she'll be remembered for is being a victim of a carjacking," he said bitterly.

Stone was sitting behind his desk. "You're wrong. That's not all she'll be remembered for," he said firmly.

Alex changed the subject. "It's killing me that Carter Gray is now some national hero when he was going to murder the president. There has to be something we can do."

Reuben said, "But if we go public, then everything else comes out. I'm not sure the country can handle that after everything that's happened."

Stone said quietly, "Carter Gray will be taken care of. I'll personally see to that."

They all looked at him curiously, but the man's expression did not invite questions.

Reuben stood. "Okay, I think it's time to make it official." He cleared his throat. "I hereby call a special meeting of the Camel Club to order. Because of their exemplary work on behalf of the United States, and their invaluable assistance to the club, I move that we admit two new members: Agent Alex Ford and Kate Adams. Do I have a second?"

"Second," said Milton and Caleb together.

"All in favor say aye!"

And the ayes carried.

Alex said, "Okay, I need to know something. Why the *Camel* Club?"

Stone answered, "Because camels have great stamina. They never give up."

"That's what Oliver says, but the real reason is this," Reuben countered. "In the 1920s there was another Camel Club. And at each meeting of that club they would all raise their glasses and take a vow to

oppose Prohibition to the last drop of whiskey. Now, *that's* my kind
of club."

When the meeting broke up, Alex stayed behind to talk to Stone in
private.

"So Oliver Stone is really John Carr," he said.

"*Was* John Carr. He's dead," Stone said bluntly.

"Oliver, you told Carter Gray that your country had taken your
family. What did you mean by that?"

Stone sat down behind his desk and fiddled with some papers lying
there. "Let's just say that I thought I'd finished my 'duties' for my
country, but apparently, my country believed that my job was not one
you ever walked away from." He paused. "It's the greatest regret of
my life that my family suffered because of me."

"Your daughter's name was Beth?" Alex said cautiously. "And she
was born in Atlanta?"

Stone stared at him. "How did you know that?"

Alex was thinking of the mistake on the NIC database as to Simpson's birthplace that she'd pointed out to Hemingway. Yet the database was right. She was born in Atlanta, not Birmingham, where the
Simpsons were from. And then he thought of the two tall, fair-haired
Simpsons and their petite, dark-haired daughter. Now Alex had a
good idea what Oliver Stone's dead wife looked like. It was clear to
him that Jackie Simpson and Beth Carr were the same person.

"It was on her official file," Alex answered.

Stone nodded absently.

Alex put his hand on Stone's shoulder. "I'm sorry, Oliver."

"Don't pity me, Alex. I've done many things in my life that I hate
myself for. I could excuse them by saying I was serving my country,
but that's not really much of an excuse, is it?"

Carter Gray had just finished his briefing with the president and was
heading back to his chopper on the lawn of the White House. It had
been a good meeting, although Brennan was making some curious—
and to Gray's thinking, disturbing—noises about a decided shift in
America's policies toward the Middle East. However, Gray stopped
pondering this when he saw the man standing at the fence looking at
him. Oliver Stone motioned over to where Reuben sat astride his In-

dian motorcycle. Then Stone pointed to the west. As Gray followed this gesture, it was clear what the man intended.

A few minutes later Gray was in a limo following the motorcycle. As he'd expected, it turned into Arlington National Cemetery. A few minutes later, with his security detail at a discreet distance, Gray stood across from Stone in front of John Carr's grave.

"I can give you ten minutes at most, John," Gray said.

"My name is Oliver Stone."

"Whatever," Gray said impatiently.

"And five minutes will be more than enough."

"Then get on with it."

"How did my daughter end up with the Simpsons?"

Gray looked a little put out by the question but said, "As you know, Roger Simpson worked at the CIA with me. We were very good friends. They couldn't have children. It seemed like a good solution. You and your wife had no family, and I couldn't just abandon the child, although there were some at the Agency who thought she should've just been shot too. I had no idea you were even alive, John."

"I don't believe you looked very hard."

"I had no involvement in what happened to you. I didn't order it and I didn't condone it. In fact, I saved your daughter from being killed."

"But you did nothing to stop the attack on me and my family, did you?"

"Did you really just expect to walk away from it all?"

"I never would've betrayed my country."

"That's not the point."

"That is *precisely* the point!"

Gray threw up a hand. "This is ancient history."

Stone pointed to the left. "Part of your history lies over there, where your wife is buried. Do you just forget that?"

"Don't you dare talk about her," Gray snapped. "Now, is there anything else?"

"Just one more thing," Stone said. "I want you to resign your position."

Gray stared at him blankly. "Excuse me?"

"You are to resign your position immediately as national intelligence director. You're no longer fit for the post."

"I feel sorry for you," Gray said, shaking his head. "I really do. You served your country capably, and if you need something to make your old age more comfortable, I'll see what I can do."

"I'll go public, tell all that I know."

Gray looked at him with pity. "And you have so much credibility, a man who doesn't even exist. And that friend of yours, Reuben. I've looked him up. He's even more incorrigible than you. And if you think Alex Ford is going to say anything, think again. He won't jeopardize his career by taking me on, and he's smart enough not to drag the country through something like this. So just go back to your little hole, John, and crawl in for good."

"All I need is for you to resign." Gray shook his head wearily and turned to leave. Stone added, "Before you go, you might want to listen to this."

Gray turned back around and saw that Stone was holding out a small tape recorder. He hit the play button.

A moment later Gray was listening to himself as he calmly talked about killing the president at Murder Mountain.

When Stone hit the stop button, Gray exploded, "How the hell did you—"

He stopped as Stone held up his cell phone. "A friend gave me this phone that's also a recorder. And being an old spy, I put it to good use." He handed Gray the tape. "I'll be delighted to hear of your resignation tomorrow morning." He started to walk off and then turned around. "We *both* served our country capably, Carter. But the way we did it just doesn't have a place anymore. And thank God for that."

Gray just stood there, his face red and his chest heaving. "I'm not a zealot, damn you. I'm a patriot!"

"Actually, you're neither one, Carter."

"Then what am I? Tell me," he said tauntingly. "What the hell am I?"

"You're wrong."

The next day Kate and Alex met for lunch. All of Washington was talking about Carter Gray's abrupt resignation.

"Oliver couldn't have had anything to do with that, could he?" Kate asked.

"I think Oliver Stone is capable of a lot more than either of us know," Alex replied quietly.

After their lunch the two walked hand in hand past a very familiar building.

"I can't seem to get this place out of my head," Alex said, staring across at the White House.

"Well, I'll just have to work extra hard on getting your mind on other things. After all, in a few years you're a free man, Agent Ford."

He looked at her and smiled. "I really don't consider myself a free man anymore."

"Am I supposed to take that as a compliment?"

He kissed her. "Does that answer your question?"

They watched as a helicopter lifted off from the White House grounds.

Alex looked at the NIC insignia on the tail. "That was probably Carter Gray making his last trip to the White House."

"Good riddance," Kate said.

"The person who replaces him might be just as ruthless," Alex cautioned.

"Now, that's a truly frightening thought," Kate said.

"It'll be okay." Alex pointed over to Lafayette Park. "So long as he's here."

On a bench sat Stone and Adelphia drinking the café.

Adelphia was talking animatedly; however, it was clear that Stone's attention was fully on the building across the street.

Alex and Kate walked off down the street, leaving the country in the capable hands of citizen Oliver Stone, and the Camel Club.

# ACKNOWLEDGMENTS

To Michelle, thanks for always being my number one fan and best critic. I'm still amazed that you read every word in every draft.

To Aaron Priest, thank you for being there for me from day one. None of this would be possible without you.

To Maureen Egen, Jamie Raab, Tina Andreadis, Emi Battaglia, Tom Maciag, Karen Torres, Martha Otis, Jason Pinter, Miriam Parker and the rest of the Warner Books gang who work so hard on my behalf. You have my thanks and appreciation.

To Lucy Childs and Lisa Erbach Vance for all the thousands of details you handle every day for me.

To Frances Jalet-Miller, your editing skills and incredible insight were on full display with this book. Thank you.

To Art Collin, my sincere thanks and gratitude for reading through early drafts.

To Dr. Monica Smiddy, thank you for the detailed and thoughtful medical advice. You make a humble writer sound like a forensic genius.

To Dr. John Y. Cole at the Library of Congress, thank you for the amazing behind-the-scenes tour of LOC and the expert knowledge of its magnificent buildings and collections.

To Mark Dimunation and Daniel De Simone with the Library of Congress for patiently answering all my questions and letting me glimpse the library's Rare Books reading room. It's a true gem.

To the USSS Washington Field Office, my utmost thanks and respect for all you do and for your willingness to share your knowledge with me.

To Jennifer Steinberg, my gratitude for always getting answers to those last-minute research questions.

To Maria Rejt, for your very helpful comments.

To Bob Schule, for reading the words, giving me incredibly good comments, educating me on energy policy and, above all, being the best friend anyone could have.

To Neal Schiff, thanks for always being willing to share your FBI knowledge.

To Charles Veilleux, thank you for the expert advice on firearms and weapons.

To Tom DePont, for help on financial issues in the novel.

To Dr. Alli Guleria, a dear friend, for always being there for us, and for educating me on all things orthodontic and Indian.

To Lynette and Deborah, for navigating the "Enterprises" straight and true.

Please see the next page
for a preview of
David Baldacci's
explosive new thriller

**MEMORY MAN**

# CHAPTER

# 1

AMOS DECKER WOULD FOREVER REMEMBER ALL THREE OF THEIR violent deaths in the most vivid shade of blue.

The stakeout had been long and ultimately unproductive. Driving home, he had been looking forward to catching a few hours of sleep before hitting the streets once more. He'd pulled into the driveway of the modest two-story vinyl-sider that was twenty-five years old and would take at least that long to pay off the mortgage. The rain had slicked the pavement, and as his size 14 boots hit he slipped a bit before traction was gained. He closed the car door quietly, certain that all inside would be asleep at this late hour. He trudged to the screen door leading into the kitchen and let himself in.

The quiet was to be expected. But the *too* quiet nature of the setting was not. He had not sensed that then and later wondered why not. It was one of many failures on his part that night. He had paused in the kitchen to pour a glass of water from the tap. He chugged it, set the glass in the sink, wiped his chin dry, and headed to the next room.

He slipped on the floor, and this time his big body tumbled. The floor was slick herringbone-patterned parquet, and he had fallen before. Yet this time was different. The moonlight had shafted in through the front window at precisely the right angle.

When he held up his hand it was a different color.

Red. Although with his special ability he involuntarily saw the first finger sticking up as a number. But not as a one that would have been the logical conclusion. No, he saw it as a zero. Which he always associated with the color purple, which was not a welcome color for him. For that reason, he did not like the number zero.

But his finger *was* red. And it had come from somewhere. And he picked himself up to find out where.

He discovered the source in the next room. It was not a thing. It was a *him*.

Johnny Sacks. His brother-in-law. A big, burly fellow like him, laid low. He bent closer, then got on his knees, his face an inch or so from Johnny's. His neck had been slit from ear to ear. There was no need to check for a pulse; there could be none. Most of his blood was on the floor. You couldn't live without it.

He should have pulled his phone and hit 911 at that very moment. He knew better. He knew not to stampede around a crime scene, for that was what his home had become by virtue of the dead man, killed by violent means.

A crime scene plain and simple. It was now a museum; you didn't touch anything. His professional mind screamed this at him.

But this was only *one* body. His gaze jerked to the stairs. One straight stack of warped plank steps up to the top and only other floor. His mind suddenly disengaged as total panic seized every bit of him, the gut feeling that life had just robbed Decker of everything he would ever have. So he ran, his boots pushing coagulating pools of blood outward like Jackson Pollock bent over a canvas. But he was using the human corpuscles of his dead brother-in-law instead of oil paint to create not a masterpiece but a nightmare.

He was destroying vital evidence, royally screwing up what should have been kept pristine. Right now he couldn't have given a shit.

He tracked Johnny's blood right up the stairs, taking the treads three at a time. His breaths were gasps, and his heart was pumping so fast and feeling so bloated it was a wonder his chest wall could contain it. He had been in danger before. He had nearly been killed before. He had never felt such terror in all his life. He was paralyzed, only somehow still moving.

He hit the hallway and bounced off one wall and then its twin as he rocketed down to the first door on the left. He never took out his gun, not even bothering to think that the killer could still be here. Waiting for him to come home.

He smashed open the door with his shoulder and looked wildly around.

Nothing.

No, not true.

He froze in the doorway as the light on the nightstand dimly illuminated the bare foot that stuck above the mattress on the far side.

He knew that foot. Intimately. He had held it, massaged it, washed it, and kissed it on occasion over many years. It was long, narrow but somehow still dainty, the toe next to the big one slightly longer than it should have been. The veins on the side, the calluses underneath, the nails painted red, it was all as it should be, except it should not be poking above the mattress at this time of night. That meant the rest of her was down on the floor and why would that be, unless...

His feet moving without his mind consciously directing them, he edged to that side of the bed and looked down, fearing what he would see and unfortunately not coming away disappointed.

Cassandra Decker, Cassie to all including and most importantly him, stared up at him from her position on the floor. Well, staring was beyond her now. He stumbled forward, and pain shot up his limbs and his knees feeling like both ACLs had just blown out. He stopped next to her and then slowly knelt, his blue jean knees coming to rest in the patch of blood that had pooled next to her.

Her neck was clean, no wound there. Her forehead was the spot.

Single-entry gunshot. He didn't know if the round had come out the back of her head. Didn't matter. The entry had ended her life. He knew he shouldn't but he used his arm to scoop her head off the floor and cradled it next to his heaving chest, her long dark hair splaying out over his arm like frozen spray from a hard breaker. The dot on her forehead was blackened and blistered.

He saw the color black as a tunnel. Not knowing what was in there. It was normally an exciting feeling. Tonight it was not.

A contact wound preceded by a muzzle's kiss. Existing only a second before the fired projectile ended her life. She would have felt no pain. Had she been asleep? Had she awoken? Would she have endured the terror of seeing her killer standing over her?

He put her back where he had found her. Now Decker simply stared down at the face that was white and lifeless, the blackened dot in the middle of her forehead to be his lasting memory of her, a grammatical period at the very *end*. Of everything. A tunnel to nowhere.

He rose, his legs screaming in agony, his other limbs curiously numb as he staggered out of the room and down the hall to the only other bedroom up here.

He did not force this door open. He was in no hurry now. He knew what he was going to find. He just didn't know what the killer's method would have been.

First, a knife. Second, a gun.

She wasn't in the bedroom, which left the adjoining bath.

The overhead light was on in there, burning brightly. The sonofa-bitch had obviously wanted him to see the last one clearly.

There she was, on the toilet. Held there with the sash from her robe wrapped around the water tank, for otherwise she would have fallen over. He drew close.

His feet didn't slip. There was no blood. His little girl had no outward signs of wounding. He drew closer, knew from her skin color and bulging eyes and the tiny hemorrhages in the whites of her eyes that strangulation had ended her young life.

That was not painless. That was excruciating. And terrifying. And she would have been staring right up at him while he slowly compressed her life away more than seventy years before it should have been due to end.

He drew closer and saw the ligature marks on her neck, ugly and blotchy, like someone had burned her there. Maybe the robe sash had been used. Maybe the guy's hands. Decker didn't know, didn't care.

Molly would have been ten in three days. A party had been planned, guests invited, the presents bought, and the damn sheet cake with chocolate inside ordered. He had gotten time off to help Cassie, who worked full time and also did pretty much everything here because his job was not a nine-to-fiver, not even close. They had joked about it. What did he know about real life? Grocery shopping? Paying the bills? Taking Molly to the doctor?

Nothing, as it turned out. Not a damn thing.

He sat down on the floor in front of his dead child, crossing his long legs like his little girl liked to do, so the bottom of each foot wedged against the inner thigh of the opposite leg. He was flexible for a big man. The lotus position, he dimly thought. Or something like that. When he was a kid it would have been simply called sitting like an Indian, but you didn't say crap like that anymore.

Her eyes were wide and open, staring back at him, but not seeing him. Like her mom.

She would always run to greet him. Certainly, not tonight. For certain not ever again.

Decker just sat there, rocking back and forth, looking at her but not really seeing her, and his baby girl sure as Heaven not seeing her daddy, either.

*This is it. Nothing left. I'm not staying by myself. Can't do it.*

He slipped the compact nine-mill from his belt holster and made sure a round was chambered by racking the slide. He cupped it in his hands. Nice little piece. Accurate with enough stopping power. He'd never shot anyone with it. But he'd wanted to.

He stared down at the muzzle with the iron sights. How many rounds fired at the police range? A thousand? Ten thousand? Who cared? He couldn't miss tonight.

He opened his mouth and swallowed the muzzle, angling it upward so the bullet would traverse the brain plate and make the end quick. His finger came to rest on the trigger guard. He looked up at Molly. Suddenly embarrassed, he slipped the gun out and put it against his right temple and closed his eyes so he couldn't see her. Again, his index finger slipped to the trigger guard. Once past it, to the trigger, then the slow, steady pull until the point of no return. He'd never feel anything. His brain dead before it could tell the rest of his body that he'd jacked himself.

He just had to pull. *Just pull, Amos. You got nothing to lose because you got nothing left. They're gone. They're...gone.*

He held the gun there, wondering what he would say to his family once they were all reunited.

*I'm sorry?*

*Forgive me?*

*I wish I'd been here to protect you from whoever did this? I should have been here to protect you?*

He held the gun tighter, digging the metal against his temple so hard he felt the barrel cut into his skin. A drop of blood appeared and then was wicked into his graying hair, hair that, he was fairly certain, had become even grayer over the last few minutes.

He wasn't seeking the courage to do it.

He was seeking the solace. He was desperately searching for the right balance. Yet could there ever be balance in taking one's own life?

Still holding the gun in place, he flipped out his phone, dialed 911, identified himself by name and badge number, and in three concise sentences described the slaughters of a trio of people. He dropped the phone on the floor.

Down below was Johnny.

Down the hall was Cassie.

Here, on the toilet, was Molly.

All in his mind forever outlined in the most vivid, spellbinding shade of blue. And he cursed himself. What he was. A freak really. The damn colors, intruding even on this! Why could he not be normal, for just this one time? Why? Did he really have to see *this* in Technicolor! Blue for him as a color was not gone forever; it would be with him every day of the rest of his life. Which might just be another minute.

And so he sat on the floor with a gun to his head and absolutely nothing left in the rest of him.

And that was exactly how the cops found him when they showed up four minutes later.

# CHAPTER

## 2

A PARK BENCH PAINTED RED.

The unsettling knife-like chill of fall draining to winter.

Amos Decker sat on the bench, waiting.

A sparrow flicked across in front of him, narrowly dodged a passing car before soaring upward, catching a breeze and drifting away. He noted the make, model, plate number, and physical descriptions of all in the car before it left him. Husband, wife in the front, and a kid in the back in a booster seat. Another one next to him, older. About ten. The rear bumper had a sticker. It read, MY KID IS AN HONOR ROLL STUDENT AT THORNCREST ELEMENTARY.

*Congrats, you've just told a psycho exactly where to snatch your very smart kid.*

Then a bus rolled to a near stop. He did the same observation. Fourteen passengers, most looking depressed and tired though it was still only midday. One was energetic, a child. He jumped and bebopped next to his exhausted mother, who sat slumped over, her fat bag perched in her lap. The driver was a newbie, her face a sheet of nervousness. Even with the power steering she fought the wheel and took the next turn so slow it looked like the bus's engine had died.

A plane soared overhead, low enough for him to ID it as a United 737, a later model because of the winglets. That number made the color silver pop out for him. The number 737 was, in his mind, a beautiful concoction. Sleek, silver, fast, bullet-like. Anything beginning with a seven gave him that reaction. He appreciated the fact that Boeing Corporation numbered all their aircraft beginning with seven.

Two men walked past. Observed, recorded. One was older, the alpha by the look of things; the other, smaller, the sidekick, there for laughs and to push around. Then he noted the four kids playing in the park cross the street. Age, rank, serial number, pecking order, and hierarchy established before age six, like a pack of wolves. Done.

Next, a woman with a dog. A German shepherd. Old, white muzzle, bad hips. Probably dysplasia, common in the breed. Cataloged. A man jabbering away on his smart phone. Zegna suit, the G for Gucci on the slick shoes, quarter-sized rock set in a gold band on his left hand, like a Super Bowl ring. Four-thousand-dollar Zenith watch rode on his right wrist. He was too small and the wrong build for a pro athlete. Dressed far too nicely for a typical drug dealer. Maybe a hedge fund manager, malpractice lawyer, or real estate developer. Memory socked away. On the other side of the street an old woman was being helped out of a van. Her left side was useless, facial paralysis on the same side. Stroke. Documented. Her caregiver had mild scoliosis and a club foot. Imprinted.

Amos Decker noted all of this and more as his mind sorted through everything that was in front of him. Deducing here and there. Speculating sometimes. Guessing other times. None of it meant anything other than it was just what he did to pass the time while he was waiting. Just like counting in color. It was by and large meaningless, just what he did. To pass the time.

He had lost the house where his family had been slaughtered. Foreclosed. They were barely making the payments with his and Cassie's salary as a part-time nurse. On his paycheck alone it was a no-go. He had tried to sell it, but who wanted to live in a house covered in blood? And he had not stepped foot in the place after he found their bodies, other than to collect his clothes and a few odds and ends belonging to his wife and daughter. The fact was they just didn't have that much. Other than themselves. And themselves were now gone.

He'd lived in an apartment for several months. Then a motel room. Then, when his job situation changed he had relocated to a friend's couch. After the friend became less friendly he had opted for a homeless shelter. When funding ran out for the place and it was closed, he "downsized" to a sleeping bag in the park. Then, a cardboard box in a parking lot when the sleeping bag wore out and the cops rousted the homeless from the park.

He had hit rock bottom, where even his closest friends might not have recognized him. Bloated, dirty, wild haired, bushy bearded, he looked like he should be living in a cave somewhere attempting to conspire with aliens. And he pretty much was until he woke up in a Walmart parking lot one morning staring at a Georgia-Pacific logo on the inside of his corrugated box and had the churning epiphany that Cassie and Molly would have been deeply ashamed of what he had become.

So he had cleaned himself up, worked a bunch of odd jobs, saved some dollars, moved into a room at a Residence Inn, and hung out his PI shingle. He took whatever cases came his way; they were mostly lowball, low pay, but they were something. And he didn't need more than something.

It was a meaningless existence, really, just like he was meaningless, really. His beard was still bushy, his hair still pretty wild, and he was still way overweight, but his clothes were reasonably clean and he showered, sometimes more than once a week. And he no longer lived in a box. Progress was always to be measured in inches, especially when you didn't have yards or even feet of success to show off.

He closed his eyes to block all these recent street observations out, though it was all still there, like a cinema screen on the inside of his eyeballs. It would always still be there. He often wanted to forget what he had just seen. He tested this several times a day. He had done his best to make it go away from the membrane of his mind. But it wouldn't. Everything in his head was recorded in permanent marker. Either he dialed it up when needed or it popped up on its own accord. The former was helpful from time to time; the latter infinitely frustrating. The latter won out over the former only because people tended to dwell longer on unhappiness.

When the cops had come that night, they had talked him out of eating a round from his pistol. He had thought many times since of killing himself. So much so that he'd gone to therapy to work around that little issue. He'd even done group counseling and stood in front of a circle of like-minded suicidals.

*I am Amos Decker. I want to kill myself. Period. End of story.*

He opened his eyes.

Four hundred and seventy-six days, twelve hours, fourteen minutes. Because of what he was the clock was spinning in the forefront of his mind, literally. That was the span of time that had passed from when he had discovered the three bodies in his home, his family wiped out. And in sixty seconds it would be fifteen minutes plus the year, months and days. And on and on it would go.

He looked down at himself. After four years as a college athlete and an extraordinarily short stint as a professional, he had kept fit as a cop and later detective. But he had not bothered with any of that after officially identifying the bodies of his wife, brother-in-law, and daughter. He was fifty pounds overweight, probably more. Truthfully, probably a lot more. Nearly six-five and a blimp with bum knees. His gut was soft and pushed out, his arms and chest flabby, his legs two meat sticks. He could no longer see even his overly long feet.

His hair was also overly long, struck liberally with gray, and smelling not overly clean. It seemed perfectly suited to conceal a mind that by never letting him down managed to let him down all the time. His beard was startling for both its bulk and its chaotic appearance. Wisps and curls and stray strands meandered everywhere like vines searching for purchase on something. But he told himself it was good for his line of work. He had to go chase scum, and scum, by definition, did not often look mainstream.

He touched the threadbare patch on his jeans and then looked down at the knees, where the bloodstains were still visible.

Her blood. Cassie's blood. Morbid to still have it there. Burn the pants, Amos. Most normal people would have done that.

*But I'm not normal. I haven't been normal since I stepped on that field and took that hit.*

The hit was the only thing he had never remembered. Ironic, since it was the catalyst for him never forgetting anything else. But it had been played relentlessly on the sports shows at the time. And even the national news felt the need to document the violence done to him for their countrywide audience. Someone told him the snippet had even been uploaded to YouTube and had more than eight million views. And this from twenty years ago. What a media star he was! And yet he had never seen it. He didn't have to. He'd been there. He'd *felt* it. That was enough for him.

And all he had done to deserve the folderol of attention was to die on a football field, not once, but twice.

He ran a furtive, mostly embarrassed glance down at his jeans. He had washed them, sometime, somewhere, but the bloodstains had not come out. Why should they be different from his brain? The pants could have—should have—been evidence. He should have let the cops take them, but they hadn't, and he hadn't offered. He kept them, wore them still. Stupid way of remembering. Asinine really. Horribly macabre way of keeping Cassie with him. Like toting her ashes in a Scooby-Doo lunch box. Sick really, but then he was sick. Really. Even though he had a place to live, held a job that paid actual money, and was functioning okay, for the most part.

He technically had been a suspect in the case because husbands always were. But not for long. The timing of the deaths cleared him. He had an alibi. He didn't care about alibis. He knew he hadn't harmed one hair on their heads, and didn't give a damn if no one else thought the same.

The real issue was that no one had ever been arrested for the murders. There hadn't even been any suspects, not a lead to come by. Nothing.

The working-class neighborhood they had lived in was quiet and the folks friendly, always offering a helping hand to others because nobody had much and everybody needed that extended hand from time to time. Either fixing a car or a furnace, or hammering a nail into a board or cooking a meal because a mom was sick or shepherding kids in a communal transportation system based on trust and need.

There were some tough nuts that lived there, for sure, but he hadn't spotted a homicidal in the bunch. Mostly bikers and potheads. But he had looked. Oh, yes, he had looked. He had done nothing else except investigate the crimes even though officially they had told him to stay the hell away from it all. But he had wanted more than anything to find and kill whoever had killed him by wiping out his family. So there was no way in hell he was staying the hell away.

But no clues presented themselves. Even with his obsessively running everything down, missing nothing. There was nothing. But there were opportunities and obstacles for a crime such as this. Doors were left unlocked; folks came and went. So access was clearly there.

But the houses were close together, so something should have been heard. But no sounds were ever heard from 4305 Boston Avenue that night. How could three people have died so quietly? Didn't violent death provoke outrage? Screams? A struggle? Something? Apparently not. The gunshot? Like a ghost whispering apparently. Zip. Nada. The whole neighborhood apparently had gone deaf. And blind. And mute.

And months later there was still nothing, far after the trail had grown cold and the odds of solving the case and catching the killer had dropped to about zero. He had left the police force then because he could no longer push paper and run down other cases and bother with precinct drama. The upper management said they were sorry to see him go, but no one asked him to stay, either. The truth was, he was becoming disruptive, unmanageable. And he was all of those things. Because he no longer cared about anything.

Well, except for one thing.

He had gone to their graves six times a day, all stacked in a neat row in plots he had hastily purchased, because who would buy a plot for a young couple and a grave for a ten-year-old? But then he had stopped going because he could not face them lying there in the dirt. He had not avenged them. He had done nothing except identify their bodies. A pitiful penance. God would hardly be impressed. He saw their graves in green. He hated the color, would not look for long at anything with that color. He almost never carried cash for that reason. He used a debit card, which never had enough money attached to it. But at least the card was black.

Their deaths had to be connected with what he did. He had put lots of scum away over the years. Some were out now. Others had friends. Just before the murders at 4305 Boston Avenue he had helped break up a local meth and crack ring that was doing its best to make everybody in the metro area an addict and thus a good customer, young, old, and every demographic in between. These dudes were bad, evil, kill you to look at you. They had friends. They must've found out where he lived. Easy enough. He wasn't undercover. And they took out their revenge on his wife and child, and his wife's brother, who had picked the wrong time to visit from out of town. But there was not a scrap of evidence against them. And without them, no arrests. No trial. No judgment. No execution.

His fault. His guilt. Led them right to his family, and now he had no family.

The community had held a fundraiser for him. Collected a few thousand dollars. Some bigwigs had kicked in some more bucks. It was all sitting in a bank account untouched. Taking the money seemed to him to be an act of betrayal for those he had lost. He didn't know why. It made no sense, but his mind was fixed on that point and so the money sat, though he certainly could have used it. But he wasn't touching it. He was getting by, barely. But barely was all he needed. Because *barely* was all he was now.

The thing though was he was biding his time. Good things came to those who waited. Well, he was willing to wait until forever. And then tack on a day if need be.

He settled back against the wood of the bench and shrugged his coat closer around him. He was not here by accident, but by design. He was waiting. Not for the biggie, not for the killer of his family to come sauntering down the street.

He was here on a job.

And as he looked to his left, he saw that it was time to get to work. He rose and headed after them.

# CHAPTER

## 3

The bar was like every other bar he'd ever been in.

Dark, cool, musty, smoky, where light fell funny and everyone looked like someone you knew or wanted to know. Or, more likely, wanted to forget. Where everyone was your friend until he was your enemy and put up his fists or cracked a pool stick over your skull. Where things were quiet until they weren't. Where you could drink away anything that life threw at you. Where you could temporarily toss aside your troubles. Where a thousand lesser talented Billy Joels would serenade you into the wee hours, and beyond.

*Only I could drink a thousand drinks and never forget a damn thing. I would just remember every detail of the thousand drinks down to the shapes of the ice cubes.*

Decker took a seat at the bar, where he could see himself in the reflection of the big mirror behind the stacked rows of Beam and Beef, Glen and Sapphire.

He ordered a dollar draft, clutched the mug between his hammy hands, and studied the mirror. Back corner and to the right. They had sat down there, the couple he'd followed into the place.

The gent was late fortyish, the girl half that. The man was dressed in the best he had. A pinstripe wool three-piece, yellow tie dotted with blue flecks in the shape of what looked to be sperms on their way to implant an egg, and a dandy pocket handkerchief to match. Hair swept back revealing a lined, mature brow—attractive on a man, less so on a woman, but then life had always been unbalanced that way. Impressive rings were on the manicured fingers. Probably stolen. His toes were probably clipped, too. His shoes were polished, but he'd missed the backs. They were scuffed, which came much closer to the man's actual nature. He was scuffed, too. And he only wanted to impress on the way in, not on the way out. After the way out, you'd never see the prick again.

She was doe-eyed and dough-brained. Pretty in a vacuous, seen-it-a-thousand-times sort of way. Like a negative of a photo badly impersonating the original or watching a 3-D movie without the requisite glasses, something was just off. The lady was naïve to the point of stupidity. So blindly faithful and oblivious that part of you just wanted to walk away and leave her to her fate.

But Decker was being paid *not* to do that. In fact, he was being paid to do the opposite of that. Which was cool with him. Whatever paid the bills.

She was dressed in a skirt and jacket and blouse that probably cost more than Decker's car. Or the car he'd once had. The bank had gotten that, too, as banks often did.

She came from real, old, unassailable money. She was so used to the privileged life that was always attached to such status that it was no big deal to her. It made her incapable of understanding why someone would work so hard to take from her things she simply took for granted and considered unimportant. That made her a potential victim every minute of every day of her life.

Such was the current moment: the shark and the dummy. Decker saw him as a six, a dirty number in his mind. She was a four, innocuous and uninteresting. Neither four nor six were prime numbers. Decker liked prime numbers. The rest were just fluff.

They touched hands and then lips. They shared drinks—he a whiskey sour, she a pink martini.

Figured.

Decker nursed his beer and bided his time. He looked at them without seeming to. In addition to the number tag, to him, she was outlined in orange, the guy in purple, the same color he associated with zero, an unwelcome digit to him. So the guy was really two numbers to him, six and zero. Complicated, but he had no control over it and he had not a shred of difficulty keeping it all straight because it was just there in his head.

Now zero was neither a prime nor a composite number. It was just there, like an outlier, lurking for some reason. Important in mathematics for sure, particularly algebra. But zero was zero. A black hole, only in purple for this guy and orange for the woman. It wasn't that he saw them exactly in that color. It was the *perception* of that color. That was the best and only way he could explain the sensation. It wasn't like they taught a class on this crap. And he had come to it relatively late in the game, so to speak.

They continued on with their lovey-dovey, hand-holding, foot-rubbing, heavy-petting afternoon fun and games. She obviously wanted more. He was unwilling to give it because you teased a mark. Rushing could only mean bad things. And this guy was good. Not the best Decker had seen, but serviceable. He probably made a decent living.

For a zero.

Decker knew the guy wasn't looking for marriage. He was waiting for an ask. A loan for a business prospect that couldn't miss. Some tragedy in his extended family that needed financial attention. He wouldn't want to do it. Hated himself for it. But this was his last resort. She was his last chance. And he didn't expect her to under-stand. Or say yes. The debate framed that way, what other answer could she give? Except, "Yes, my darling. Take double. Triple even. Daddy will never miss it. It's only money after all. *His* money."

An hour and two more pink martinis later she left him there. Her parting kiss was tender and moving, and he reacted in just the right way until she turned away and his expression changed. From one of reciprocal tenderness and love, to one of triumph and some might even say cruelty. At least that's what Decker would say. The color purple and the number six were flowing off this guy like a miniature tsunami. Dirty purple water full of sixes with the occasional zero thrown in is what he saw in his head.

Decker had a job to do, and now was the time to punch the clock. He carried his beer over to the table in time to put a massive hand on the man's shoulder and push him back into the seat he was just about to vacate.

Decker sat across from him, eyed the man's untouched whiskey sour—predators didn't drink on the job—and then raised his own beer in praise.

"Nice work. Like to see a real pro on the job."

The man said nothing at first. He eyed Decker up and down and sideways, sizing up both him and his response. His nose then wrinkled at the other man's unkempt appearance and odor.

"Do I know you?" he said at last. "Because I don't see how that's possible."

Decker sighed. He had expected something a bit original. At least to take his mind off other things. It was not to be. "No, and you don't have to know me. All you have to do is look at these."

He pulled the manila envelope from a pocket inside his coat and passed it across.

The man hesitated but then took it.

Decker drank his beer and said, "Open it."

"Why should I?"

"Fine, then don't open it. No sweat off here."

He reached to take the envelope, but the man jerked it out of reach. He undid the binding and slid out the half-dozen photos.

"First rule of a con, slick," said Decker. "Don't play on the sidelines while you're on a job. And when I said you were a pro I was being charitable."

His hand reached out and he tapped the photo on top. "She doesn't have enough clothes on and neither do you. And by the way, that particular act is illegal in pretty much all states south of the Mason-Dixon."

The man glanced up, his look one of caution. "How did you get these?"

Again, Decker felt disappointed by the query. "What were you expecting, privacy? You want privacy, jump in a coffin and let them bury you. Then maybe you get left alone."

He shouldn't have said this because his mind immediately jumped to the color blue, to the three bodies back at the now foreclosed-upon house. He pushed through it and said, "Now, it's just a matter of negotiation. I'm authorized to give you fifty thousand bucks. In return, you move to another state, permanently. You have no further contact with the lady. You write this one off and move on to someone else."

The man smiled, slid the photos back and said, "If you thought these were a real problem for me, why not just show them to her? Why come here and offer me a way out with cash?"

Decker sighed once more and for the third time felt disappointed. This guy was just not a challenge. He collected the photos and put them back neatly in the envelope.

"Read my mind, slick. Exactly what I told the family. Thanks for validating my opinion. The girl's very religious by the way. What you're doing to the lady in that third picture is a deal killer, in addition to the fact that she's your *wife*. Have a good one."

He rose to leave but the man clutched at his arm. "I can hurt you," he said.

Decker took the man's fingers and bent them back until he gasped, and then and only then did Decker let go.

He said, "I'm fat but I'm two of you and a whole lot meaner. I don't have to have a pretty face to do what I do. But you do. So if take you out back and smash it in, what does that do for your future cash flow? You see my point?"

The man held his injured hand and paled. "I'll take the money."

"Great. I have the check for twenty-five grand right here."

"You said it was fifty thousand!"

"That was only if you pulled the trigger when I asked. You didn't. The consequences are that your return goes down by half."

"You son of a bitch."

Decker sat back down and slipped a piece of paper from his pocket. "Plane ticket. One-way. For as far away from here as you can get without leaving the lower forty-eight. Leaves in three hours. A condition of the check clearing is you being on it. They'll have people there to confirm, so don't do anything stupid."

"Where's the check?" demanded the man.

Decker pulled out another piece of paper. "One more condition. You need to sign this."

He handed the paper across. The man ran his gaze down it. "But this—"

"This ensures the lady will never think of you again, except in a very bad way. Which means even if you try and slink back here it'll be a no-go."

The man's brain ran through what was happening, what this all really meant. "So you're blackmailing me with the photos and the fact that I'm married to get me to sign this? And if I don't sign you'll show her the photos and tell her I'm married and trust that will be enough to get me off her?"

"What a genius you are."

The man sneered. "I have a dozen more just like her. And far better looking. She wanted me to sleep with her. I kept putting it off. You saw the photos. I have filet mignon at home. Why would I settle for hamburger, even if it does come with a trust fund? She's a dumb shit. And she's only fair-looking on a good day, even with all of *daddy's* money. I don't know why I even bothered. I could get better tail than Jenny Marks at the place down the street. And I wouldn't have to listen to her baby talk. Actually, she's not a dumbshit. She's a moron."

Decker took back the unsigned piece of paper and slid the photos back in the envelope. He put them all away in his coat pocket.

"What are you doing?" the man said incredulously.

In answer Decker pulled out a miniature digital recorder and hit the Play button. The man's words were clear.

"I'm sure she'll enjoy your description of her," said Decker. "What kind of hamburger by the way? All-beef? Organic? Or just moronic?"

The man just sat there looking stunned.

Decker put the recorder away and pushed the one-way ticket toward the guy. "We'll let you keep this. Be sure your butt is on the plane. The next guy they send out will be even bigger than me and it won't just be your fingers he cracks. It'll be you."

The man said pitifully, "Are you telling me I get none of the money?"

Decker stood. "How does it feel to be slicked, slick?"

# CHAPTER

## 4

Decker sat on his bed in his one room about the size of a prison cell. For dealing with clients he used the dining room of the Residence Inn as an office, where his monthly payment included a daily buffet breakfast. They were definitely losing money on him with that arrangement. He would just pick up entire plates of food from the buffet and carry them to his table. He could have used a backhoe instead of a fork.

He had gotten his check from Mr. Marks's emissary. A buddy on the police force had recommended Decker to the rich guy to handle this delicate matter concerning his vapid daughter who was always falling in love with the wrong guy. He'd never met with the old man, only his reps. That was okay. He doubted Marks would have wanted Decker soiling his fancy furniture. They had met at the breakfast bar—two young slicks in thousand-dollar suits who declined to even sample the coffee there. They were probably more into double espressos spit out from those shiny little machines manned by a barista. He could tell from their expressions that they knew exactly how good they had it and how not good Decker had it. Decker had worn his best shirt to the meeting, meaning the other one.

Daddy Marks had authorized up to a hundred grand to get rid of the albatross around his little girl's neck. After sizing up the con, Decker had told the slicks he could get it done for a lot less. And he had. The price of a one-way ticket. You'd think Daddy Warbucks would have bonused him at least a percentage of the six-figure savings. But he stuck to the letter of their agreement and Decker just got his flat hourly rate, though he'd padded that considerably and made a nice payday for himself. Yet a percentage would have been good.

Probably how the rich stayed rich. But it had been worth it, to see a con conned. And he figured Jenny Marks would be in the same boat in a few more months and he'd get called up again. Maybe he should ask Daddy for retainer.

He left his room and made his way to the dining room right off the inn's lobby. It was early and he was the only one in the room other than eighty-year-old June, who was enjoying her golden years by shoveling home fries onto a platter at the buffet stand. He sat at the same table every morning. He conducted his client meetings at this very spot.

After loading up his plate he sat down to eat.

His first forkful was halfway to his mouth when he saw her come in.

She would be forty-two now, same age as he was. She looked older. Her job just did that to a person. It had done so to him.

He lowered his gaze and his fork and salted everything on his plate four times over, including the pancakes. He was hoping that a man of his considerable size could shrink to invisibility behind a wall of protein and carbs.

"Hello, Amos."

*Well, apparently not.*

He said nothing and shoved a congested forkful of eggs, grits, bacon, home fries, and ketchup down his throat. He chewed with his mouth open, hoping that the disgusting sight would prompt her to hit a U-turn and go back where she came from.

No such luck.

She sat down across from him. The table was small, and she was also small. But he was not. He was huge. He took up most of the table just by being there.

"How're you doing?" she asked.

He stuffed more food into his mouth and smacked his lips together. He didn't look up. What would have been the point? There was nothing that she could possibly say that he would want to hear.

She said, "I can wait this out, if that's how you want to play it. I've got all the time in the world."

He finally looked at her. She was stick-thin because of the cigarettes and the gum, which she always substituted for food and drink.

In nearly ten years he couldn't remember food or drink going down her throat. He was probably having more food at this one meal than she put away in a month.

Her hair was a pasty blond, her skin the same, and her nose a little crooked—some said from an encounter with a mean drunk when she was a beat cop. Her small chin seemed overwhelmed by her disproportionately large mouth, where uneven and nicotine-stained teeth lurked like sleepy upside-down bats in a cave.

She was not pretty. Her looks were not what made her memorable. What made her remarkable was the fact that she had been the first female detective on the Burlington police force. As far as he knew she was still the only one. And she had been his partner. They had made more arrests leading to more convictions than anyone in the history of the department. Some on the force thought that was just great. Others thought they were full of themselves. Starsky and Hutch, one rival had called them. Decker never knew which one he was supposed to be, the blond or the brunette.

"Hello, Mary Suzanne Lancaster," he said, because he somehow couldn't *not* say it.

She smiled, reached over, and poked his shoulder. He winced slightly and drew back a bit, but she didn't seem to notice. "You even got the middle name. I didn't know you knew it."

He looked down at his food, his limited chitchat quota exhausted.

She ran her gaze over him, and when she was done Lancaster seemed to silently acknowledge that all reports of Decker having hit rock bottom were spot on.

"I won't ask how you've been, Amos. I can see not too good."

"I live here instead of in a box," he said bluntly.

Startled, she said, "I'm sorry, I didn't mean it that way."

"You need something?" he asked. "I have a schedule."

She nodded. "I'm sure. Well, I came by to talk to you."

"Who did *you* talk to?"

"You mean how did I know you were here?"

His look told her that was obviously his question.

"Friend of a friend."

"Didn't think you had that many friends," said Decker. It wasn't a funny line, really, and he certainly didn't smile. But she forced a chuckle as a potential icebreaker but then caught herself, realizing, probably, that it was stupid to do so.

"Well, I'm also a detective. I can find out things. And the city isn't *that* big. It's not New York. Or LA."

He smacked his lips and shoveled in some more food, and his mind started to wander back to colored numbers and things that could tell time in his head.

She seemed to sense his withdrawal. "I'm sorry for everything that's happened to you. You lost a lot, Amos. You didn't deserve this, not that anyone does."

He glanced at her with not a single emotion evident in the look. Then he looked away again. Sympathy was not going to hold his attention. He had never sought sympathy mainly because his mind didn't really get that particular sensation. At least it hadn't after the hit. He could be caring. *Had* been caring and loving with his family. But sympathy and its even more irritating cousin empathy were not in his wheelhouse. At least not now. Probably not ever again.

Perhaps sensing that she was losing him again, she quickly said, "I also came to tell you something."

He ran his gaze up and down her. He couldn't help himself, so he said, "You've lost weight. About five pounds you couldn't afford to lose, not that you could afford to lose any." He flicked his gaze over her. "And you might have a vitamin D deficiency."

"How do you figure that?"

"You were walking stiffly when you came in. Bone ache is a classic symptom." He pointed to her forehead. "And it's cold outside but your head is sweating. Another classic. And you've crossed and uncrossed your legs five times in the brief time you've been sitting there. Bladder problems. Another symptom."

She frowned at this very personal going-over. "What, did you start medical school or something?" she said crossly.

"I read an article a few years ago while I was waiting at the dentist's office."

She said, "I guess I don't get out much in the sun."

"And you smoke like a rocket, which doesn't help anything. Try a supplement. Vit D deficiencies lead to bad stuff. And quit the ciga-rettes. Try a patch." He glanced down and saw what he had seen when she first sat down. He said, "You also have a tremor in your left hand."

She held it with her right, unconsciously rubbing at the spot. "I think it's just a nerve thing."

"But you shoot left-handed. So you might want to check it out."

She glanced down at the slight bulge on the right side of her jacket at the waistband, where her pistol rode in a belt holster.

"Did you remember that from our years together or did you note the position of my sidearm?"

"You never pulled your gun in all our years together. Neither did I. Yes, as a beat cop. But not as a detective sergeant. I saw the bulge. But I remembered it, too."

She smiled. "You have any more Sherlock Holmes stuff to throw at me? Want to check out my knees? Look at my fingertips? Tell me what I had for breakfast? I can certainly tell what you had." She said this all jokingly, hoping to draw him out, getting him back to old times when sometimes he could be downright loquacious, especially after a good bust and a stiff drink or two.

He took an elongated sip of coffee. "Just have it checked out. Could be something else. More than a tremor. Bad stuff starts in the hands and the eyes. It's an early warning, like a canary in a coal mine. And firearms recert comes up next month. Doubt you'll pass with your grip hand going wacky on you."

Her smile fell away at this abrupt segue laden with an astute obser-vation that she had obviously not thought about. "I will, thanks, Amos."

He looked down at his food and drew a deep breath. He was done, just waiting for her to leave. What could she tell him, really? He closed his eyes. He might just go to sleep right here. Running off the con scum at the bar had earned him enough to chill for a while.

She idly played with the button of her jacket, shooting glances at him. Preparing for what she had really come here to do. To say.

"We made an arrest, Amos. In *your* case."

Amos Decker opened his eyes. And kept them open.